THE
BIRTHDAY
PARTY

WENDY DRANFIELD

Bookouture

Published by Bookouture in 2022

An imprint of Storyfire Ltd.
Carmelite House
50 Victoria Embankment
London EC4Y 0DZ

www.bookouture.com

ISBN: 978-1-80019-988-0
eBook ISBN: 978-1-80019-987-3

ONE

MAPLE FALLS, VERMONT

The warm morning sunshine streaming through the window of the spacious kitchen is promising so much for the summer break: lazy mornings and hazy evenings, neighborhood barbecues, trips to visit friends, and the annual summer vacation. All school books and extracurricular activities will be long forgotten until the weather turns cooler.

Squinting at the brightness, Kathy Hamilton feels a migraine brewing. They always start with a sensitivity to light, and although it's not even 9 a.m., the heat is already rising outside, which doesn't help. The temperatures have been creeping up for a week now, and they're on day four of an early-summer heatwave. The A/C is doing a good job of keeping the house cool, but it's misleading. When you step outside, it feels like stepping off a plane in Barbados.

Her eyes settle on five-year-old Charlie's fine blonde hair, which is backlit by the sun, making her look like an angel in a nativity production. The strawberry-blonde shade reminds Kathy of Mitch's hair when they first met, although his has turned darker with age and is more sandy brown now than the blond of his youth.

She tenses as her husband leans in to kiss her lips. She offers her cheek as a compromise, to show she does still love him but a kiss on the lips is too intimate right now. The disappointment on his face leaves her feeling like *she's* the one in the wrong.

She glances at Fay to see if she noticed. Now that she's sixteen, it's difficult to fool her, but she's preoccupied with taking tiny bites of her scrambled eggs with a look of disgust planted firmly on her face. She's already dismissed the toast in front of her: carbs have become the enemy, so she's sticking to protein. Fay has only recently started caring about her appearance, which is completely unnecessary at her age and with her athletic figure. She also has the most gorgeous long chestnut hair, inherited from Kathy's mother, but she ties it back because she gets teased by the boys at school about the red tone. In a certain light, it can look auburn.

In contrast to Fay, Charlie's taking the time to enjoy each mouthful of her cereal, while laughing at the bad knock-knock jokes Mitch is telling her. When he runs out of them, Charlie wipes away her milk moustache with her sleeve and looks at Kathy. "How long now until the birthday party?"

Kathy smiles, ignoring her poor table manners. The birthday party is at Mitch's brother Scott's house. Scott's twin boys—the girls' cousins—turn six today, and this party is all Charlie has talked about for weeks. "It starts at one and now it's nine, so count it with me on your fingers."

Charlie drops her spoon into her bowl, splashing milk onto the counter, and lifts her hands.

Kathy counts the hours until one o'clock on her fingers. "How many fingers is this?"

"Four!" says Charlie.

"That's right." Kathy smiles. "You just need to be patient."

Charlie wriggles in her seat and resumes eating her cereal as Mitch strokes her head. "Well done, Charlie."

Everyone calls her Charlie, thanks to Megan, but Kathy prefers her given name of Charlotte. It just sounds better to her, although she eventually gave in to shortening it, the same as everyone else. Megan watches the girls when Kathy and Mitch want a date night or need to work late. She lives in the next town over, Glenwood, and Charlie loves her. She was here last night for the first time in a couple of weeks and spent the whole evening in the backyard playing various games with Charlie as the sun went down. She's due back again later today to collect Charlie from the birthday party while Kathy and Mitch are at work.

Megan was raised differently to Kathy and her family. She works at a sports bar on the edge of town; she often swears in front of the children and her arms are covered in tattoos. But despite that, there's something magnetic about her. Kathy admires her carefree attitude around people, never stopping to think about how she's being perceived. And she has a great sense of humor. Her quick, witty comebacks are always delivered with a smile so as not to offend, even though they cross the line sometimes. In that regard she reminds Kathy of her mother, Connie, who at seventy is just as feisty as she ever was.

It's clear Megan enjoys the family atmosphere at their house, because she always stays longer than necessary. Perhaps she didn't get that growing up. Kathy doesn't know and she doesn't like to pry, especially as Megan's a little shy around her. She's probably the only person Megan watches her language with.

Mitch slams the cupboard door shut, causing Kathy to wince because of her emerging headache. She's dreading attending the party later and isn't intending to stay long.

"Another migraine?" He comes over and gently rubs her back.

His warm hand is comforting, and Kathy sees Fay looking at

her, concerned. She's a sensitive girl who notices everything, despite sometimes trying to act as if she doesn't care about any of them.

"Maybe it's time you saw the doctor again," he suggests. "She might be able to change your medication."

She smiles. "I'll make an appointment for next week."

"Do you think I can read my story out to everyone at the party?" asks Charlie. "Mr. Barren says it's the best one I've ever written." Mr. Barren is her beloved teacher. He moved here a few months ago to work at the school, and he's encouraged her creative writing skills.

Fay puts her phone down and pushes her barely touched breakfast away. "How would he know it's the best story you've ever written? I mean, he clearly hasn't read the fifteen million other stories you bore us with daily." She says it with a smile playing at her lips. She likes to tease Charlie, and, unlike her, Charlie enjoys being teased.

"You're just mad because I named the smelly character after you," Charlie shoots back.

To her credit, Fay laughs.

Mitch grabs his cell phone and car keys from the side table by the front door. "I've got to go to work or I'll be late for my first showing." He kisses Charlie on the cheek. "Enjoy the party, honey. Don't make the clowns cry with those horror stories you write."

Charlie giggles. "I'll try not to."

He rubs Fay's shoulder as he passes, knowing a kiss wouldn't be appreciated, before approaching Kathy again. Placing a hand on her forehead, he says, "You look pale, Kathy. Promise me you'll phone the doctor?"

"I will."

He replaces his hand with his lips before leaving. She knows she should feel grateful to have such an attentive husband, but she feels numb, unable to appreciate much anymore. The marriage counseling isn't working, and she suspects their relationship will soon end in tears, opening their lives to public scrutiny. She watches him leave the house.

"See you all tonight," he shouts before slamming the front door closed behind him.

Mitch is in real estate. And with Maple Falls being a small but affluent town surrounded by vast scenic landscapes—forests, lakes and mountains—it's a desirable place to live. It may be sleepy in the suburbs, but with a lively downtown it appeals to families of all ages. At least that's what Mitch tells buyers who are new to the area. In reality, the town is a little run-down. Filled with character, yes, lively... not so much. The old families—Kathy's included—outnumber the new, making things slow to change.

Unlike Kathy, Mitch doesn't come from money, but he worked his way up from nothing and now sells the most expensive homes in town, as well as the surrounding area, making some serious commission. They met while studying at the University of Vermont. Kathy grew up here, but he's from Connecticut originally and chose Vermont purely for the business degree he eventually dropped out of. Something her father never lets him forget.

Fay pulls a backpack over her shoulders. "I'm outta here."

"What have you got planned for today?" asks Kathy. "Are you coming to the party later?"

Fay high-fives Charlie. "No way, that's for kids. I'm going to Jenna's." That's all the detail she'll give, and Kathy knows not to try asking anything else. Mitch is convinced Fay has a boyfriend, but if she has, she's keeping him secret for now. Maybe that's why she's started having issues with food; she's trying to impress someone. Hopefully her therapist will nip that in the bud, along with the increasing anxiety she's been experiencing lately.

Fay's backpack is bulging and Kathy wonders what she's got

in there. When Kathy was younger, she'd sneak clothes out of the house so she could get changed out of the respectable ones her mother made her wear before she arrived at high school. Her parents were strict and wouldn't allow her to have a boyfriend or to wear anything that might attract the attention of boys, but Kathy's more relaxed with Fay. She doesn't want to run the risk of her daughter hating her. "Be home by six for dinner."

Fay's attention has already diverted to her phone again. She's out of the door and on her bike within a minute. Kathy watches through the window as she cycles down the drive. The house instantly feels emptier. Looking at Charlie, she sighs. "So it's just me and you now, kiddo."

Charlie carefully climbs down from the breakfast bar stool. "How long until the party now?"

Kathy rolls her eyes in playful exasperation. "About ten minutes less than the last time you asked! You can kill some time by getting out of those smelly PJs and choosing a dress to wear."

Charlie crinkles her nose. "I'm not wearing a dress. I want to wear my cowboy boots for when I ride the pony."

For some reason Charlie has it in her head that there's going to be a pony at this party, but Kathy can't imagine there would be. A house full of excitable children is enough work without adding animals to the mix. Kathy watches her run up the stairs and winces as she imagines her falling and hurting herself. "No running in the house!"

Charlie immediately slows down until she disappears out of view.

Kathy sighs. It's time to load the dishwasher, but when she stands, the pain in her head doubles in protest. Her hand instinctively reaches for her temple and she's forced to sit back down again. Now she's alone, tears threaten to fall and she's overcome with a feeling of hopelessness as she tries to blink them back. Because instead of being excited for the start of the summer break, Kathy feels uneasy.

TWO

When there's just thirty minutes to kill before she needs to drop Charlie off at the party, Kathy calls her mom. She sits on her white couch with the phone to her ear and a cup of coffee in her free hand.

"Good morning, Kathy. How are you?"

Hearing her mother's voice should probably relax her, but she's always slightly wary of her. "Hi, Mom. How are you?"

"Oh, you know; in pain, same as usual." Her mother had a stroke in February and is only just out of a wheelchair. Connie Hamilton's not the kind of person who can suffer in silence.

"Sorry to hear that. Can I do anything?"

"No, no. I'm just in a bad mood." Her mom sighs. "Your father's spending the day at the country club to get away from me, and I can't say I blame him."

Kathy smiles at the thought of her dad escaping to play golf. "I was calling to check whether you or Dad will be at Scott's party this afternoon. I'm guessing he won't be."

Her mom snorts down the line. "No, darling. I've got plans that are far more exciting than watching Scott and Cindy Bowers get drunk and sloppy."

Kathy doesn't blame her for not being tempted. "Well, I'm dropping Charlie off and then heading to the refuge, so I won't be staying at the party long."

"I know, dear, you've already told me. You're letting Megan Carter collect her. Why can't your husband do it?"

Your husband. Not *Mitch.* "Because he's working today too."

A groan. "If you're not careful, Charlotte will pick up that woman's potty mouth one day and come home with seventeen tattoos."

"I don't think so," Kathy says, diplomatically.

"I'm telling you, Kathy, that girl is a bad influence on her, and on Fay too. And she smokes like a chimney."

She's one to talk, considering Kathy has caught her with a cigarette behind her back more than once over the years. "Come on, Mom. Leave Megan alone. Can't you just try to get along?"

"I do!" Connie exclaims. "She doesn't have a clue how I really feel about her, which is a true testament to my manners."

Kathy takes a deep breath. "I've got to go. See you at church in the morning?"

"Of course. I'm brimming with excitement to see which rehashed sermon we have to sweat through next." Although her mom jokes about it, she's highly religious and has lived her life very carefully so as not to upset God. She doesn't mind upsetting everyone else though. "Take care, darling. Kiss the children for me."

Kathy puts her cell phone down and realizes, not for the first time, that she never feels better after talking to her mother. She wonders if that's normal as she heads upstairs to check on Charlie. She peers into her room and sees her kneeling on the floor next to her bed. Charlie only agreed to wear a dress today if she could wear it over shorts and cowboy boots. Kathy smiles. Hopefully people will realize she dressed herself and this isn't Kathy's idea of style. She listens in as Charlie talks to a plastic pony while brushing its mane. "When we have stables, I'll visit you every single day and I'll plait your hair with ribbons and feed you hay. We'll ride down to the creek behind Uncle Scott's house and play in the water so that you never get too hot. There's an apple tree down there and you can eat as many apples as you want."

Fay went through a pony obsession too around the same age and begged them to get her one. They settled for a cat in the end—Mr. Hairy Ears, a gorgeous Maine Coon. He eventually went to live with Mrs. Hendricks down the street. Probably because Mrs. Hendricks cooked him fresh prawns for dinner every day in a bid to entice him. They see him walking past sometimes and he'll always throw the house a cursory glance, but that's as close as he gets to acknowledging the love and money they put into him.

"It's time to go, honey," Kathy says.

Charlie drops everything and jumps up. "Finally!" she says, before running for the stairs.

"Wait! Let me fix your hair." Kathy grabs a brush and ties her hair into pigtails, in the hope of keeping it relatively tidy and off her neck in today's heat. She uses white ribbons to secure them. Then she slathers Charlie's arms, legs, neck and face in sun block. "Close your eyes."

Charlie scrunches her face up tight, making it harder to apply the lotion. Kathy laughs. "Not helpful, sweetie." When she's done, she kisses Charlie's cheek. "All good?"

Charlie nods and runs ahead of her down the stairs. Kathy winces again. "Slow down!"

Once they're in the car and Kathy pulls away from the house, Charlie starts singing in the back seat. Her voice is bright and melodic and it doesn't bother Kathy's headache at all. She even sings along with her until a passing neighbor spots her.

"How excited are you?" she asks through the rear-view mirror.

Charlie grins, showing the gap where her front teeth used to be. "More excited than astronauts who went to the moon for the first time."

Kathy laughs.

"No, wait. More excited than the people who discovered the first dinosaur bones in the old ages!"

She's clearly been paying attention at school.

"Actually, I'm excited as—"

"Okay, okay! I get it. You're excited." Kathy laughs.

Within minutes they pull up outside Scott's house, and she hears her phone buzz in her purse. It's a text from Mitch.

Don't forget our appointment later. Love you.

How could she forget? Her smile fades as she thinks about her crumbling marriage, but she doesn't get long to dwell on it as Charlie starts wriggling to get out of her car seat. Kathy goes to help with the clasp. "Don't forget it won't be me or Daddy picking you up later, because we have work. And keep your hat on in the sunshine, okay? And don't eat too much candy or you'll be sick like at the last birthday party you went to, remember?"

Charlie nods excitedly, making Kathy smile. She kisses her cheek again, unable to resist. "Have fun today, sweetie."

She tries to hold her hand as they walk up the drive, but Charlie, fidgeting with excitement, slips away to run off ahead of her. Within seconds she's disappeared around the side of the house to get to the backyard beyond. "Be careful and stay away from the pool!" Kathy calls. Her plea goes unheard. Charlie can't swim yet—it's on the long list of things to teach her over summer—but all parents have been assured there will be a life-guard watching the children today, the teenage son of a neighbor. Despite that, Kathy has made Charlie aware of how dangerous swimming pools can be and she knows to stay away until she has her lessons.

The midday sun is intense as Kathy walks up the long path that meanders to the front door. This house is almost double the size of her own, and the driveway fits six cars. The front yard is landscaped with beautiful mature trees providing shade and she can hear carnival music from within. She can tell there are a lot of people here already from the loud outbreaks of laughter, but there aren't as many cars parked out front as she expected; looks like the majority of guests chose to leave their cars at home and let their hair down.

Despite being a birthday party for six-year-old boys, it's the first of many parties to be held over the summer and will probably draw the biggest crowd because no one has set off on their vacations yet. Everyone from the twins' school has been invited —teachers, parents and pupils—as well as all the neighbors and Scott's co-workers, and it sounds like most people have accepted. Luckily the neighboring houses are well spaced apart, so those who would rather not spend the afternoon drinking too much in the sun won't have to listen to those who do.

According to Charlie, there have been promises of circus entertainers, inflatables, pool games and everything else a young child could dream of. Kathy can't help wondering how much this is costing.

She opts to enter the house first—assuming that's where Cindy will be—as she wants to drop the boys' gifts off. Inside, adults of all ages are clumped together chatting, already drinking liquor from the smell of it. Seeing others enjoying themselves helps her relax. Work really is done for the summer.

Walking through the large, impeccably clean and stylish living room, she spots Cindy in the kitchen at the rear of the house. She's filling buckets with ice to keep beer bottles cool. The skin-tight yellow summer dress she's wearing accentuates her gym-honed curves. Her cleavage is heaving against the thin material, straining to break free. Kathy's tempted to warn her, but her sister-in-law already thinks she's a prude, so she lets it go.

"Hey, you made it!" says Cindy. She comes over for a hug.

Cindy is married to Scott, Mitch's only sibling. The couple are both younger than Mitch and Kathy, at thirty-eight, and have been married for nine years. They only moved to Maple Falls a few years ago, for the excellent schools and safe neighborhood. The town's welcome sign proudly declares that Maple Falls *breeds good people*, and it's true that crime rates are low compared to the national average. But, regardless, Cindy has confided that she hates living here because of how small the town is. She's used to city living and assumes everyone here is secretly related and involved in incestuous affairs, so she looks down her nose at them, not giving a second thought to how offensive that is to Kathy, whose whole family is from here.

Luckily, Kathy's not easily offended. At least not by someone whose opinion she doesn't respect. Knowing Cindy feels this way, she suspects the only reason she's invited so many locals to her home today is in order to show off. The house is worth almost two million dollars and the finishes are high-end. Scott has his own IT firm and Cindy's a stay-at-home mom with two nannies for support. They're one of the few couples in this neighborhood who don't attend church, insisting they're proudly atheist. Kathy doesn't care whether they go to church or not, but she often wonders why they use their opinions about religion as a conversation starter in a town like this. Mitch says they're just a combative couple who enjoy arguing.

"These are for the twins." She hands over two gifts neatly wrapped in blue paper, and looks around. "Where are they?"

Cindy waves a dismissive hand. "Probably setting fire to something out back." She's only half joking. "If they're this bad at six, what are they going to be like when they hit puberty?" She sips a glass of what smells like vodka and orange with ice.

Kathy smiles sympathetically. Austin and Thomas do seem out of control sometimes, and they've always been boisterous, but then she has no experience with sons. Charlie's only four months younger than them, but she's much better behaved most of the time. And she may have been excited to attend her cousins' birthday party, but Kathy knows she wants to steer clear of them while she's here. They've previously threatened to push her in the pool, something she's terrified of.

"Where's Charlie?" asks Cindy.

Kathy takes a deep breath. "She ran straight out back to see if the pony's arrived yet. Do you really have one booked?"

Cindy rolls her eyes. "Our star attraction has not only arrived, he's crapped all over my roses, and you can bet the mess will make it into the house before the day's through." She sighs. "Are you staying for the whole afternoon? We have plenty of food."

"No, sorry. I have to go to the refuge this afternoon. I have a mountain of paperwork to get through."

Cindy raises her eyebrows but holds her tongue. She doesn't approve of Kathy volunteering at the domestic refuge for women, believing that if a woman allows herself to be hurt, she only has herself to blame. They've argued over it so many times they both know not to discuss it anymore.

Kathy's real job is teaching at the junior high, but Connie always instilled the need to help those less fortunate and is on the board of several local charities herself, so Kathy has always volunteered where she was needed. The refuge uses her organizational skills in the office. With such a small budget to run the place, they need all the help they can get.

"Megan's collecting Charlie at four," she says. "She should be exhausted by then."

"I'm sure we all will be. Here, help me take these out and

come say hi to everyone." Cindy passes her one of the ice-filled buckets and heads out to the backyard.

Kathy takes a deep breath, mentally preparing herself to ignore the pain in her head and paint a smile on her face, not unlike the clowns present.

THREE

It takes Kathy's eyes some time to adjust to the bright sunlight reflecting off the water in the oval swimming pool. She places the bucket of beer and ice on the deck and retrieves her sunglasses from her shirt pocket. The vast backyard is quickly filling with children, and most of them are playing with silver or blue balloons. Each time one pops, the sound goes straight through her like a gunshot.

While Cindy distributes ice buckets, Kathy walks around to see who's here. She only spots two children from her class and gives them a wave, but she recognizes a lot of the adult guests and happily makes small talk about the weather, plans for the summer break and how her mom is. She and her family are well known thanks to the Hamilton name, which both Connie and Kathy opted to keep rather than take their husband's names upon marriage.

Connie's great-grandfather made money through his involvement in building the railroads in the area, and that wealth has increased with each generation that followed, thanks to well-placed investments and some good business acumen. Over the generations they've always given generously to the town through various philanthropic ventures, meaning the Hamilton family are respected in Maple Falls and even have some buildings named after them—the library being one. As Connie once said to Kathy, "Why would I take Jack's last name when I have a perfectly good one myself?"

Kathy often wonders whether her father and her husband regret marrying Hamilton women.

To her right, on the lawn, is a cotton candy machine with a line of children waiting to take their turn. One boy is licking remnants of the spun sugar off his fingers. The pool and sunloungers are empty so far, but with the heat creeping up, it won't be long before someone jumps in. She spots Charlie at the rear of the yard, near the woods beyond, riding a beautiful white pony that's being led around the lawn by its female handler. At first she tenses, worried Charlie could fall, but she's sitting in a proper child's saddle that looks perfectly secure, and the handler is giving her her full attention.

Somehow Charlie already looks disheveled. Her—now messy—pigtails poke out from underneath a cheap cowboy hat and she smiles at the camera as the pony's handler snaps a couple of quick photographs.

It doesn't take long for Kathy's skin to prickle in the direct sunlight, making her wonder whether she slathered enough sunblock on Charlie's arms and legs. To her left, a woman dressed as a Disney princess is painting faces in the full glare of the sun. She's sweating profusely thanks to the cheap polyester costume. Kathy retrieves a parasol from an empty table and positions it over her, giving her some shade.

The woman looks up, surprised. "Thanks. I feel like I'm going to spontaneously combust in this thing." She motions to her dress and laughs, but the redness in her cheeks suggests she's struggling.

"Would you like a water?"

"I have some." She nods to a bucket of melted ice filled with bottled water and soda cans. The child in front of her has the beautifully painted face of a tiger, and Kathy wonders why the woman's wasting her artistic talents at children's parties. Then again, perhaps there's money to be made working for rich parents like Scott and Cindy.

"Hey, Kathy." It's Trish, one of Kathy's neighbors from two doors down. Being a teetotaler, she has a glass of Coke in her hand. "Are we still on for a playdate on Wednesday? Maisie wants to show Charlie how to braid her hair."

Kathy smiles. "Sure. Is ten okay?"

"Ten works for us. I'll bring my donation for your fundraiser too."

Kathy's raising money for a new engine for the local fire department. "Great. By the way, I need you to come clothes shopping with me next weekend. I can't go on vacation without new beachwear. I swear I've gained ten pounds this month."

"Count me in," says Trish. "I need some summer dresses. This heatwave is killing me. The weather man said it's going to last through next week too."

Kathy groans. "I hope not. Have fun this afternoon." She moves on, and as she passes a table filled with gifts wrapped in various shades of blue, Scott and Cindy's boys rush up to her.

"Can we open our birthday gifts yet, Aunt Kathy?" asks Austin, the taller of the pair. He has chocolate ice cream smeared down his chin and she just knows that at least one child will throw up by the end of the party. She's seen a photograph Cindy sent her of the birthday cake that's arriving later. It's in the shape of a football and is covered in blue icing.

She smiles at them. "That's not up to me, boys."

They look disappointed. Thomas says, "But it's our birthday!"

"I know, honey. I'm sure you won't have to wait too much longer." She kneels down. "I can't stay, so I need you to take special care of Charlie for me, okay?" But they lose interest in her and run off to the pool with Austin shouting, "Charlie smells!"

Thomas dives into the water, splashing everyone nearby, and Kathy hears Cindy scolding him. She can't help worrying they'll pick on Charlie once she leaves.

"Hi, Mrs. Hamilton."

She turns around to see Fay's therapist. "Hi, Christine. I didn't know you'd be here." They've only ever chatted at the clinic when Kathy has dropped off or picked up her daughter. It's an awkward relationship, shrouded in secrecy, because unlike her, this woman knows Fay's innermost thoughts.

"Cindy's a friend of a friend, so I'm a plus-one," says Christine. "How are you?"

Even though Kathy must be at least five years older than the therapist, she feels herself clamming up in case anything she says is judged in respect of Fay's anxiety issues. "I'm fine. How are your sessions with Fay going? I mean, I don't expect you to give me details, of course, but Fay won't talk about them at all, so I have no idea if she's finding them helpful."

With a sympathetic look, Christine pushes her blonde curly hair behind her ears. "She finds it difficult to open up, but she's certainly present in the sessions. I think she'll find them useful over time." She pauses. "She's a special girl."

Pride makes Kathy unexpectedly well up. She swallows. "Yes, we think so. She has a lot of potential. She's a cheerleader, you know? And always top of her class."

"I don't just mean in an achievement sense," says Christine. "She's very perceptive for her age."

Kathy wonders what she's implying. Over by the outdoor grill she spots Scott, and is relieved to have an excuse to get away. "I better go check in with my brother-in-law, as I'm not staying long."

"Of course. Say hi to Fay for me."

Kathy walks away, trying not to show how tense she feels.

FOUR

Kathy approaches Scott at the grill. She has to wave her way through a cloud of flies hovering around the raw meat that sits uncovered on a side table. Flames dance around the sizzling beef patties and hot dogs, and the grilled onions smell irresistible. Her mouth starts watering at the thought of eating something, but she's already had a quick chicken salad for lunch.

Scott is in his element. He's only three years younger than Mitch and the resemblance is uncanny. Scott probably works out more—he has an employee gym in his office building because he's obsessed with keeping fit—but they're both built similarly, with broad shoulders and a slim waist. Mitch prefers to dress smart, even when he's not working, and has a short, tidy haircut, whereas Scott's sporting a T-shirt and shorts with flip-flops and he wears his hair slightly longer. But it's mostly in personality that they differ. Mitch is a little uptight compared to his laid-back brother, although Kathy doesn't see that as a bad thing.

There's an empty beer bottle on the table next to Scott, which isn't a good sign. He's supposed to be giving alcohol a break. She puts a hand on his back and leans in. "You haven't managed to burn anything yet then?"

He smiles when he sees her. "Kathy! Thanks for coming. You might want to eat something from this first batch, because once I've got another beer in me, it's all going to hell."

She wishes he was joking. A nervous glance around reassures her there are enough parents here to watch out for the children if Scott and Cindy do get drunk. "I've already eaten, thanks. I just wanted to say hi before I leave."

He raises his eyebrows. "Already?"

"I have to be at the refuge. Mitch sends his apologies; he has to work too. He said if he finishes early he'll be sure to stop by."

Scotts turns away, but not before she registers his disappointment. They may be brothers, but there's a disconnect between them. She's never got to the bottom of why they struggle to get along. Her guess would be money. They grew up with nothing and it seems to be an unspoken competition between them as to who can earn the most. She wishes they would just grow up and realize family is more important, but whenever she tells Mitch that, he replies with "That's easy for you to say."

"Did he sell that house over on Wicker Lane yet?" asks Scott. "I'd be interested to know how much he gets for it in the end."

That property has been on Mitch's books for too long. No one wants it for some reason. "I don't think so. All I know is he's always busy." She doesn't know how much money Mitch is making, but his cell phone rarely stops ringing. She worries he's trying to prove to her and her parents that he's not a deadbeat living off her family money and can make his own. She can't get it through to him that he doesn't need to prove anything to her.

"I was hoping he'd make an effort to show up today," says Scott. "We never see him anymore."

She smiles sadly. "Don't take it personally. He's still

building his business and you know better than most how much time and energy that takes."

He nods. "Sure. But you're the only family who's turned up. Cindy's parents are cruising somewhere in the Atlantic, and I know your parents aren't obligated to attend, but the boys would've loved to see them."

With no parents of his own, there is a noticeable lack of family here today. It dawns on her that perhaps that's why he and Cindy overcompensated by inviting anyone they know. Neither Scott nor Mitch talk about their parents much, and all she really knows is that their father passed away years ago and their mother moved back to Ireland shortly after. For reasons unknown to her, Mrs. Bowers doesn't stay in touch with her sons. Kathy feels bad for them, but her family have their own issues. The Hamilton name might be well thought of in Maple Falls, but the family itself is fractured. Her aunts don't stay in touch with her mom or Kathy, so her cousins are strangers to her.

"My mom's been struggling with her health ever since the stroke," she says, "so I think she just wanted some alone time. But I'll make sure we all get together at some point this summer. Thanks for inviting Charlie, by the way, she's been talking about nothing else for weeks. And I'd like to say thanks for hiring a pony, but she's going to have to be dragged kicking and screaming off that thing later." She laughs.

"Hey, if you can't have a pony at a kids' birthday party, what's the point?" Scott smiles. "Charlie's welcome here any time, you know that. I mean, sure the boys tease her and all, but we'd keep a close eye on her. She needs to get to know her cousins properly. I want us all to be close."

"Thanks. How are you anyway? Work okay?"

He nods. "Same as usual. Cindy wants me to downsize my business at some point soon, but she doesn't appreciate that means she'll have to rein in the spending."

"Maybe that would be a good idea anyway." It's out before she can take it back.

He looks her in the eye. "You've noticed, then?"

Kathy nods. "It doesn't take a detective to figure out Cindy has a spending problem. I mean, your house is beautiful and she has impeccable taste in interior design, but you don't need to spend a lot of money on expensive watches, children's gifts and birthday parties. And not everything needs to be designer."

He looks away. "I know. At first it was fun being able to splash the cash and buy whatever we wanted. I was as bad as her. But I don't need half the stuff she comes home with. I just don't know how to get her to stop."

Kathy does. "She needs something else to focus on: a job, or volunteering. Or she could do away with one of the nannies and spend more time with the boys. They'd love that." She surprises herself by being so honest with him, but she cares about him and doesn't want to see him back where he started, with nothing.

"You talk about us to Mitch?" he asks without looking at her.

"Of course not. I'm sorry, I shouldn't have said anything."

He stops turning meat on the grill. "Actually, I appreciate your honesty. Maybe you could ask Cindy to help with your next fundraiser? Give her some responsibility, something she can sink her teeth into. Just don't make it obvious."

Kathy smiles, but she knows Cindy won't agree to that. She's not a bad person; she just has no interest in volunteering. "I'll be sure to ask her." She takes a deep breath and pushes her hair off her sweaty neck. "It's so hot already! I don't know how you can stand next to this thing on a day like today."

He picks up a fresh bottle. "That's what the cold beer is for."

She checks her watch and sees it's past 1.30 already. "Listen, have fun today. Just..." she nods to the beer, "take it slow.

Make sure you eat something. There's going to be a lot of children here in your care."

To his credit, he's not offended by her advice. "Don't worry, there's a big-ass steak here somewhere with my name on it. And I'll keep a close eye on Charlie for you. She'll be fine." He hugs her goodbye, holding on for a second longer than usual, and then turns back to the grill. She gets the feeling he's unhappy, but then Austin runs over and asks him if he and Thomas can open their gifts yet.

Looking around for Charlie, Kathy notices she's no longer on the pony. The sun is so bright she has to shield her eyes despite her sunglasses, but she can't see where Charlie went. Then she spots the bouncy house taking a pounding, and she smiles. She'll be on there. Kathy doesn't want to disturb her. The kids are starting to get louder already, and her headache feels heavier with each shrill scream of excitement. She walks back into the cool house, past one of the clowns, who's on his way to the yard. The painted grimace on his face makes her shudder. She's never understood why clowns are popular at children's parties.

The living room TV has a baseball game playing, and she spots some teachers from school standing around gossiping. Martha Burton calls her over and her heart sinks. She was hoping for a quick getaway.

"What do you think, Kathy? Is Cindy trying a little too hard to impress? I mean, I've heard there are *fire-eaters* coming later. For a kids' birthday party!" She turns to the other teachers and rolls her eyes in disgust.

Kathy doesn't get involved in gossip as she doesn't want to be on the receiving end. Besides, this is her family Martha's talking about. "The children are enjoying themselves, so where's the harm? They'll remember this party for years."

Martha sips her white wine and takes a large handful of salted peanuts from the coffee table. "It's obscene if you ask me.

My kids are happy with just a couple of friends and a sleepover. I've taught them the value of money."

Says the woman who was addicted to online gambling for three years. "I've got to go, ladies. Have a good afternoon, and don't do anything I wouldn't do."

They giggle, and as Kathy heads to the empty powder room, she wonders why adults revert to childlike behavior at parties. She's relieved she doesn't have to stay a minute longer than necessary.

FIVE

Kathy fans herself with a women's magazine from the waiting area as Mitch arrives for their marriage counseling session bang on 4.30. He's never late for anything, and she appreciates that. His tie has already been discarded, and he's rolling up his shirt-sleeves because of how warm it is. It takes a second before she notices he's wearing a pale blue shirt, not the navy one he left the house in this morning. It's not unusual for him to carry a spare around with him in the summer. He likes to look presentable when showing houses. When he leans in to kiss her cheek, she can smell the soft apple aroma of their shampoo. Maybe he stopped by the house for another shower before coming here.

Jan, their therapist, appears at the door to her office. She smiles and gestures for them to come in and take a seat on the plump cream couch by the window. They sit next to each other, a sign of solidarity. They don't do this at home anymore, each having their favorite, separate, chair. Jan positions herself opposite them with a notebook and pen in her lap, ready to take notes if necessary.

When Mitch suggested they see someone to work through

their issues, Kathy was skeptical. She's not a fan of any form of therapy and it was a difficult enough decision to let Fay see someone. The level of trust people place in their therapists makes her uneasy. Who says they have all the answers? Who knows whether they even have the client's best interests at heart? They have access to your innermost thoughts and secrets and that's something she's uncomfortable with. Focusing on people's childhoods, as if that holds the key to everything, doesn't sit well with her either. She knows from experience that nothing good comes from looking back.

She finally relented in order to try and save their marriage, but insisted they see someone who doesn't know her family. Jan is based in Glenwood. It's far away enough to avoid being spotted by anyone they know, but not too far for them to drive to straight from work.

"I'm sorry about the heat," says Jan. "The air conditioning is due to be fixed this afternoon, and not a minute too soon." She's in her late fifties and has a reassuring motherly vibe about her. "So how have you both been since our last session?"

"Fine," says Mitch with a sigh. "Keeping busy with work and the kids."

Kathy nods; she has nothing to add. She's already starting to sweat and wishes she'd worn a dress instead of pants. She can feel the heat coming off Mitch. It makes her move away from him slightly.

"Is there anything specific either of you want to discuss today?" asks Jan. "Any conflicts since we last got together that you'd like my help resolving?"

Kathy looks at Mitch, who hesitates before placing his hand on hers. The look on his face tells her something bad is coming. She braces herself.

"You don't let me kiss you anymore," he says.

She's taken aback. Not just because he's noticed, but because he cares. "I do."

"No. This morning at breakfast you turned away from me again. Even just now you stiffened when I touched your hand."

She doesn't know what to say.

Jan looks at her. "Is there a reason you don't want to be kissed?"

Of course there is, and they both know why, but she doesn't want these sessions to be the same every time, so she's determined not to rehash everything again. "No, not really." She looks at Mitch and rests her hand on his. "You're reading too much into it. I'm fine."

He withdraws his hand and she can tell he's hurt. That wasn't her intention.

"How does this lack of intimacy feel for you, Mitch?" asks Jan.

He runs a hand through his thick hair. "Honestly? I feel like Kathy's changing, and because of that our family dynamic has shifted. The kids have noticed it, I'm sure. Well, Fay at least. It's not just the physical intimacy that's changed; I don't care about that. Kathy just refuses to open up to me. Or to you."

"Let's be careful with our use of words," says Jan. "You say she 'refuses' to, but perhaps she's just unable to right now. Once the trust in a relationship has been broken, it can take time to rebuild it."

Before Kathy can speak, Mitch continues. "The problem is that Kathy's been brought up too well to air her dirty laundry in public, even to a therapist. And that's frustrating for me, because she never drops her guard. Everything happens inside her head and she doesn't let anyone in, not even me."

Kathy tries not to roll her eyes when he mentions how she's been brought up. "You just have a chip on your shoulder about wealthy people. You always have."

He doesn't deny it. "Why shouldn't I? You and your parents come from old money and they look down their nose at someone like me who wasn't born into a respectable family.

Your mom is exactly the same as you when it comes to hiding emotions. Her expression doesn't reflect what she's really thinking. She's like a smiling assassin. I actually prefer the open scorn of your father. At least I know where I stand with him." He's getting louder.

Jan interjects. "Did you grow up in Maple Falls, Mitch?"

"No. I'm from Connecticut. My dad was a drunk, my mother a... It doesn't matter. They're not around."

Kathy feels the need to explain. "He grew up with no money and barely any love. His parents weren't family-oriented at all. If he made a mistake as a child—shoplifting, fighting, lying —he was on his own. He was raised to be independent and he was expected to deal with his own problems and pay his own way from a young age."

Mitch lowers his eyes.

"His father never wanted to work or support his family," she continues. "As a result, Mitch and his brother have worked hard to turn out nothing like him, which is admirable, but my family is different. They look after their own."

He scoffs. "By that you mean they hide their secrets to protect the family name. And even though I'm their son-in-law, it's painfully obvious that Connie and Jack still don't consider me family, even after all these years. Your mom almost had a heart attack when I took your name."

Kathy crosses her legs. "Don't be so dramatic."

"It's unusual to take the woman's last name," says Jan. "Why did you do that?"

"It was my idea," says Kathy. "The history of the Hamilton name, and the fact that my mom had no brothers to carry it on, meant she kept it when she married my dad and suggested I do the same. But it meant that when we had Fay, we didn't know whether to name her Hamilton or Bowers, after Mitch. I suggested that both Fay and Mitch take the Hamilton name, so we were all the same and for the lineage to continue as long as possible." She smiles. "Boys are hard to come by in my family, so we have to do what we can. I'm sure my mom would've kept trying for a son if she hadn't needed a hysterectomy."

"I wish I hadn't bothered taking Kathy's last name," says Mitch. "Her mother hates me for it, even now. She accuses me of using it to get ahead. Thinks I'm a fraud because of it. And sure, maybe it's opened doors for my business, but so did the work I've put into it." He takes a deep breath and lowers his voice. "Kathy's the apple of her parents' eye, and maybe that's how it should be, but it's hard to always be the wrong one in the relationship."

Kathy hates this. She hates bringing it all up in front of a stranger. It has nothing to do with the real reason they're here. She's already told him she'd happily change all their names to Bowers if it stops this resentment. She shifts position. "Let's not talk about this. We've been together twenty-three years, Mitch. Our eighteenth wedding anniversary is coming up. We should be celebrating that, because the important thing is that we still love each other."

He fixes his handsome brown eyes on her, and she remembers what a thrill that would give her when they first started dating at college. He was only eighteen, she was twenty-one. She hadn't had a boyfriend since high school, deliberately keeping her distance from men and focusing on her studies instead. But after meeting Mitch, she fell in love with his zest for life. He had a determination to succeed, but knew how to enjoy himself in the meantime. She doesn't understand how it all went wrong.

"Is love enough anymore?" he asks.

She opens her mouth but doesn't know what to say. Has he given up? A flutter of panic fills her chest. Feeling trapped, she wants to get out of here.

She zones out as Jan tries to reassure them that all marriages go through ups and downs, especially ones that have lasted this long. She suggests they go on more date nights, just the two of them, but they've already tried that several times, and while it's resulted in physical intimacy, it's the trust that's gone from the relationship.

And Kathy's starting to believe it isn't possible to get that back.

SIX

They took separate cars to their session, and Kathy arrives home before Mitch. With no sign of the heatwave easing any time soon, she lets herself into the house, grateful for the cool interior. She looks around for the girls. It's almost six, but no one's home. She should start dinner, but she can't face cooking. Maybe they can order in tonight, depending on who gets home when. She retrieves her cell phone from her purse.

Perching on a breakfast bar stool, she calls Fay, but there's no answer. She's probably on her way back, so Kathy decides against leaving a message. She tries Megan next. She was due to collect Charlie at four, and Kathy's a little concerned that they're not here. Again, no answer.

Mitch walks through the door. "I'm going for a shower."

She frowns. "Another one?" That would be his third today.

Noisy banging outside is followed by Fay walking through the front door. Her bare shoulders are pink from the sun and her lovely chestnut hair is tied back, with just a few escaped strands sticking to her face. "Hey." She goes straight to the fridge to grab a soda.

"Good day?" asks Mitch.

"I guess. Is Charlie out back?"

"She's not home yet," says Kathy. "Megan must've let her stay longer at the party. I wish she would've told me, though."

After a long gulp of her drink, Fay puts it on the counter and shakes her head. "They're not at the party."

"How do you know?" asks Mitch.

"Because I've been there since," she makes a thinking face, "about three."

"I thought you weren't going?" Kathy's hands tense around her phone.

"Changed my mind. There was nothing else to do. Megan must've picked Charlie up early and taken her somewhere else."

Kathy frowns. "I don't know. It's unlikely Charlie would have wanted to leave the pony before she absolutely had to."

Mitch pulls his phone out. "I'll try calling Megan."

"I just did," says Kathy. "There was no answer."

He lets it ring, but when Megan still doesn't answer, he shoves his phone back into his pocket in frustration. With a serious expression he asks, "When was the last time either of you saw Charlie?"

Kathy has a heavy feeling building in her chest. She tries to think. "I dropped her off at the party, but I'd left by two, maybe a little earlier."

He turns to Fay. "And you?"

"At breakfast this morning. She definitely wasn't at the party when I got there." Kathy can tell that Fay's starting to panic, because her eyes are widening and she's placed her phone on the counter, temporarily forgotten. "Can we go back there and look for her?"

He nods. "Sure. She could've been hiding or playing in the house. Let's go."

Scott and Cindy only live two blocks away, and with Mitch driving, it takes less than four minutes to get there. Fay's out of the car and around the side of the house first, with Mitch walking slower. Kathy tries to ignore her trembling hands as they head out back.

They meander their way through the adult guests, the majority of whom are starting to look sunburnt and a little worse for wear. The sun has shifted to behind the woods, and Kathy notices that the clowns and entertainers have all left. There aren't as many children here now, but there could be some upstairs in the twins' rooms, playing video games.

Scott appears in front of Mitch with a smile on his face. "Hey! You made it." He claps his brother on the back, genuinely pleased to see him.

"Have you seen Charlie or Megan?" asks Mitch.

"Sure." Scott must pick up on the tension in Mitch's face, because he frowns. "What's wrong?" He looks at Fay, who's shielding her eyes from the sun and scanning the backyard in the hope of spotting her sister. "Fay? I thought you'd already left?"

"Charlie's not home yet, so we've come to collect her," says Fay. She absently waves to one of her friends, who's in the pool.

Cindy approaches them. She's wearing a sunhat to protect her face, but her cleavage is bright red above a white line of unburnt skin that peeps out under the dress's plunging neckline. She wobbles as she leans in to hug Mitch, making sure to press her chest into his. Kathy tries not to roll her eyes. She's clearly drunk. The glass she's holding has nothing but a cocktail umbrella in it. "Charlie left a while ago," she says.

Mitch glances at Kathy before looking back. "With Megan?"

Cindy shrugs. "I guess. I was surprised she didn't want to stay longer, to be honest, especially because we got the pony in just for her."

"Let me fix you a drink," says Scott to his brother. "And some food. I have a huge ribeye steak that I was saving for later, but I'll split it with you." He offers a hopeful smile, but Mitch doesn't return it.

"Thanks, but we're eating at home once we have Charlie. She should've been back two hours ago." He turns to Fay. "Go check the house. They could be upstairs somewhere."

Fay heads for the patio doors.

Turning to Kathy, Mitch says, "If they're not here, Megan could've taken her to the playground." He looks around and shares a few words with one of Scott's friends, who asks about work.

Kathy spots Charlie's teacher, Mr. Barren, waving to a group of guests as he leaves the party. He opts to exit around the side of the house instead of through it. He's gone before she can ask him when he last saw Charlie. Her gaze drifts up to the cloudless sky as something catches her eye. It's a helium-filled balloon that has managed to get away. It's drifting higher in the sky, and something about the slowness of it fills her with dread.

"Did you get through your mountain of paperwork at the refuge?" asks Cindy with a hint of sarcasm.

Kathy looks at her and nods.

Fay returns, but the look on her face suggests she's worried. "They're definitely not inside, and I can't get a straight answer from the boys about when they last saw her."

Mitch moves toward them both. "I'll drop you home and then drive around town to find them. If they're not at the playground, I'll check the ice-cream parlor." Charlie's favorite place to go after school. "Keep calling Megan, okay?"

Kathy nods, but a sinking feeling in her stomach makes her feel sick. She turns to Fay and notices her daughter's eyelid is twitching. It does that when she's anxious, so Kathy offers a reassuring smile. "We can order pizza ready for when they get home."

"Enjoy your evening," says Mitch to his brother and Cindy.

A look of annoyance crosses Scott's face, but he bites back

his obvious disappointment that Mitch isn't there to see him and his family. "I'm sure she'll be fine. Let me know when she's home safe." He turns and walks away.

Kathy and Fay follow Mitch to the car.

"Mom? What if something bad has happened to Charlie?"

Kathy swallows, unsure how to respond.

SEVEN

Detective Chase Cooper knocks on the solid oak door in front of him and takes a step back. With dusk approaching, the sun is casting a golden glow on the neighborhood. He surveys the landscaped yard, the two expensive cars in the driveway, and the neighbors' houses, coming to immediate assumptions about the kind of people who live on this street. Most people would think that makes him judgmental, but it's his job. He's been doing it for almost twenty years, and experience has taught him that first impressions are usually bullshit. This house, those cars, that's what this family want him to see. What he's looking for is the secrets bubbling beneath.

He turns when the door opens and smiles widely at the woman who stands there. Dark chestnut hair sits on her shoulders, and she's modestly dressed, even in this heat. He already knows she's forty-four, same as him. "Kathy. Long time no see."

She offers an anxious smile, and he gets a glimpse of the teenager he knew at high school. The girl who stole his heart and refused to take him seriously. She must've known then that he could never provide this kind of house—this kind of lifestyle —for her.

"I had a feeling they'd send you," she says. "Thanks for coming so quickly. Come in."

He follows her inside, past the kitchen on the right and on to the spacious open-plan living room and dining area beyond. The oak sideboards are filled with family photographs. He'll need to take one of those with him. That usually upsets the mother. Out past the dining room is a generous backyard filled with mature shrubs and trees framing a square lawn. Surprisingly, there's no pool as far as he can tell.

A teenage girl hovers nearby and he has to do a double-take. It's like looking at sixteen-year-old Kathy. "I'm Fay," she says.

He smiles at her. "Hi, Fay. I'm Detective Chase Cooper." A guy has joined them and Chase recognizes him from the real-estate signs around the neighborhood. He heard a long time ago that this was the guy Kathy had married.

They shake hands. "Mitch Hamilton. I'm Charlie's dad."

Chase is reminded that he took Kathy's last name. He doesn't know if he could do the same; it would make him feel like he's pretending to be something he's not. Only because of what that name means to the town. If she were called anything else, it wouldn't be an issue for him.

Mitch Hamilton looks pale, despite the tan. The blood has left his face and he has sweat accumulating at his hairline, even though it's cool inside. This could be a sign of distress, or guilt. "Can I get you a drink—coffee, water?" he asks.

Chase looks at the empty whiskey glass in Mitch's hand. "Not right now, thanks. Mind if I take a seat?"

"Of course," says Kathy.

The couch alone is bigger than his kitchen. He chooses a leather armchair, and the couple sit opposite him. The girl remains standing. Her eye makeup is smudged and her cheeks are pink, presumably from a day spent in the sunshine. She looks on the verge of tears.

Chase speaks to Kathy. "It's nice to see you again. I wish it were under different circumstances, but it's been too long."

She smiles, properly this time. They had a bond back then. Teenage love. He doesn't know why it ended so abruptly. He just knows he wasn't ready for it to be over.

Mitch clears his throat, oblivious to the history between them. "How much do you know?"

Chase pulls out his notebook and pen, ready to focus on the case at hand. "Only what you told the dispatcher on the phone: you're unable to locate your five-year-old daughter and you believe she's with the babysitter." He looks at his notes. "A Megan Carter?"

Mitch nods. "The last time any of us saw Charlie was when Kathy dropped her at a birthday party over on Lexington Lane. My brother's kids' party. Kathy left there before two, and Megan was supposed to collect Charlie at four. I've driven around town looking for them, but they're nowhere to be seen and Megan isn't answering her cell phone or her door."

"And what do the people at the party say?"

Kathy speaks up. "Scott's wife said she thought Charlie left with Megan earlier this afternoon but she doesn't know what time. We didn't ask anyone else because we thought they'd be home by now." She's clasping her hands together, her knuckles white. She's obviously starting to fear the worst, but she's doing well to contain her panic. "I wouldn't have been surprised if they'd gone for ice cream or to the playground after the party, so I wasn't expecting them to come home bang on four, but when Mitch and I arrived home at six, they still weren't here."

Chase checks his watch. It's almost eight o'clock. Not too early to consider the child missing, considering the parents have lost contact with her. He needs to locate the babysitter and he needs to head to the party, to question the remaining guests before they all leave. A checklist of tasks is formulating in his head, causing adrenaline to quicken his heart rate. "What was Charlie wearing?"

Kathy describes her outfit. "Pink cowboy boots, yellow shorts under a red dress with zebras on, and a cowboy hat. She has blonde hair. It was tied into pigtails with white ribbons."

He writes it all down. "I'll need a recent photograph of her."

"I have lots on my cell phone I can send you."

"Thanks. Any of Megan too?"

She shakes her head. "Sorry."

He holds his notebook out to her. "Can you write down Megan's home address and cell number for me?"

Kathy hesitates. "She lives in Glenwood and works at the sports bar on Alma Road near the edge of town." She passes the notebook to Mitch, who writes everything down before handing it back to him.

Chase thinks he might know who Megan is. He's been in that bar a few times. That part of town is a stark contrast to where the Hamiltons live. He knows because his line of work takes him there daily. "How well do you know Megan?"

Mitch says, "She's a friend of the family. She's dependable and I don't think she'd deliberately cause us this kind of upset. She certainly wouldn't harm Charlie, if that's what you're thinking." He rubs his jaw. "Maybe she's stranded somewhere with no cell service or battery life left. She could have car trouble."

"But if her phone battery was dead, it wouldn't ring," says Fay, behind them. "It would be a dead line. Mom said it rang out."

The kid's right. Chase thinks that if Megan was stranded somewhere with car trouble, she'd have made contact by now. Someone would've stopped to help. A patrol car would've spotted them. "What does she drive?"

"An old Chevy Aveo, navy-colored," says Mitch. "I'm sorry, I don't know the license plate."

"That's easy for me to get." Chase stands up. "Can I look in your daughter's bedroom?"

Kathy frowns. "Why? She's not in there."

He doesn't suspect she is, but he has to be sure there are no signs of foul play in there, and no clues as to her disappearance.

"I'll take you," says Fay.

He follows her upstairs. "Any ideas where your sister might've gone?" he asks. "Has she ever confided in you that she was thinking about running away from home?"

Fay opens a door off the spacious landing and motions for him to go in. "No way. Charlie loves us. She has no reason to run away."

He walks into the room. It's full of toys. Most of them are horse-themed. There's a small desk with lots of crayons and coloring books scattered around. He picks up the top book and rifles through it. No running-away notes drop out. He opens the drawer, but it just contains more crayons and plastic farm animals. Her princess-themed bed is neat and covered with stuffed animals neatly lined up near the pillow for bedtime. He smiles. "I bet she loves this room."

He turns to look at Fay, but she's crying silent tears. "Please find her tonight."

He pats her shoulder reassuringly. "I'll do my best." He doesn't need to linger in here; a thorough search can be done at a later date if necessary. Closing the door behind them, he follows Fay back downstairs. To Mitch he says, "I want to pay your brother a visit and question the guests. You said he lives on Lexington Lane?"

Mitch nods. "Right. Twenty-two-seventeen."

That street is even more impressive than this one. "Before I go, I need you all to clarify what you were doing today, so I can piece together everyone's locations." He doesn't say it, but he's checking their alibis.

Kathy takes a deep breath. "The four of us had breakfast together here before Mitch left for work just after nine."

Fay speaks up. "I left the house after Dad and cycled to my friend's house. Jenna Carpenter."

Chase knows the family.

"We hung out at hers until we went to the party."

"Did Jenna's parents go too?" he asks.

"No. They weren't home when we left, but they weren't at the party."

He makes a note of everything before looking at Mitch. "You're a realtor, is that right?"

"Right." Mitch hesitates. It's only a second, but Chase notices. "I was working all day, until Kathy and I met at four thirty over in Glenwood for a pre-scheduled appointment."

Kathy says, "I was home with Charlie until just before one, when I dropped her at the party. I left there by two, probably earlier, and drove straight to the women's refuge. I volunteer there."

He nods. "What was your appointment in Glenwood for, if you don't mind me asking?"

Kathy and Mitch share a look, and an awkward silence settles over them. Behind him Fay says, "They're in couples therapy. Although I don't know why they bother, it's clearly not working."

"Fay!" Mitch doesn't like her honesty.

Kathy looks away, embarrassed.

Chase doesn't react. "What did you do after your session?" he asks.

"We came back here, to eat dinner together," says Mitch. "And that's when we realized Charlie and Megan hadn't returned."

He knows the rest. "Okay, thanks for that. It helps me create a timeline." He takes a deep breath and looks at Mitch. "What do you think has happened to your daughter?"

Caught off guard, Mitch stumbles over his words. "I... I don't... I mean, who knows?"

"Have either of you upset anyone lately? Had any business deals go south? Had any threats made against you or your family?"

They exchange another look, but this one appears to be of genuine confusion.

"No," says Kathy. "Not at all. We haven't fallen out with anyone."

Chase nods. "And there have been no ransom requests of any kind?"

Mitch laughs. "Are you kidding me? Why would there be a ransom request?"

"Because, looking around, I can see you clearly have money, and everyone knows Kathy's family has money. Maybe someone took Charlie to blackmail you."

"Oh my God." Kathy lowers her head.

He feels bad for suggesting it, but it's perfectly plausible. "Look, I'm not saying she's been kidnapped. It's just one possibility I have to keep in mind, amongst many others." He stands up. "Call me the minute you hear from the babysitter." He hands Kathy his card, acutely aware that she now has his number again after all these years. Back then, there were no cell phones, just a landline in the middle of the kitchen or living room. Less private.

"I want to come with you," she says.

"Me too," says Mitch, but his cell phone beeps with a message. "Shit, I forgot about my final house tour." He runs a hand through his hair. "I've been trying to sell this place for months and these guys seem interested." He looks at Kathy. "Do you mind?"

She shakes her head. "Try to be quick."

"Of course. I'll meet you both at Scott's afterwards."

"Not necessary," says Chase, slipping his notebook into his

pocket. "I don't need either of you to come along. I'll keep you posted."

"Please," says Kathy. "I want to come. I can smooth it over with Scott and Cindy. They don't know the extent of the problem yet, so they'll probably be hostile to a detective showing up out of the blue and asking them personal questions. Fay can stay here in case Charlie and Megan come home."

Fay nods.

Something in Kathy's expression makes him agree. Maybe she wants to reveal something while her husband is out of earshot. "Fine. Mr. Hamilton, it's best if you come straight home afterwards. We'll keep you updated."

He leads them outside, then watches as Mitch takes off in his car without any reassuring words to his wife, or even a goodbye kiss.

Kathy slides into the passenger seat of his ancient Honda Accord, a far cry from her husband's brand-new Lexus. He's not embarrassed. It's fully paid for, as is his small house. He doesn't owe anyone anything, and how many people can say that these days?

As she buckles in beside him, he remembers the driving lessons he gave her one summer, well before she got her license. She always played her music full blast, making him have to shout instructions.

He tries not to smile at the memory as he pulls away from their house.

EIGHT

The sun is vanishing behind the horizon as Kathy and Chase drive to Lexington Lane. Being so close to him again after all this time is surreal for her. He smells the same, and it reminds her of summer days spent lazing around the creek together, getting to know each other where no one would stumble across them. He's in need of a shave and a haircut, which doesn't surprise her, as he always liked to say his thick black hair looked best messy, and he was right. It's sprinkled with some gray now, though. She looks out of the passenger window, afraid. These are things she shouldn't be noticing.

Apart from her time at college, neither of them moved away from Maple Falls, but they've only bumped into each other occasionally over the years, and from afar: across the grocery store parking lot, or at different pumps at the gas station. They'd wave quickly, but never talk. She didn't give him the opportunity. She would see him driving around town as a patrol officer in his twenties, before he made detective in his early thirties. They don't mix in the same circles and she actively avoided him after they graduated high school. She knows he must have questions about how their time together ended, but now's not the time to answer them. She fights the memories and tries to concentrate on the here and now. On finding Charlie.

"Fay looks so much like you, it's unreal." He glances at her with a playful smile. The smile that started it all.

She has to look away. "She has my mother's hair, that's for sure."

"So do you. How is your mother? Relieved you ended up with someone like Mitch, I'll bet."

She turns to him to see if he's angry about Mitch, about where she lives and what she has, but he isn't. He's still smiling. He's not the angry type, never was. He wasn't jealous of anyone at school and he was right not to be. Chase Cooper would do anything for anybody. He was reliable and irresistible in his treatment of her. That's what makes being with him now so difficult to bear. She doesn't want to be reminded of that time. She can't be. Not with everything that's going on in her life now. She's determined to keep a distance between them. "How's Shannon? I heard you married soon after high school."

His eyes return to the road and she regrets her question immediately. She knows full well that Shannon Watts—head cheerleader—was cheating on him through their seven-year marriage. Even after their divorce, she kept coming back, using him until she found someone better. He helped raise the baby she had with one of the cops he worked with, until Shannon eventually left him and Maple Falls for good about five years ago, taking her three-year-old son with her.

"I'm sure she's fine," he says. "Wherever she is."

She checks his wedding finger: no ring. She doesn't know if he's seeing anyone else, but she's pretty sure he's never had any children of his own. Being a teacher at the local junior high, and with Charlie in kindergarten and Fay in high school, she'd know if he had. Knowing what a great father he would be makes that a travesty in her opinion.

Feeling horrible for lashing out, she changes the subject.

"How worried are you about Charlie? Do you think she'll turn up? Or are there sex offenders living nearby that I should know about?"

He takes a hand off the steering wheel and touches her bare wrist. His hand is warm and rough, but his touch is tender. "She's probably playing hide-and-go-seek with your friend Megan, and maybe they got lost out in the woods. Don't worry, I'll find them."

He's trying to keep her calm, but she can tell he's taking this seriously. Is he aware of something she isn't? She checks her phone: no messages. When they approach the house, she nods. "This is it."

Chase looks at the house and pulls over.

There are fewer cars in the driveway now. As they enter the house, she feels weighed down by dread. She wants this to be discreet, to avoid the rumor mill, but she knows it's impossible with the number of people who were here earlier. She leads him through the house, empty now, and they find Cindy sitting on Scott's lap at a table outside, with about eight other guests. A few children are in the pool, including the twins, but it's much quieter now the sun is almost set. Music plays low in the background.

"Kathy?" Scott moves to stand up, gently pushing Cindy off him. Cindy's eyes are glazed as she takes in Kathy, then Chase, clearly confused. She's smoking a joint, something Kathy's never seen her do before.

"Sorry to bother you again, Scott. Could we have a word in private?" She implores him with her eyes, hoping he'll understand that what she has to say isn't for public consumption.

"Sure, no problem." He leads her and Chase inside to his empty study and closes the door behind them. "What's going on?"

Chase remains silent. Observing.

Trying to keep her voice even, Kathy says, "We haven't been able to find Charlie and Megan."

"What? But they haven't been here since..." Scott shakes his head. "I don't remember what time they left, but they didn't stay for food. I would've served them." He looks at Chase. "Are you a cop?"

Cindy slips into the room and Chase shakes hands with both her and Scott. "Detective Chase Cooper from Maple Falls PD. And you are?"

They give their full names. He makes a note.

"Mrs. Hamilton is concerned at how long her daughter's been missing. Do you mind if I clarify a few things about Charlie's attendance at today's party?"

"Oh my God. She hasn't been abducted, has she?" asks Cindy. Her hand goes to her mouth. "What if someone's raped her?"

Kathy closes her eyes and tries not to react. She knows Cindy wouldn't speak those thoughts aloud if she weren't drunk and probably stoned.

Chase ignores her. "I need you both to tell me exactly where Charlie and Megan were the last time you saw them today. And what time that was."

"I didn't see Megan at all," says Scott. "I've been busy with the grill, so I only saw Charlie briefly when she first arrived."

"What about you?" Chase turns to Cindy.

She places her glass on Scott's polished oak desk, and Kathy finds herself thinking about the ring it will leave on the wood. "I last saw Charlie..." She's trying to think. "You know what? I only know when I didn't see Charlie. Does that make sense?"

"What do you mean, Cindy?" says Kathy, irritated.

"Well, I know she wasn't here for long after you left. I thought maybe she was feeling unwell and assumed you came back for her shortly after."

Kathy feels Chase's eyes on her as she says, "What do you mean? You said you saw Megan collect her."

Cindy shakes her head. "No, I'm sorry but I didn't say that. You told me Megan was going to collect her, so when you showed up earlier with Mitch and Fay, asking where she was, I said I assumed Megan had already been."

Kathy rubs her temples, trying to keep her frustration at bay. "You're confusing me. How much have you had to drink?"

Scott puts his hands on his hips. "What's that got to do with anything, Kathy? She's not drunk."

Chase steps in. "Let's stay focused. So you're saying neither of you saw Megan Carter here today?"

They shake their heads.

"And were you both here all afternoon?"

Scott says, "Right. Both of us. The party started at one, so we had to be."

Cindy frowns at her husband. "No, you went out for more supplies, remember?"

"Sure, but I was only gone about forty minutes, if that." He crosses his arms.

"What time was that?" asks Chase.

"I don't know, maybe three o'clock?" says Scott.

"No," says Cindy. "It wasn't that late, because Helen's children hadn't arrived yet and they got here at three, after basketball practice."

Scott rolls his eyes. "Jesus, Cindy. Are you trying to make me look bad?" He sighs. "Okay, then I probably left just before they arrived. But I came back with meat and salad, remember?"

Chase stares hard at him without speaking.

Scott slips his hands into the pockets of his shorts and pulls out a small piece of paper, a look of relief on his face. "Here. It's the receipt from the store."

Chase takes it from him and Kathy leans in to read it,

squinting at the small font. It shows he was at Marty's Meat Market at 2.44 p.m.

"Thanks for your help." Chase gives it back to him and turns to her. "Can I have a word?"

Kathy pries her eyes away from Scott and follows Chase out of the house.

He checks no one is around before saying, "If no one saw the babysitter, that means she didn't turn up to collect Charlie, which in turn could mean someone else is with your daughter."

Kathy's mouth goes dry.

"I'm sorry," he says, "but I have to assume the worst has happened, because everything now depends on acting fast. It could be that she's gone off with a friend's family, not a stranger, but the fact that people have been coming and going from this party all day and the front door isn't locked means I need to act swiftly. I'm going to brief my department, get permission to raise an amber alert and get some backup to interview the guests. I'll drop you home first."

Her hands are trembling and she feels nauseous. Everything about this situation feels wrong, like she's watching it happen to someone else. "I'll send Mitch to Megan's house again as soon as he's home. They could be there now."

Chase shakes his head. "No. I'll go there myself. The best thing you can do right now is to stay home, take care of Fay, and make a list of the parents of all Charlie's friends so I can contact them later if necessary to see if she went home with one of them."

"But that wouldn't explain why Megan never showed up."

He fixes his blue eyes on hers. "It could be that she did show up, and that your brother-in-law and his wife are lying."

She opens her mouth but closes it again.

"Is there any animosity between your husband and his brother?" he asks.

"Only normal sibling rivalry." She takes a deep breath,

suddenly overwhelmed. "I can't believe this is happening." Tears quickly accumulate, so she looks away, but she can't stop them from falling.

Chase steps closer, wrapping his arm around her shoulders. "Please don't cry, Kathy," he whispers into her ear. "I'll get your daughter back. I promise."

A car door slams shut behind them and Mitch approaches. "Why are you hugging my wife?"

Chase takes a step back from her and looks at Mitch. "She's a person, not a possession, Mr. Hamilton. I'm just consoling her."

A couple from the party appear at the front door behind them, about to leave. Kathy doesn't want them to overhear anything. "Let's go, Mitch. I'll update you in the car."

Chase asks the couple to stay for questioning while Kathy leads Mitch to his Lexus.

"You never told me you knew the local detective," he says.

She can feel his stare. "We went to high school together. I haven't talked to him since then."

"Just be careful what you say to him, because if Charlie doesn't come home, there's a good chance he'll blame us and start prying into our lives. My reputation is on the line here, Kathy."

My reputation is on the line here, Kathy.

Last time she heard those words the situation didn't end well, but she never thought she'd hear them from Mitch. She sinks into the passenger seat and watches Chase walk back into the house, closing the door behind him.

NINE

SUMMER 1993

The sun has set, making it dark in the playground. Sitting on a swing, Kathy is contemplating using her savings to run away from home. It's the only solution she can think of to the problems in her life. A boy's voice gets her attention. She looks up. Chase Cooper from school is walking toward her.

"Aren't you too old for playgrounds?" he says.

She rolls her eyes. "Says the sixteen-year-old boy in the playground."

He laughs and takes the swing next to hers. She's become more aware of Chase over the last few months. He's been stopping to chat to her in the hallways at school. Seeking her out in the cafeteria. Her friends think it's hilarious that someone like Chase Cooper thinks he has a chance with her. He's not in her league, apparently. Their attitude annoys her to the point of distancing herself from them. Sometimes they're too much like her mother.

"Trouble at home?" His face is serious now, making her think that's why *he's* here. After all, it takes a troubled kid to know one.

She sighs. "My parents keep threatening to disown me. To

cut me off and let me see how much I'll miss their money when it's gone."

He frowns. "Why? You're a straight-A student who does a million extracurricular activities and is heading straight for college. What have they got to be unhappy with?"

She looks away. He makes it sound like she's perfect. "They always find something to complain about: I'm ungrateful for my life, my skirts are too short, my hair isn't tidy enough. Or I'm not acting like a Hamilton should."

He snorts. "Sounds like they need a real problem in their lives if that's all they've got to worry about."

She glances at him. It's well known that Chase has spent time in foster care, but she doesn't know why. Although she knows him from school, they've never spent time alone together. He flicks his black hair out of his eyes, and she realizes he's changing. His jaw is becoming more angular and his shoulders broader. He's always been cute, but now he looks like he could be in college already. Older than her somehow. When did that happen? She looks away. "I should probably get home."

"Why? So you can get into another argument about crap that doesn't matter? I'll bet you've only been missing for what, a half-hour?" He pauses before adding, "How about we give your parents something real to worry about?"

She smiles. "How?"

He pulls her swing toward his. Their knees and shins touch. "Hang out with me for a couple of hours. I'll keep you safe, but they don't need to know that."

She likes the feel of him against her, and having his undivided attention, but she feels bashful all of a sudden. "I don't think so. My parents already think I'm attracting the wrong kind of attention."

"Yeah?" He grins. "Well, they're right about that."

The soft white glow from the only light in the playground highlights his dark blue eyes, and she's surprised by her attraction to him. Her mother would definitely disown her if she brought Chase Cooper home for dinner. Kathy smiles at the thought.

A dog barks behind them, and she turns to see Mr. Wilby from her street. He works with her mom on the church's fundraising committee. He's walking his dog, but he's stopped to look at them with a frown on his face. "Everything okay, Kathy?" he shouts.

Kathy quickly pulls her swing well away from Chase's hold and pets the Jack Russell that's yapping at her ankles. "Yes, thanks, Mr. Wilby. I'm going home in a minute."

He nods slowly. "Don't stay out too late." Giving Chase a hard stare, he walks on reluctantly, calling his dog to follow him.

When he's out of view, Kathy feels Chase looking at her closely. When she turns to him, he fixes a smile on his face, but not before she notices disappointment in his eyes. She feels horrible for pulling away, but Mr. Wilby could report back to her mom.

He stands up, taking a few steps away from her. "You're right. You should probably get home before the cops turn up to arrest me."

She smiles sadly. "He won't call the police on you, Chase."

After a few seconds' hesitation, he leans in to her and whispers, "Let me know if you ever want to piss off your parents." He grins with a sparkle in his eyes that's irresistible and then walks away, into the darkness.

Her arms are covered in goosebumps, but it's not a cold night. She watches him leave, wishing more than ever that he'd turn around and come back for her.

He doesn't. Not this time.

TEN

After dispatching an officer to Megan Carter's apartment to see if she has turned up, Chase arranges for an amber alert to be issued for Charlie Hamilton. He needs all media outlets to know who he's looking for, and an amber alert is the quickest way of disseminating information and getting the public's help in finding a child before the worst can happen. If it hasn't already.

At the house where she was last seen, Chase has interviewed the remaining party guests, catching them before they leave. He needs their memories to be fresh, but so far no one has offered any insight into Charlie's whereabouts. Most people last spotted her on the pony near the woods. Detective Frank Brown, from his department, is talking to the final few guests.

When Chase's cell phone rings, he answers it immediately.

"Detective, it's Officer Letts. There's no answer at Megan Carter's apartment, but her Chevy is parked outside the complex."

Interesting. Why would her car be there if she's not? "Understood."

"Want me to hang around?" Letts asks.

"No," says Chase. "I'll head over there now. You can swap places with me and help Detective Brown at the house on Lexington Lane."

"Sure thing."

Chase tells Brown where he's going and then slips into his car to make his way to Megan Carter's address. It's dark when he pulls up outside the apartment complex, and a couple of guys hanging around on the corner under a street light scatter when they see him get out of his car. They know who he is and he knows what they're doing, but he doesn't have time to worry about them.

He locates Megan's car and tries the handle. Locked. He shines his flashlight inside. It's empty apart from a few fast-food wrappers discarded in the back. The fact that her car is still here suggests she never left to collect Charlie. But then why isn't she answering her door or her phone?

The complex has no security doors. The stairways to each apartment are open to the elements, so he climbs the stairs until he finds Megan's place. Looking around for any surveillance cameras, he's disappointed to find there are none. The owner clearly doesn't care what happens to his tenants as long as they pay their rent. He knocks hard on Megan's door and listens for any movement from inside.

Nothing.

He leans down and performs the mailbox test. If she's dead in there, he'll know it when he pushes it open and sniffs. Plus, the flies will tell him. But there's no smell or flies, and he can't see much from out here, so he bangs loudly and shouts, "Maple Falls PD. Open up."

The door next to Megan's opens and an old guy dressed in khaki pants and an open shirt appears. "What's the goddam problem?"

Chase flashes his badge and the guy leans in for a good look. "Detective Chase Cooper. And you are?"

"Bryan."

"Well, Bryan, I'm looking for your neighbor, Megan Carter. You seen her today?" He can hear the guy's TV coming from the apartment behind him: canned laughter and a game show host on full blast. That must drive his neighbors nuts.

"Sure, she picked up a few groceries for me this morning."

"What time did you last see her?"

"She dropped them off at eleven. I banged on her door a little later to ask if she wanted coffee, but she must've gone out again, because she didn't answer. Why? She okay?"

"That's what I'm trying to find out." He figures that if she fetches groceries for this guy, they must have a good relationship. "You wouldn't happen to have a key for her door, would you?"

After a brief hesitation, Bryan pulls a set of keys from his pocket. "Sure. I'm prone to falls, so she suggested we have access to each other's places in case anything happens to one of us."

Chase admires the community spirit. "How long has she lived here?"

"Moved in January this year. She's a good neighbor. Comes and goes quietly, even though she works late at the bar."

Chase takes the keys from him and unlocks the door.

"She'll kill me for letting a cop into her place," says Bryan, "but I want her to be okay."

"I appreciate it. You should stay here, just in case."

The old guy raises his eyebrows in surprise. "In case of what?"

Chase doesn't answer. Instead he slowly opens the door and shouts again, "Ma'am? I'm from Maple Falls PD. I'm coming in."

Slowly walking forward through the tiny kitchen, he enters the living room and immediately sees a woman collapsed on the floor next to the couch. "Shit."

She's on her front, lying next to a patch of dried vomit, and from here he can't tell if she's dead or alive. Her black hair obscures her face. He runs to the bedroom and bathroom to see if anyone else is present, clocks an open fire-escape window and rushes back.

Kneeling down, he rolls her gently onto her left side to feel for a pulse in her neck; that's when he sees the bruising. Staying calm, he focuses on the heartbeat. It's weak. He pulls out his cell phone and calls for an ambulance.

"Megan?" says Bryan behind him. "Is she okay?"

Judging by the blood matted in her hair and the bruising around her neck, Chase thinks she's in a critical condition. "Stay back! I don't want your DNA anywhere near her."

With an ambulance dispatched, he leans in to listen to her breathing. She's wheezing, but she doesn't appear to be gasping for air. There's still hope.

"Megan?" he says into her ear. "There's an ambulance on the way, honey." He winces. They're not allowed to call people honey anymore, but he can't help it. "It won't be long. You just hang on in there. You're safe now. I've got you."

She groans slightly, clearly in pain, but noise is good. It means she's fighting to stay alive. But it's clear the ambulance can't come quick enough.

ELEVEN

With Megan in the ambulance on the way to the hospital, Chase drives through the dark to return to the scene of Charlie's disappearance. The large house on Lexington Lane is backlit with floodlights as officers search the backyard. It has an eerie effect on the front of the house, which stands in quiet darkness apart from the light spilling out through the windows and open doorway.

He checks the time before going in; 10.30 p.m. They haven't searched inside the property yet, and he's mindful that the couple's twins might be scared by a team of officers moving around their home so late. But it has to be done now. If he waits until the morning, the family could—unwittingly or not—destroy evidence overnight.

Detective Brown's car is still out front, and Chase finds him in the living room, which smells like a bar. Empty glasses cover almost every surface, and potato chips have been ground into the wooden floors. He's glad Scott and Cindy haven't cleaned up yet, as each glass and food dish is a rich source of DNA and fingerprint evidence. Chase fills Brown in about his discovery at

Megan's apartment, and then focuses on the search. "Glean anything from the guests?"

"Nothing useful," says Brown. "The booze doesn't help. Half the people I talked to can't even remember what time they arrived." He shakes his head. "Must be nice to be able to spend the weekend drinking."

Chase smiles.

"From what I can tell, our missing girl was last seen either on the pony or in line for the pony. Nothing of significance has been found in the yard, and the K9 unit is searching the woods beyond. Conditions are dangerous, though, on account of the dark. The handlers don't want their dogs getting trapped in anything or falling into water. I think the thorough search will have to wait until first light."

He nods. "Get the forensics guys into the house. I want all the glasses, plates and door handles dusted for prints, just in case we need to place someone at the party who tries to deny being here."

"Sure thing." Brown heads outside as he gets on his cell phone.

Scott Bowers approaches Chase. "When do you think you'll be done outside? We've put the kids to bed, but they're upset by all the commotion."

"I'm sorry for the inconvenience, Mr. Bowers, but we need to search the house next."

Scott crosses his arms, a look of annoyance on his face. "Seriously? At this time of night?"

Cindy appears from the living room. She's already in pajamas and a robe. "Why on earth would you want to search our house? We've already looked for Charlie inside, and my boys are asleep upstairs! You can't wake them at this time of night, especially after the day they've had."

Chase lets her complain. "I'm sorry. It has to be done now. We won't be more than an hour or two." The truth is, it will take longer than that, but he doesn't want to piss them off any further and have them demand he get a search warrant. "Try not to worry. We'll leave your house in the same condition as we find it." Better, probably, looking at the mess and knowing how thorough and professional his team are.

She eyes her husband. "What's going on, Scott? Do you know something I don't?"

Scott holds his hands up. "Of course not! They can search wherever they want. Jeez, Cindy, a little support wouldn't go amiss."

"Listen," says Chase. "It's standard protocol to examine the scene of a person's disappearance. It doesn't mean I suspect either of you were involved, but the sooner I rule you out as persons of interest and know for sure whether or not Charlie was harmed inside the house, the sooner I can narrow down my search and find her."

Cindy shakes her head. "I can't believe this is happening. And in *our* house! I never even saw her inside today."

"Just because she was last seen in the yard doesn't mean she didn't slip inside to use the bathroom or to watch TV. We'll be thorough but fast." He's about to turn away when he adds, "Do me a favor and don't tidy anything away until we've finished."

Cindy looks surprised by the suggestion that she'd tidy. "I've got cleaners coming in the morning."

That gives his team time to do their thing. Technically, the house isn't a crime scene unless the dogs or officers find something to suggest otherwise. If they do, Cindy will need to cancel the cleaners altogether. Chase leaves the couple standing together and goes out to the officers in the backyard. He gives them the all-clear to come inside. The last one in brings a German shepherd with him.

"A dog?" says Cindy, her eyes wide. "You think we have a dead body in our house?"

"Not necessarily, but maybe a blood trail. I'm just covering all bases. Again, I'm sorry for the inconvenience. I'm just trying to find your niece as fast as possible."

A young boy wearing blue and red Marvel pajamas appears at the top of the stairs. His nose and cheeks are tinged with sunburn. "What's happening, Mom?"

Cindy looks at Chase with disgust. "See what you've done? They'll probably have nightmares about this for years." She runs up the stairs to lead him back to his room, but Chase hears him say, "Can I play with the dog?"

As the uniforms get to work, Chase's cell phone rings.

"Hey, Chase. It's me. Where are you?"

The familiar female voice takes him by surprise, and he almost groans out loud. He moves to the empty study. "Shannon?" His ex-wife, the woman he started dating after Kathy's rejection. He was young and stupid and should never have got involved with her, but having said that, it wasn't all bad. She just wasn't Kathy.

"Yeah," she says with amusement in her voice. "Long time no see."

What a stupid thing to say. "Well, when you skip town with your kid and no forwarding address, it's kind of hard for me to keep in touch." Not that he'd want to. That was five years ago now. There have been a few women since, but nothing serious. In a town like Maple Falls, it's hard to find a woman you either didn't go to school with, aren't related to, or didn't arrest at some point.

She laughs. "I always did enjoy your sense of humor."

"What can I do for you, Shannon? I'm busy."

"I'm outside your house. I thought you'd be home by now, but I forgot you like to work all hours." She pauses, before saying, "Look, Patrick and I need a place to stay."

He sighs. Patrick was three when she took off, and Chase missed him a lot more than he missed Shannon. "No way. Not my place."

"You want to see us homeless?"

He thinks of the boy, who must be eight years old by now, and feels a pang of guilt. But Patrick isn't his responsibility. He won't even know who Chase is after all these years, despite spending more time with him than with his real dad. "What about Luke?" he says. "I would imagine he'd love to see his son again after all this time. Surely he'd take in the mother of his child."

"Wow, you're never going to let me forget I cheated on you, are you?"

Not likely. She was sleeping with Luke, his first detective partner, behind his back. When she got pregnant, she tried to pass the baby off as Chase's. He would've fallen for it if Luke hadn't insisted on a DNA test. But still Chase didn't kick her out. How do you ask a pregnant woman to leave? Especially one as vulnerable as Shannon. She's never been good at taking care of herself. He watches the large German shepherd pass from the living room to the kitchen, his handler keeping up with him. "I've got to go."

"No, wait! Don't be mad, but I've still got a key to your place, so I've already let myself in."

He shakes his head in annoyance. He should've changed the locks a long time ago.

"Patrick's settled in front of your TV under a blanket," she says. "You can't make him sleep in the car, Chase. That's not fair on him."

He knows he has no choice. "One night. That's it. Tomorrow you can stay at the women's refuge, if you've got nowhere else to go."

She laughs down the phone. "I knew you'd be happy to see me back."

He ends the call and runs a hand through his hair. Maybe it'll be nice to have some company around the house. He can teach the kid to ride a bike or something.

Detective Brown approaches him. "No hits from the dogs so far, and the officers haven't found anything of interest yet."

Chase nods. He notices Scott standing by the front door, as if he wants to flee. He's watching closely as the officers climb the stairs. Is there something he's hiding up there? Is there a reason Cindy asked him if he knows something she doesn't? Scott sees him watching and walks away, toward the kitchen.

TWELVE

The first thing that hits Megan is the bright lights, quickly followed by a searing pain in her head. Her throat feels as swollen as it did after her tonsillectomy back when she was in seventh grade. With her neck too stiff to move, she waits for her eyes to open to see where she is, because this doesn't sound like home. There are machines beeping and people talking in the distance. A ringing in her ears disorientates her as a feeling of panic builds in her chest. She senses a presence close by.

"Megan?" A male voice. "Megan, you're in the hospital. The pain you're experiencing will ease shortly once the meds kick in."

Her vision clears, and she sees a man in blue scrubs under a white coat standing over her.

"Great, you're awake. How are you feeling?" he asks.

A nurse to her right offers her a glass of water with a straw in it. She tries to sit up, but winces with the pain. She feels like someone's squeezing her throat. That's when the coughing starts. It's excruciating and makes her gasp for breath. She can't imagine ever wanting to smoke another cigarette.

"Take it slow," says the nurse. "My name's Derek and I'll be taking care of you."

She manages to sip the water and then swills it around her dry mouth. It's refreshing, but tough to swallow because of the burning sensation in her throat.

"I'm Dr. Anders," says the other guy, leaning over her and shining a light in her eyes. "You were found home alone with some nasty injuries, Megan." He pulls her eyelid wide. "I'm sorry to have to tell you that it appears you've been attacked. I imagine you're extremely uncomfortable right now?"

No shit, Sherlock. With an effort, she clears her throat. "No more pain meds. I'm a recovering addict. Trying to be clean of everything." Her voice is raspy.

He glances at the chart in his hands. "Sorry, I wasn't aware of that." He looks back at her with sympathy in his eyes. "It's not feasible for you to recover from your injuries without some pain medication. But I'll make sure I control the dosage carefully, and you need to tell me if the pain becomes unbearable so I can reassess. How does that sound?"

She knows from her support meetings that having medication prescribed for an operation or serious injury isn't the same as falling off the wagon. It's a necessity. Her six-month sobriety will still be intact. But she's worried all the same. She'll need to be careful she doesn't become dependent on it. The pain is still intense with the medication he's given her, so she has no option but to agree. She nods, wincing at the throbbing that tears through her throat.

"Good," he says. "You've had a blow to the head, which has been treated but will take some time to heal."

She involuntarily swallows, making her wince.

"You have some external bruising to your neck, but it's mostly internal, which isn't unusual. Your throat will feel tender for a few days, maybe up to a week, and there might be some ringing in your ears for a while. Plus, you may find yourself drooling a lot today."

She wipes her mouth just at the thought of it.

"You were lucky: my initial tests have found no sign of any brain, heart, artery or spinal damage, or internal bleeding, but I need you to keep me informed of any changes you notice that worry you, even after you're released. If this was attempted strangulation, you may experience delayed symptoms, which can quickly escalate, so please take this seriously: stay alert to new symptoms and give your body time to recover. You understand?"

She looks into his kind eyes. She doesn't understand any of this: why she's here, who hurt her, how he can say she's been lucky. But she whispers, "Yes," without crying.

"Now, I imagine you have a lot of questions, but I have a detective here waiting to speak to you. He says time is of the essence, otherwise I would've had him wait. Do you feel up to giving him a few minutes?"

The beeping from the heart-rate monitor to the left of her bed speeds up. She's mistrustful of cops.

A man in dark blue jeans and a pale blue shirt with the sleeves rolled up, tie pulled askew, steps forward as the doctor retreats. "Hi, Megan. I'm Detective Chase Cooper from Maple Falls PD. I'll try to keep this brief, as I can see you're in pain, but the sooner I get some answers, the sooner I can find out who did this to you." He smiles. "Does that sound okay?"

She rests her head back on the pillow and stares at him. She's seen him before, in the bar where she works. They've shared a few conversations. He probably doesn't remember her. He looks more tired than usual.

Detective Cooper takes her silence as consent. "We found you at your apartment last night. You were face down on the floor near the couch. Do you have any idea what happened to you?"

Last night? Without a window in her hospital room, she hadn't realized it was Sunday already. She glances at the clock above the door: it's after 10 a.m. Trying to think back, she vaguely remembers someone taking her by surprise, approaching her from behind, sudden and threatening. "I was home alone. Someone must've got in while I was folding laundry." Her voice is still hoarse, and she has to keep clearing her throat, causing more pain. "I remember feeling like someone was behind me, but before I could turn, there was a pain in my head. I must've blacked out. Later on, I woke up on my couch and vomited, but apart from that, I couldn't move. I remember thinking I needed to get out of there, but... I don't know what happened next. I don't know how I got here."

He nods sympathetically. "You were brought here in an ambulance. And as Dr. Anders said, your injuries suggest that someone attempted to strangle you." He pauses, letting her absorb the information.

She blinks, not knowing what to say. She notices the doctor leaving the room when approached by a nurse.

"I don't want to alarm you," says Detective Cooper, "but I want to be completely honest, as it'll help my investigation." He pauses. "I think whoever did this intended to kill you, because otherwise he would've stopped once you'd blacked out from the blow to your head. To strangle you while unconscious suggests he didn't want you to survive. I think he would've been successful too, if he hadn't been disturbed by your neighbor."

"Bryan?"

The detective smiles. "Yeah. He knocked on your door to see if you wanted to join him for coffee. I think that scared your attacker enough to make him flee out of your fire escape, or else the guy thought he'd already choked you enough to kill you. Maybe both. So I have to ask: can you think of anyone who might want to harm you, Megan? Do you owe anyone money for drugs or... anything else?"

She looks away, ashamed. "I haven't used this year at all, and I don't owe anyone anything."

"Listen," he says, his voice soft, "I'm not here to judge you, but it's my job to ask these questions. It helps me rule certain people out."

She looks at his earnest face and can imagine there's nothing he hasn't heard before in his line of business. "I understand. But there are no drug dealers, pimps or johns in my life. I may have used drugs and alcohol in the past, and I may be a bartender who's covered in tattoos and lives in a shitty apartment, but I'm not the kind of person who seeks trouble, Detective. I'm too busy surviving."

He smiles. "I hear you. How about relationships: are you dating anyone right now, or have you recently split with someone?"

Megan hasn't been in a relationship for a long time. "No. There's no one."

He makes a note. "I know from seeing you at the bar that you get a lot of unwanted attention. Maybe you can think of one guy in particular who didn't deal with rejection well, or someone who got a little handsy one time. Or maybe even a jealous girlfriend who thought you flirted with her partner."

Sure, there have been guys she's had to kick out of the bar or warn to keep their wandering hands to themselves, and women who've deluded themselves that she's interested in their loser boyfriends, but she can't think of any serious threat. "No one springs to mind. If I had any idea, I would tell you. I'm not covering up for anyone. The truth is there are very few people in my life." She's annoyed to feel tears in her eyes. She wants to be stronger than that.

He nods and offers her a reassuring smile. "Okay. That helps, because now I know I'm probably looking for an opportunistic assailant. Maybe he followed you home after your morning visit to the grocery store and thought he'd take a chance you lived alone." He changes focus. "Did you recognize anything about the person who crept up behind you: a smell of aftershave or perfume, perhaps, or a reflection of them in a mirror or window? Did they say anything at all before they struck you?"

"No. It happened just as I realized someone was in my apartment."

"Do you remember what time that was?"

She leans over to take a sip of water, but she can't reach the glass. Derek is on the other side of the room updating her chart and doesn't notice, so the detective hands it to her, putting the straw to her lips. The water feels amazing, but the pain from swallowing ruins it, making her want to ration herself. She lies back again. "It was afternoon. I was doing some chores before collecting Charlie." She stops. "Shit, Charlie! Is she okay? Did Kathy collect her from the party?"

Detective Cooper takes a deep breath. "This is why I needed to speak to you urgently. I'm afraid Charlie Hamilton hasn't been seen since yesterday afternoon."

"What?" Her blood runs cold and goosebumps prickle her arms. She tries to sit up properly, but Derek rushes over, gently pushing her back.

"No sudden movements. You're wired to these machines and it's not good for your blood pressure, or mine." He smiles.

She lies back and looks at the detective. "So, what, she's out there all alone somewhere?"

The detective chooses his words carefully. "She never made it home from the party and no one has seen her since around two o'clock yesterday afternoon. So far there's no trace of her. Until you were located, we were all hoping she was with you."

Her head pounds harder as she tries to control the panic creeping through her body. "What happened? Someone must've seen where she went. I need to get out of here."

Derek objects. "If you leave now, you won't last ten minutes before you're brought back in. You need to rest until we know you're well enough to leave."

"I have a whole team out looking for her," says Detective Cooper. "The best thing you can do is rest and try to remember any small detail that might help with finding out who attacked you."

"But I don't know who it was."

"Maybe you'll remember something once you're on the mend." He pauses. "I need to know whether you think your attack and Charlie going missing could be linked. It's probably unlikely considering you don't suspect anyone you know of hurting you, but to me it looks like someone didn't want you to collect her yesterday, giving them an opportunity to snatch her without anyone immediately raising the alarm."

"I don't know whether it's linked," she insists. Her mind is racing. "How are the Hamiltons coping?"

"They're beside themselves with worry, as you can imagine. I haven't told them we've found you yet; I wanted to wait until I'd spoken to you and got an update on your condition. I'll be calling Kathy shortly. I'm sure she'll come visit you once she knows where you are."

Just this short conversation has Megan feeling drained. Exhaustion sweeps over her, making her unable to focus. She relaxes into the bed, powerless against the sudden fatigue. "You have to find Charlie," she mumbles.

THIRTEEN

Kathy didn't sleep last night. It didn't feel right to rest while Charlie is missing. She only really dozed before jolting awake regularly, so she's relying on caffeine to keep her awake at this point. As a result, she feels shaky. Eating something would help, but she's worried she'll vomit it straight back up, especially as they're currently driving. As a child, she always suffered with travel sickness.

Last night was distressing without Charlie at home. Kathy missed reading her a bedtime story and tucking her in. Her cozy bedroom is filled with everything a child could ever want, and it seems unbearably empty without her. The house was so quiet. Kathy's parents wanted to come over, but they would have been of little comfort, and no doubt they would have clashed with Mitch. She told them it was best to stay away for now. Until she and Mitch have a better understanding of what's happening.

Scott told them about the search of his place, which he said went on until three this morning. Nothing was found inside or outside as far as he knows. But how does a child just vanish with no trace? And what about Megan? There has to be a reason that she's missing too. They must have been abducted together.

Kathy's stomach flips with dread at the thought of the alternative: that Megan has abducted Charlie. She doesn't allow the thought any credence. She doesn't believe Megan would put them through that. It's obvious she loves Charlie and wouldn't let any harm come to her.

Mitch was out until late, searching everywhere he could think of for them. He's clinging on to the hope that Charlie wandered off on her own and just needs finding, but they both know that doesn't explain why Megan didn't arrive to collect her. Kathy heard him get home at five this morning, and even then he didn't sleep. He sat in the kitchen, scouring his phone for potential sightings mentioned on the comments pages of the online news sites. It broke her heart to watch him.

Neither she nor Fay wanted to attend church this morning, not after seeing Charlie splashed across all the news channels on TV thanks to the amber alert, but Kathy's mom talked her into going. She thought it would offer them a brief respite from the worry. Mitch has never been one for attending church, but he always accompanies her if she asks him to. He knows her faith is important to her, and, who knows, maybe he'll find some comfort there too.

As he pulls into the parking lot, Fay says, "Do we have to? Everyone's going to stare at us. We could still turn around and go home."

Everyone in town knows what's happened. Their landline didn't stop ringing last night, with friends and co-workers wanting to reach out. Mitch has disconnected it now, and they've agreed with Chase to be contactable on their cell phones only, where they can screen calls.

Kathy turns in her seat. "Reverend Stanley called me earlier and said he wants to see us. He thought we might find comfort in being here amongst our friends."

Fay looks unimpressed, but she gets out of the car when they do. Kathy tenses when she sees people turning their heads to look at them. Some effort is made to stare discreetly, but it still makes her feel exposed.

"How are you holding up, Kathy?" asks Philippa, the school secretary.

She forces a smile. "I'm okay, thanks."

"I'm so sorry to hear what's happened. I'll be praying she's found today, safe and sound."

Kathy nods, unable to speak. Philippa walks back to her family and enters the church.

It's a beautiful Sunday morning and not too hot yet, but the hint of what's to come later is obvious. The sun is bouncing off the cars, causing glare, and the birds are singing in the cemetery. As she looks at the graves, Kathy has a terrible premonition of coming here in a couple of weeks to bury Charlie's body. It makes her stop in her tracks as she's overcome with grief.

Mitch's phone rings. After checking the number on the screen, he declines the call and silences his ringtone. It can't have been Chase or he would have answered it. Her own phone is set to vibrate so she can be alert for updates. Mitch takes her hand and whispers, "Let's get this over with."

She lets him lead her inside, where the stagnant air is already too warm. They find her parents seated near the back of the room, saving space for the three of them. Her dad offers her a sympathetic nod. Her mom kisses Fay's cheek when she sits next to her, then says, "Take your sunglasses off, sweetie. You're in church now."

"I can't," whispers Fay. "My eye is twitching like crazy."

Kathy only briefly glances at her parents, not wanting to see the sympathy in their eyes. It might crumble her resolve not to cry in public. Mitch nods to them from his position at the end of the pew.

"How are you?" asks her mom, leaning in.

"Stressed and tired," says Kathy quietly. "I don't know if coming here was the right thing to do. It feels like everyone's talking about us."

Reverend Stanley walks past to close the heavy oak door. On his way back to the front, he stops and leans in to her and Mitch. "I'm so pleased you came. I hope today's sermon brings you some comfort and that our prayers bring your daughter home."

Mitch mumbles, "Thanks."

"If you would like to see me afterwards, please feel free to stay behind." He smiles before walking away.

People chat quietly while fanning themselves with sunhats, and there are glances over shoulders at Kathy and Mitch. She hears the woman in front whisper to her friend, "I was at the party. I'm so glad it wasn't my daughter. I mean, can you even imagine?"

"No," says Kathy loudly. "You can't even begin to imagine what it's like."

The women don't look back at her, but their backs stiffen and they sit deadly still while Reverend Stanley delivers his sermon. He starts with Charlie, and Mitch's hand finds Kathy's. They both squeeze, trying to give each other strength.

"I wish to begin by asking God to bring Charlie Hamilton home to her loving family as soon as possible. She's an innocent child who deserves to live a long and happy life with her parents and her sister."

He doesn't mention Megan, and Kathy can't help feeling that was uncharitable. Everyone knows Megan is missing too. But she's not from Maple Falls and she's certainly not the kind of person these people would have in their lives, so to them she probably doesn't matter. Kathy feels a stab of guilt. She wishes she'd spent more time getting to know her.

"Let us now pray for Charlie's safe return," Reverend Stanley says solemnly.

Everyone lowers their eyes, and the large room is silent as he recites a prayer.

Kathy lets her concentration wane. Her mind is occupied with trying to piece together what could have happened at Scott's party in such a short time frame. Who from that party could have been capable of taking her? And why?

"Am I being punished?" Mitch whispers next to her.

She looks at him. His eyes are red and he's hanging his head, not wanting to make eye contact with anyone. Her heart goes out to him. Squeezing his hand tighter, she whispers, "No, Mitch. You can't think like that. This isn't your fault."

He rubs his eyes and remains silent as the reverend moves on to his planned sermon. Kathy glances at her mother and is shocked to see tears in her eyes. Her mother never cries. She has to look away as she realizes things must be bad if even Connie is emotional.

The longer the minister talks, the warmer Kathy gets. The wooden pew is hard beneath her, and she feels claustrophobic with so many people squeezed around her. "Stay here with Fay," she whispers to Mitch. "I need some air."

Several people watch her leave, probably hoping for tears. Or is she being unkind? Maybe they're genuinely worried about her. Once outside, the fresh air feels good and she takes a deep breath.

A woman sitting on a bench stares at her cell phone until she spots Kathy. She stands and slowly approaches. "I'm sorry about your daughter, Mrs. Hamilton. I hope she's found safe." She sighs. "I was at the party on Saturday."

Kathy's first instinct is to walk away. She doesn't want to talk to a stranger about Charlie. But neither does she want to appear rude, so she remains where she is.

"It all appeared a little unsavory to me, if I'm honest. Not what a children's party should be."

Kathy turns to her. "What do you mean? How can a children's birthday party be unsavory?"

The woman waves away a persistent fly. "Everyone was drinking too much. The men were boisterous and the women were loud. There was a lot of flirting going on between couples. I don't know, it just felt like the kids were being neglected. Left to their own devices. I remember saying to my husband that I didn't feel comfortable and wanted to leave early."

Kathy thinks of how Cindy was behaving, and how there was definitely an adult party vibe, but the children all seemed happy and safe. They had plenty of entertainment to keep them occupied. "Did you see anything in particular that concerned you?" she asks.

"Only the drunks." The woman pauses. "What about you? Who do you suspect?"

Kathy looks away. "I didn't see anything that made me worry about Charlie. She was having fun when I left."

"Did you know everyone present, or were they mostly your brother-in-law's friends?"

Kathy turns back to her, suspicious. "Who are you? I don't remember seeing you there."

The woman pulls a card out of her pocket. "Susan Cartwright. I'm an investigative reporter. Little girls going missing bothers me."

Alarmed, Kathy starts to walk away. She feels stupid for letting her guard down.

"I'm sorry, Mrs. Hamilton, but I wasn't lying," says Susan behind her. "I may not have been at the party, but I'm repeating what some of the guests told me, and I wanted your opinion. I'm trying to find your daughter."

Kathy doesn't stop until she reaches Mitch's car.

Susan is still following her. "If you decide you want to talk, call me." She slips a card under Mitch's windshield wipers. "I'm not from the tabloids. I'm trying to figure out what the hell's going on in this town."

Kathy pulls the card out. "Stay away from me and my family. The police will find my daughter."

With a sympathetic look, Susan says, "You really believe that? Charlie's not the only girl who's been abducted from this town recently. Remember Olivia Jenkins? She's still missing after eight months." Before Kathy closes her door, she hears Susan say, "Call me when you realize you need help."

She watches the woman walk away. Is this her life now, running away from reporters? She leans back against the headrest and tries to control her breathing.

FOURTEEN

Back at the house, Kathy peers out through the closed blinds covering the kitchen window and studies the three news vans outside. The rival reporters are swapping information and she recognizes Tammy Arlette from the local TV news, but the woman from the cemetery isn't there as far as she can tell. Mitch managed to dodge them all when they arrived home from church, but she wishes they would just leave her family alone. Having them camped outside makes her feel like a criminal. Her house is even being shown on TV.

Just past them is a police cruiser with a uniformed female officer watching the house. Chase insisted it was for their protection, but she wonders if he suspects that she or Mitch had anything to do with Charlie's disappearance. Just the thought of it makes her heart flutter with dread. The officer checks in on them periodically, bringing updates from Chase, who's too busy to call regularly himself right now. That gives Kathy hope that he's doing everything he can to find Charlie. Not wanting to be spotted, she steps away from the window.

She can tell Mitch isn't coping well. He's taken up smoking again after a long hiatus, and can't seem to sit still. He decided to go and oversee the renovation property he and Scott have partnered on, just to get out of the house. The contractors were booked weeks ago and it would cost too much to put the whole schedule back at short notice, so it makes sense. She doesn't mind him going. At least he has something to distract him from this nightmare.

Her cell phone rings. It's Chase.

"Hey," he says. "How are you holding up?"

She tenses, assuming the worst. She hasn't heard from him since a brief visit to the house last night to get some more information. "Have you found her?"

"No, not yet. I'm just checking in to update you. Is Mitch there?"

"No, he's had to go to work."

Fay appears from upstairs, wanting to hear whatever news there is. Kathy knows she managed a few hours' sleep last night, because she checked in on her more than once, but she still looks exhausted. Unfortunately, Fay's managed to convince herself that Charlie's been murdered, and now her anxiety is taking control.

"We've found no trace of Charlie at your brother-in-law's property, which I think is a good sign, because if she was harmed or taken against her will, there should be some evidence of that." He doesn't elaborate. "But I want you to know that I've located Megan."

The solemn way he says it makes her heart drop into her stomach.

"She was attacked at her home yesterday. It happened before she could leave to collect Charlie."

Kathy gasps. "Is she okay?"

"She will be. It looks like someone strangled her. I don't know yet if it's linked to what's happened to Charlie. She doesn't remember much. It could be a coincidence, but I'm not ruling anything out at this stage."

"*Strangled?* Oh my God, Chase. I can't believe this is happening. Things like this don't happen here." But she remembers what Susan Cartwright said: Charlie isn't the first girl in Maple Falls to go missing. Things like this do happen here—they happen everywhere—and Kathy knows she's been naïve to believe otherwise.

He hesitates before adding, "Megan doesn't have anyone with her at the hospital. I'd like to contact her family so that someone's there for her. Do you have her mom's number?"

Kathy has never met any of Megan's family or friends, and it dawns on her that she's never actually asked about them. Megan doesn't volunteer many details about her life, so Kathy doesn't like to pry. "Sorry, I don't. Are you sure she's going to be okay?"

"The doctors think she'll be fine. Physically, at least."

"I can't imagine who would do that to her." Her thoughts lean toward an ex-boyfriend, or maybe a customer from the bar. "Have you managed to interview all the guests from the party yet?"

"We're still working through them and your list of Charlie's friends. So far no one remembers seeing Charlie leave the party. The latest anyone saw her, although this is the estimate of someone who'd drunk a lot of bourbon, was around two o'clock. Apparently, Charlie was getting her face painted, so I spoke to the woman who did it."

Kathy remembers the woman in the princess costume who was overheating.

"She couldn't tell me much because she didn't notice where Charlie went after she'd finished with her. I guess it's to be expected with the number of kids present."

Her shoulders drop with disappointment. She doesn't know how long she can go without them finding her. What must poor Charlie be going through? If she's lost, she'll be hungry and terrified. If she's been taken... Kathy closes her eyes against the thought.

"I'm organizing a thorough search of the woods behind your brother-in-law's house. It's possible she wandered off on her own. We sent dogs in briefly last night, but they didn't find anything."

Kathy would prefer that to be the reason for her disappearance but she doesn't think Charlie wandered off, not when she had a pony to play with. And Chase isn't stupid. He must think her body could be dumped there. Tears quickly materialize. "My mind is racing with all the terrible possibilities. This is unbearable, Chase."

"I know it is. I'm sorry. Just trust that I'm doing everything I can. I have officers canvassing the neighborhood asking who and what the neighbors might've seen that afternoon. I'm checking to see if anyone has home security footage I can watch too." He sighs. "Did you get any sleep last night?"

"No. Neither did Mitch."

"That's understandable." He pauses. "I have an officer stationed outside Megan's hospital room to protect her in case her attacker comes back. Now that you know where she is, will you drop by and pay her a visit?"

Kathy wonders if Megan wants any visitors other than her own family. "Sure."

"I was wondering how long you've known her," says Chase. "Because it's my understanding that she lives in Glenwood and works in the sports bar on the edge of Maple Falls—which, forgive me for saying, isn't a place I would expect you or your husband to frequent, so I was wondering how you guys met."

She watches Fay wander into the kitchen, losing interest in the phone call. Moving to the patio doors in the dining area, she explains how Mitch met Megan first. "Mitch's job involves entertaining people: developers, buyers, other realtors. He finds himself in bars all over town as he sweet-talks people into deals. He met Megan at the bar a while ago and got talking to her over several visits. When he told her we were looking for a babysitter, she volunteered for some extra cash. She's wonderful with Charlie."

"Right." Chase sighs. "Listen, I've got to go." He sounds stressed.

"Is everything okay?"

"Yeah, it's just..." He hesitates. "Shannon arrived back in town last night, with no warning. She and her son are now my uninvited house guests."

Kathy is taken aback. "I thought that was over a long time ago."

"That makes two of us." He doesn't elaborate. "Listen, I'll keep you updated on the investigation, and if you need me for anything, just call."

"Thank you." Putting her phone on the coffee table, she goes to find Fay in the kitchen. Her daughter is leaning over the sink, hyperventilating. Rushing to her, Kathy doesn't bother asking what's wrong. She tries to comfort her instead, to slow her breathing.

"She's dead, isn't she?" asks Fay through gasps.

"No, that's not why he was calling. They've found Megan."

Fay snaps her head up. "Was Charlie with her?"

Kathy feels tears running down her cheeks. "No. Megan was attacked at home before she left to fetch Charlie, but she's going to be okay."

The news makes Fay worse, and Kathy knows what she has to do. She phones the clinic, gives her name and asks for an emergency appointment.

The receptionist is sympathetic, but has bad news. "Christine has a full day scheduled already. I'm sorry."

"Please," says Kathy. "My daughter is struggling. You must have seen the news?"

After a few seconds, there's tapping on a keyboard before the receptionist says, "Does twelve fifteen work for you?"

"Yes. We'll be there. Thank you."

"You're welcome. And I'm so sorry about your little girl. I'll be praying for you."

She tries to say thank you, but it comes out as a barely audible whisper.

Returning to Fay, she slips an arm around her shoulder, careful not to smother her with a hug, as Fay hates feeling claustrophobic. "Christine will see you at lunchtime. Until then, Charlie needs you to be strong, honey. Can you do that for her?"

Fay looks down at her hands, a tear dropping into her lap. "I hate feeling out of control." She has hiccups now as she regulates her breathing.

Kathy closes her eyes. "I know. Trust me, I hate that feeling too."

FIFTEEN

Progress Notes—Confidential

Client's description of the issues they are experiencing

Client detailed certain expectations from her parents, which she feels have added to increasing feelings of anxiety over recent months. She described her parents as overbearing, with a strained relationship with certain family members that causes tension at family gatherings, making her feel a strong sense of dread on those occasions. Her mother can be "over-protective" and "too worried about other people's opinions". Her father is "always working".

Client feels she has to act a certain way, achieve high grades, participate in a variety of activities she has no interest in, and present an air of respectability at all times. She says this makes her feel exhausted and unmotivated, as if she's pretending to be someone she's not, which makes her question whether being herself isn't good enough for them.

With the family currently experiencing a high level of stress, she feels unable to control her anxiety symptoms at present.

Therapist's observations

Client mentioned changes to her diet, limiting certain foods in order to lose weight, possibly to gain approval from peers or someone else. Some sense of rebellion is beginning over her hair, which she keeps tied back. She talks of wanting to cut it all off in a dramatic change to look less like her mother, so perhaps she's seeking her own identity, or she's looking to shock her mother into noticing her as an individual.

Goals/objectives of client

To practice self-care when feeling overwhelmed. To speak to her parents at the time something upsets her instead of letting it build up, unspoken. To keep taking her medication.

Assessment of progress

Although client was tearful at times, I don't see anything of particular concern other than her dietary changes and increasing anxiety. Her current low dose of medication is acceptable and I have emphasized the importance of taking it regularly, as it would appear she sometimes skips it when she's feeling well.

Client left the session feeling "better" for having spoken to someone outside the family and agreed to return before our next session if she feels overwhelmed again.

Any safety concerns

None.

Next appointment

Next week.

SIXTEEN

After dropping Fay off at the clinic, Kathy drives to the hospital. When Chase emphasized that Megan was alone and injured, she felt sympathy, of course, but also a little awkward about visiting her. Would Megan even want her there? In the end, she decided to go regardless. It's not like there's anything useful she can be doing instead. Work is over for summer, Mitch is out looking for Charlie when he's not at one of his properties, and Chase doesn't want her help with the search.

As well as the reporters turning up at her door, there have been random visitors dropping by with home-cooked food and sympathetic looks, but she still manages to feel alone. She'd like to be able to lean on her mother for support, but suspects it would come with recriminations and arguments. She needs to stay active, to distract herself from the terrible thoughts running through her mind. She keeps imagining Charlie's lifeless body being discovered in its hiding place. Closing her eyes against the image doesn't help, it just becomes more vivid.

Walking through the sterile corridors of the hospital, searching for Megan's room, she passes a young woman in a pink hospital gown. She looks gaunt and scared, and Kathy gets the urge to hug her. She doesn't, of course. Whenever she visits someone in the hospital, she's reminded to feel more content with her life because she's lucky not to be in here. She's lucky to have reached forty-four never having had an operation.

Her only two experiences of overnight stays in hospital were distressing. The first was filled with emotional trauma on top of the physical, and the second brought all that back up, making her want to flee the minute she'd given birth. If those experiences had gone differently, perhaps she would have had another child—they would have loved a son—but she couldn't face it. She consoles herself with the thought that, knowing her genes, a third child would've been another girl anyway. Up until last year, she and Mitch had been considering adopting a boy, but they don't discuss that anymore.

When a nurse points her to the right room, Kathy notices a police officer sitting outside. He's scrolling through his cell phone, but looks up every few seconds. Kathy tells him she's a friend of Megan's and that Detective Cooper has approved her visit. The officer nods as if he's expecting her. He watches closely as Kathy hesitates by the door.

Megan is lying flat on her back, and Kathy can't tell whether she's awake or not. Sensing her presence, Megan lifts her head. She looks surprised as she says, "Oh, hi."

Kathy steps forward, to the bed. Megan's black hair, with noticeably lighter roots, is in need of washing. There's dried blood around her hairline. As Kathy draws near, she's unable to contain her shock at the purple bruising around Megan's neck. Putting one hand to her mouth and her other hand on Megan's, she says, "Oh my goodness. You poor thing."

Megan grimaces. "I know, right? This will ruin my sex life for a while. Although my nurse tells me some guys are into this shit." As soon as she says it, she blushes hard, but Kathy knows she's just using humor to mask her fear of what's happened to her.

An awkwardness fills the room, and Megan uses the controls to raise the back of the bed, putting her in a half-seated position and closer to eye level. Her tattoos become visible as her hospital gown sleeves pull up. "Have they found Charlie?" she asks, with concern on her face.

Kathy shakes her head. "No. There are no clues and no sightings of her. It's like she just vanished into thin air." Her voice hitches, and she clears her throat. "I just had a text from Chase—Detective Cooper—saying they're searching the woods behind Scott's house again. They have sniffer dogs and will ask for volunteers to join the search if she's not found by the end of the day."

"So they're expecting her to be found dead." Megan closes her eyes against tears. "I should be there. I want to help find her."

"You need to get better first. There's no point you going out there just to collapse. Besides, Chase doesn't want our help."

Wiping her eyes, Megan looks desperate. "But I feel so helpless! I can't believe this is happening. The thought of her alone out there, or with a... stranger." She's trying to put a brave face on it, but a tear manages to escape. "It has to be someone who was at the party. I mean, isn't that obvious to the cops? They should be background-checking every person who attended, every neighbor who recently moved in. One of Scott's friends must be a sex offender!"

Kathy reaches for a tissue and hands it over. "Don't let your mind go there, Megan. I'm trying hard not to." She takes a seat next to the bed. "Do you have any idea who might have attacked you?"

"No. Like I told Mitch, I don't have any enemies—"

"Mitch?" Kathy interrupts. "When did you speak to him?"

Megan looks like a rabbit caught in the headlights. "He was here about an hour ago. I thought that was why you were here now. To sort the arrangements."

Kathy's confused. "What do you mean?"

"He said I can come stay with you when I'm released tomorrow. Just while I recuperate and until Charlie's found."

Kathy can't stop her mouth from dropping open in shock. "He said *what?*"

Megan tries to sit up straighter, but winces with the pain. "Sorry, I thought you knew. He gave me the impression that you both thought it was a good idea."

Kathy hears the blood rushing to her head in anger. Imagine what people will say when they realize she's let the babysitter move in. Why can't Megan stay with her own parents? She grabs her purse. "I need to speak to him."

Megan looks both mortified and disappointed by her reaction. "I'm sorry. I didn't mean to upset you. I don't want to be anyone's charity case."

Knowing it's not her fault, Kathy tries to reassure her. "You didn't upset me. I just don't like it when Mitch makes decisions without discussing them with me first." She sighs, dropping her purse back on the bed. She looks over her shoulder at the police officer outside the room. "Do they think your attacker might return?"

"Who knows? The cop thinks that whoever did this to me intended to kill me, so maybe. It's horrible to think someone wanted me dead." Megan's voice is raspy, and she keeps having to sip water.

Kathy can't believe this has happened to someone they know. What if Megan's would-be killer tracks her down at their house to finish what he started? Does Mitch not realize he's putting his family at risk by letting her stay with them? "Why don't you want to recuperate with your parents?"

Megan looks away. "I can't. I mean, I only have a mom, but I'm not in touch with her anymore. She disowned me back when I started using drugs. I don't blame her or anything; I was a lost cause back then."

Kathy's heart sinks. "I'm sorry." She doesn't want to pry; they're not close enough for that. If Megan really is alone, it would be the right thing to do to have her stay with them temporarily. But Kathy's no nurse. She can only offer so much. And with school being closed for summer, she'll be home all day with her. It'll be awkward. It's alright for Mitch; he'll probably keep going to work to distract himself from waiting for news. She takes a deep breath, trying to calm her speeding heart rate. "What else did Mitch say while he was here?"

Megan sinks back into the bed. "Not much. He doesn't want me to talk to the cop about any of you, just about what happened to me."

That doesn't surprise Kathy. He always paints her as the intensely private person, but he's the one harboring secrets. He's the one she's been protecting for months now.

"He said he'll pay for a lawyer if I need one."

Kathy frowns. "Why would you need a lawyer?"

"It may come as news to someone like you, Mrs. Hamilton, but cops can't always be trusted. If they want to close a case fast, they'll pin the crime on anyone who looks like an easy conviction. I'm sure it won't be long until Detective Cooper asks to search my apartment for signs of Charlie being hurt there." She pauses. "But only after he searches your house first."

Goosebumps run up Kathy's arms at the thought of the police searching her private things. "Chase is a good person. He's not like that. He'll be doing everything possible to find Charlie and the real kidnapper."

"So you know him personally?"

She nods. "We went to school together, though that was a long time ago. He can search our home if it helps him find Charlie. Mitch and I have nothing to hide."

Megan raises her eyebrows. "You don't?"

Kathy's cheeks flush hot with annoyance. It's time to leave.

SEVENTEEN

The mid-afternoon sun is beating down on Chase's neck, making it sting. He takes a sip of his bottled water, warm now, as he watches the search team advance through the woods behind Mitch's brother's house. They move one slow step at a time before stopping to look left, right, forward; then take another step, almost in unison.

It's too hot to be outside today, and the canopy of leaves above isn't dense enough to block the sun's rays in most places. At least the team are almost at the creek now. It's usually cooler there, and a great place to hang out with your girlfriend when you're a teenager with no privacy at home.

Chase thinks of Shannon. He found her naked in his bed when he eventually got home late last night. She was asleep, but she obviously thought she could worm her way back into his life. Maybe if she'd caught him on a different day, she could have, but not now. He slept in the spare room, and before he left for work this morning, he asked her to find somewhere else to stay. Something tells him she won't go quietly.

Patrick was wary around him, confirming the boy doesn't remember the first three years of his life. Chase had time to show him a few magic tricks before he left for work, and the kid finally lost all fear of him when he handed over his detective badge. He promised they could play cops and robbers when he gets home from work later, because deep down, Chase knows Shannon has no intention of leaving. She's done this too many times before. Besides, it might be good for Patrick to be in town for a while. Maybe it's an opportunity for Luke to seek some kind of custody arrangement so that the boy has a responsible adult in his life. He knows that Luke's tried numerous times before to get custody, but then Shannon bailed on them. She's a problem Chase needs to solve, but right now, that's not as important as finding his missing girl.

He squints against the glare of the sun as he looks in the direction of the creek. Beyond that is the seedier part of town, where Chase spends most of his days. That's not to say there's more crime there than there is here. It's just not as well hidden.

His cell phone rings for what must be the tenth time in an hour.

"Sorry to bother you, Detective." It's Maureen, the dispatcher. "I've got another reporter on the line. He wants a statement for tonight's bulletin."

Chase sighs. "Tell him and any other reporters who call that I'll be holding a press conference this evening. They'll have to wait for that."

"Understood."

He slips his phone into his pocket as Detective Brown approaches. They're not exactly partners, but they do buddy up when necessary. The sweat patches under Brown's arms are spreading. "No sign of her yet," he says. "I'm starting to doubt she came this way."

Chase chews the inside of his cheek as he considers their next move. "How else would the abductor have got her out of the party undetected? It's not like one of the guests could've walked her off the property without someone seeing them together."

Scott's yard backs unsecured onto the woods beyond. Unlike his nearest neighbors, he hasn't fenced it off. It would be easy for someone to hide amongst the trees, lying in wait. Especially since practically the whole town knew of this party, which was planned months in advance. And from what Chase has learned from interviewing the guests, it would seem Charlie was last spotted on the white pony that was giving rides near the woods. Elaine—the pony's handler—told him the little girl had taken her third turn on the horse and then gone straight to the back of the line, waiting for another. But she never got another turn. Charlie disappeared, and when she didn't see her again, Elaine assumed she'd gone to get some cotton candy.

"Maybe she really did wander off on her own and fell into the creek," says Detective Brown.

Chase nods. "The other team are over there now, and I have divers on standby if we don't find anything here."

"Did you manage to get any home surveillance footage from the neighboring houses?"

"No. Everyone thinks this town is so safe they don't need smart doorbells and cameras." He scoffs. "If it's so safe, what are we doing here? Why is there even a police department? We should be redundant."

Brown snorts. "I know, right? They all think it won't happen to them until it happens to them. I drove by a five-year-old girl playing in a front yard this morning on my way to work. She was completely alone and would've been an easy target."

Chase shakes his head.

"That's not even the worst of it. I rolled up alongside her in my car and she came over without me even saying anything. We made small talk before I lectured her about stranger danger. If I was a perp, I could've just snatched her! No one came out of the house to check on us. No blinds were twitching at the neighbors'. I mean, a five-year-old girl literally went missing yesterday, but this family still let theirs play outside unsupervised!"

"Rich folk think they're invincible, that it won't happen to them," says Chase. "Besides, everyone's glued to their cell phones. As long as the kids are quiet, the parents keep scrolling. This is why witnesses are so hard to come by nowadays."

"Yet the minute we put a foot wrong, there they are in the blink of an eye, recording their little social media videos."

Chase isn't bitter about that. Some of his co-workers need recording, the things they get up to. In his opinion, if there's nothing to hide, those videos aren't worth worrying about. "I need a motive for Charlie's disappearance, and I'd bet you a hundred bucks it's linked to Megan Carter's attack."

Brown agrees. "You solve one, you solve both."

Chase turns when he hears the sound of branches snapping behind them. Scott Bowers raises his hand as he approaches. "Hi. I'm just coming to lend a hand. I'd like to join the search for my niece."

Chase crosses his arms. He doesn't want family members dropping DNA anywhere around here. It could muddy the waters if Charlie is eventually found dead. "Thanks, but we don't need anyone else right now."

Detective Brown walks back toward the volunteers, leaving them to talk.

Chase takes the opportunity to question Scott away from his wider family. "So what do you think happened to Charlie?"

Scott rubs the back of his neck and sucks in his breath. "I wish I knew, man. My wife's in bits worrying that someone we invited into our home—someone we trusted—took her."

Chase watches him carefully. "Did you invite anyone with a criminal background? Anyone who's done time?"

Scott laughs. "How am I supposed to know? I mean, we only know what people tell us, right? But I don't think so."

"Was there anyone present you didn't recognize?"

"Sure, a few people. And the entertainers, of course."

He means the two clowns, the cotton-candy operator, the pony handler and the face-painter. The fire-eaters cancelled at short notice, apparently. All the entertainers were considered persons of interest, but Chase has already questioned and cleared everyone but the clowns. "Who booked the clowns?" he asks now.

"Cindy booked everything. My business keeps me busy, so I let her do anything that involves the kids, especially with the size of parties expected nowadays. When I was a kid, the only good thing about a birthday was the fact that our dad would try not to beat us. He'd make a special exception." Scott smiles bitterly. "Kids these days don't know they're born."

Chase waves away a cloud of flies. "Oh, I don't know about that. I still attend households that sound similar to yours growing up." He didn't know Scott and Mitch were physically abused. He wonders if Kathy does. "I don't have contact details for the clowns you used. Would you get your wife to text them to me urgently?"

"Sure."

Someone appears from the direction of the backyard. It's Mitch. He looks at Scott as he approaches. "What are you doing here?"

"I wanted to help with the search," says Scott, somewhat defensively. "Where have you been?"

Mitch takes a final drag on his cigarette before dropping it in the dirt and stepping on it. He picks up the dead butt. "Some people have to work on Sundays." He turns to Chase. "I'm free for the rest of the day. What can I do?"

Chase senses tension between the brothers. "We're all good here."

Mitch shakes his head. "I don't care. I have to help. I'll just join the end of the line." He moves forward, but Chase holds up a hand.

"No, I can't get your DNA mixed up with anything we find here." He looks at both of them in turn. Scott rubs his face, disappointed, and Mitch clenches his jaw. Chase clarifies. "Think about what happens if this gets to court and your DNA is found on her clothes, or on a weapon found out here. Any potential suspect I arrest will have their defense team blame you in order to get off. I need a clean crime scene."

"So you think she's dead?" Mitch whispers, the color fading from his cheeks. He unbuttons the collar of his shirt.

"Honestly? No. I think if she were dead, we would've found something by now. Most abductors do what they want with the child within the first few hours, then they discard the body, knowing that every minute they keep it they risk getting caught."

Mitch's hands go to his head and he briefly turns away.

"It's been approximately twenty-five hours since Charlie was last seen," says Chase. "In my experience, that means she's either been taken somewhere alive, or she's wandered off and hurt herself."

A helicopter approaches and hovers overhead, temporarily obscuring the sun and sending leaves and dirt flying around them. It drowns out all other sounds. When it eventually passes, Chase turns back to Mitch. "That's here for Charlie. So you can be certain that I have all available resources dedicated to finding her. The best thing you guys can do is stay home and be there to comfort your families and take calls from anyone who might get in touch with you about sightings and rumors. Because some people don't like talking to the police; they'd rather speak to the family of the missing child."

Mitch lets that sink in, before nodding. "Kathy and I have been talking about it, and we'd like to offer a reward for information leading to Charlie's whereabouts."

Chase takes a deep breath. "That's not a good idea."

"Why the hell not?" says Scott. "It's worth a try. I'll contribute a few grand."

"Not yet, okay? We'll just be inundated with false information from people attempting to claim the reward. It could do more harm than good." Mitch doesn't look convinced, so Chase adds, "Trust me on this and hold out for now. It's something we can try a few days down the line if necessary. But I'm hoping we won't need to."

Eventually Mitch nods. "Fine. What about the assault on Megan; have you got any leads on who did that at least?"

Chase ignores the attitude. "Nothing yet. No one saw any strangers coming or going from her apartment, and I don't have anything to prove it was linked to Charlie's disappearance, but I have to prioritize finding your daughter first. That's more time-sensitive."

Mitch doesn't press for details. He understands what Chase is saying. "If you need to speak to her again, you'll find her at our house once she's released from the hospital tomorrow morning."

Scott's head snaps around so fast to look at his brother that Chase is distracted from his own confusion. "What? Why?"

Mitch looks at Chase instead of Scott. "She doesn't have any family to stay with, and Charlie's disappearance has hit her hard. She's blaming herself because she wasn't there to collect her. We want to take care of her, just until she's well enough to take care of herself."

Scott's shaking his head in disbelief. "You need to be careful. She might get used to living there."

Chase is trying to read Scott's reaction. "You sound like you don't have a very high opinion of Megan Carter."

Mitch flashes his brother a warning look that shuts him up. "Whatever," says Scott. "I need a drink. You coming?"

Mitch nods. Before he leaves, he says to Chase, "Call me as

soon as you find anything, or if you need volunteers. I'm serious: I want to help."

Chase nods and watches them walk away. From behind, it's difficult to tell them apart, yet their personalities couldn't be more different.

EIGHTEEN

Kathy struggles to acknowledge Mitch when he finally returns home late afternoon. She's still angry at him for inviting Megan to stay with them, so she only manages a brief smile before they compare updates from Chase. But when he hugs Fay and takes the time to ask how her therapy session went, she finds herself thawing toward him.

"I'm going back next week, but Christine said I can call in whenever I feel a panic attack coming on," says Fay, tying back her long hair. She's sitting at the breakfast bar. For some reason, the family spend more time in the kitchen than anywhere else in the house. "She's kind of cool, you know? I feel like she really cares about me."

"That's great, sweetie," Mitch says. "I'm glad we got you a therapist. It's good to talk about your feelings with a professional, especially if you're completely honest and open with them."

Kathy wonders if that's a dig at her strained participation in their couples therapy, but when he comes up and pulls her in for a hug, she realizes she's being too sensitive. Being in his embrace gives her strength. It makes her feel like they can get through this together. She kisses him before he pulls away to make a drink.

Fay sips her soda before asking, "What happens if Charlie isn't found? Like, if she never comes home and we just never find out what happened to her?" She keeps her eyes low.

Kathy goes to her and kisses her forehead. "We just have to take it one day at a time. Remember what you were told about not looking too far ahead and assuming the worst?"

Fay nods. "I guess. It's easy to say that, though."

There's a knock at the door, and they all visibly tense. Is it the police? Mitch opens it to Reverend Stanley.

"I'm sorry to trouble you at home," he says. "It's just that I didn't get a chance to talk to you at church this morning and... well, I wanted to see if I could be of any help."

Mitch looks at Kathy, who nods. "Come on in, Reverend." She leads him outside to the deck, and notices that both Fay and Mitch opt to stay indoors. He's been a minister at their church for around five years now. She'd age him at around fifty, and although he's pleasant enough, she's never really felt close to him, not in the way she did with Reverend Holbrook, who was always so warm and kind. "Please, take a seat."

"Thank you."

"Can I get you a drink?"

Before he can answer, Mitch has placed a jug of lemonade on the glass table in front of them, along with two glasses. Kathy smiles up at him. "Thanks."

He squeezes her shoulder. "You don't mind if I make a few calls, do you? I think I might finally have a buyer for Wicker Lane, and the guy seemed interested in the Glenwood house too."

Kathy shakes her head. The Glenwood house is the renovation project Scott went in on with Mitch. The first time they've partnered on anything. Scott's not overseeing any of the work; he just invested money. When Mitch leaves, she pours

Reverend Stanley a drink and then sits back. Her hands shake a little. "I suppose everyone's talking about us?"

He smiles faintly. "It's to be expected. But I haven't heard anything negative. There's a feeling of disbelief that this could've happened here. And the community just wants to help."

She believes him. "I know. It's just that we're in such a terrible situation that I can't imagine how anyone *could* help." A tear rolls down her face.

Reverend Stanley leans forward. "Sometimes a kind ear is all you need to put things into perspective and regain hope. From what I understand, there are no signs that Charlie's been hurt. Have faith that she'll be returned home unscathed. That's what I'll be praying for."

Kathy knows he means well, but he doesn't have children. Perhaps it's easier to have faith in something when it's not your loved one who's missing.

"How's Fay coping?" he asks. "Because I'm happy to see her one-on-one if she needs more support."

"Fay's seeing a therapist, so she's already got someone to talk to. She gets on well with Christine. They've built a good level of trust, I think."

"Christine Stiles?"

"Yes."

He nods. "I know Christine and her partner well. They're a nice couple." He sips his lemonade before asking, "Are you seeking comfort from your parents?"

She takes a deep breath. "Not really. I'm hoping Charlie will be back before I get that desperate." She attempts a laugh.

"You know, Connie was visibly upset after you left church earlier. She stayed behind to pray with me. Your father was worried about her."

Kathy feels guilty. "I guess they're just as affected. They love the children."

"I know all families have their tensions, but don't shut them out in your time of need. This is a time for bonding, for dismissing past problems and giving each other strength. It's what Charlie would want."

She looks at him. "Charlie loves going to church. She told me you're kind to her and that you remind her of Santa Claus."

He leans back and blushes. "Well, I've never been called Santa before."

Is it modesty making him blush? "You've given her some thoughtful gifts over the last few months."

He frowns. "No. I don't think so."

"Yes, she showed me. The plastic horse with a pink mane. A stuffed animal. That's why she thinks you're like Santa. Well, that and the white hair."

He shakes his head. "No, you must be mistaken. Perhaps she accidentally brought them home from the playroom at church?"

Kathy's confused. Is he accusing Charlie of stealing?

Voices drift out from the house behind them, and Kathy recognizes Cindy's. She stands up. "Sorry, Reverend. It looks like I have another visitor."

He puts his drink on the table and stands up. "No problem." He takes her hands in his, which are sweaty. "I'll pray for her every day until she's home safe."

Kathy offers a smile, but she doesn't feel it. Reverend Stanley exchanges a few words with Mitch before he leaves the house.

Cindy's carrying a ceramic dish and wearing sunglasses, presumably hiding her hangover from yesterday's party. "Sorry to call by unannounced, but I just had to see you." She hugs Fay first, then Kathy. She's dressed demurely today; there's no hint of the sunburn that covers her chest.

She leaves her sunglasses on, but shudders, clutching her

elbows. "You need to turn your A/C down; it's like a morgue in here!"

No one replies, and Kathy's aghast at the insensitive comment. Cindy eventually realizes she's said the wrong thing and quickly changes the subject without apologizing. "How are you coping? I can't stop thinking about you all."

Kathy crosses her arms. "We're just about managing. Waiting for news. There's not much else we can do, is there?"

"I've been watching the news unfold online," says Cindy. "They've issued an amber alert, and there have been sightings of her as far away as Texas."

Mitch shoots her a sharp look. "We don't need to hear about every hoax sighting, thanks."

But Fay's eyes light up at the news. "Then we need to go to Texas! We could bring her home."

"No, Fay. It won't be her," says Mitch. "And if it is, don't you think the police would already be on their way?" He shakes his head at Cindy. "See what you've started?"

Cindy's defiant. "I'm sorry, but I'm just repeating what people are saying online. How do you know it isn't her?"

"Yeah, Dad. We should go."

"No!" he shouts.

They all look at him, surprised by his anger.

"Should we also go to New Hampshire, where she's been spotted in a mall?" he says. "Or to Washington, where she's supposedly eating ice cream by the sea with an old woman?" His voice is rising. "Or how about Hawaii, where she's being forced to have sex with rich men? Because that's also what it says online." He walks away from them, through the living room and out to the backyard.

Cindy sighs. "I didn't mean to upset him"

Fay fights back tears as she runs upstairs. Kathy's left alone with her sister-in-law. "Everyone's a little sensitive right now. Perhaps you should leave."

Cindy's eyes widen. "But I'm family! I'm Charlie's aunt. Don't you think this is upsetting for me too?"

"Come on, Cindy. How many times have you visited her in the last six months? When do you ever ask how she's progressing at school? When have you ever invited her over to spend time with your boys?" Scott's made the effort, but Cindy never has.

Cindy is speechless, until: "She's welcome whenever she wants. I assumed you knew that."

Kathy has heard enough. "I have things to do. Thanks for the food. I'll get the dish back to you."

Cindy removes her sunglasses, revealing bloodshot eyes and dark circles. "What's really going on, Kathy? Because something doesn't add up. How can Charlie be at my house one minute and gone the next? It just doesn't make any sense."

Kathy feels her face flush with anger. How should she know what happened? "Where was your husband around the time she vanished?" she retorts. "Did he really go out for more food mid afternoon, or did he drive his niece away somewhere?"

Cindy gasps. "How dare you! If you want to point fingers, how about you tell me where you were yesterday afternoon. Because I know you weren't at the refuge."

Kathy gasps and looks for Mitch, but he's still outside.

"A friend of mine told me she spotted you after you left the party. You were headed home, the opposite direction to the refuge. At first I assumed you lied because you didn't want to spend time with us. But now I'm starting to wonder. Because as far as I can see, you're the person with the biggest reason to want Charlie gone."

Kathy is trembling. She can feel her world about to come crashing down.

"Go home, Cindy." Mitch strides back inside. "Stay away from my family. That goes for your asshole husband too."

Kathy has never been so relieved to hear him shout.

Cindy slips her sunglasses back on and heads to the front door. "You guys are crazy. I wouldn't be surprised if Charlie ran away from you."

Before she knows she's going to do it, Kathy has hold of the dish Cindy brought and is at the front door, throwing it onto the driveway. It smashes upon impact, sending red sauce and lasagna sheets across the concrete and up Cindy's legs. She regrets it instantly.

Cindy looks back at her in horror. "The unflappable Kathy Hamilton has finally let her guard down, I see. And it turns out you've got a screw loose."

Mitch is gently pulling on Kathy's arm, but it's too late. She sees her neighbor, Mrs. Patterson, watching. Embarrassment overwhelms her as she turns away.

Mitch closes the front door on the mess and pulls her to him. "I'm so sorry, Kath," he says.

She looks up at him. "I don't know how much more I can take."

He squeezes her tight, but it doesn't help. Because she has a horrible feeling that their secrets are about to be exposed.

NINETEEN

The swelling in Megan's throat has significantly reduced thanks to all the fluids she's been drinking, but the bruises will take longer to heal. Dr. Anders thinks they could stick around for weeks. That's okay, she can button her shirts up to hide the worst of them. He says her head wound is, thankfully, superficial, although the blood made it look much worse. He confirms she can be released in the morning, as long as she continues the bed rest for a few days and then takes it easy as she gets back to her normal routine. But how can she return to normality while Charlie's missing? Not knowing where she is is devastating, and her body feels like it's in a state of heightened anxiety while she waits for news. The nurses keep telling her to try to relax, as it's affecting her blood pressure.

Staying at the Hamiltons' house will be strange. Mitch is relatively easy-going, but Kathy keeps her wall up. That's why Megan still calls her Mrs. Hamilton, despite Kathy insisting she shouldn't. Megan has no idea what Kathy really thinks of her, and she wouldn't normally care, but she genuinely wants to know. She could tell Kathy wasn't thrilled at Mitch's offer to let her stay with them, but she was gracious enough to accept it, and for that Megan is grateful. She wouldn't feel safe alone in her own apartment right now. Not until the cops find out who did this to her.

She leans her head back against the hospital pillows and realizes the sun will be setting soon. This will be the second night Charlie's missing. Is she outside somewhere alone and lost? She's scared of the dark, so Megan really hopes not. But the alternative makes her shudder. She switches on the light that's sitting on the nightstand. She was in this hospital not that long ago, on Christmas Day. An unexpected overdose. She had been doing so well, but sometimes the depression takes her unawares and cocaine is the only thing she's found that numbs it.

A tear rolls down her cheek. She can't rest not knowing where Charlie is, who she's with. The guilt is unbearable. If she had been able to fight her attacker, she would've been at the party to collect Charlie.

She unmutes the small TV on the wall when she notices that a press conference at the police station is about to start.

Detective Cooper leads Kathy and Mitch to the front of the room, where they stand a short distance behind him. Kathy is visibly nervous. She's wearing pale pink pants and a white silk blouse, looking down at the ground and clutching a tissue. Mitch, dressed the same as always in a crisp shirt and suit pants, stares defiantly at each journalist behind the camera before fixing his steely gaze into the lens. It makes her feel like he's looking directly at her.

The cop clears his throat. "Thanks for joining us, folks. For those who don't know me, I'm Detective Chase Cooper from Maple Falls PD. Behind me are Mitch and Kathy Hamilton, Charlotte Hamilton's parents."

Megan feels butterflies in her stomach.

"Charlotte, known as Charlie to her friends and family, has been missing since around two o'clock yesterday afternoon. At this stage we don't know whether she wandered off on her own and hurt herself, or whether she was taken by someone, but she was attending a party at twenty-two seventeen Lexington Lane." He stops to take a breath. "Having interviewed almost all the guests present, and searched the woods and creek behind the residence, we appear to have no leads. If you have any information relating to Charlie's disappearance, we would ask that you get in touch with us as a matter of urgency. It might be something that you consider small, such as a car speeding away from the neighborhood at that time, or maybe you spotted a discarded item of child's clothing on your morning run. Everything will be treated seriously and confidentially."

He sips some water in front of him before continuing. "All media outlets have been provided with a recent photograph of Charlie, which should appear on your TV screens now. This was taken shortly before her disappearance, and she was wearing the outfit she's dressed in here."

Charlie appears, straddling a white pony and smiling at the camera. She looks adorable and so happy.

"She actually had her face painted shortly after this was taken," says Detective Cooper. "She chose a rabbit, so her face was mainly white, with black whiskers and a pink nose. As you can see from her photograph, she's missing her two front teeth, and the face-painter said she drew bunny teeth on her bottom lip."

Megan chokes back a laugh, imagining what Charlie looked like as a rabbit. She wipes her eyes, then clutches her hands together.

"However," continues the detective, "the paint could've been washed off by now, so please concentrate on her outfit. She's only five years old, six in October, so we obviously want to see her reunited with her parents as soon as possible."

He turns to look at Kathy and Mitch. Megan can hear him asking if they want to say anything. Kathy shakes her head and presses the tissue to her eyes and nose. Mitch takes a step closer to the mics. "Please get in touch with either the police or us direct if you can think of anything out of the ordinary that happened on Saturday afternoon. We want our daughter back safe with us as soon as possible. She's an innocent little girl who deserves to be at home, and her older sister misses her greatly." Overcome with emotion, he turns away.

Megan's eyes well up and she reaches for a tissue from the nightstand. Mitch is an exemplary father.

Detective Cooper asks the journalists if they have any questions. They're out of view of the cameras, but Megan can hear their questions. One man asks, "Do you have any potential suspects at all, Detective?"

"Not at this time, no."

She can tell it pains him to admit that.

"Is this latest disappearance linked in any way to the disappearance of Olivia Jenkins eight months ago?"

"I don't believe so, no."

Megan remembers Olivia's disappearance. She was seven years old when she was snatched after getting off a school bus mid afternoon. She hasn't been seen since. Her mother tried to keep the case relevant in the news, but the media moved on quickly. They don't like hanging around trailer parks for long; their viewers aren't interested in the people who live there. She feels a flurry of panic building in her chest. Is that what's going to happen to Charlie's case? Or will the fact that the Hamiltons are well known, well connected and come from a more affluent neighborhood mean Charlie never gets forgotten? The police are sure to pump more resources into finding her.

She considers the possibility of the two disappearances being linked. Could it be the same person who took Olivia?

"Where were Mr. and Mrs. Hamilton at the time of their daughter's disappearance?" asks another reporter. "I understand they weren't present at the party. Is that correct?"

Chase nods. "They were both at work at the time."

Megan notices he doesn't mention she was supposed to collect Charlie for them. He told her beforehand that he doesn't want to drag her into this story, because he thinks there's a risk the focus will be shifted away from finding Charlie and onto why Megan was attacked. He explained that if he finds proof of a link between the two incidents, he'll have to go public in the hope of securing new information, but until then he's keeping her attack under wraps as much as possible. She quickly realized it's because he thinks the public will assume she was responsible for whatever happened to Charlie. The press would start hounding her and looking into her background. The fact that Chase doesn't want that to happen tells her he doesn't suspect her of any involvement.

A woman speaks up next and Megan recognizes her voice. She's from the local TV news—Tammy something. "I understand Mrs. Hamilton was volunteering at the women's refuge that afternoon, is that correct?"

Kathy looks up for the first time. There's surprise in her eyes and Megan wonders why. Kathy stares hard in the direction of the question.

"That's correct," says Cooper.

"Then why," continues Tammy, "do I have sources telling me she didn't actually turn up at the refuge at all that day?" She pauses for effect. "Where was she really that afternoon, Detective?"

Mitch's head snaps left to look at his wife as a chorus of excited mumblings can be heard off camera.

Megan sits a little straighter in bed. Has Kathy lied about her alibi? Why the hell would she do that?

Despite looking surprised himself, Detective Cooper resists the temptation to turn around and stare at Kathy. Instead, he ignores the question and asks if anyone has any others. The inevitable happens.

"Would Mrs. Hamilton like to answer the question?" asks a guy.

Kathy walks off camera, closely followed by Mitch, leaving the cop by himself. "That's it for now. Please call in with any information you may have. Our main priority is getting this little girl back to her family."

Detective Cooper is trying to keep people focused, but Megan knows that once the finger of suspicion has fallen on someone, it's impossible to shake it off.

TWENTY

"What the hell is going on?" says Mitch, incredulous. "You made us look terrible!"

Kathy remains silent, cursing herself for putting them in that position.

Chase leads Mitch away from the reporters who are emerging from the briefing room. "Keep it down." He takes them to a small, windowless interview room and closes the door. "Take a seat. Both of you."

Kathy's hands are shaking. She feels like she's about to be arrested. Sitting next to Mitch, she glances at a discarded newspaper in front of her on the table, next to a dirty coffee mug. She does a double-take at the black-and-white photograph under the headline *Local professor offered tenure at university.* She must be staring too hard, as Chase pulls the paper away and dumps it on a spare chair. She looks up at him. "I'm sorry."

His eyes are wary. "What exactly are you sorry for, Kathy?"

She can feel Mitch's eyes on her too. "I was supposed to go to the refuge, but I had the opportunity to have a couple of hours alone at home, and I couldn't resist." She turns to Mitch, who's clearly angry. "I had a migraine, remember? I just needed to lie down for a few hours, because once I got to the party, the music and afternoon sun made it even worse."

"Why didn't you tell me?" says Mitch. "Why didn't you tell *him*? It would've saved us a hell of a lot of embarrassment."

Because she knew she'd be judged for it. "I felt bad for taking some time for myself. I'm expected to do everything, and there's no one else to do it if I can't. You're rarely at home these days, and you leave all the kids' stuff to me, even though I work full-time too. And the refuge staff rely on me, so I felt guilty for letting them down. But I just needed some peace and quiet. And I'm not going to apologize for it, because those few hours of silence were bliss." She looks at her hands. "Obviously if I'd known Charlie was being abducted, I would've stayed at the party."

Mitch puts his hand on hers but doesn't say anything.

"Cindy knows I didn't go to the refuge," she says. "I guess she must've told that reporter. All because she was angry at me for throwing her out of the house."

Mitch removes his hand. "I'd like to say I can't believe she'd go against us like that, but it doesn't surprise me. She's worse than my brother."

Chase is rubbing his temple. "You shouldn't have lied, Kathy. It's going to make my job harder."

"Why?" she asks.

"Because now I have to treat you both as suspects," he says sharply. "Something I was trying to avoid."

Mitch shakes his head in disgust. "That will waste so much time. Meanwhile my daughter's alone out there with some sex offender!"

"We don't know that." Chase takes a seat opposite them and pulls out his notebook. "Kathy, did anyone see you arrive home after leaving the party? Any neighbors maybe, or passers-by?"

She tries to think. Mrs. Patterson wasn't around, but that doesn't mean she wasn't watching from behind her blinds. "Not that I saw. I got home about two fifteen and went straight to bed."

"How long were you asleep?"

"I didn't actually fall asleep, I just rested." It really was bliss to have the whole house to herself in complete silence. It's so rare for her to get that kind of downtime, and it's only when she gets it that she realizes how much she needs it occasionally. "I left the house at a quarter to four for our appointment in Glenwood."

"Did anyone call you during that time?" asks Chase. "Because I can check your phone records."

"No."

"No unexpected visitors?"

She shakes her head.

Chase sighs. "So you have an alibi that can't be corroborated. Perfect."

She doesn't know how to prove she had nothing to do with Charlie's disappearance. "Why would I take her, Chase? What on earth would I gain from all this? You know how private I am. Yet now I have reporters hounding me outside my own home and cameras constantly focused on me. This is my worst nightmare."

He doesn't comment. Instead, he turns to Mitch. "Okay, your turn. I need the names of whoever you were with yesterday."

Mitch drops his hands into his lap. "I was showing a house to a couple over on Wicker Lane. I got there just after eight." He looks away.

Chase says, "I already know about that. It was *after* you reported Charlie missing and I came to your house. What about earlier on? I thought you said you were working all day?"

There's no hiding the fact that Mitch's face has turned ashen. Beads of sweat are accumulating on his upper lip. He wipes them away. "I wasn't with clients during the day, I was just checking out the homes I have on my books. And there was work being done at one of the houses I'm renovating, so I went to oversee that."

"Okay, so I need the names and numbers of the contractors who were working at the time. Anyone who can confirm you were there and how long for. And I want the contact details for the couple you showed around the house on Wicker Lane. Once I have all that, I'll have Detective Brown verify everything."

"You told me you had a full day of house tours scheduled," Kathy says to her husband.

Mitch is tense. "I'll get you those details, Detective. In the meantime, you need to be looking closely at everyone who was at the party. I've been told her teacher was present—Mr. Barren. I don't know his first name. He's a single guy, new to town, and Charlie never stops talking about him. Have you questioned him yet?"

Chase clearly doesn't appreciate being told how to do his job. "Almost everyone has been questioned."

"So who are your main suspects? Because focusing on us is going to slow down the investigation."

"I'm not at liberty to discuss suspects with you."

"But you do have some?" asks Kathy.

"Like I've told you both before, we've found no evidence of what happened, so we don't know whether Charlie was abducted or whether she wandered off by herself. We're staying open-minded."

"Sounds to me like you should be working harder." Mitch stands up. "Are we free to go?"

Chase crosses his arms. "That depends. Is there anything else either of you wants to tell me? Because now would be a good time considering the heat is going to be on you after what happened in there."

Kathy can feel sweat in her armpits. Her hands are

clenched. Chase is going to discover everything, she just knows it. He won't ease up until Charlie's found. As Mitch moves for the door, she remains seated and takes a deep breath. "Charlie's adopted."

"Kathy! What the hell?" Mitch is fuming. He slumps back down in the seat next to her.

"I'm sorry, but he'd find out eventually anyway. It's not like it's a secret." Mitch shakes his head and she turns to Chase. "She's only been living with us for six months."

"She's adopted?" Chase looks surprised. "Why wouldn't you tell me that from the beginning?"

Her mouth is bone dry. "We thought you would assume we don't love her because we're not her biological parents. You might have thought we weren't careful with her; that we don't care that she's missing." She pauses. "Or that we had something to do with it."

Mitch is fidgeting next to her, clearly uncomfortable.

"But we *do* love her. We're her parents now. Besides, we didn't know she'd be missing this long, so it seemed irrelevant before." She feels like she's bargaining with her freedom. "Chase, you have to believe that we had nothing to do with her disappearance and that we want her home safe. She's such a loving, bright little girl who's already been through so much."

Chase studies them both silently. Eventually he says, "You've got to stop keeping things from me; you're hampering the investigation. Knowing she's adopted means I can check out whether her biological parents might've been involved in her disappearance."

"No," says Mitch. "They're dead. She doesn't have any biological family left. That's what we were told when we adopted her."

"Who else knows she's adopted?"

"All our friends and family," says Kathy. "And the school and all Charlie's friends."

"Megan Carter?"

"Of course. It isn't a secret, we just didn't see the relevance in you knowing. Every time we have to explain to someone that we're not her biological parents, it feels like we're reinforcing the fact. We feel like her real parents. She's fit into our family so well, and Fay adores her."

"So Fay knows?"

"Of course."

"And how did she react when she found out she was getting a new sister?"

"She was anxious at first, of course, but they get on so well that it's never been an issue. Charlie is a lovable little girl, Chase. I can't imagine anyone wanting to hurt her."

Mitch rubs his eyes, and clears his throat. She can tell he's struggling to keep himself together.

Chase stands up. "I guess it doesn't make much difference that she's adopted. I just wish you'd told me before the press conference so I could've told them. You're new to all this—being scrutinized by the media—so I understand how these mistakes can happen. But you need to be careful now, because we need the public on our side if we're to get Charlie back. I'll have to issue a statement to confirm she's adopted before any reporters find out for themselves through your acquaintances. Otherwise they'll make it appear as if you tried to hide it."

Kathy shakes her head at the thought of everything being in the papers.

"If I were you, I'd stay away from all reporters. Give no-comment answers to any questions they throw at you as you come and go from your house. Now they have a hint that your alibi was false, they're going to spin this story from a different angle and you two could be in for a rough ride."

Kathy closes her eyes at the thought that things are about to get a whole lot worse.

TWENTY-ONE

Chase's cell phone rings and he frantically rushes to silence it. Sliding low in the driver's seat, he watches Scott's house. There's a huge maple tree obscuring his view of the driveway, and with the sun now set, it's dark out, so he's relying on street lights, but he can just about tell who's coming and going.

After his meeting with Kathy and Mitch, his gut tells him that one of them—or maybe both—is holding back on him. It's disappointing that Kathy won't trust him. Sure, a lot of time has passed since they were close, but he feels like it's more than that. Maybe her husband is controlling her in some way. Or maybe she's covering for herself or someone else. His stomach dives just thinking about the possibility of her being involved in Charlie's disappearance. He doesn't want to believe it, but he's been a cop long enough to know that most serious crimes, like murder and kidnap, are committed by people who know the victim: friends, co-workers and family members. He has to remain objective and not let his past feelings for Kathy skew his logic.

So, following his instinct, he left the station shortly after them and watched as Mitch drove straight here, without Kathy, who headed in the direction of their home. Chase wonders what's going on in Scott's house. It's past nine, so Mitch should be home with his own family. Maybe he's confronting Cindy about going to the press with Kathy's false alibi. Or maybe he's discussing Charlie's whereabouts with Scott. Chase fully intends to look into both brothers carefully. He considers the teacher Mitch mentioned. Mr. Barren wasn't named as a guest by anyone else at the party, so he hasn't been questioned as far as Chase knows. He'll make sure that gets rectified.

He glances at his phone to see who called. It was Detective Brown. He shoots off a quick text.

Surveilling Mitch Hamilton. Text me instead.

Within seconds, he gets a response.

I've left a message for the couple Hamilton was showing a house to on Saturday night. Also, the press conference has generated a lot of calls. Working through them all. Will update if anything useful.

It doesn't surprise Chase that the public want to play a part in solving Charlie's disappearance. Everyone's an armchair detective these days. But he's banking on one of the family's friends or neighbors coming forward about something out of the ordinary that may have happened that day. Something that made them stop and think, "Huh. That was weird."

He sees movement to the left. Mitch is leaving Scott's house. Whatever he came for didn't take long, suggesting it was most likely an angry outburst at Cindy, or Mitch blaming his brother for Charlie being taken from his property. It's too dark to read the guy's expression from here, and he gets straight in his car before driving off. Chase decides to follow him at a distance, putting two cars between them. The darkness helps obscure him.

When it becomes clear Mitch isn't driving home, Chase sits a little straighter in his seat. This is the part of the job he loves: surveilling suspects. Catching them in the middle of something and piecing everything together. He's a little disappointed when Mitch pulls up outside an apartment complex in Glenwood. It's not Megan's, but it's not far away either. Mitch is inside for all of five minutes before getting back into his car.

"What are you doing?" Chase mumbles to himself. "Covering your tracks maybe?" He makes a note of the street, but he didn't see which apartment Mitch went into, so he can't check who lives there.

This time Mitch does drive home, and with the blinds closed at the house, Chase can't see what's going on inside. He sighs and checks his watch. It's probably time for him to go home too, but he doesn't want to be there if Shannon hasn't left. He could do without the drama. If she has left, there's a good chance she's taken half his stuff to sell, like last time. He thinks of Charlie Hamilton. Happy to avoid his personal life in order to find her faster, he heads back to the station.

Detective Brown brings Chase a black coffee and takes a seat across from him. Brown's desk is covered in paperwork, which is bad considering they're meant to be going paperless. "Want to hear what people have been calling in about?"

"Sure," says Chase, sipping the coffee.

But they're interrupted by Luke Phillips, and he looks pissed. "So I hear you and Shannon are back together? You're back to bringing up my boy, who for some unknown reason I'm not even allowed to talk to." He crosses his arms.

Detective Brown raises his eyebrows at Chase, but remains silent.

"No, actually," says Chase, leaning back in his seat. "She turned up out of the blue, let herself in and told me afterwards."

Luke doesn't look convinced. "Is Patrick with her?"

"Of course." Chase remembers his promise to play cops-and-robbers with Patrick before bedtime tonight, but that's out of the window now. He feels a pang of guilt for letting the kid down. "You can stop by to see him whenever you want."

Luke scoffs. "There's no way Shannon would let me in."

"Then we'll sort a time when I'm home. I'll let you in."

Luke's arms drop. "Seriously?"

"Sure. Your boy's growing up fast and he needs his dad in his life. Your issues with Shannon are nothing to do with me, and I'm not interested in taking her back. I've actually asked her to leave."

"Good for you," says Brown.

"Think she will?" asks Luke.

"Not immediately, no." Chase pauses. "I don't think it's good for Patrick to only have her in his life. He needs somewhere to settle. He needs to be enrolled in school. I don't want to tell you what to do, Luke, but if I were Patrick's dad, I'd lawyer up and seek some kind of custody arrangement. I mean, she's not beating the kid or anything, but I don't think he's a priority in her life."

A determined look crosses Luke's face. He nods. "I'll make a call." He starts walking away before turning back. "Thanks."

Chase nods. When Luke has gone, he turns to Brown. "So where were we?"

Brown looks like he wants to give Chase some unsolicited advice about Shannon, but he thinks better of it. "Okay. So, we've had the usual psychics who say they'll tell us where the girl is for the special reduced rate of a hundred bucks. Non-refundable if their intel is bogus, of course."

"Oh, of course." Chase rolls his eyes.

"And we've had the weirdos who obviously just want to be involved in the case." Brown discards the written notes onto his desk as he goes through them. "Ah, this woman said she heard a girl scream out by the meat market Saturday afternoon, but that could've been anyone." He's about to go on, but Chase stops him.

"Wait. Scott Bowers—the uncle—was at the meat market at..." He tries to remember. "Around two forty." He takes the slip of paper from Brown. It has the caller's contact details on. He checks his watch and sees that it's nearing ten. "Think it's too late to call her?"

Brown shrugs. "What's the worst that can happen?"

Chase smiles and picks up Brown's desk phone, punching the number in. It takes several rings before he gets an answer from a wary woman.

"Hello?"

"Michelle?" he asks.

"Yes. Who's this?"

"Detective Chase Cooper from Maple Falls PD. I'm sorry to bother you so late, ma'am, but I'm following up on your earlier call to us. I believe you heard a scream during your trip to the meat market on Saturday?"

"Oh, okay."

"Could you tell me what time that was?"

She exhales. "Let me think. I'm pretty sure I was there between one forty-five and probably two fifteen, maybe a little later."

The hairs on his arms stand up.

"I was loading my trunk with groceries when this loud, piercing scream rang out through the parking lot. I looked up, waiting for a second one, but there was only that one."

"Could you tell what direction the scream came from?" He can pull CCTV from the store and check if the nearby businesses have cameras, but it would be useful to know what direction he should be looking at.

"No, it kind of reverberated across the lot, so I looked in all directions."

"Did you see anything at all? A car speeding off, or a child being dragged along by someone?"

"There were cars coming and going every few minutes, but I don't remember anyone speeding off or a child being dragged." She laughs nervously. "I mean, I definitely would've noticed that."

He tries not to bombard her with questions, but he has to know exactly what she witnessed. "Did you hear a door slam shut after the scream?"

"Er, I don't know, sorry. I only listened for a few seconds before returning to my groceries. At the time, I just assumed it was a child having a tantrum—that happens all the time in the store. God knows my daughter used to throw all kinds of theatrics when I refused to buy candy."

"And you're sure it was a girl, not a boy?"

"Right. That was my impression. I could be wrong, though."

"Sure. Did anyone else look up or investigate the scream?"

"Not that I could tell, but I really wasn't paying that much attention to anyone around me. Of course, with hindsight I would've phoned the police immediately, but it was only when I saw you on the news tonight, and the look on her poor parents' faces, that I put two and two together."

He nods. "I understand. Well, you've been very helpful. Thanks for calling in."

"No problem. Goodnight."

Chase puts the phone down and looks at Brown, whose eyebrows are raised in anticipation. "Get the surveillance footage from the meat market for that afternoon. And from the nearby stores too."

"Sure thing."

He doesn't know if this is a false lead, but the fact that Scott Bowers was present at the same location and within thirty minutes of someone hearing a girl scream means he needs to get it checked out.

TWENTY-TWO

The morning sunshine is bright, making Kathy wince as she peers out of the kitchen window to spy on the reporters. Monday has rolled around fast, and the weekend would normally be a distant memory as the week got off to a busy start, even during the summer break. She planned to take Charlie shopping for vacation clothes today. They were going to go for lunch at her favorite diner after and have the ice cream sundae reserved for special occasions. Kathy thinks of all the times she told Charlie she couldn't have one because it was bad for her teeth. Now she wishes she'd given in every single time. She blinks back tears.

This is the second morning of waking up without Charlie, and the reporters have grown in numbers since yesterday evening's press conference. She daren't look at the papers this morning or watch the news. Mitch reminded her that she's most likely the headline now, for misleading the police about her whereabouts.

The thought stopped her from sleeping, so she spent the night in Charlie's room. She expected to remain alone in there, but Mitch came to find her. There were no recriminations from either of them, just tears for Charlie and prayers that she'd find her way home to them. The guilt is the hardest emotion to bear. If only one of them had stayed at the party with her. If only they'd both attended it and been the family Charlie so desperately needed. But they didn't. Eventually they fell asleep on her bed, clutching each other tightly.

"Where are they?" says her mom behind her.

Kathy turns to look at her. Since her stroke, she's aged noticeably. Being seventy, she was already looking a little gray and weathered, but now she walks slower and there's a frailty to her movements: a shake of the hand, watery eyes, jewelry askew. Normally always polished in appearance, she now forgoes her custom silk scarves, and opts for comfortable flat shoes over her favorite low heels. It's sad to watch her decline this way. The stroke really affected her physically, but mentally she's as sharp as ever.

What's been surprising is the effect it's had on Kathy's dad. Jack Miller isn't a man who often shows his softer side. That's not to say he's a bully, but Kathy's never seen him cry, for instance, and he doesn't tell her he loves her. But since his wife's stroke, he's become quieter, less bullish and more reflective. When he arrived earlier—the first time at the house since Charlie went missing—he hugged Kathy hard and she could swear he was choking back tears. It made her uneasy. She needs his strength at a time like this. "I'm sure they won't be long, Mom."

Her dad walks in from the backyard. "I don't know why we bought you this house if you're not going to maintain it, Kathy." He leans against the door frame. "You need a gardener if your husband is never going to mow the lawn. I'd be embarrassed for my neighbors to see my yard looking like that."

Kathy takes a deep breath. It's true the house was a gift to celebrate her pregnancy with Fay. At the time, Mitch was only just finding his feet in the realtor world and she was earning less than she does now, so they were extremely grateful. But that makes her parents think they get a say in how she and Mitch take care of the place, so they're always looking for something to criticize. "He likes doing it himself when he has the time. Besides, we really don't care what our neighbors think of us, Dad."

"Oh, good Lord," says her mom dramatically. "She's turned into one of *those* people, Jack. I thought we raised you better than that, dear. I mean, what's next: a huge trampoline in the yard sitting amongst a collection of rusty old cars housing feral kittens?"

Biting her tongue, Kathy turns back to the window, not wanting to argue with them. Charlie would love a huge trampoline in the backyard.

Her dad approaches. He squeezes her shoulder gently. "Sorry, honey. I'm just trying to distract myself by talking crap. Don't listen to me. I'm not good in situations like this."

She puts her hand on his and turns to face them. "You have to be nice to Megan. Both of you. She's been through a terrible ordeal."

Her mom raises her eyebrows. "Well, it's her own fault. I mean, what does she expect, living the life she leads?"

Kathy stares at her. "What do you mean?"

"Working at that awful bar, getting those ugly tattoos. And don't even get me started on the way she dresses. I bet there's a long line of men who come and go from her apartment; I doubt the police will ever get through the list of potential suspects."

"Mom! Stop it. Don't you dare victim-shame anyone! And if you say any of that to Megan, you won't be welcome here anymore. I'm serious." She can feel her blood boiling. "By that logic, you're basically saying it's Charlie's fault she's been taken."

Her mom looks surprised. "Not at all. She's a child. She can't help it if some despicable loser who can't get a woman his own age kidnapped her!"

"Give it a rest, Connie," says Jack. "Now's not the time."

"Fine. Then tell her what we've decided, before Megan arrives."

Kathy looks at her dad. "What do you mean? What have you decided?"

He crosses his arms. "We're going to offer a reward for information. Twenty-five thousand dollars to start with."

Kathy's mouth drops open and she's overcome with gratitude. "The police don't think that's a good idea."

Her dad waves away the thought as if it's preposterous. "Oh, please. How can it not be a good idea? If life's taught me anything, it's that nothing motivates people more than money. If a buddy or a neighbor of the perp knows something, they're far more likely to come forward if they'll be financially rewarded. It's an incentive. I don't care what the cops say."

She agrees with him and it gives her fresh hope. Stepping forward, she hugs him tight. "Thanks so much, Dad."

"What about me?" says her mom, coming over with that annoying smile on her face, the one that says *I know I've done wrong but you have to love me anyway*.

Kathy hugs her too. "I appreciate it. But let me tell the detective. I can talk him around to our way of thinking." She turns back to the window as a car pulls into the drive. "Mitch and Megan are here."

She steps back from the window as her mom takes a seat on the couch. She would rather her parents weren't here for this, but she can't just ask them to leave. Especially after what they've just promised. "Please don't be mean to her. And don't stare at the bruising on her neck or the gash on her head. I don't want to make her self-conscious."

Her dad walks toward the back door. "I'm going to mow your lawn. Mitch can thank me later."

That's so typical of her father. He'd rather do manual labor than get in the middle of an awkward situation.

Fay must've spotted Mitch's car too, because she emerges from upstairs. Her hair needs washing and she looks tired and sweaty. She's not coping well, so Kathy's booked her in for another therapy session in a couple of hours.

The key turns in the lock, and Kathy can hear some commotion from the reporters outside. It sounds like they're throwing questions at Mitch. Not for the first time, she thinks it should be illegal for the press to harass victims' families during the worst time of their lives.

"Ready?" she says to her daughter.

Fay nods sullenly. "I guess. I still think it's weird, though."

"I couldn't agree more," says Kathy's mom behind them as the lawnmower starts up in the distance.

Kathy fixes a smile on her face as the front door opens. Megan enters behind Mitch. He's carrying a suitcase she knows is full of belongings from Megan's apartment, because they were stopping by there on their way here.

"Hi, Megan," she says, a little too high-pitched. "Come on in."

Megan tentatively steps forward, and blushes when she sees Kathy's mom smiling at her from the couch. Mitch has to coax her out of the doorway and into the kitchen. Her neck is less swollen, but it's still not back to normal. Her face is pale and her hair is tied into a messy topknot. She's not dressed for the heat, wearing gray sweatpants with an oversized cardigan over a white vest. She looks like she's just got out of bed, which of course, she has.

Kathy glances at Fay, who hasn't seen Megan since Charlie vanished. She has tears in her eyes and she gasps as she notices the bruising.

Megan steps toward her. "You don't need to worry about me. I'm not in as much pain as you probably think I am. I mean, I was at first because it hurt like a bitch—" She looks at Kathy. "Shit, sorry."

"It's fine." Kathy tries to smile reassuringly. It's nothing Fay doesn't hear at school.

Megan turns back to Fay. "I'm going to be fine. I just need a few days' bed rest and then I'll be out of your hair."

"I don't care what happened to you," says Fay bitterly. "You should've been with Charlie! She would never have been taken if you'd done your job!" She's wiping tears away from her eyes with her sleeves.

Kathy is mortified. "Fay! Stop that. It's not Megan's fault."

"How do you know? Don't you think it's weird that Charlie would go missing at the exact same time *she* gets attacked?" She doesn't give Kathy time to answer before she's turned back to Megan. "People online are saying you probably sold her to someone for human trafficking! Or you have some sleazy boyfriend who's raping her right now!"

"Fay! That's enough," says Mitch firmly. "I've told you before you can't believe any of those conspiracy theories online." He looks at Kathy. "News has broken about Megan's attack. The reporters outside couldn't get enough photographs of her. So much for your cop friend keeping it quiet."

Kathy doesn't think Chase would have leaked it.

Megan has tears in her eyes now. "I didn't have anything to do with it, Fay. You have to believe me."

"No, I don't. I don't even know why you're staying with us. You're only the babysitter, and now that Charlie's probably dead, you're not even needed anymore!" Fay runs upstairs and slams her bedroom door closed behind her.

"I'm so sorry," says Kathy. Fay's anger is confusing. It doesn't make sense to blame Megan.

Kathy's mom gets off the couch. "I'll give you folks some

privacy for this strange situation you find yourselves in." She heads out the back door, into the yard.

Megan remains silent, her eyes on the floor. She clearly feels as awkward as Kathy does. The next few days are going to be difficult.

Grateful to have a reason to get out of the house for a while, Kathy grabs her car keys and purse. "I'm taking Fay to her session. She's getting worse."

Mitch looks at his watch. "It's a little early, isn't it?"

"I don't care!" she snaps. Everything's getting to her now. She just wants Charlie to walk through the door, and it's becoming clear that that might never happen. Regaining her composure, she adds, "I'll stop by the store while I'm out. I'm making beef tacos for dinner, Megan. Is that okay?"

Megan nods. There's disappointment in her eyes.

There's nothing Kathy can do about that. She can't help needing to escape. This whole situation is spiraling out of control. "You're welcome to help yourself to anything in the kitchen during your stay, but is there anything specific you'd like me to pick up? Or do you need a toothbrush? Any toiletries? Medication?"

"No, honestly, I'm fine. I'll eat anything and I brought some toiletries from home. Mitch has my meds." She blushes.

"She thinks it's a good idea if we keep them somewhere safe," says Mitch.

Kathy realizes that Megan's afraid of having the pills around her. A shot of sympathy makes her want to hug the girl, and it reminds her that Megan is suffering too.

Mitch notices the sound of the lawnmower for the first time. "For God's sake, is Jack mowing our lawn again?"

Kathy nods. "Sorry, I can't deal with my parents right now. I need some air."

Shaking his head, Mitch picks up Megan's suitcase. "I'll guess I'll show you to your room. I'll send Fay down, Kathy. Try to speak to her therapist after to see if she's coping okay. Because it really doesn't feel like it."

Kathy nods, and escapes through the front door. The warmth of the morning sun does its best to reassure her, but there's nothing reassuring about having Megan staying with them.

TWENTY-THREE

Progress Notes—Confidential

Client's description of the issues they are experiencing

Client arrived extremely upset and explained the tension in her household feels unbearable. She believes her parents are keeping secrets from her, which is making her question whether they're trustworthy. This is having a significant impact on the parent–child relationship. It's noteworthy that she doesn't entirely trust me yet, which shows she finds it difficult to make meaningful connections, perhaps because of secrecy at home.

At present she doesn't feel close to either parent, so I suggested confiding in a close friend, at which point she asked if we were friends. She then turned her attention to asking me about how to become a therapist and what qualifications I have. This could be an attempt at deflection or a way to relax her mind from her own worries. When she tried to probe me with questions about my private life, I moved the subject back to her.

Therapist's observations

Client is still limiting her diet and now declares herself vegetarian. No one else in the house forgoes meat. If she starts losing weight, I will raise this with her parents. She wanted to show me the definition in her abdominal area, expecting praise. I told her a healthy weight was more admirable. She appeared somewhat disheveled this time, although she hadn't cut her long hair short as she previously stated she wanted to do.

I explained the client confidentiality rule again to emphasize I will protect her privacy and not reveal the content of our sessions to anyone else, in order that she trust me with more details at future sessions. However, I'm not sure she was convinced her parents won't find out what she tells me. I explained the exceptions to this rule but I don't believe them to be a factor for consideration with this client. I will build on her trust in future sessions, making sure she sees me as an adult who will never let her down.

Goals/objectives of client

Client agreed to educate herself on nutrition and to practice meditation techniques using the information pack I gave her.

Assessment of progress

Client left the session feeling "more relaxed" but "dreading going home" because "it will all start up again". I've provided her with some exercises she can do when feeling out of control, and suggested she tries to focus on her school work. I believe she has the coping mechanisms in place to handle her current stress levels.

Any safety concerns

None.

Next appointment
    Within a week.

TWENTY-FOUR

With Fay dropped at the clinic a little early, Kathy has time to wander around the grocery store for an hour or so. She's hoping that performing a routine task like this will distract her from the overwhelming urge to break down.

She grabs a shopping cart and stops dead when, on the noticeboard near the entrance, she sees Charlie's sweet face grinning at her. She gasps. She wasn't prepared for it. It's a missing person flyer, something she never expected to see a member of her family on. But half of it is already covered by ads for dog-walkers, mobile hairdressers and other mundane services. Chase's team must have distributed these, but to know they're already being overlooked just two days into her disappearance makes her want to cry.

She takes a deep breath and diverts her eyes, trying to ignore her trembling legs. As she pushes the cart around the aisles, she can't remember what she needs. She throws random food items into it, trying to predict what Megan likes to eat and drink. Stopping in front of the liquor aisle, she considers buying a large bottle of vodka. Never much of a drinker—although she likes the odd glass of wine in the evening, and champagne at special events—she's suddenly overwhelmed with a craving for the sharp taste. Maybe it would help her sleep.

She places a bottle in her cart before immediately taking it out again and putting it back on the shelf. Best not go down that road. She focuses on the regular food her family likes, and it's only when she puts Charlie's favorite snack bars into the cart that she realizes they might go uneaten. Forever. A chill runs through her and she has to lean against the shelf when her legs go weak. She swallows back tears as the thought of never needing these again threatens to overwhelm her.

Should she buy them to prove her faith that Charlie will come home? Or is buying them tempting fate that she's dead? Her throat suddenly closes up at the thought of having to throw away Charlie's favorite food. Then she thinks of her clothes and toys. Will she have to give them to charity, or should she bin them? What does one do when a child dies? She thinks about Charlie's bedroom. How it will need emptying and redecorating in a way that never reminds them of her. Will Mitch collapse under his grief and leave the family home? Would that be the best thing for all of them? Could she start afresh without him? Who would get custody of Fay? And what about poor Megan?

She puts her hand to her chest as she tries to calm down, but her heart is pounding so hard she worries she'll have a heart attack from all the pressure she's under.

Other shoppers pass her, and all of them look twice. Some she recognizes, but others must have seen her on the news. No one is brave enough to say anything, and for that she's glad. She takes a couple of deep breaths, trying to regain control. She only looks up when she senses someone staring. It's Charlie's teacher. She tries to smile, but Mr. Barren walks away before she reaches him.

For some reason, it angers her. Why won't he say hello? She abandons her cart and walks quickly past the refrigerated milk, finding him in the bread aisle. When he looks over at her, she feels stupid for following him and she doesn't know what to say.

"I'm sorry for what you're going through," he offers. He's dressed casually in cargo shorts and a T-shirt.

"Thank you. You were at the party, weren't you? I saw you leave later on."

He nods, placing his basket on the ground at his feet. "It's hard to believe something like that would happen in this town."

"Something like what?"

"A child vanishing." He looks at her like she's stupid, before his eyes soften. "When I was considering applying for my role at the school, I looked into whether Maple Falls was somewhere I'd want to live. Most people confirmed that it's a quiet, safe town with low crime rates. So it's a shock to learn Charlie might have been abducted."

She finds it unlikely that a thirty-something single male would care much about crime rates. "Did you talk to her at the party?"

"No. I think I saw her getting her face painted, but we didn't speak." He picks up his basket. "If I can do anything to help, just say the word."

If Charlie had seen him there she would've told him about her latest story. She'd been talking about it at breakfast. Is he lying? Kathy remembers the way he left the party the minute she turned up the second time. And Mitch was right when he said Charlie never stops talking about him. "She loves you, you know."

He smiles. It appears genuine. "Children get attached to their teachers. She was always a joy in class, telling stories to whoever would listen."

Kathy goes dizzy. "You said *was*."

"What?"

"You used the past tense. Do you know she's dead?" What if it was him? What if he abused his position of trust like so many do? Her hands are shaking as she clutches her purse tighter. "Did you take her?"

His eyes are wide with surprise. "Of course not! Mrs. Hamilton, you've got the wrong idea. I didn't even speak to Charlie that day. I'm a teacher, for God's sake. I'd never hurt a child!"

A full minute of silence passes between them as Kathy tries to judge whether he's lying.

Someone touches her shoulder, making her jump. She spins around and sees Martha Burton, the former online gambler, standing there with a dopey smile across her face.

"Hi, gang! Fancy meeting you two in here like this. I usually bump into fellow teachers in the liquor aisle." Martha laughs at her own joke.

"I've got to go," says Mr. Barren, taking his opportunity to escape. "It was nice seeing you both."

Kathy watches him walk away. Is she jumping to conclusions?

"Something I said?" asks Martha.

Kathy doesn't answer. Her eyes wander down to Martha's shopping cart. There are two large bottles of champagne, various dips, finger food, a pack of balloons and some beer.

Martha follows her gaze. "Oh, we're having a party this afternoon. It feels like my whole summer is booked up with parties already!" She must realize by the look on Kathy's face that she's said the wrong thing. Awkwardly, she adds, "It's not a child's birthday party. My friend's dating a professor, and he's got tenure at the university. So we're going to celebrate."

Kathy feels like everyone is carrying on as normal, as if there isn't a predator in their midst. She doesn't know who Martha's friend is, but she asks, "What's the professor's name?" She already knows the answer to that. It was in the paper.

"Evan Harris. There's a chance he might propose to her tonight, so obviously I'll be there to catch it on camera."

Kathy looks away.

"Look, I wasn't going to ask, because I don't want to upset you, but have they found any sign of Charlie yet? I'm constantly updating the news page on my phone, waiting and praying that they'll find her alive. I mean, I know she's not been with you long, but you must be distraught about losing her so soon."

Kathy's hands twitch at the thought of slapping this ignorant woman. "I didn't *lose* her, Martha. She's not some item of clothing left behind in a restaurant. She's a five-year-old girl who was abducted. And save your prayers for someone else, because I don't want them."

Martha gasps. "I've got to say, Kathy, that's not very charitable. I thought you'd believe in the power of prayer."

Kathy walks away, biting her tongue. She fights tears as she heads to her car. She parked in the corner furthest away from the store so she could stay out of view while she waits for Fay's therapy session to be over.

It's only when she's seated and sure no one else can see her that she lets her tears fall, and they quickly turn into heavy, gasping sobs.

TWENTY-FIVE

A tap at the window makes Kathy jump. She reaches for a tissue to wipe her eyes and nose before she faces whoever is insensitive enough to disturb her when she's clearly upset.

It's Chase. Relieved, she opens the door and gets out of the car.

"Hey," he says. "Sorry to bother you, but I saw you leave the store. Are you okay?"

After a few seconds' hesitation, she steps forward without saying a word. He pulls her into an embrace as she breaks down. Stroking her hair, he murmurs, "It's okay, Kathy. Let it out. It's good for you."

They could be sixteen again, back at the creek and far from prying eyes. Their summer that year was perfect; the following one would have been too if it wasn't for what happened. She finds comfort in his strong but tender embrace. He was always the ideal height for her chin to rest in the dip of his warm neck.

Eventually she pulls away, glancing around to see if anyone spotted them. He follows her gaze, and when she looks back at him, he retreats a step, reading her mind. He'll know she's worried what people will think. He should be too, given his position, but she can tell he isn't.

"Is there any news?" she asks.

"No. I'm sorry. You'll be the first to know. How's Fay coping?"

"Not well. She has a therapist. I dropped her there before coming here."

He smiles. "You rich people and your shrinks. I always found Jack Daniel's listened to my problems at a pinch of the price." He nudges her arm to show he's only joking.

She smiles as she wipes her eyes. "I wish I could help her myself, but she's at that age where she'd rather keep things from me. She respects Christine. It sounds like they're building a good rapport. I know it's sometimes helpful to have someone to talk to who isn't involved in the family."

He nods. "I want to update you on why I'm at the grocery store, because it's not to grab lunch."

She tenses, suddenly not wanting to hear what he has to say. "Tell me in the car."

He walks around to the passenger side as she slides into the driver's seat. Closing the door, she takes a deep breath.

He faces her. "A woman at the meat market heard a single scream, possibly female, in the parking lot at around the same time Scott was here picking up supplies on Saturday afternoon."

She shudders, and goosebumps appear on her arms.

"I haven't been able to pinpoint the exact time Charlie went missing, but I believe, based on witness accounts, it's between one forty-five and three p.m. We're in the process of securing the store's surveillance footage from that afternoon, and I've come to check which other businesses around here might have cameras or witnesses. But seeing as I've got you alone without your husband, I'd like to ask you whether there's anything I should know about your brother-in-law or his wife. Because I want you to stop holding out on me, Kathy. You need to trust me with whatever you know."

She looks at her hands. "I don't know anything negative about Scott. He's hard-working, a great dad to his boys. I get along with him just fine."

"But he and Mitch have some tension?"

She raises her eyebrows, surprised he knows. "It's just a brother thing. They're in competition, I think, each trying to outdo the other financially. Plus, they're both trying to prove they're not their deadbeat father."

"You know, I checked out Mitch's financial background, as a matter of course."

"Really? Why?"

"I'm trying to find a motive for Charlie's disappearance, and because there are no signs yet that she was abducted by a stranger, I have to look at the people in her life. It's nothing personal. I'd do the same with any other family."

She turns away, embarrassed that Chase is looking into something so private. It also makes her feel like she can't trust him because he's not trusting them. But if she can't trust Chase Cooper, who can she trust?

"From what I can tell, he made a lot of money last year. As did his brother. Neither of them has ever been bankrupt, and they're certainly not strapped for cash, which means I can rule out certain motives. That they arranged for Charlie to be kidnapped, for instance, to try to extract money from you or your parents in the form of a ransom request."

She shakes her head. It sounds so outlandish to her. "I know neither of them is capable of that, but I understand you have to satisfy your suspicions. And as for the money Mitch makes, I don't think it will ever be enough to fulfill his constant need to prove himself." She pauses. "You're not considering either of them for Megan's attack, are you?"

He looks away, and that tells her he is. "Again, I'd need

motive. Megan probably would've said by now if she suspected it was one of them."

"They're not violent, Chase. Just because they were beaten as children doesn't mean they'd hurt anyone."

"So you know about that?"

"Of course! Mitch is my husband, we've discussed our childhoods over the years." She suddenly clams up. The truth is she *has* kept something from Mitch, and for the first time she considers whether he's kept anything from her. She feels naïve to have assumed he hasn't.

"Does Megan ever interact with Scott?"

She shakes her head. "Not really. They've bumped into each other at our house a couple of times, but I don't think I've ever heard them have a proper conversation." Chase sits quietly for a moment, so she takes the opportunity to ask him a question. "Tell me honestly: do you think Charlie's disappearance could have anything to do with that other little girl going missing last November?"

"Olivia Jenkins? No, I don't think so." He doesn't expand, and Kathy has to trust that he would be looking into it if there was a link.

"I don't even remember much about what happened to her," she says. "Isn't that terrible?"

"Not many people do. She wasn't declared newsworthy for long." He looks at her. "Her mom was a drug user who had some questionable boyfriends, so Olivia suffered because the public didn't care for her mother. I didn't work that case, but I know my department has done everything they can to find Olivia. Just because the media don't show it doesn't mean it's not happening."

She feels terrible for Olivia's mother, suddenly wondering whether she should get in touch to offer support. "I have something I need to tell you," she says, "and you won't like it."

He groans. "What now?"

"My parents are putting up a twenty-five-thousand-dollar reward for information that leads us to Charlie."

He looks away and rubs the stubble on his jaw. "Well, knowing your parents, I guess I can't dissuade them."

She's relieved he's not annoyed. "Can it really hurt? Surely it will act as an incentive for anyone who's not yet come forward?"

"Maybe. But it can also alert people across the country that you guys have money, which will bring out all the crazies wanting to claim it. As I already told Mitch, we'll be inundated with false tips, taking our attention away from the real leads and overwhelming our team."

Her shoulders sag.

"But what the hell? At this stage, I'm willing to try anything to get her home. I'll get a press release issued by the end of the day." He checks his phone. It's silently flashing. "What's the deal between you and Scott's wife?" he asks. "It was pretty nasty to go to the press about you not being at the refuge on Saturday."

She takes a deep breath. "It was, but I'm not mad at her. Cindy and I normally get along fine. We're not best friends or anything, but we usually keep it civil. She's annoyed at me for not staying at her party." She looks at him and smiles. "She thinks I'm a snob. Just like you do."

His blue eyes light up playfully. "Shit, you still remember that? If I remember rightly, I never said you were a snob. I just said you were high maintenance."

She surprises herself by laughing. "I remember that conversation like it was yesterday. We were having our first fight."

"I blame your mom. The minute she caught sight of me sniffing around you, as she so eloquently put it, she wanted me out of your life."

"No," she protests, but that's exactly how it was.

"I wasn't stupid then and I'm not stupid now, Kathy. You

were always too good for me. I knew it deep down—maybe that was part of the thrill of dating you—but I thought you could see past all that money and status bullshit. But then... you disappeared. Out of my life, at least."

"I didn't disappear, I just took a step back. My parents and I were fighting a lot. I had so much pressure on my shoulders. You know what they're like."

"Yeah." He nods. "They *are* snobs. They must love Mitch, with his million-dollar listings and fancy cars."

She scoffs. "You'd think so. But they can't get over where he started in life. He's more similar to you than you know."

He's quiet for a while. Finally, he says, "You know your mom offered me a thousand bucks to stop seeing you back then?"

"What?" She turns to face him properly.

He nods and looks away. "Obviously I told her what she could do with her money, but when you stopped returning my calls, I assumed they offered you something you couldn't resist."

She shakes her head emphatically, devastated that he would think that. That he's spent all these years believing that was what she was like. She takes his hand. "No, Chase. That couldn't be further from the truth."

He looks into her eyes. "So what *is* the truth? What happened, Kathy?"

She squeezes his hand, but remains silent. She can't give him the answers he craves. Because if she did, he'd never want to speak to her again.

TWENTY-SIX

SUMMER 1993

Kathy has butterflies in her stomach. She's on the verge of leaving the playground through sheer nervousness when she spots Chase walking toward her. Having lost interest in her closest friends lately, feeling she's grown apart from them and the shallow things they obsess over, she's agreed to spend the afternoon with Chase. It's not a date, at least she doesn't think so, but it *is* the first time they've arranged to meet up.

She looks around to see if anyone's paying attention to her, but the few mothers present are busy watching their children play. Besides, she's hiding beside a tree in the shade, seeking solace from the hot sun so she doesn't burn.

"Hey," he says as he approaches. "Are you ashamed to be seen with me or something?"

Her eyes widen, worried she's offended him. "Not at all! It's just so hot today and—"

"Relax, I'm joking." He smiles, and it disarms her.

His eyes are intense, and he's standing closer than he ever has, as if they're girlfriend and boyfriend. She's not used to boys being this familiar with her. The other boys at school mask their fear of the girls with immature jokes and pranks, all bravado but no guts. God forbid they ever build the courage to actually ask one of them out.

Taking her hand, he says, "Come on. Let's get out of here." He gently pulls her behind him as they enter the woods. He's walked here from the other side of town, and his hand feels sweaty in hers, but she doesn't mind.

"Where are we going?" she asks.

"To the creek. No one ever goes down there, so you won't be spotted by anyone who knows your folks."

"I don't care if we're spotted," she says, her voice giving away her guilt. "We're not doing anything wrong."

He glances at her, squeezing her hand gently. "Not yet, anyway."

A thrill runs through her entire body. She's excited, but worried that he's expecting something from her. Apart from hanging out with boys from church and attending one dance with an unbelievably boring kid her mother approves of, Kathy has no experience with boys or sex. She's been instructed that that can wait until she's married.

When they finally reach the opening in the canopy, the sun glistens off the small creek. It's a beautiful place to spend a couple of hours. "I never knew this was here."

"I practically live here," he says.

She looks at him. "Why?"

He looks away. "It's peaceful. No drama." He sits on the grass next to the water and pulls off his T-shirt, laying it down beside him. Looking up at her, he says, "So you don't get dirty."

She smiles. Who'd have thought a sixteen-year-old boy could be thoughtful? She tries not to stare at his tanned torso as she sits next to him. He rests his weight on his left shoulder, lying beside her. Any fear she had has vanished. She feels relaxed around him. They talk about school; the teachers who give the worst grades and the kids who are destined for Ivy League colleges. How meaningless school dances are and who's rumored to be sleeping with who. How the summer break will be over in a flash if they're not careful and don't make the most of every day.

Kathy eventually lies back, looking up at the sun through a canopy of lush green leaves. It really is secluded here, with no sounds other than the birds in the trees and the occasional faint rumble of a train passing by the other side of the creek, over near the old brewery.

"I called in sick to work today," says Chase.

She turns to him, their faces close. "Where do you work?"

"At the auto repair shop on May Street."

She hadn't realized, but it makes sense that he would need a part-time job. "Why did you call in sick?"

"Why do you think?" he asks.

The butterflies in her stomach start up again. The more she looks at him, the more she wants to kiss him. But she can't. It would only lead to a whole lot of trouble for both of them. It wouldn't be fair on him. She sits up. "Chase. I didn't come here to do anything. I just wanted to get away from my life for a few hours."

He's silent behind her, until she feels his hand gently running down her back. "I don't want anything from you other than your company."

She looks at him properly. His hair needs cutting and his clothes are worn, he doesn't do well at school and his parents are nobodies, so why does she feel drawn to him?

Afraid of what will happen if they stay next to each other, she gets up and walks to the water. Slipping her sandals off, she dips her feet in. "It's so cool."

He walks up behind her. "I dare you to get in."

She laughs. "No way! I can't walk home in wet clothes. My mother would freak out."

He whispers in her ear, "So don't get your clothes wet."

She watches as he pulls his sneakers off, followed by his

jeans. She turns away, not wanting to stare, until she hears him dive into the deepest part of the creek, in the center. He emerges with his black hair clinging to his face, and a quick head swipe soaks her top with cold water. "Stop it, it's freezing!"

"You'll soon get used to it. Come in."

She thinks about what her parents would say if they could see her down here with him. If someone caught them together. Looking around reassures her there's no one here, and part of her is disappointed. Maybe it would be good for them to know. "Turn around," she commands.

His face lights up. "You're coming in?"

"Only if you turn around. I need privacy."

He turns around while she undoes her skirt and pulls her top over her head. "I can't believe I'm doing this." She wades into the deeper water, getting used to the temperature, and then dives under. Feeling for Chase, she uses his body to pull herself up and takes a deep breath.

He smiles as he pushes her wet hair back from her face. "I didn't think rich girls knew how to have fun."

She wipes the water from her eyes. "You're obviously a bad influence on me."

The sun is beating down on them and the water feels perfect against her skin.

Chase moves closer. He takes her face in his hands and fixes his eyes on her. "Am I the bad influence, or is it the other way around?"

She doesn't know what he means, but she doesn't care, because he slowly leans in, his blue eyes fastened intently on her face. He brushes a thumb over her lips before kissing her. His own lips are soft and they move slowly but intensely. She kisses him back, aware of the electricity between them. Aware that something special is finally happening to her.

She knows she'll never forget this moment.

TWENTY-SEVEN

With hair wet from her shower, Megan walks slowly around the Hamiltons' empty house. Her neck is still stiff so she has to avoid sudden jolts, but if she's careful, she can manage the pain. Kathy and Fay are still out and Mitch has reluctantly left to show buyers around a house. Connie and Jack wanted to stay behind in case the cops came with news of Charlie, but thankfully Mitch told them it would be better if they left. There's clearly tension between him and Kathy's parents, which is fine with Megan, as she doesn't want them here while she's recuperating, watching her every move. They probably think she's going to steal something. Connie thinks Megan's stupid, but she's not, she can see right through the fixed smile. She knows that the woman is judging her.

She walks into the kitchen and opens the huge silver fridge. It's already packed with food and drink, so there was no need for Kathy to go to the store. She sighs at the thought that Kathy's never going to let her wall down. Staying here was a mistake.

A knock at the door makes her close the refrigerator and go to the front window. The reporters have switched their cameras on, filming whoever's standing there, but she can't see who it is from this angle. She walks to the door in case it's the detective and opens it a crack, careful not to get caught on film.

"Good morning." The minister looks at his watch. "Actually, it's good afternoon now!"

She doesn't smile. "What do you want, Reverend?"

"I'm just checking in on the Hamiltons."

"They're all out."

"That's okay. I'd be happy to lend you an ear if you have anything you'd like to talk about? I understand you've been through something distressing yourself."

She looks at the casserole dish in his hand. There's a pink stuffed rabbit on top with a goofy smile. Charlie would love it.

"Oh, this is from one of my volunteers. They wanted me to pass it on." He holds it out and she gets the impression he's desperate to come in. If he weren't a minister, she'd assume he was being nosy and inserting himself where he's not wanted. Maybe Kathy has been relying on him for emotional support and he thinks Megan needs the same. But she doesn't. She's used to relying on no one but herself.

Megan doesn't go to church, she wasn't raised that way. It doesn't mean she doesn't have faith, but she doesn't feel the need to listen to guys like this preach at her in a stuffy old building. "You should come back when Kathy's here," she says. "Later this afternoon."

Flashes go off behind him and the female reporter from TV steps forward.

"I've got to go, sorry." Megan closes the door on him and watches his shadow walk away.

In the living room, she switches the TV on and finds a news channel. They're still covering Charlie's disappearance intermittently, but they're not currently showing live footage from outside this house. Her appetite for lunch vanishes as she watches Charlie's adorable face pop up on screen. She can barely tear her eyes away when her cell phone buzzes with a message. It's her boss from the bar.

Sorry, Megan. I feel like a piece of shit but I've found someone to replace you. I don't have the luxury of waiting for you to be well enough to return. Maybe I can find you some part-time hours once everything's settled down.

She shakes her head. "Asshole." She badly needs that job, but once she'd told him she couldn't say when she'd be well enough to return, it was inevitable he'd fire her. Wiping her eyes, she tries to control the growing craving for a high. On the TV, the scene changes to show police dogs combing every inch of town. It makes the craving come in waves, taking over her entire body. She gently rubs her sore throat.

This is why Mitch let her move in. He knows she's at risk of using again. She has an uneasy feeling he's not letting her stay here out of the kindness of his heart. The drinks cabinet catches her eye and she looks over the expensive bottles of whiskey. Her mouth waters at the thought of getting drunk. It's a shame Mitch didn't think to keep this out of her view.

She switches the TV off and pulls her cell phone out of her sweatpants pocket. The numbers she wants are deleted from her phone, and have been since her OD at Christmas. But she knows them off by heart. She pauses, thinking how strange it is that she can't remember the phone number of her friends or her doctor, but she knows those of her drug dealers. Is she really that dependent? Her mouth waters again. Her mind is imagining that rush of adrenaline as the coke works its magic.

A sudden desire to see Charlie's bedroom gets her off the couch. She knows which room it is and no one has said she can't go in there. She wouldn't listen to them if they did.

As she opens the door wide, she's confronted with Charlie's character. The pink comforter on the bed, the plastic ponies positioned in their stable, the many soft toys Megan has bought her. It's all here. And so is Charlie's smell. Only faint, but it's the smell of baby shampoo, crayons and candy.

Megan sits on the bed, touching the pillow with one hand and pulling out a school notebook with the other. Inside, Charlie has described her favorite person in large, messy writing.

```
She  has  black  hair  and  brown  eyes  and
freckles.

Her hands are soft.

She  buys  me  ice  cream  and  paints  my
nails shiney colors.

She  needs  looking  after  like  my  china
dolls.

I feel warm and happey when I see her.

My favorit person is Mommy.
```

Underneath is a photograph of Megan, taken six years ago by a friend. She looks happy and relaxed, and her bump is fully visible.

Megan suddenly feels a craving for something much stronger than cocaine; a craving for her daughter. She needs to be well for when Charlie's found, because as soon as she has her back in her arms, she's taking her away from this town. Away from this family.

Because they've proven they don't deserve her.

TWENTY-EIGHT

Chase allows himself a lunch break in order to check on Patrick. He takes him on a trip to the grocery store, where he lets the kid choose whatever food he wants for the next few days. But things go downhill the minute they get home. Shannon's been stringing him along about a house she wants to lease downtown. Apparently it's a sure-fire thing, but she needs time to get together some money for the deposit and first month's rent. Or, according to her, Chase could loan it to her and she'd be out of his hair sooner. He suspects she has no intention of using what-ever money he gives her on a house.

"You're so boring!" she says in a mocking voice. Because he hesitated when she asked him for money, she's launched into one of her scathing personal attacks. "You don't smoke, take drugs, drink much. You don't even raise your voice when you're angry! And I'm betting you haven't got laid in years. What's wrong with you? Don't you have any passions besides working?"

He doesn't react. It's not worth it. "Been arguing with Luke this morning, I see?"

She turns away from him. "He's a piece of shit."

"He's not. He wants his son in his life. You have no reason

to keep Patrick from his dad, Shannon." He turns to the living room to check the kid isn't listening. He's sitting in front of the TV playing with a cheap toy he chose at the store. A plastic squad car with realistic siren sounds. Chase didn't make him pick that one.

"Whatever. I need a shower." Shannon brushes past him without even stopping to say hi to her son. She was still asleep when they left for the store earlier. She's not a morning person.

Chase sighs. He takes a seat next to Patrick and pulls out a small card from his wallet. "Here." He hands it to the boy. "If you ever feel like you or your mom need help, this is my number."

Patrick takes it from him and studies it. "I don't call 911?"

Chase smiles. "You can if you forget this, but this number will get you straight through to me."

The boy looks up at him, his eyes sad. "Are we leaving today?"

"I don't know, kid. I'm not sure what your mom has planned. But even if you're not in Maple Falls anymore, call me if you need help. Got it?"

Patrick nods and slips the card into his pants pocket.

Chase wonders if it'll end up in the washer. "Try to memorize my number if you can." He wanted to buy the kid a cheap cell phone but suspects Shannon would sell it. As he stands, he says, "I've got to go back to work. Don't stare at the TV all afternoon. There's a kid lives next door about your age, always playing in the yard. Introduce yourself, okay?"

"Okay."

He leaves the house, wondering if they'll still be there when he returns.

Chase is trying not to worry about Patrick when he pulls up outside a single-story house about two miles from where the birthday party was held. The yard is overgrown but the house looks like it's had a new coat of white paint. It's so bright he has to slip his sunglasses on. It's as hot inside his car as it is out, because the vehicle's A/C has been bust for months. He pulls his tie a little lower from his neck in a bid to cool down.

Slamming the car door shut, he slowly approaches the house while glancing at the neighboring homes that stand close by on either side. With it being early afternoon, there are a few kids riding bikes up and down the street and a dog barking non-stop in the distance. He pulls the screen door open and knocks three times on the door behind it. Low music drifts out through the open windows.

The door opens to a middle-aged man with round cheeks and thinning curly hair. To Chase, he looks like a clown even without the makeup. "Help you?" the guy asks.

Chase flashes his badge and introduces himself. "Are you Jim McClean, otherwise known as Bobby the Clown?"

"Yeah, why?"

"I'm investigating the disappearance of Charlotte Hamilton, and I understand you were hired as a children's entertainer for the birthday party she was last seen at?"

Jim's eyes dart from side to side, anywhere but fixing on Chase. "Sure, but I didn't take her, man. I didn't have anything to do with it."

Chase holds his hands up. "No one's saying you did. We've been interviewing all the guests from that day, including the entertainers. You're the second-to-last person on my list." This guy's reaction is interesting, but not unusual. Just speaking to a cop makes some people nervous, whether they have anything to hide or not. Chase wanted to speak to him sooner but Cindy Bowers wasn't as forthcoming with the guy's number as he'd expected. "Can I come in for a second?"

"That depends. Got a warrant?"

He crosses his arms. "Do I need one?"

Jim appears to think better of aggravating a cop and steps aside. "I've got nothing to hide."

The house is cooler than outside, as most of the drapes are closed. It smells a little musty, and the cigarette packet on the couch tells Chase why. He peers beyond the living room into the small kitchen, where a clown's costume is drip-drying from one of the cabinets. Water is pooling on the floor beneath.

"Mind if I take a seat?" he asks.

"Go ahead."

He rolls his sleeves up and sits on the couch. No sooner is he seated than a large white cat jumps into his lap. It wiggles its ass in front of Chase's face, displaying a huge set of balls. "Hey, boy."

"Oh, he can't hear you. He's deaf," says Jim. "He's not even my cat, but he likes to keep me company sometimes."

Chase strokes the cat's head and it immediately purrs. Jim takes a seat across from them. "I assume you've seen the story play out on the news?" says Chase.

"Sure. It's sad. And I knew you'd turn up here eventually. I know what people think of clowns: if we're not terrifying kids, we're abducting them, right?"

"I sure hope not, Jim."

The guy hesitates, unsure of Chase's response. "The mom actually wanted a magician, but Mike was out of town so he gave her my number. I wasn't supposed to be there, so it's not like I could've planned something in advance."

Chase didn't know that.

"Look, I turned up, entertained the kids, accepted my hard-earned money and left. I couldn't even pick the missing girl out of a line-up, there were that many kids there. I sure didn't recognize her picture on the news."

To Chase, that confirms Charlie wasn't there long enough to be noticed, because other guests have said the same. That helps him narrow down the time of the abduction. "What time did you and your guy start and finish?"

Jim looks confused. "What guy?"

"The other clown. There were two present that afternoon."

"I don't know anything about him. I work alone. I mean, I saw another clown briefly, but I didn't speak to him. I just assumed the lady hired two clowns."

That's interesting. Cindy only gave him the contact details of this one. "You didn't recognize him?"

"He was wearing a mask, man. How could I recognize him?"

"Well, it's a small town and there can only be so many clowns working kids' birthday parties—" Chase stops. "Wait, a mask? Don't clowns usually use makeup?"

"Right, and for good reason. That guy must've been sweating his ass off under that rubber. No wonder he didn't last long." Jim sighs. "Listen, if he wasn't hired by Mrs. Bowers, then he was probably one of the dads dressing up for a bit of fun. He definitely wasn't a professional clown, put it that way."

He's probably right, but Chase's instinct tells him this could be a good lead. He needs to find out which guest decided to dress up so he can rule them out as a person of interest. Sitting up straight, he asks, "How do you know it was a guy? Could it have been a woman?"

Jim considers it before shrugging. "I just assumed it was."

"Were they tall, short? Medium build?"

"I don't know, man. I didn't take a goddam photograph."

Chase gently moves the cat to the floor so he can focus on this new lead, but it jumps straight back onto his lap, rubbing its face across his stubbly jaw. "So how long were you at the party?"

"I was there from the very beginning. Mrs. Bowers warned me she wanted her money's worth. Rich people always do." Jim rolls his eyes. "So I got there at one and I was exhausted by the time I left at four."

Chase writes it all down, trying to stop the cat from chewing his pen. "What about the other guy?"

"I can't remember. I wasn't paying much attention."

"But you said he didn't last long."

Jim takes a deep breath. "He didn't get there on time and he was gone before me, which tells me it was just some guy—or woman, if you like—dressing up to please their kids. He probably got changed in the bathroom and then pretended he'd missed the clown, like playing Santa at Christmas. Other than that, I can't tell you anything else about him. I had kids to entertain, man, and those rich kids are hard work. I had nightmares that night about being eaten alive by a bunch of screaming zombie children."

Chase laughs.

"No, I'm serious! I'm getting too old for this shit."

He doesn't think this guy was involved in Charlie's disappearance, but he's glad he paid him a visit. He stands up, ignoring the cat's protests. "Thanks for your time. I'll be in touch if I need any more information."

"No problem."

He leaves through the front door and heads back to his car, wiping fur from his shirt. He opens the door but doesn't get in yet, knowing it's going to be hot in there. Instead, he calls Detective Brown. When he answers, Chase asks, "Have any of the guests we've interviewed mentioned the clowns at all?"

"Only to say there was one."

"There were two, apparently. But the clown who was hired by Cindy didn't know who the second one was. I need you to call all the guests again as a matter of urgency and find out if anyone knows who was wearing the clown costume. They used a mask instead of makeup, so it's likely a parent of one of the kids. But if it isn't..."

"He could be our guy?"

Chase doesn't want to get his hopes up, but his stomach flutters with excitement at the thought of finally having a possible suspect. "Could be."

"I'll get straight on it."

He leans against the car. "Thanks. Did you run a check for local registered sex offenders yet?"

"Yeah. The ones who aren't currently incarcerated are under the watchful eye of their parole officers, and all have credible alibis for that day."

Chase knows from experience that registered offenders are less likely to be the cause of missing children than undetected offenders hiding amongst the child's family, but it's always worth checking. The lack of evidence in this case so far—no dropped clothing, no blood trails, no eyewitnesses—tells him it was either someone from the family who took Charlie, or someone who knew the family. Because they've been able to plan her abduction in advance. Snatching a child from a birthday party takes balls unless you know exactly where she's going to be at what time, and what the escape routes are. That would account for the lack of evidence; there's none of the sloppiness you'd see with an opportunistic grab.

"Did you manage to speak to Mitch Hamilton's contractors yet?" he asks.

"I've spoken to the foreman," says Brown. "At first he corroborated Mitch's story. Said the guy turned up at the Glenwood renovation property in the afternoon and was on site between one and four."

"How convenient."

"Right? But get this. As I was talking to him, I felt there was something wrong. He was twitchy. The kind of guy who sucks at poker. So I ask him straight if he was asked to cover for Mitch, and he looks away, suddenly avoiding all eye contact. I give him the spiel about a little girl needing to get back to her family, and he tells me about his own little girl. I can tell he's worried he'll lose his job by talking, so I go easy on him. Ten minutes later, he finally breaks and tells me Hamilton asked him to lie. Turns out he didn't stop by the site that day, not while this guy and his team were there anyway. They were on site all day until finishing early at four because it was the weekend."

Chase shakes his head. "Son of a bitch. Why would Mitch Hamilton try to cover his tracks?"

Detective Brown laughs. "I assume that's a rhetorical question."

Chase doesn't laugh. This is Kathy's child her husband may have harmed. Sure, Charlie's adopted, but he knows how desperate Kathy is to get her home. Does she have any idea her husband is giving false alibis? He thinks about how she lied too, and shakes his head. "Have you heard back from the couple he was supposedly showing a house to that night?"

"Not yet. It was a guy called Evan Harris. I'll try him again."

Chase nods. "Something tells me we're getting closer to finding Charlie."

"Yeah." Brown sighs down the line. "But I don't think she'll be alive when we do."

"Don't do that, Frank."

"What?"

"Don't give up on her. She needs us." Chase stands straight. "Let's see if we can find out what Mitch was really doing that day. And before he realizes we're onto him." With renewed enthusiasm, he ends the call and gets straight into his car, ignoring the intense heat inside.

TWENTY-NINE

Kathy fixes Fay a late lunch. She doesn't ask her how her therapy session went, because she doesn't want to talk about Charlie right now in case her daughter gets upset again. She just wants them to experience a couple of hours of normalcy, if that's even possible.

Mitch has taken it upon himself to print hundreds of missing person flyers that he's pinning up and handing out around town to make sure people have as many images of Charlie in their heads as possible while they're looking for her. He added the reward money and seems certain that will get people calling. He hasn't told Chase what he's doing, but Kathy feels better that he's being proactive instead of waiting for news that never comes.

With Mitch out, it means she and Fay are alone with Megan for the first time. Megan is upstairs in her room, and Kathy daren't knock to see if she needs anything.

"This bread is gross," says Fay as she picks out the cheese and salad leaves, dropping the bread back onto the plate. She hasn't even tried a bite.

Kathy knows there's nothing wrong with the bread. She also

knows not to make a big deal out of it. "Let me get you some more cheese and some tomatoes so you can turn it into a proper salad."

"No, I'm not even that hungry."

Disappointment and fear swell in Kathy's chest. She's noticing how bony Fay's forearms have become over the last month or so. Her hands are looking too big for her and she's deliberately wearing baggy clothes. "I bought some of those potato chips you like. They're in the cupboard if you find your appetite."

Fay stares at her cell phone, probably reading about fake sightings of Charlie again.

A noise on the stairs makes them turn. Megan smiles at them as she reaches the bottom step and stops. Her eyes are puffy and her smile is weak. It looks like she's washed the crusted blood out of her hair. "Mind if I get something to eat?"

Kathy glances at Fay, bracing herself for another barrage of abuse. But Fay barely looks up, so she says, "Of course not. Do you like cheese?"

"Sure, but I can do it." Megan walks over and leans against the counter.

"It's no problem." Kathy fixes another sandwich and spills a bag of potato chips on the side of the plate, the way Charlie likes it. She hands it to Megan.

"Thanks."

Fay looks up. "I'll have a bag."

Kathy hands one over and tries not to watch as Fay opens it and starts crunching on the cheese and onion chips while reading the pack for the calorie count. They're not nutritious, but it's better than nothing. To Megan she says, "How are you feeling?"

"I've got a headache I can't get rid of, but apart from that, I'm just exhausted. It's impossible to sleep until Charlie's home."

Kathy nods. She wants to tell Megan what Chase told her earlier, about the scream at the grocery store, but she can't do it in front of Fay. It's better she doesn't know. But now would be a good time to tell both of them about the reward money. "Mom and Dad are offering a twenty-five-thousand-dollar reward for any information that leads to Charlie's whereabouts."

Megan looks more surprised than Fay. "Really?"

Fay doesn't look up from her phone, but she's smiling. Kathy knows she'll be glad.

"Do the media know?" asks Megan.

"Detective Cooper will be issuing a press release. He says we shouldn't raise our hopes, but it might lead to some new information coming in." Kathy can tell Megan is relieved. She's also probably wondering why her parents would do that for Charlie, but hopefully this is a step in the right direction for all of them.

Putting a brave face on, Megan looks at Fay. "Who're you messaging?"

Surprisingly, Fay answers. "Just some boy."

"Oh yeah?" Megan puts her plate on the breakfast bar next to her. "Is he cute?"

Kathy watches with interest as Fay blushes. "Not really. I mean, I guess."

"Got a picture?" Megan presses more than Kathy would. Fay tips her phone in Megan's direction. "Ooh, blond hair and blue eyes. A dangerous combination. He looks like a really young Brad Pitt."

"Eww. No thanks. Brad Pitt's *ancient*."

"Let me see," says Kathy.

Fay hesitates before showing her. "I'm not dating him or anything. We were working on a science project together."

"Yeah, right," teases Megan with a glimmer in her eye. "That old chestnut. He actually looks a lot like my first boyfriend."

Fay's interest is piqued. "What was his name?"

"Curtis. He was the love of my life. I've never forgotten him. He treated me like sh—" she catches herself, "like garbage, which of course made me love him even more." She sighs. "You never forget your first love. Isn't that right, Mrs. Hamilton?"

Kathy smiles. "You've got to stop calling me that, please. It makes me feel like an old woman."

"I will if you tell us about your first love."

Fay is staring hard for her reaction. Kathy doesn't normally talk about things like this, but she finds herself wanting to, which surprises her. Maybe it's because they can forget Charlie's missing, even if only briefly. "Mine treated me like I was his everything."

Megan takes a seat next to Fay and picks at her sandwich as she listens. Fay leans in. "Why didn't you marry him, Mom?"

"It's complicated. We were only your age: sixteen, seventeen. Those relationships rarely last beyond high school."

"Was he your first kiss?" asks Fay.

Kathy feels heat in her cheeks as she remembers it vividly. She remembers the way Chase would take her face in his hands and pause to stare at her as if she was the only girl he would ever consider kissing. The only girl he ever noticed. Then his full lips would touch hers and she'd be overcome with spine-tingling lust. She's never felt that thrill since. Not with anyone else. She thinks of the hug they shared earlier in the parking lot of the grocery store. Would it feel the same if he kissed her now? Probably not. You can't recreate those blissful teenage experiences. That's what makes them so memorable.

"He was. And I can tell you it's much better to wait until you've met the right boy before you start kissing them. It'll mean a lot more and you won't end up regretting it."

Megan winks at Fay. "She has to say that because she's your mom. I say kiss as many frogs as you have to so you know you haven't settled for a toad."

Fay smiles. Then her phone beeps and she gets up. "Can I go to Jenna's house? Her parents are home all afternoon, so we won't be alone."

Kathy goes to the window. The news vans are still there, but the reporters have learnt to wait inside their vans now, where they can run the A/C. "Sure. But don't stop to answer any questions, and stay at the house so I know where you are. No talking to strangers. And keep your phone on you at all times. Do you have your alarm?" Chase gave them a handful of personal alarms, and Mitch beat himself up about the fact that he'd never thought of it himself. Kathy pointed out to him that Charlie wouldn't have been carrying one anyway, not at her uncle's house. A cousin's birthday party is not where you expect anything bad to happen.

"It's in my pocket," says Fay. "Call me if there's news." She's quickly out the door.

Kathy's tempted to make her stay here with them until Charlie's found, but it's not fair on her. Jenna's a kind and responsible girl and her parents go to their church. They'll take care of Fay. At least that's what she has to believe.

An awkward silence falls over the room, so Kathy rinses some dishes before loading them into the dishwasher.

"It was Detective Cooper, wasn't it?"

Kathy turns, blood once again rising to her cheeks.

Megan's smiling. "All girls love dating someone they shouldn't, someone who's off limits."

"Why would he be someone I shouldn't have dated? We were both young and free."

Megan drops her crusts onto her plate. Charlie never eats hers either. "Sure, but you come from this," she gestures to the house, "and he's from my world. Don't get me wrong, he's a good guy. I've served him a few times in the bar and he's never got drunk or hassled any women. Not in front of me, anyway. But I can't picture you two together."

She doesn't say it unpleasantly, more matter-of-fact, the way Connie would speak. But it annoys Kathy all the same. "So you're judging me for growing up in a wealthy family?"

Megan raises her hands in protest. "Not at all! Some people get lucky with their parents, others don't. I was just saying you two aren't an obvious pairing. But he *is* cute. I can understand the attraction. Mitch is more..."

"More what?"

"You know, one of the great pretenders. New money."

Kathy frowns. That's how her dad describes him too.

"He's one of those guys who came from nothing and made it big," explains Megan. "But he's so terrified of being judged for where he's from that instead of being proud of his accomplishments, he pretends he's always been rich, and that he belongs over here in affluent suburbia." She goes quiet and eats a couple of chips. "Sorry. I probably shouldn't be speaking so freely about your husband. My customers always tell me I'm too opinionated. I didn't mean any offense."

If Kathy's parents said that to her, she would blow up at them and accuse them of being snobs. Hearing it from Megan makes her see it in a different light. How many other people have observed this about him? Kathy doesn't know what to say, so she changes the subject. "Has Mitch been keeping you updated?"

Megan's smile slides and she looks down. "Yeah. No news yet."

Kathy considers telling her why Chase was at the grocery store earlier, but doesn't think it's worth worrying her unless something comes of it. "Have you thought about making contact with your mom to let her know what's happened?" she asks. "I'm sure something like this would bring you back together, help her forget whatever it was she was unhappy about. You were almost killed. I'm sure that'll put everything into perspective."

Megan shakes her head slowly, looking away. "She would've seen my picture on the news by now, and she has my number. She could've got in touch if she cared about me."

Kathy's about to ask another question but this time Megan changes the subject.

"By the way, your minister stopped by earlier. I think I was rude to him, because he wanted to come in but I wasn't in the mood to have someone watch me cry." She smiles sadly.

"That's okay. I don't really want to see him either."

"No?" Megan's surprised.

"No. I just want to be left alone. The only person I want to hear from is Chase, and that's only if he's telling me he's found Charlie alive and well." Kathy's voice catches. Megan looks like she could cry too.

Voices outside make them look up.

Mitch rushes through the front door, slamming it closed behind him. He throws the remaining flyers onto the side table and they scatter all over the floor. "They're like a bunch of goddam vultures!" He notices the two women in the kitchen. "Sorry. I'm just sick of them hassling me outside my own house. Why don't they do some actual investigative reporting and find Charlie?"

"I think that's what they believe they're doing," says Megan.

He looks at her. "What do you mean?"

"Isn't it obvious?" She glances at Kathy before looking back at him. "They think one of us was involved in her disappearance."

Kathy's stomach flips. She has to pray that Megan's wrong.

THIRTY

Chase has been fielding phone calls all afternoon. As lead investigator, every credible sighting of Charlie that gets called in to the station is transferred to him so he can decide whether or not to follow up on it. Unfortunately, not one of the sightings has led to anything concrete yet.

His latest tip has brought him near to the school where Kathy works. It wasn't as dramatic as a sighting; just a mention of Charlie's teacher, Stuart Barren. One of the women at the birthday party said she was talking to him and got an uncomfortable feeling. Apparently, she noticed he was paying close attention to all the kids, especially the ones in their bathing costumes in and around the pool. With Mitch also mentioning the guy, Chase thinks he's worth checking out. If anyone was going to dress up as a clown to entertain the kids, it's likely a teacher would.

After three loud knocks, the front door opens and Stuart Barren stands there. His inquisitive smile fades as he recognizes Chase. He must've watched the press conference. "I guess it was just a matter of time. Come on in, Detective."

Chase follows him inside, amused by his reaction. People

really do sit at home waiting for a knock on the door from the police. It makes him wonder why they don't just get in touch themselves and get it over with. The teacher's house is small but neat. Everything is tidied away and the TV is off. It looks like he was reading a book before Chase interrupted him.

"Can I get you a drink?" asks Stuart.

"Sure. A glass of water would be good. It feels like this heat-wave's not going to break anytime soon."

He goes to the kitchen, returning with a glass of tap water.

"Thanks."

"I knew someone would suspect me eventually." Stuart doesn't take a seat or offer one to Chase. "It's an occupational hazard, you know? Teachers being suspected of pedophilia. I guess priests have the same problem."

Chase raises his eyebrows. "There's usually no smoke without fire, but I understand what you mean. I've interviewed almost everyone from the party, so I'm obliged to interview you too. It's nothing to do with your profession. I left a message on your cell phone asking for a call back."

"I didn't get it. Maybe you have the wrong number for me."

Chase stares hard. "I got it off your criminal record. Have you changed your number since your DUI?"

Without blinking, Stuart says, "Yes, actually. But you're here now, so ask away."

Chase knows from his background check on the guy that he doesn't have any other arrests or convictions. He puts the glass on a sideboard and pulls out his notebook. "What time did you arrive and leave the party?"

The teacher takes a deep breath. "I was there from maybe two until just after six."

Chase makes a note. "Did you see any of your pupils there?"

"Yes. Charlie, of course, as well as Rebecca Gates and Robert

Glassway. I don't recall seeing anyone else there, but to be honest with you, it was too hot for me outside. With my coloring, I need to stay out of the sun, so I spent most of the time indoors."

He's pale with blond hair, whereas Chase can get away with sitting in the sun all day. He never burns; just gets a darker tan. "What's your relationship like with Charlie?"

Finally Stuart takes a seat. Chase copies him. "The same as with all my students. She's a nice girl who mostly behaves. Her strengths are writing and math. Her weakness is listening in class. She's chatty, so she's always talking." He smiles. "She's funny, though, so it's hard to be mad at her."

Chase nods. "Ever spend any time with her one-on-one?"

"Of course not. I didn't even speak to her at the party. She was busy having fun."

"Did you see any adults interacting with her in a way that made you take notice? Because witness statements suggest she went missing around the time you arrived."

Stuart is silent as he thinks. "No, not at all. I only noticed her while she was getting her face painted." He stands up. "I'm sorry I can't be of more help. I'd love to see her back with her family. I want her back at school next semester too. And I don't want to believe I've moved to a town where this kind of thing happens."

Chase gets up too. He's clearly not going to get anything else out of the guy. Not unless he brings him in for questioning. "Thanks for your time. If you see or hear anything that could help in the search, get in touch." He hands him a card and leaves the house.

Outside, a quick check of his cell phone shows he has a message from Detective Brown.

Evan Harris has confirmed he was at the house on Wicker Lane with Mitch on Saturday night. If you want to speak to him face to face he said you need to get to the university by four. He's a professor of psychology there.

Chase checks his watch. He should just make it.

Chase has never visited the university before as it's not in his jurisdiction, and he's in awe of the size of the place. As he drives through the grounds, he realizes it must be spread over hundreds of acres. It's filled with impressive buildings, mature trees, well-tended shrubs, coffee shops and lawned areas for students to sit out and relax in. This is a world away from anywhere he's spent time at, and he suddenly understands the extortionate tuition fees some colleges demand. There's barely anyone around, what with it being mid June, and the place reminds him of a movie set awaiting its actors.

Parking his crappy car in a spot under a huge maple tree, he feels like he's going to get a ticket for bringing something so old into the grounds. It takes a while to find the professor's office, with the help of several staff pointing him in the right direction, which means he only just makes it there for four o'clock. The professor's door is wide open, and Chase spots him behind a huge desk, packing his briefcase. He's tall, slim and tanned, and he looks like he's just stepped off a tennis court, with a sweater hanging over the shoulders of his short-sleeved white polo shirt.

Chase knocks on the open door. "Professor?" When he looks up, Chase says, "Hi. I'm Detective Cooper."

The professor smiles widely. "Hi, Detective. Come on in."

"Thanks. Do you prefer Professor or Doctor? Sorry, I'm not knowledgeable in these things and I wouldn't want to cause any offense."

"Evan is fine, really."

Chase nods. "This is some campus. I bet the students love studying here."

"Well, some of them appreciate it," Evan says diplomatically. "Others... not so much. Where did you go to school?"

"Oh, my education stopped at high school, I'm afraid. College never really appealed to me. I couldn't wait to get a full-time job and earn my own money."

Realizing they have nothing in common, the professor glances at his watch. "I should really be leaving for an appointment, so I hope this won't take long."

"Not at all. I just have a few questions about Saturday night. I know I could've done it over the phone, but I like an excuse to get out of the station." Chase smiles.

"I don't blame you. Please, take a seat." Evan sits behind the desk as Chase takes the less comfortable-looking chair. "So I guess we should get straight to it. I was at one of Mitch Hamilton's properties on Saturday night in Maple Falls, and I believe that's what you want to discuss?"

"Right," says Chase, appreciating the professor's willingness not to waste time. "I'm sure you've heard about the disappearance of Charlotte Hamilton?"

Evan nods. "It's terrible. I take it she hasn't been found yet?"

"Not yet, no."

He takes a deep breath. "An eighteen-year-old female student went missing from the university just last year. It was a horrible time, with her friends breaking down in tears during lectures, and an eerie feeling of mistrust spread quickly through the campus. No one knew who might have been involved." He shakes his head. "She was later found dead in her home town over in Connecticut. It shook us all up, so I can't imagine how a five-year-old's parents are feeling right now."

Chase remembers the case. The woman's boyfriend was responsible and was recently sentenced to life in prison because of the state of her remains.

"You know," says Evan, "I only found out after the showing

that Mitch's daughter was missing. I don't know how he managed to remain composed, considering it was the evening of her disappearance."

Chase raises his eyebrows. "Really? He didn't mention it?"

"No, which I thought was strange, in hindsight. Maybe he was expecting her to be home by the time he finished work. But then that was only the second time we'd met him, so maybe it's not surprising he didn't want to talk about it with us."

"Us being?"

"My partner came along. We don't live together, but I'm looking to upsize and I wanted her opinion. I've been offered tenure, so I feel it's time to treat myself."

"I think I read about that in the news," says Chase. "Congratulations. It must be nice to know you've got a job for life."

"It is. I may be in my mid fifties, but I must admit I feel a little more secure in life now." Evan laughs.

"So how did Mitch Hamilton seem during his time with you? Was it all business as usual, or were there any signs of the stress he was under?" The appointment was at eight, so Charlie had only been missing about six hours by that point, but if Mitch had anything to do with her disappearance, Chase thinks cracks might've been showing already.

The professor takes a deep breath and leans back in his leather chair. "I won't lie: it was all a little rushed. But we'd already seen the house once, so I just assumed he didn't want to repeat himself. I remember he was sweating lightly, and he seemed a little desperate to sell. It put us off, actually, because we thought he must be hiding something about the house."

"What do you mean?"

"Well, it's been on the market for a while, and there must be a reason for that. We thought Mitch's nervousness was a sign he wanted it sold as fast as possible, before we found anything out."

"Like what?"

"Oh, you know, like it being the scene of a horrific murder or something." Evan laughs again.

Chase's mind starts whirring. "When you say he appeared nervous, in what way do you mean?"

"The sweating—although it had been a hot day—as well as the look on his face. His smile didn't quite reach his eyes, and I felt like he was just humoring us. He said he only had limited time because he had to be somewhere."

"Do you know where?"

"I didn't ask, but when we were leaving, he drove off in the direction of Glenwood. I assumed he had another showing. I know realtors work hard for their commission, and they're always hustling."

Chase is silent while he digests everything. Kathy and Mitch had already been to Glenwood that afternoon, for their couple's therapy session at four thirty. So why go back in the evening? And alone?

Evan rises. "I'm sorry, Detective, I really should get going. Unless there's anything else you need clarifying?"

"What time did you leave the house?"

"By nine, I believe."

Chase stands and offers his hand. "Thanks for your help. And congratulations again on getting tenure."

He works his way down the long oak-filled corridors and out to the exit, thinking about where Mitch could've gone after the showing. Because he told Chase he'd gone straight home.

THIRTY-ONE

"I'll be glad when this weather breaks. It's insufferable."

Kathy looks across at her mother, who's sipping a brandy opposite her on the deck. She's never seen so much of her in one week, and it's comforting to know that she wants to be here at such a distressing time. But she's also annoyed by what Chase told her: that her mom offered him money to stay away from her. She can't raise it with her, though. There's no point. Her mother is a law unto herself, and Kathy doesn't have the energy to argue. It's too hot and she's too drained. She also hasn't yet told her mom that Chase is the detective in charge of Charlie's disappearance.

Kathy's dad is out buying them a new lawnmower. That's his way of showing his support. Mitch is upstairs on his laptop, and Megan disappeared as soon as Connie arrived. Kathy wonders what it's like for her to suddenly become part of someone else's family, if only temporarily and from the outside looking in. Will she be judging the way she and Mitch live? What they eat? How they treat Fay? What about her first night tonight: will she be listening to what they say to each other in the privacy of their bedroom? Does she even trust them?

A bee lands on her wine glass and she absently waves it away. She probably shouldn't be drinking at all, but it's just the one. The heat is starting to recede now it's early evening, but it still feels stifling. Warm air fills her lungs when she takes a deep breath, and every move leaves her feeling sticky. She'd give anything to dive into the cool, secluded creek behind Scott's house. It's horrendous to think that those amazing memories of her and Chase in the water at sixteen will now be replaced with images of the police and their dogs searching for Charlie's body. That whole area is ruined for her now, whether or not Charlie's found alive. She squeezes her eyes closed to push back the tears.

"What will happen if Charlie's never found, Mom?"

Connie looks at her, surprised by the question. "Of course she'll be found. Especially once news of the reward spreads. You have to stay positive, for Fay."

Kathy's heart sinks. How can she stay positive when there are no leads and there's no information about what happened that day? And it's all very well to offer platitudes, but no one's providing actual advice on *how* to stay positive, on *how* to exist during Charlie's disappearance. Food tastes like cardboard, and all she wants to do is drink herself into a blissful stupor, so she can only imagine how Megan feels.

"What does your gut instinct tell you?" her mom asks. "Is there anyone you suspect might have been involved?"

A few names run through Kathy's mind: Charlie's teacher, Scott, Mitch, even Reverend Stanley, which is ridiculous and a sign that she needs to leave the detective work to Chase. She shakes her head. "I haven't a clue what could've happened. If this were someone else's family, I would assume someone at the party abducted her. But most of the people who were there are well known to us. I can't imagine any of them having anything to do with it. To be honest, I can't imagine anyone in Maple Falls having anything to do with it."

"That's because you're too trusting," says her mom. "You've

never been able to tell when people are using you. I mean, some of your boyfriends have been..." She doesn't finish the thought. Instead, she softens and reaches across the table to touch Kathy's hand. "She'll come home. You just have to have faith. I'll ask Reverend Stanley to visit you again."

Kathy doesn't reply. It's difficult to have faith when the worst has happened.

"You know, this is why I always wanted a boy."

She looks at her mom. "What do you mean?"

"Well, aside from the fact that he could carry the family name, a boy is much less likely to be abducted than a girl."

Kathy rolls her eyes. "Boys get abducted too, Mom. They just don't make the news as much."

Voices drift out to them from inside the house. Kathy stands and leans to look through the patio doors. Chase is here. He's talking to Mitch in the hallway. Her mouth goes dry and she struggles to swallow.

"Who is it?" asks Connie.

"The detective." She walks into the house and her mom follows her.

Chase smiles when he sees her and takes a step forward. When he looks over her shoulder, his smile vanishes. "Mrs. Hamilton." He nods. "Nice to see you."

Kathy turns to her mother, who looks like she's swallowed something unappealing. "Detective." The animosity is obvious, and Kathy wonders whether her mom realized Chase had become a cop. She had him down as a criminal all those years ago—certainly not good enough to date her daughter—so it must come as some surprise to see him here now after all this time. But Connie's good at pretending. She fixes a smile on her face. "What a pleasure to see you again. And you joined law enforcement. Smart move, considering..." Thankfully, she doesn't finish her thought.

Chase laughs good-naturedly despite knowing how she

really feels about him. Kathy knows it must take a lot of self-control not to say what he really thinks.

"I've been calling you for updates, but you never answer your phone," says Mitch. His neck has gone blotchy in places. It happens when he's stressed. Kathy can tell he's terrified that Chase is here to deliver bad news.

"I'm sorry I missed your calls. My phone is ringing constantly at the moment and I'm prioritizing leads from the station." Chase looks at Kathy. "I'm sorry to just drop by like this, but I need to ask some more questions."

There's an awkward silence as Megan appears from upstairs. "Any news about Charlie?" It's obvious from her worried expression that she's fearing the worst too.

"Not yet," says Chase. "I don't have any leads on who attacked you either, I'm afraid. How are you feeling now? You look a little better."

Her shoulders slump. "I'm okay. I still haven't remembered anything that would help your investigation."

Kathy can tell this is agonizing for Megan. She should be down here with them listening to Chase's update. She'll go up and see her soon. Have a proper talk at last. It's long overdue.

Megan reluctantly returns to the guest bedroom, and Connie says, "I'll make myself scarce. Leave you folks to it."

She walks slowly to the backyard as Kathy leads Chase to the living room. Mitch sits next to her. "Did you find anything on the security footage from the stores in town?" she asks.

Chase shakes his head. "My team have been through everything handed over and there were no sightings of anyone resembling Charlie. I'm sorry. I have to assume it was just a child having a tantrum."

She hesitates before asking, "Did you see Scott on there?"

"Yes. It was as he said. He went into the meat market, purchased a few items and got straight back in his car after. Alone."

Mitch stands up. "I can't believe there's still no sign of her. Are you sure your team are working hard enough on this? I mean, normally there's something to go on by now: an item of clothing, fingerprints, a convicted predator living in the area. Have you even looked into that?"

Chase nods. "We've done everything that needs to be done in order to locate a missing child."

"If that were true, you'd have found her!" Mitch's voice gets louder. "Someone must have seen what happened. People don't just vanish into thin air."

"Mitch, calm down," Kathy says.

"It's okay," says Chase. "I understand your frustration. This case remains my top priority. Just because we don't currently have a lead doesn't mean I'm not spending every hour of my day looking for your daughter." He pauses, staring at Mitch. "Which is why I need you to come to the station for further questioning."

Kathy thinks she's heard wrong. She looks at Mitch, then back at Chase. "What? But we've already told you everything we know."

"I only need to question Mitch." With sympathy in his eyes, Chase adds, "Your husband's been lying to us."

She frowns. Lying about what? She looks up at Mitch again, expecting him to deny it, to shout at Chase. But he doesn't.

Eventually Mitch nods. "Does it have to be at the station? This could kill my business if word gets out I've been brought in."

She can't believe what she's hearing. He sounds so cold, so calculated.

"It does, I'm sorry." Chase stands. "We can go in my car."

Mitch looks at Kathy, and the blotches on his neck are getting redder. "Stay here. Tell Fay to come home. I don't want reporters finding her at her friend's place and giving her the news."

Megan rushes down the stairs. She must have been eavesdropping. Confronting Mitch, she shouts, "What did you do? Where is she? Where's Charlie?" She slaps his face hard before Chase grabs her arms and moves her away.

"Stop that!" he says.

Mitch grabs a baseball cap from the hallway and looks at Kathy. "It's not what you think. I'll be home soon." He leaves the house.

Chase appears confused by Megan's reaction.

Kathy puts an arm around her. "He hasn't done anything, Megan. He's just being questioned, that's all."

Megan pulls away. "I don't know how much longer I can cope with this." She climbs the stairs, unable to hold back her sobs.

When they're alone, Kathy takes Chase's hand. "Please tell me it wasn't him." She lets the tears escape now.

He rubs her hand with his free one. "I don't know yet. I'll tell you everything once I've interviewed him, I promise. I'm sorry. I wouldn't do this if it wasn't necessary." He pauses. "Megan seems more upset than a babysitter should be. What gives?"

Connie clears her throat behind them, making them both turn in her direction. Kathy feels like she's been caught red-handed, like a teenager again. She pulls her hands away from Chase and steps back.

"Is this how law enforcement comfort victims these days?" says her mom. "Things have certainly changed since my day."

"Stay out of it, Mom. He's trying to help us." Kathy sees the hurt on Chase's face. He's probably thinking he got a lucky break not marrying into this family.

"I have to go." He leaves, closing the door behind him.

"You never told me *he* was the investigator." Her mom comes to stand next to her. "If you had, I would've suggested you consider whether Chase Cooper might be the culprit."

Anger is swelling in Kathy's chest. "Stop being ridiculous. Why would he take Charlie?"

"Here you are being naïve again, Kathy. I warned you about being too trusting. Chase Cooper pursued you like a fox preys on a rabbit. But he couldn't have you back then. Maybe he's jealous of Mitch and the life you have with him. Maybe that jealousy has him framing your husband for Charlie's murder. I mean, he clearly has the power to do that."

Kathy shakes her head, looking away from her mother. "Chase isn't like that. You've got him all wrong. You always did."

"I do hope so, Kathy. Although to be honest, I don't know which would be worse: your ex-boyfriend or your current husband being Charlie's abductor." She puts a hand on Kathy's shoulder. "I'm sorry. I don't mean to upset you. Let me make some coffee. I'm sure we'll be needing it to get through this evening."

With barely contained anger, Kathy says, "No. I think you should leave. I just want to be alone for a while."

Her mom looks surprised. "I'm sorry. I shouldn't have been so blunt." She tries to laugh it off. "Don't listen to me." She moves toward the kitchen.

"I want to be on my own." Kathy sees the hurt in her mom's eyes, but she doesn't back down.

Her mom collects her purse and slowly walks to the front door, the consequences of her stroke still visible. Before she opens it, she says, "I'm always here for you, Kathy. No matter which one of them has betrayed you."

When she's gone, Kathy thinks of Chase. He would never harm anyone, and certainly not a child. She's only ever seen him angry once, but he had good reason. He was hurt. She tries to think. Was that reason enough to hurt her in return after all these years?

Surely not.

THIRTY-TWO

SPRING 1994

Kathy's a freezing-cold bag of nerves, because tonight is all about her and Chase. Although they've been dating for months, it's been in secret. It was thrilling at first, lying to her parents about where she was going after school, pretending she was taking extra study sessions with her friends, but now she just wants to be with him all the time, and it's frustrating that they can't do that. They haven't been able to hang out by the creek over winter, so they're struggling for places to go that won't get them seen by prying eyes, especially as she's ready to spend the night alone with him.

As a solution, Chase has booked them an overnight stay at a hotel in Glenwood. She's thought of nothing else since he told her. But then, all she ever thinks about is Chase. It distracts her from school work to the point of getting a B in math for the first time ever. Her mom noticed that. She threatened to talk to Kathy's therapist to find out what's causing her to "wreck" her education. Kathy managed to convince her it was just the result of not studying hard enough. She doesn't need her mom interfering with her therapy. Apart from when she's with Chase, it's the only other place she can be herself. Her therapist is just about young enough to understand the pressure she's under, unlike her parents.

She looks up at the sky. The moon is bright tonight. It illuminates the hotel in the darkness. The wind whistles through the phone booth she's sheltering in outside the lobby; it's the only warm and dry place to wait for Chase, who was supposed to be here a half-hour ago. She can't wait inside because she doesn't want to be recognized. Word could get back to her mom. Sometimes it feels like everybody knows her parents.

She hugs her coat round her tightly, trying to hold back the excitement that's building. She can't imagine what it's going to be like to sleep next to him, to wake up with him. To be naked together. Although she's nervous about it, this is the person she wants to be with forever, so she knows she's doing the right thing. She's been conditioned to believe sex is for marriage, but that seems such an old-fashioned way of thinking about it. Although if Chase proposed to her tonight, she would wait. It would be difficult, but worth it. That's how sure she is that he's the person for her.

But a proposal's not going to happen. They're far too young to get married, and her parents would never agree to it. She needs to be out of their clutches before she goes public with Chase. Even if that means they cut her off financially.

Headlights suddenly cut through the dark, lighting up her face. He's here. She leaves the booth and stands by the parking lot with a smile on her face. Finally. Her backpack drops to the floor and a thrill runs through her.

The car pulls up alongside her and the window slowly winds down. Shock makes her take a step backward.

"Get in the car, Kathy." It's her mom.

She shakes her head, devastated. How did she even find out? "No."

Her mom gets out and opens the passenger door. "Now."

Kathy feels hot, shameful tears in her eyes. "I always do

what you want me to do. I'm almost an adult now. Let me do what I want for a change. *Please*." She feels like she's begging.

Her mom checks no one is watching them from the hotel and then crosses her arms. "Your boyfriend's not coming. He's been arrested for stealing a car."

Kathy gasps. How does her mom even know she has a boyfriend, never mind who he is? "That's not true."

"I'm afraid it is. He's at the police station now. He got pulled over by a patrol officer who was looking for the stolen car. He begged the officer to cut him some slack and explained that he was on his way to spend the night with some girl, trying to gain sympathy. But he was stupid enough to give your name. Luckily, the officer handled it discreetly by calling me, because your father would've disowned you for hanging around this hotel like a cheap hooker."

Kathy can't stop the tears from falling. Her mother can be so mean. "I don't believe you," she whispers.

"How would I know where to find you otherwise?"

She doesn't have an answer. It must be true. How could Chase be so stupid, tonight of all nights? And why steal a car? He told her his boss at the auto repair shop was letting him borrow one. He must've lied. She feels her heart flutter in disappointment. What else has he lied about?

Her mom's expression softens and she drops her arms. "Look, you've been led astray by a liar, Kathy. The officer told me that Chase Cooper has a record. It's not the first time he's been pulled over, and he usually has a different girl riding beside him each time. You're just one in a long line and you shouldn't accept that kind of disrespect. You're a Hamilton. Imagine what Reverend Holbrook would think if he knew why you were here."

Kathy's mouth has dropped open at the news that Chase has been cheating on her all this time. She feels like her heart is being torn from her chest. How could she be so gullible? Chase made her feel like she's the only person in his life.

In a softer tone, her mom says, "I know you're feeling hurt right now, darling, but he's just a boy. You'll get over this. I'll get you in to see your therapist this week. That will help you put this little incident into perspective." She hugs her, and the scent of her expensive perfume fills Kathy's nose. "I promise I won't tell your father any of this ever happened. We'll pretend we've been out for dinner together. On a girls' night. You can wipe that awful makeup off on the way home."

After a few seconds, Kathy pushes her away. Shame and embarrassment burn her face. She feels cheap. Worthless. How is she ever supposed to trust anyone again? If Chase can betray her, anyone can. He appeared so sincere. She'd been planning for their future together. She loves him.

She lets her mom guide her to the car, but she can't sit next to her in the passenger seat. She couldn't bear the sympathetic side glances. She chooses the back seat instead and sobs all the way home.

THIRTY-THREE

Chase sits at the table opposite Mitch Hamilton in the windowless interview room. With no breeze and no comforts, it's a room designed to make people want to talk fast in exchange for getting out. Detective Brown is next door, watching through the camera that's positioned high in the corner. He's listening for anything Chase might miss and he'll provide a second opinion of the guy's behavior.

"You sure you don't want a drink?" Chase asks. "Not even water?" He could do without this guy passing out from thirst. It's just gone 7 p.m. on what has been the warmest day this summer yet, and with no A/C in here, the room feels oppressive.

Mitch shakes his head. "Let's just get this over with." He looks downcast. There's no bravado or claims of innocence. Instead, he looks disappointed in himself. Is that because he hasn't been clever enough?

Chase has done a criminal background check on both his names: Mitch Hamilton and Mitch Bowers. There are no convictions and just one arrest—stealing from a grocery store as a teenager—but the charge was dropped. "Just confirm what you said on the way here: that you're happy to talk without your attorney present, and that you understand you can have an attorney present at any point."

"I understand that I've waived my rights for now. I want to hear why you've brought me in before I decide whether I need my lawyer."

Chase nods, then sips his own water before saying, "You told me and your wife that you had been working all day on Saturday, and that's why you couldn't collect your daughter from the birthday party."

Mitch doesn't look up. He must know what's coming.

"So why don't you tell me exactly where you were all day, because I know you didn't visit the contractors you mentioned. Despite your attempts at convincing the foreman to vouch for you, he did the right thing and told us he didn't see you at all that day."

Now he has the guy's attention. Mitch shakes his head. "This isn't something I really want to discuss with you."

Chase laughs, incredulous. "Well, this may come as a shock to you, Mr. Hamilton, but suspects in a child's abduction don't get to pick and choose who they talk to."

In a surprising display of anger, Mitch bangs his fist on the table. "I was *not* involved in my daughter's disappearance!"

He's obviously rattled, which is exactly how Chase wants him.

As he leans back in his seat, Mitch's demeanor changes again. "You dated my wife, didn't you? She said she knew you from high school, but I can tell by the way you look at each other that there was more to it than that. Is that why you've brought me in here? Some stupid high-school crush keeps you up at night, and now you've decided to frame me for this?"

Chase feels his hands clenching. He doesn't anger easily, but this guy has hit a raw nerve. "You're the one being questioned here, not me."

Mitch is persistent. "Did you kill our daughter, Detective? To get back at the woman who rejected you? Or to punish me for marrying her?"

Chase laughs. "That's quite a theory. But I'm not the person who has no credible alibi for that day." Mitch breaks eye contact and Chase decides to change tack. He softens his tone. "Listen, just tell me what you were doing that day and we can both go home. I don't want to be in here any more than you do."

Rubbing his eyes, Mitch sighs heavily. "I spent most of the day out at the overlook hiking trail, about fifty miles north of here."

Finally, the truth. Chase knows the trail. It's in the middle of nowhere. "Why? Because it's secluded and a great place to hide a body?"

Mitch glares at him. "No."

"What time were you there?" He picks up a pen.

"I got there at about eleven. I stayed until it was time to drive to Glenwood to meet Kathy for marriage counseling."

"Can you prove you were there that afternoon? Did anyone see you?"

"A couple of hikers walked past my car, but I didn't know them."

If he has to, Chase has other ways to confirm whether he was there or not: phone records, CCTV from the area, tracking down witnesses. "So why did you go there instead of to work?"

"Because I needed some space to think, somewhere I could be alone for a few hours. I've been working non-stop for years, trying to build my business, but the pressure's becoming unbearable. On top of that, there's the fact that Kathy and I are on the verge of..." He doesn't finish.

Chase looks away out of respect. He hadn't realized their relationship problems were that serious.

"Look. Things aren't good between us. I was out there thinking about what to do about it. Whether it's better to keep working at trying to resolve things or whether it makes sense to just walk away for good. Move on and start afresh." Mitch takes a deep breath. "It's just so goddam easy to make mistakes. If only we could rewind time, you know?"

Chase nods thoughtfully. "What did you do?"

Mitch lowers his eyes. "I was an asshole. I got drunk and slept with... a bartender."

It takes Chase a few seconds to realize where this is going. His mouth opens in surprise. He had no idea. "Megan Carter."

Mitch is silent for a minute, before confirming it. "Right. I got to know her in the sports bar where she works. When a house sale I'd been relying on fell through, I got wasted there. Kathy was out of town for a few days visiting friends with Fay." He looks up at last. "I was a fool. I spent the whole goddam weekend drunk in bed with Megan."

Chase tries hard to hide his surprise.

Mitch shakes his head. "She reminded me of Kathy when we first met, which confused me, because they're so different. And she was easy to talk to. She's street smart with a healthy dose of cynicism that you only get from growing up in a broken household, and her lifestyle attracted me: no responsibilities, late mornings and even later nights. She doesn't care what people think about her and she laughs a lot. I just needed to blow off some steam and be someone other than Mitch Hamilton for a few days."

"You wanted to be Mitch Bowers again. No money, no pressure, no expectations."

Mitch snorts at the realization that Chase is right. "Damn. I never imagined I'd want my old life back."

"Did Megan know you were married?"

"I stopped wearing my ring to the bar when I realized I was attracted to her. I guess I knew something might happen one day. But I didn't..."

Chase leans in. "You didn't what?"

"I didn't think she'd get pregnant." Mitch looks him in the eye but remains silent, letting him put two and two together.

Chase has to stop himself from shaking his head as he realizes what Mitch is implying. "Are you saying Charlie's *not* adopted? That she's your biological daughter with Megan?"

Mitch looks away, and Chase sees him for what he is: a lying, cheating asshole who's nowhere near good enough for Kathy Hamilton.

THIRTY-FOUR

Megan is watching the reporters from the kitchen window. They're focusing their attention on her attack now, after seeing her arrival here yesterday, and they're basically blaming her for it. Apparently being a female bartender who lives alone in a certain part of town is an open invitation for sadistic freaks to enter your home and try to strangle you to death.

She swallows. Her throat is still sore, but it's gradually healing and not as painful as the headache she can't seem to shift. She could take some of the painkillers the doctor prescribed her, but she doesn't want to ask Mitch or Kathy for them. She wants to be able to cope without them, but it's becoming more difficult to avoid temptation with each new article she reads about Charlie's disappearance. Some websites are now blaming her for that too, saying she faked her injuries to hide the fact that she took Charlie and did something to her. It makes Megan want to go outside and confront the reporters, but she's resisted so far.

None of them have figured out that Charlie's her daughter, but it's just a matter of time if they track down anyone who knows her in Glenwood. She has no friends in Maple Falls other than the Hamiltons.

Still peering out, she says, "Have you noticed how their numbers are dwindling the longer Charlie's missing? And they're arriving later and leaving earlier each day that passes. They're already losing interest. They must think she's never going to be found."

"That'll soon change when the images of Mitch and Chase driving away together are released," says Kathy behind her. "Hiding behind a baseball cap just makes him look guilty of something."

Megan turns, surprised at the comment. "Do you believe he could've had anything to do with it?"

Kathy hesitates. "No. I don't."

"Then why'd he lie about where he was that day?"

Kathy sighs. "Maybe he's seeing someone else and doesn't want either of us to know."

Her honest responses make Megan feel as though they're finally having a real conversation. That Kathy's finally seeing her as someone other than Charlie's irresponsible mother, or the woman who slept with her husband. She looks at Kathy properly. Her hair isn't blow-dried, and she's wearing minimal makeup. Normally so pristine, she looks like she's suffering. Megan decides it's time they had an honest conversation at last. "How did he first tell you about me?"

Kathy meets her gaze. "He came home the day after Christmas and told me someone he knew was in the hospital. You'd overdosed?"

Megan nods, feeling her cheeks redden. "It wasn't intentional, and I haven't touched anything since then." She'd fallen off the wagon big-time. Christmas is a difficult time of the year for fractured families, and she'd been unable to resist using. She'd convinced herself she could control it. "When child services showed up at the hospital and said they were taking

Charlie from me, I knew I had to call Mitch and sort my life out."

"I'm not judging you," says Kathy. "Addiction is a disease. My volunteer work at the women's refuge means I see what it does to people from all walks of life. Some of the women are there because their partners can't get off the stuff. Some of the women turn to it in the hope that it'll erase their trauma."

Megan laughs bitterly. "It never does, though. That's the problem. It starts with just weekends and builds from there. Then it becomes a crutch. Something you need to get you out of bed in the morning. 'Mama's little helper' is what a woman I know calls it. It becomes daily, then you sell it to make money to buy it. Then you risk prison. I entered rehab before it got that bad, but I still managed to slip up last Christmas. Never again, though."

There's sympathy in Kathy's eyes. Hugging her mug of coffee as if she's cold, she says, "Mitch explained he'd had a brief fling with a younger woman six years ago and it resulted in a daughter." She shakes her head. "When I realized he'd been visiting that child every month for five years without me knowing, I felt so stupid. So utterly naïve. I mean, how does someone not notice that?"

Megan remains standing, but crosses her arms. "You run a busy household, you work full-time and you volunteer. Besides, when you don't expect someone to be lying to you, there's no reason to suspect them of anything."

Kathy sips her coffee. "Was it a difficult decision to let Mitch change her last name to Hamilton and pretend we'd adopted her?"

Tears quickly fill Megan's eyes, but she wipes them away. "Of course. I want Charlie with me full-time. I want to make her breakfast, take her clothes shopping and read her a bedtime story every night. I understand that the fact I gave in to my addiction on Christmas Day suggests otherwise, but I love her more than anything." She wipes her nose with a tissue. "And when it's a choice between child services taking her permanently or Charlie going to live with her well-off father, it was obvious what needed to be done." What she doesn't say is that last names can be changed back. She should be Charlie Carter, not Hamilton.

"You know," says Kathy, "my mother wasn't at all surprised when I told her Mitch had cheated on me, almost like she'd expected it to happen eventually. She was more surprised when she met you for the first time back in February, like you weren't who she'd expected him to cheat with. Probably because she thinks he's always been after my money, so she expected him to pick someone wealthy." She shakes her head. "She told me not to let him give Charlie the family name."

For Megan, that stings. It confirms that the old woman hates her, and for no valid reason. "Is that why she had the stroke, do you think? From worrying that this whole situation would reach her bible-bashing friends and they'd all be gossiping about her?"

Kathy winces and Megan realizes she's being harsh. It's hard not to be when she's considered a lowlife. But it took two people to make Charlie, and she was single, unlike Mitch. He lied to her.

"My mother's old-fashioned. Try not to take it personally. Even though Mitch was unfaithful, she talked me into staying with him. She doesn't believe in divorce. Besides, she didn't want him getting half of what's mine." Kathy looks at her. "Mom and Dad bought us this house when I became pregnant with Fay, and it's worth a lot more now. They don't think he deserves a penny of it."

"I imagine you have family money he would be entitled to also?"

Kathy nods. "There's no prenuptial agreement. But to be honest, I don't care about all that, and he has his own money now anyway. I didn't want to divorce him, not really. I married him for a reason, and I thought we could get through this, but it's been hard to look at him in the same way now I know what he's capable of. I think that at this point, I'm staying with him for Fay really." She smiles sadly. "We always put the children first, don't we?"

Megan nods, but she's consumed with guilt for letting her addiction take precious time away from Charlie. For a while she was incapable of putting her daughter first, and she'll always regret that.

"How did you cope with letting Charlie live with us?" asks Kathy. "I mean, I know you get to visit her regularly, but it's hard to give up a child, no matter what the circumstances. I can't imagine seeing Fay that infrequently."

Kathy looks emotional at the thought of it, but Megan decides to keep quiet about her thoughts on getting Charlie back to live with her eventually. She'll go to court for custody if she has to. Although she's not sure how successful she'd be until she has at least a year clean of drugs and alcohol. Even then, it's debatable whether a judge would favor her over Mitch. But she has to try. If she gets the opportunity. She tries not to think about what happens if Charlie's never found. "It helps that you've been good to us. I mean, I can't imagine many wives would let their husband's secret child move in and then let the woman who cheated with him visit."

Kathy puts her cup down. "Charlie shouldn't suffer for her father's indiscretion. I see a lot of children at school who carry the emotional bruises of parents at war. It's not fair on them." She looks away, and it's hard to read her expression. "He told me it was just one weekend and that he's never cheated on me since. He explained he wanted to be in Charlie's life, to make sure she doesn't go without. I couldn't deny him seeing his daughter, but I won't lie to you, it's been hard on me. I..." She trails off.

"What?" Megan presses.

"It's just that sometimes I feel like you two could still be seeing each other, especially now you've moved in." Kathy tries to laugh. "I guess my paranoia gets the better of me."

Megan genuinely feels sorry for her. "Let me put your mind at rest on that one. It *was* just that one weekend. I didn't know he was married. I didn't even know his last name. He was just some guy in the bar who paid me some attention when I was at my lowest. I could've gone home with anyone during that time, to be really honest with you. There wasn't anything special that made him the lucky guy." She smiles weakly.

"But what about now? Now you know him better and you've seen him caring for your daughter. Isn't there any attraction between you? I mean, he and I are going through marriage counseling, and I don't even know if we're going to make it, so it makes sense that he'd turn to you for..." Kathy wells up.

Megan goes to her and places a hand on her back. She's surprised by her feelings at seeing Kathy upset. "I'm sorry. I didn't know you guys were in counseling. The only thing that keeps me coming here is Charlie. It has nothing to do with Mitch. I lost all respect for the guy when I found out he'd lied about being single." She tries to make light of the situation. "Besides, he's old. I'm only twenty-seven, and what is he now, like, forty or something?"

Kathy laughs as she uses a tissue to wipe her eyes. "Forty-one."

"Exactly. Believe it or not, I can do better than Mitch Hamilton. No, he was definitely a mistake that I don't intend to ever repeat. Haven't you ever slept with someone and regretted it?"

Kathy tenses. The answer is yes, but she can't open that can of worms. "I've regretted *not* sleeping with someone before."

Megan thinks of Detective Cooper. It must be him. She's noticed the chemistry between them. She wonders if he knows Kathy's still holding a torch for him while trying to make her marriage work with a guy who's disrespected her in the worst way. "Why don't you want Chase to know that Mitch and I are Charlie's parents? I mean, you haven't kept it from your parents; only Fay, which I totally get. Fay doesn't need to know her dad's an asshole." She assumes it's because Kathy's ashamed to have someone like her linked to her family.

"It's for exactly that reason: Fay. She's already suffering with anxiety. She's at such a delicate age, I didn't want to make things worse for her." Kathy pauses. "But also because it's humiliating." She lowers her eyes. "It's humiliating that I married someone who would do this to me. Maybe if Chase wasn't the detective assigned to us, I would have been honest from the outset and avoided all this extra drama. But we had no way of knowing Charlie would be missing this long. We had no idea how this was going to play out. I believed she'd be found overnight."

Megan takes a deep breath. She can understand why it would be humiliating for Kathy to admit that to the love of her life. "I bet your mom didn't want people knowing either. Am I right?"

Kathy nods.

"Well, like I said, you don't have to worry about me and Mitch hooking up ever again. He can't even look me in the eye anymore. I'm just his dirty little secret who he's probably hoping overdoses sooner rather than later in order to leave him and his family alone."

Kathy suddenly clutches her hand. "I'm so sorry your daughter's missing, Megan. I'm so sorry I didn't take better care of her that day. I should've stayed with her. You should've been invited to the stupid party." She's crying now. "I love her, you know? Obviously not in the same way you do, but she's a lovely little girl who has so easily blended into our family. Whether Mitch and I save our marriage or not, Charlie is always welcome in my home. You both are."

Megan can't hold back her tears this time. No one's ever been this kind to her. She leans in and hugs Kathy. "Thank you for saying that. Charlie loves you too. She never stops talking about you all when I'm with her. She's had the best time living here." So good that it's made Megan feel guilty for wanting to take her away from all this. Pulling away, she looks into Kathy's watery eyes. "We need to do everything we can to find her, Kathy, because I don't want to trust Mitch or the cops with my daughter's life. I'm sick of being let down. It's time we did something ourselves."

Kathy's nodding. "That's exactly how I feel. I hate just sitting here waiting for news."

A weight lifts from Megan's shoulders when she realizes she and Kathy can come together to try to find Charlie. It makes her feel a step closer to ending this nightmare.

THIRTY-FIVE

"I'm telling you all this because you have to see that I would never harm her," Mitch says in the stifling interview room. Sweat accumulates at his temples. "I love Charlie just as much as I love Fay."

Chase tries hard to hide his contempt for the guy. "How did Kathy react when she found out you not only cheated on her, but you had a secret child too?"

"She surprised me. I thought she'd want a divorce, but it actually helped having Charlie live with us. Kathy treats her exactly the same as Fay. She turned to the church for guidance, and she told her parents." He shakes his head. "They already hated me because I was broke when I met their precious daughter. After I dropped out of college, they labeled me a loser and tried to talk her out of marrying me."

Chase nods. He knows how that goes. "So you told everyone that Charlie was adopted and Megan was the babysitter. Why? Why not just come clean?"

Mitch runs a hand through his hair. "I have my business to think of, and Connie didn't want the family name being brought into disrepute. Besides, Kathy's a private person. She felt it would be humiliating for the whole town to be talking about what I did, and that they'd see her as some kind of doormat who was happy to accept it. At the end of the day, we both agreed Charlie would be better off with us at that time. Megan was struggling with her addiction and it was Charlie who called the ambulance when she overdosed."

Poor kid. Chase thinks of Patrick. Shannon's an occasional user, but it wouldn't surprise him if she ended up addicted to meth one day. "And Megan just agreed to let Charlie live with you?"

"It was either that or child services take her, and we all know how that ends. I agreed to pay for all Charlie's expenses, and for Megan's apartment too, on the proviso she stays clean. And Kathy and I agreed she could visit Charlie whenever she wanted to. Charlie was confused at first, but she's a smart kid, she could see her mom was struggling. Besides, she and I already had a good relationship, so for her it was just about spending more time with Dad. I don't think she realizes it's permanent; she's too young to understand the implications."

"How did Fay take the news?"

Mitch takes a deep breath. "She thinks Charlie's adopted. We didn't want to tell her, because she's already going through some stuff and seeing a therapist. We didn't want to add to her anxiety. You've probably noticed she's too thin. If she finds out I cheated on her mother, she could hurt herself or something." He looks guilt-ridden. "She's going to hate me if this gets out."

"But teenagers are pretty perceptive," says Chase. "You don't think on some level she already knows? That she hasn't heard you and Kathy arguing about it late at night? I'm just trying to gauge whether there's a chance she's told someone about it, and maybe that someone doesn't think you deserve Charlie. It's a possible motive for her disappearance."

Mitch goes pale at the thought that his secret could be the

reason for Charlie's abduction. Quietly he says, "If Fay knows, she hasn't let on to me or Kathy."

"Maybe now would be a good time to tell her, before a reporter finds out." Mitch doesn't respond. "Do your brother and his wife know all this?"

Mitch nods.

"And how do Kathy and Megan get along?"

"Enough to get by. They don't talk much. There's no tension between them, but Megan keeps her distance, knowing that she's the other woman. Kathy's too well bred to be anything but nice. They have a shared responsibility for Charlie, so they make it work." He stands up and takes a few steps around the table to stretch his legs. "Can't you see now that none of us would want Charlie hurt? We all love her."

Chase disagrees. He thinks this actually gives Mitch a motive to harm the child. And to try to kill Megan. They're a drain on his finances and a wedge between him and Kathy. And what about Megan? Could she be hiding Charlie in order to blackmail Mitch? Maybe she needs money. There have been no ransom requests yet, but she could be biding her time. She's managed to wrangle her way into their home somehow. Is that so she can stay one step ahead of his investigation by being close to the action?

Mitch is getting antsy. "So can I leave now? I should be out looking for my daughter."

"Just one more thing. Where did you go after your house tour the night Charlie disappeared?"

Mitch frowns. "What do you mean?"

"You showed Professor Harris and his partner around the house on Wicker Lane at eight that evening. What did you do afterwards?"

"I drove straight home because I wanted to see if there was any news on Charlie."

Chase crosses his arms. "You didn't drive to Glenwood?"

"What? No."

The professor said he'd seen Mitch drive off in that direction, which is the opposite direction to his home.

"Oh, wait. I went to the liquor store." Mitch's face reddens. "I needed something to calm my nerves. I only had two slugs before realizing it wasn't going to help the situation. I tossed it into a trash can before driving home. I didn't want to drink in front of Fay and Kathy. At that point I was trying to appear composed so they didn't see how worried I was."

It's a reasonable excuse, but Chase is going to check with the liquor store clerk anyway so he can confirm a time. "You have any listings out that way?"

"No."

"But that's where the house is that you're renovating, right? The one where you originally said you'd been that afternoon."

Mitch looks confused. "Right. But we've established I *wasn't* there."

"I know. I'm just getting things straight in my head." Chase wonders whether Mitch went there after the showing. And if so, why. "Okay, you're free to go. I appreciate your honesty. But next time I ask you a question, it'll help me find Charlie quicker if you're straight with me. Because all this back-and-forth has slowed down my investigation and possibly put your daughter at risk of greater harm."

To his credit, Mitch nods. "I understand. I've never been in this position before, so I wasn't sure who to trust."

Chase watches as he leaves the interview room and walks down the long corridor to the exit. Under his breath he mutters, "That makes two of us, buddy."

THIRTY-SIX

Car headlights illuminate the dark kitchen and hallway before a key in the lock makes Kathy tense. She stands up and meets Megan's gaze. There's an understanding between them now: Megan is privy to whatever Kathy is. They're in this together.

"I'll just stop for one." That's Scott's voice. He must've collected Mitch from the police station and now he's coming in for a beer.

Kathy's disappointed. She wanted to quiz Mitch as soon as possible. "Hi, Scott."

He walks over to hug her. "How are you holding up?" He nods at Megan before glancing at the bruising on her throat. Scott's always been stand-offish toward her, and Kathy knows it's because he thinks she seduced his brother on purpose so she could have his child and drain his finances. It's a ridiculous thought, from a man who believes everyone values money as much as he does.

An awkward silence fills the room as Mitch notices Megan. "Do you mind giving us some privacy?" He sounds tired rather than annoyed.

"Actually, Mitch, we both want to know what happened at

the station." Kathy looks at Scott. "Would you mind pouring some coffees? I think we could all do with some caffeine."

Scott looks surprised. He's not used to Kathy asking him to do anything. "Sure." He heads to the kitchen.

"Come take a seat." Kathy leads Mitch into the living room and they wait while Megan helps Scott fetch the drinks. Scott's chosen a beer for him and Mitch. Kathy notices that Megan has spilled some of her coffee because her hands are trembling slightly. She must be dreading this. She and Scott take an armchair each.

"Where's Fay?" asks Mitch as he kicks his shoes off.

"I've agreed she can spend the night at Jenna's. She doesn't know you went down to the station, but you should call her before she goes to sleep, because photographs of you in Chase's car are starting to appear online."

"Shit," says Scott. "Don't the reporters know he was just answering questions? Trying to be helpful?"

"The press wants one of us to be Charlie's abductor," says Megan. "It'll sell more papers."

Scott shakes his head and looks at Mitch. "I told you she'd be trouble."

"What did you say?" Incredulous, Megan leans forward.

Scott turns to her. "This is all your fault. You know that, right?"

Her eyes widen. "How do you figure that?"

"If you'd looked after your own child, she wouldn't have been at the party that day. She wouldn't even be living here."

Kathy gasps. He's out of line. She's about to say so when Megan speaks up. "If *you* didn't invite sleazy men to your party, she wouldn't have been taken! I mean, just how many criminals do you hang out with, Scott? And is there a reason for that?" She raises her voice. "How do I know it wasn't *you* who took her?"

"How dare you?" Scott stands up and walks to the corner of

the living room while he cools down. "I wish I'd never had that damn party. Charlie going missing has me questioning how well I know people. I can't sleep from the guilt. This doesn't just affect you three, you know."

"Oh, *you* can't sleep?" says Megan. "How the fuck do you think *I* feel?"

"Everyone shut up!" says Mitch firmly. "This isn't doing anyone any good." He sighs. "I've told Detective Cooper everything. He knows Charlie is mine and Megan's."

Kathy raises her eyebrows in surprise, and is overcome with relief. He should've told Chase from the very beginning. They both should have.

"Thank God," says Megan before realizing the implications. "I expect the press will have a field day with that. I'll be public enemy number one for sleeping with a married man."

Mitch looks at her. "I need to speak to my family, so I'd appreciate it if you'd go to your room."

She glares at him. "What am I, a child? Screw you."

Kathy speaks up. "Stay here, Megan. Scott, you're out of line. She's suffering enough without you blaming her for what's happened. Don't you think she already wishes she'd never met our family?"

Scott looks away. "This is so screwed up."

Kathy tries to get things back on track. She looks at Mitch. "Why did you lie about your whereabouts on Saturday? What were you doing?"

Mitch glances at Megan. "I don't feel comfortable talking about this in front of other people."

Megan rolls her eyes.

"Well guess what? I don't feel comfortable with any of this," says Kathy firmly. "So deal with it, and for God's sake tell us what happened at the station."

He's surprised by her attitude. "I took a ride out to the overlook hiking trail on Saturday to get some alone time. I needed to think about... our marriage."

It's like a dagger piercing her heart. He's considering leaving the family. Divorcing her. Kathy swallows, not knowing how to respond. Megan looks away. Scott sips his beer, but it's clear that he's squirming. Did he already know? She doubts Mitch would've confided in him.

"I'm sorry, Kathy, but you made me say it," says Mitch. "Things have been tough since I told you about Megan and Charlie. The guilt is stressful."

Quietly she says, "I wasn't trying to make you feel guilty. That's never been my intention."

"That's the worst part, though." He focuses on her. "It's not even you making me feel guilty. I see the repercussions of my actions daily. I stare at Charlie and wish she was ours, not mine and Megan's. I see Megan struggling to cope with her daughter living with us. I catch Fay looking at me sometimes when she thinks I haven't noticed. Is she putting everything together in her head? And if so, does she think any less of me?" He pauses. "And then there's your parents."

"But Mom never even mentions it," Kathy says, and it's true.

"Oh, come on, she doesn't have to. The minute you told her about my affair, she had a gleeful look in her eye that tells me everything I need to know. She was waiting for me to screw up, and I proved her right." He turns to Megan. "This is going to make me sound like a bastard, and I'm sorry, but every time you come over here, I regret what I did."

Kathy glances at her. He's being honest at last, but can Megan cope with the brutality of his words? Kathy's instinct is to go to her, but she holds back, not wanting to make her feel worse. Looking back at Mitch, she realizes she doesn't recognize her husband anymore.

"It's got nothing to do with you, Megan. It's about what I

did to my family," he continues. "I broke Kathy's trust and now I feel like I'm walking on eggshells around all of you. I wish Kathy and I could go back to how we were, but marriage counseling has proven that's never going to happen."

Kathy's heart rate quickens. He's not the same person she fell in love with. He's deeply unhappy. He spends so much time pretending to be something he's not that it's ruining him. She sits up straight, trying to find an inner strength. They can discuss their marriage another time. Right now, she wants answers about Charlie. "So you were there all afternoon until our counseling session?"

He nods, exhausted by his outburst.

"So why did you have a different shirt on when you arrived for that?"

He goes still. "I guess I changed. It was hot. I don't remember."

It was a hot day, but he's leaving out the part where he came home for a shower. He smelled fresh when he kissed her in the waiting room. "Did you have a shower before changing?"

He looks blank. "I don't remember. So much has happened since then, why does it matter?"

"I'm just confused, because when we got home *after* the counseling session, you wanted to go for a shower straight away. That would've been three showers in one day."

He rubs his face with his hands.

"What's going on, Kathy?" asks Megan, frowning. "Do you know something?"

Mitch scoffs. "There's nothing to know! I always carry a spare shirt with me, so I changed when I got hot. After our counseling session, I wanted a shower so I could relax for the evening, but that was when we realized Charlie was missing."

Scott rests his beer on the coffee table. "Kathy, are you seriously insinuating that Mitch killed Charlie, showered, changed and then turned up at your counseling session like nothing had happened?"

Kathy looks at the ground. She doesn't think Mitch is a killer. But does anyone think that of their partner, even when it's true? "It's just been bothering me, that's all." She looks at Mitch. "So Chase was happy with your new alibi?"

He gives her a sharp look. "It's not a new alibi, Kathy, it's the truth. I didn't say where I was the first time he asked me because you were in the room and I didn't think you'd want the local detective to know we were having marriage problems. It could get back to your parents."

That's true, but Kathy's mom knows they're in counseling. She just doesn't know it's not working.

"I was doing you a favor," he says. "But that was before I knew you and the detective used to have the hots for each other."

She shakes her head in disappointment. He's resorted to cheap digs.

"Guys?" says Scott. "What's the point of all this? We shouldn't be turning on each other. You should be focusing on Charlie and I should be taking care of my own family. The boys have been rattled by her disappearance, especially because it happened in their own backyard. Cindy's adamant she wants to sell the house and move."

Kathy's not surprised. She'd probably want to do the same. She takes a deep breath. "So what happens now? Is Chase happy none of us were involved?"

Mitch nods. "I think so. But if the press is running photographs of me being taken in for questioning, it's going to make the public turn on us. My business will be ruined. Who's going to want to be alone in an empty house with a suspected child killer?" He fixes his eyes on hers. "The reporters are going to be relentless in trying to find people to spill any dirt they might have on us. And it only takes the attention away from finding Charlie."

Kathy shivers. "Then we'll need to find her ourselves."

Scott looks doubtful. "If the cops haven't found her, you have no chance."

The room goes quiet.

"Don't give up on her," says Megan quietly.

They all turn to her.

"It hasn't even been three days yet," she says. "She could still be alive."

"She's right," says Kathy. "We have to—"

A knock at the door interrupts her. There's some commotion outside, with raised voices, and Kathy spots blue and red flashing lights. Scott reluctantly goes to answer the door and Kathy hears him say, "What do you want now?"

Chase walks into the living room and stares at them. She wonders if they look suspicious all together like this. "I'm sorry to bother you folks again," he says, "but I'd like to search the house with some of my officers."

Mitch jumps up. "For God's sake, Cooper, this is harassment!"

"No," says Chase. "I just need to be sure nothing happened here."

"You'll need a warrant," says Scott.

Chase pulls a piece of paper out of his pocket and looks at Kathy. She notices the regret in his eyes. She has time to feel grateful that Fay's staying overnight with her friend.

On shaky legs, she stands up. "Where do you want to start?"

THIRTY-SEVEN

To Kathy it feels like the night is never-ending. Four police officers and two dogs are assisting in the search of her house. She can hear them upstairs banging around. Chase said they'd be careful, but one of them has already knocked a framed family portrait off the wall by the stairs, smashing the glass. The photograph was taken before Charlie came to live with them, so she's not in it. As she carefully picks up the shards of glass, Kathy can't help feeling it's a bad omen. That it's not just the glass that's broken, but the family looking back at her too. It makes her wonder whether Charlie was the glue holding them together.

Megan approaches. "Let me help. I have a lot of experience with picking up broken glass." She smiles.

"Thanks. Be careful." Kathy slowly stands. Her body feels heavy with exhaustion. She needs an uninterrupted night of sleep, but as soon as she has the thought, she feels guilty. Is Charlie sleeping wherever she is? Or is she being kept awake by God knows who? She fights back tears and heads to the kitchen, dropping the glass into the bin.

Mitch stands facing the window. The blinds are closed so

he can't see the news vans. She notices he has a whiskey in his left hand and it makes her want to console him. She rubs her hand across his back, but he tenses before saying, "You think I took her, don't you?"

She sighs. "If I thought that, you wouldn't be in my house right now, Mitch."

He scoffs. "So this is how it starts. *My* house. I guess I was just a roommate all this time?"

"That's not what I meant." She takes his whiskey from him and downs it. It stings her throat. "I think it's time you started putting Megan's feelings before your own. She brought Charlie up single-handedly for five years, so imagine how this feels for her. She should be the person Chase calls with updates. She should be the person we're taking care of. But if all you want to do is drink and wallow in self-pity, then you're no use to any of us."

He's silent for a few minutes. "You're right. I'm sorry." He turns to her. "That's all I ever say now, isn't it?" She doesn't answer, so he takes her hand in his. "I wouldn't blame you for giving up on me. I think I've given up on myself."

She studies his face. "If you want to give up on yourself, there's nothing I can do about it. But don't ever give up on your children. They need you. Stop thinking about what this is doing to you and your business. Think about what it's doing to Fay. Think about how to get Charlie home." She pauses. "Neither of them care about how much money you make, Mitch, they never did. They need you to be a father. It's as simple as that, so stop overcomplicating things."

He looks away, so she places the empty glass in the sink and walks out of the kitchen. She knows now that it's inevitable they'll split. Their private business is out there for the whole town to judge, and she resents him for putting them in that position. But even if Charlie had never gone missing, news about his affair was bound to get out eventually. They were naïve to think they could raise Charlie without hurting both her and Megan. She has to console herself with the knowledge that their intentions were good. But that doesn't help Megan or Charlie right now.

She's found the contact details for the reporter who spoke to her in the cemetery the morning after Charlie vanished. As an investigative reporter, Susan Cartwright seemed adamant she could help. Kathy intends to call her, but she won't be telling Chase or Mitch. This is something she wants to do with Megan.

Upstairs, she finds Chase alone in the master bedroom. It's strange seeing him in her private space. "Found anything?"

He looks up from his position on the floor. He's feeling under their bed. Embarrassment ripples through her. The bed is unmade, carelessly discarded clothes are draped over chairs and she hasn't vacuumed since Friday. He must think she's a slob. Unlike Cindy, she opted not to have a cleaner once Fay was old enough to pick up after herself. She prefers that the girls learn how to do their own chores.

"No." He stands up. "I'm sorry about this. I wouldn't do it if it weren't necessary."

"But why is it necessary? Mitch told you where he was that afternoon. If he's not a suspect, does that mean I am?"

Chase crosses his arms. "The truth of the matter is that everyone's a suspect until I find Charlie." He rubs his jaw. "I want you to be honest with me for a second, Kathy. Do you think Mitch could've been involved?"

She hesitates. Exhausted by constantly going back and forth in her mind, she doesn't know what to believe. She doesn't know who to trust. "I don't think so. But..."

"What is it?"

She tells him about Mitch's change of shirt and how he wanted to shower for a possible third time on Saturday evening. As soon as it's out of her mouth, she regrets it, because Chase writes it down, so she adds, "It would be completely out of character for him to hurt anyone."

"Well, we don't know that Charlie's been hurt. I'm considering the possibility that someone could be keeping her hidden in order to profit from a ransom or a reward."

She doesn't know how to respond to that.

"Has Mitch ever dressed as a clown?"

"What?" She laughs at the idea. "Not that I know of."

"So you haven't spotted a clown mask around the house at all? Or in the garbage?"

So that's what they're looking for. "No." It dawns on her then. "You think it was one of the clowns from the party who took her."

"It's something I'm looking into. Cindy hired one of them and he checks out, but a second clown appeared for a short time and no one knows who he was. Cindy was adamant she only paid one of them before they left. But that's just between you and me. I haven't released that information to the press yet, because I don't want the guy destroying the mask and costume before we locate him. No one from the party has admitted to dressing up that day."

Her blood runs cold as she remembers walking past a clown on her way out of the house. Could she have stopped him from abducting Charlie? But he wasn't wearing a mask; his face was covered in make-up.

"Does your husband go to Glenwood much?"

She's confused by the question. The longer this day goes on, the less she's able to concentrate. "I don't know. I think he has a listing near there, as well as the fixer-upper he's been working on. Why?"

"But no family or friends out that way?"

"No, Scott's his only family, and he doesn't hang out with anyone else other than developers and contractors. Between working long hours and spending time with me and the kids, he doesn't really get time." She thinks of Megan. He had enough time to sit alone in a bar on more than one occasion. She has an uneasy feeling that Chase knows something he isn't letting on, but she can't bring herself to ask him about it. "I think it's best you liaise directly with Megan from now on. She deserves to hear any news before I do."

He raises his eyebrows. "You sure?"

"Yes. She's Charlie's mother, after all. Have you got any leads on who might have attacked her?"

"No. All I know so far is that whoever it was came and went through an open fire escape. And now that I know she's Charlie's biological mother, I'm treating the two incidents as if they're linked, so I'll be questioning the people in her life: co-workers and customers from the bar, her family if I can find any. It opens up a new avenue for potential suspects."

"So why are you so intent on blaming my husband for this?"

He looks disappointed by the question, but she stares at him, waiting for an answer. Her mom's words play out in her head: Chase could be fixated on framing Mitch for this either because *he* took Charlie, or because he's holding onto some anger for what happened when they were younger.

"I'm just doing my job," he says wearily.

He looks exhausted and pale, like he needs a long sleep followed by a hearty breakfast to give him some energy. She softens. "I'm sorry, Chase. I just don't know who I can trust anymore."

He nods. "That's to be expected. Everyone in your life becomes a suspect, right? You see them through different eyes. Things you previously ignored, or didn't pay close enough attention to, become sinister."

She thinks of Reverend Stanley and the gifts he gave Charlie. Or did she steal them? Then she thinks of Charlie's teacher. But Chase has never raised him as a suspect, so it can't be him. She rubs her forehead. It's exhausting suspecting everyone.

"You have to follow your instincts, but you know me, Kathy." Chase takes a step toward her, but stops at one. "I only have your best interests at heart."

She'd like to believe that, but it's been so long since they were close. So long that she doesn't really know him anymore. And with Shannon living with him again, he's got other priorities. She changes the subject. "When Charlie comes home, she'll live with Megan again. Mitch can go back to being a part-time dad. It's not that I don't want Charlie in my life—I'd love to still see her regularly—but she needs her mother. Mitch and I will support them both wherever they need help." She worries about explaining the whole sorry mess to Fay, but is hopeful that Christine can help her cope.

Chase is clearly surprised. "Has something happened to make you feel this way?"

"Only that I've seen how wrong it was for me to pretend to be Charlie's mom. Megan made a mistake when she overdosed, but that doesn't mean she should be punished for it by watching her daughter grow up with another family. It must've been awful for her." Kathy feels herself giving in to the sobs she's been trying to hold back. Her heart is breaking into pieces because she feels keenly what Megan's going through.

"Hey, it's okay." Chase pushes the bedroom door closed, then comes over and sits her on the bed. He crouches down in front of her as she tries to catch her breath. His voice is low. "I have no problem keeping Megan updated, and your husband, but I see how this is affecting you, and it worries me, Kathy. Is it just the fact that Charlie's missing that's making you feel this bad, or is there something else?"

She meets his gaze and feels his warm hand on her knee. He has a reassuring way about him that makes her feel he can help her fix all her problems. Taking a tissue from her pocket, she wipes her eyes and nose. "Isn't it bad enough that Charlie's missing?"

"Sure, but I've got to be honest: she's only been with you for six months, so I'm surprised you have such strong feelings for her already. Are you sure there's nothing else you want to tell me?"

There's plenty she wants to tell him, but not about Charlie's disappearance. She can't help him there. This case is bringing up old memories and all the feelings from that time when she had to stop seeing him. She tilts her head to the ceiling, trying to keep tears back. "I wish I could tell you everything. I'm so sick of keeping secrets. I want to talk about it all, but I can't." She breaks down again, her breathing becoming shallow as the enormity of everything threatens to overwhelm her.

"It's okay, take some deeper breaths." Chase patiently counts in and out for her until she manages to normalize her breathing. "I hate seeing you so upset."

When she feels her panic abating, she says, "Sorry for being emotional."

He sits back on his heels. "Hey, if you can't break down around me, who can you?"

There's something in that. She doesn't do this in front of Mitch, ever. There's something about her history with Chase that makes her drop her guard. She takes his hand. "I wanted to be with you so bad that night. More than anything else I ever wanted. Even after you stood me up."

As he realizes she's talking about when they were teenagers, he drops the detective part of his persona. "I didn't stand you up, Kathy. I was arrested for something I didn't do." His eyes are sincere. "Do you ever ask yourself why that happened, and on that night of all nights?"

She searches for answers in his face and suddenly suspects why, but she doesn't want to believe it. "It doesn't matter now."

"You practically disappeared after that night. You turned into a home-schooled church mouse, sticking close to your parents and dropping your friends. You were the talk of the school for a while. I couldn't understand it, because you always loved being around people, you were sociable and adventurous." He tucks a stray strand of hair behind her ear. "We planned to travel the world together, do you remember? Did you at least manage to do that before you got married?"

She shakes her head. "No. I spent all my time studying to get into college. That's where I eventually met Mitch. He came from no money and his parents were awful. Maybe he reminded me of you." She swallows. "Although I introduced him to my parents, I didn't tell them anything about him for a long time. He was presentable and said all the right things—his attempt at trying to fit into my life—so they assumed he came from a good family. But in reality, he was my small rebellion. My way of getting back at my parents for being so judgmental."

Chase smiles with a glint in his eye. "I hate to break it to you, Kathy, but the whole point of a rebellion is to do something big. Make a statement. You did it all wrong. I mean, your mom would've died if you'd married *me*. Just sayin'."

She finds herself laughing. "I guess it just wasn't meant to be. Not after what happened following that disastrous night." She looks down at her hands.

Chase strokes a tear away from her cheek. "What did happen? You've never explained; all I know is that it must've been pretty bad to give up on me." He smiles.

She wants to smile too. But she can't. Not when she thinks of what happened and how it changed the course of both their lives.

THIRTY-EIGHT

FALL 1994

Staring at her bedroom ceiling, Kathy feels like this room has become her prison ever since her mom caught her at the hotel waiting for Chase. A few days after he stood her up at the hotel, she went to school with puffy eyes and a hardened heart, determined not to speak to him. He didn't show up anyway. The following week, he was there with fading bruises all over his face. He made multiple attempts to get her alone to explain himself. He claimed he was on his way to the hotel when he was arrested in the car his boss had loaned him, not a car he'd stolen. He said the arrest wasn't his fault and he promised he didn't have any other girlfriends, but he wouldn't offer an explanation for the bruises.

It didn't matter what he said. What they had was already ruined. Not only by him not turning up that night, but by how Kathy dealt with her crushing disappointment.

She'd never been in love before, so she wasn't prepared for the level of distress she experienced after finding out Chase was a cheat and a thief. Her therapist confirmed what her mom had been telling her: that she was better off not seeing him again, that he'd caused her too much psychological damage. Her mom confided in her dad what had happened, because he couldn't understand why Kathy was so miserable. He wanted to kill Chase for luring her to a hotel in the first place. His disappointment that she went there has shifted their relationship. She's not the apple of his eye anymore. It makes her feel worthless.

She feels panicky as her chest tightens. She drops her math book on the bed; there's no way she can concentrate on it right now. She wants to forget everything that happened back then, but it's all she can think about.

Loud shouting outside her bedroom window makes her jump. She hesitantly walks over to peer out from behind the drapes, careful not to be seen.

"Kathy, please, let me in," shouts Chase. "I know your parents are out. Just give me five minutes."

Her heart flutters with both excitement and dread. Her mom pulled her out of school a few months ago. She was concerned for her mental and physical health, or so she said. Kathy feels it's more likely she's worried about rumors ruining the family name. She's home-schooled now, and apart from church on Sundays and some volunteering with her mom, she stays close to home. Her mom has recently suggested she stops going to church, so she's going to be even more of a prisoner. She's counting down the days to graduation and starting college. To moving into dorms and being away from her parents and the people in this town.

She walks down the stairs and leans against the back door, near to where Chase is standing. He must see her shadow through the glass. "This is the last time I'm going to come here, Kathy. Is that what you want?"

No.

"I didn't steal that car, it was a set-up! I don't understand why you don't believe me. I thought you felt the same way as I do." He's silent, until: "But I get the message. You're too good for me."

She winces.

"Was I just an easy way to piss off your parents?" She hears him lean against the other side of the door and he lowers his voice. "Can't we start over? Just you and me? I'll rent an apartment and we can live together, away from both our families."

She's helpless against her tears. She'd love that. She'd love to move in with him. The temptation to open the door is overwhelming, and she panics at the thought of him leaving here today and never coming back. Of giving up on her. But she can't go out to him now, even if she wanted to. He won't want her once he realizes things have changed. She's not the person he fell in love with anymore.

"Get away from my house before I call the police!" Her dad's voice. She cringes as she realizes her parents are home already.

Straining her ears, she tries to hear what her mom says to Chase. She can't make it out, but eventually she hears Chase shout, "No way! I don't want..." She can't work out what he's talking about.

"The cops are on their way," says her dad aggressively. "I suggest you get out of here and stay away from my daughter, or you'll be staring down the barrel of my gun."

Chase's shadow hesitates, but she sees his face turn to the door. "I get the message, Kathy. I won't try again." She watches him walk away from the house before sinking to the floor in a fit of sobs.

She's still crying when her mom comes into the kitchen. Connie pulls out a chair from the dining table and leads her to it. "He's acting the fool, darling. He's probably been dumped by his other girlfriends and now he realizes what he's lost by lying to you." She doesn't know that Chase comes to the house regularly, at least twice a month. It's the first time he's been caught. And it sounds like it's the last time he'll try.

Pushing some random textbooks in front of her, her mom

says, "Come on, get on with your school work. It's a good distraction. I'll make you a chamomile tea."

Kathy's dad walks in, red-faced with anger, and although he doesn't say anything, his disappointment is evident. As usual, his eyes linger on her stomach for just a second too long.

Her cheeks burn with shame as her hand automatically goes to comfort her growing baby.

THIRTY-NINE

When Chase opens his eyes to the early-morning sunshine beaming through the crack in his drapes, he turns to check the other side of the messy bed. There's no one there. He reclaimed his bedroom last night after telling Shannon that if she won't leave, she'll have to sleep downstairs on the couch and let Patrick have the spare room. Still, he half expected to find her in his bed.

It's hot already. He pushes the sheet off his bare torso and thinks about the search of Kathy's house last night, which didn't finish until 2 a.m. It included both of the couple's vehicles, the double garage and the backyard. It was fruitless. No clown mask was discovered, or anything else that suggested Charlie was harmed in the house or by someone who lived there.

The reporters were quick to double in number when they realized what was happening. What with that and the reward money being made public, Kathy's street was swarming with news crews by the time he left to come home. There was a definite disappointment in the air when he finally emerged with none of the residents in cuffs. He didn't answer any of their questions.

After a long, cool shower—he skips shaving as there's no time—he dresses for work, grabs his badge and unlocks his gun safe. Once holstered, he heads downstairs.

"Chase, look!" Patrick is in front of the damn TV again. Some cartoon Chase has never seen before is playing loudly.

"Morning, buddy." He leans in and kisses the boy's forehead. "Just do me a favor and turn it down for me? I'm getting a headache."

Patrick does what he's told and goes back to staring at the screen.

Chase is surprised to find Shannon in the kitchen. He assumed she'd still be asleep. She's wearing nothing but a long T-shirt and sipping something from a mug. Even though he can't see it, he can smell it's not coffee.

"Listen," he says, trying not to look at her long bare legs. "I want to run something past you."

A smile lights up her face and she puts her mug down, pushing her blonde hair behind her ears. "You want us to stay?"

His heart sinks. He takes one of her hands in his. "Sorry, no. I want to help you find work, and pay your first couple of months' rent somewhere more suited to you and Patrick."

She leans forward and kisses him on the lips. She tastes of vodka. "It would be much cheaper for you to let us live here. Move me back into your bed and let's live together like old times."

Shannon isn't a bad person—she has her qualities—but he isn't interested in reliving their failed marriage. He's taken her back so many times over the years that it's clear they're not meant to be together, no matter how much he'd like to be able to offer her kid a stable home. He drops her hand. "That's not going to happen this time."

Her eyes darken instantly, reminding him of her temper. "Why? Because of Kathy goddam Hamilton? I saw you on the news with her. I bet you're flavor of the month again now she needs rescuing."

He shakes his head in disappointment. "I'm trying to find a missing child. That's it. And my personal life is none of your business anymore. I meant what I said the other night: I want you to leave. And because you're not willing to accept help, it has to be today."

She brushes off his comments. "I think I'll stay a little while longer."

"No, Shannon. You're not hearing me. This fucked-up cycle of ruining other people's lives has got to stop. If it's not me you're playing, it's Luke. At the same time you're messing up Patrick's childhood, and you're not even making yourself happy. It's time for things to change."

She looks away, but not before he sees tears. She's actually listening to what he's saying for once. "I don't know how to mother him, Chase." She wipes her cheek with her hand. "I feel like he's not mine. I never even wanted kids."

He always knew she didn't want children, which is why he was surprised he married her. Because he wanted at least three kids back then. "So let Luke raise him. You'd be a free agent who could travel wherever you wanted. Luke wants a relationship with his son. Patrick would be well cared for."

"It's not that I don't love him," she says quietly. "I do. But I don't want to be tied down. At the same time I don't know how to leave him behind. That's why I always take him with me."

"That's not fair on him," Chase says. "It would be fairer to let him live with his father until you get your life on track. Find whatever it is that's going to make you happy. Because you're not happy in Maple Falls and you're not happy with me."

She looks at him as another tear slides down her cheek. "I had some of my happiest moments with you. That's why I keep coming back whenever I hit rock bottom."

He rubs her arm. "I'm always going to be a friend you can

rely on, but I've got to live my own life. You're capable of more than just moving from one place to the next, dodging work and dragging Patrick around. After all these years I still don't know what you're running away from, but let him settle here. At least you'll always know where he is, and I bet you'd be welcome to visit him whenever you're in town. I'd make sure Luke takes care of him."

Shannon's sobbing now. He goes to hug her as Patrick appears in the kitchen doorway. The poor kid looks scared.

"It's okay," Chase says. "Your mom forgot bread at the store." He pulls away from her and crouches in front of Patrick. "Do you want pancakes for breakfast?" Before the boy can answer, Chase's phone rings. He can see from the screen that it's Detective Brown. "Just give me one minute and I'll make you the best pancakes you've ever tasted. Okay?"

"Can you make them square like SpongeBob SquarePants?"

He laughs. "I can try."

With a smile on his face, Patrick runs back into the living room. Shannon is wiping her face dry with a dirty dishcloth.

Chase answers his phone. "Hey, Frank. What's up?"

"We've got a body."

His stomach dives with dread. "What? Who? Not a kid?"

"Afraid so."

He feels like retching. He genuinely hoped to find Charlie alive. "Where?"

"Behind the old brewery next to the railroad tracks. I've got the whole team dispatched."

"I'm on my way."

Before he can end the call, Brown says, "Cooper? I think you should know in advance that the child's head is missing."

Chase leans back against the wall, trying to steady himself as a sinking feeling threatens to floor him. He reaches for his forehead. "Oh my God."

FORTY

Megan tries to get comfortable in the passenger seat of Kathy's
Mercedes. Kathy is driving them to a coffee shop on the edge of
town, where they've arranged to meet with the journalist who
approached her outside the church. She's agreed to help them
find Charlie, but she told Kathy on the phone that she needs to
ask them some probing questions they might not like. Megan is
prepared to tell her anything she needs. She fiddles with the
A/C, trying to get it right. Her throat was sore and dry again
this morning, and the bruising still looks terrible; when Kathy
noticed she was trying to hide it with the collar of her shirt, she
gave her a beautiful silk scarf to tie around her neck. Megan
hadn't a clue how to make it look any good so she accepted
Kathy's help.

"You okay?" asks Kathy now, glancing at her.

Megan nods. "Those reporters unnerve me." They nearly
ran two over when trying to back out of the driveway. "How do
we know this woman is any different to the rest of them?"

Kathy sighs. "Well, she doesn't hang around outside the
house for one thing. And she said she's still looking into the
disappearance of Olivia Jenkins, even though it's been eight

months, which suggests she's serious and not in it for a cheap headline. Let's just wait and see what she has to say before we make our minds up."

Megan nods. "How come Mitch didn't want to come?"

"He'd already planned to have a talk with Fay." Kathy hesitates. "He's coming clean to her. He wants her to hear it from him that Charlie wasn't adopted and that you two..."

She doesn't have to finish. Megan feels alarmed at the prospect of returning to the house later to an angry sixteen-year-old girl screaming at her. She remembers how hot-headed she herself was at that age. A patrol car passes them with flashing lights. There's a much bigger police presence in town since Charlie vanished. It comforts her to know they really are looking everywhere for her daughter.

"But to be honest, I didn't tell him what we were doing," says Kathy. "I just said we wanted some fresh air. I think it's best we keep this meeting to ourselves."

Megan studies her face. "You don't trust Mitch or Cooper?"

"It's not that. I just want to feel like we're doing something productive. Let them do things their way and we'll do things our way."

Megan smiles. She didn't think Kathy had it in her.

"Here we go." Kathy pulls into the parking lot and they make their way to the entrance.

Although Megan's never met Susan, she spots her right away. It's still early, but the breakfast rush is over and the coffee shop is almost empty now everyone's at work. The woman is dressed smartly in a white shirt and black pants. She looks like a serious reporter. Her long hair is swept back into a ponytail and she's wearing glasses. "She's over there."

Kathy looks in the direction Megan nods, and they hesitantly approach her. Megan feels butterflies in her stomach. Could this woman really help them, or is she just trying to get an exclusive on life inside the Hamilton house?

"Hi, Susan," says Kathy.

The woman looks up from her cell phone. "Mrs. Hamilton, hi." Standing up, she shakes Kathy's hand before turning to Megan. "Miss Carter?"

She nods. "Megan."

They all take a seat before Susan speaks. "I've ordered coffee, is that okay? If not, I can change it."

"That's fine, thanks."

Megan lets Kathy do the talking.

"Okay, so thanks for reaching out," says Susan. "I've been following your daughter's disappearance closely, Megan. First of all, I want to say how sorry I am that you're going through this. I've spent a lot of time with the parents of missing children and I've seen how hard it is to cope. Add to that the fact you were attacked by an unidentified assailant, and I'd assume you're going out of your mind right now."

Megan is wary, but she gets good vibes from the woman. "It hasn't been easy. But I'm lucky to have Kathy and Mitch supporting me."

Susan nods and a young guy brings their coffees over. "Sugar and sweetener are on the table," he says. "Let me know if I can get you anything else." He walks back to the counter, but not before glancing over his shoulder. He recognizes them.

Tearing open a sweetener and pouring the whole thing into her coffee, Susan says, "I read Detective Cooper's press release about you and Mr. Hamilton being Charlie's biological parents." She pauses. "I'm up to date with Cooper's investigation, and I understand he doesn't have any serious suspects right now. So I want to delve a little deeper into your private lives." She glances from Megan back to Kathy. "It might be uncomfortable, as I know there have been some false starts with alibis that didn't quite check out."

Kathy squirms.

"But the more open and honest you are with me, the more I

can help you and Detective Cooper's investigation. Anything I find out will be shared with him. I'm not here to beat him at anything; that's not how I work."

Megan chews her lip before asking, "What's in it for you? Why do you want to help us? Do you have a big exclusive lined up with a national newspaper or TV producer?"

Susan leans back and smiles. "You're right to be wary, it's smart. I work for the *Vermont Daily News* as an investigative reporter. I'm all about unraveling the secrets in small-town America, and I've been looking into missing child cases ever since I joined the paper. I even helped find one child alive: a twelve-year-old boy from a town south of here."

Megan's heart flutters. Is she that good?

"It's what I love doing. I'm not in it for the salacious gossip, although my editor would probably prefer that I was. I've been liaising closely with the mother of Olivia Jenkins, and I feel like Charlie's disappearance could be linked. But even if it didn't look that way, I'd still be investigating the case." Susan looks away, out of the window that overlooks the parking lot. Megan thinks she sees a sadness in her eyes.

"It's personal for you, isn't it?" asks Kathy, leaning forward.

Susan looks at them. "My sister's boy was abducted nine years ago. He's never been found and my sister couldn't bear the not knowing. She took her own life four years ago. So I get what it's like for you, Megan. I'm part of a family with a missing child. I see what it does to people. I've felt that overwhelming disbelief and heartache."

"I'm sorry to hear that." Kathy excuses herself and heads for the restroom.

"So can I ask you some questions about your life?" asks Susan.

Megan sips her coffee and relaxes a little. "Sure, what the hell? I've got nothing to hide."

"Great." Susan pulls out a laptop. "I understand you're adopted, is that right?"

Megan nods, surprised. "How did you know that?"

"I have my ways." She turns her screen so Megan can see it. "Are these your adoptive parents?"

Megan sees the names of the couple who raised her from birth. Her dad left her mom when she was only ten, so her mom was left to take care of the difficult years alone. She was there through Megan's puberty, teenage angst and emerging drug addiction. "Yeah, that's them. I'm not in touch with either of them, though. My mom disowned me years ago because of my drug problem, and my dad moved on with a new family after divorcing my mom. I'm not interested in reconnecting with him, but maybe once Charlie's back with me I'll give my mom a call and let her see her grandchild." The thought gives her some hope. Her adoptive mom coped as long as she could and Megan doesn't wish her any ill-will for kicking her out. An addict's family have difficult decisions to make and she probably thought cutting Megan off from a loving home would shock her into getting clean. It worked for a while, but Megan never found the courage to reconnect with her.

Susan pulls the screen away. There's sympathy in her eyes. She hesitates before taking a deep breath. "I'm sorry to be the one to tell you this, but your adoptive mom passed away last year."

Megan's mouth drops open. She feels blindsided. She wasn't prepared to hear that. Silent tears instantly appear and she doesn't try to hold them back. She rubs her mouth as she tries to take it in. "How?" she whispers.

"She died of a stroke. She was cremated down in Pennsylvania, where her remaining family lives. I'm so sorry, I thought you must have known. I assumed someone would have informed you."

Megan wipes her eyes with her sleeve. She tries not to feel

anything. She wants to process it later when she's alone in her room. Because if she doesn't get Charlie back, this means she's completely alone in the world. Hers was a closed adoption, so she doesn't know anything about her biological parents. She gets a sudden craving that's hard to ignore. She hides her shaking hands in her lap, under the table. "Okay. What else do you need to know?"

Susan glances over her shoulder. "Your relationship with the Hamiltons. Forgive me for saying, but it seems a little strange to me. I get that Mitch is Charlie's dad, but is there anything about them that seems off to you? Anything that you've been asked to keep quiet?"

Megan shakes her head. "No. Kathy's as straight as they come, and Mitch tried to be fair when taking Charlie in. They asked me to keep it a secret that I was Charlie's mom, but I think we all knew that wouldn't last long. We were just trying to come to an arrangement that suited us all and benefited Charlie." She looks Susan in the eye. "I don't believe either of them had anything to do with Charlie's disappearance."

"What about visitors to their house: Scott and Cindy Bowers, business partners of Mitch, friends of the couple, anyone else who visits regularly?"

Megan tries to think, but her mind is clouded by the news of her latest loss. "They haven't let many people in while I've been staying with them. Apart from Kathy's parents, Mitch's brother, and the minister, I haven't seen anyone else there."

Susan makes a note. "And you have no suspicion of anyone in your life or theirs who might be capable of this? Anyone who maybe stared a second too long at Charlie in the past? A teacher or a neighbor? Or any exes of yours who didn't want to go quietly?"

Megan scoffs. "It's been a long time since I've had an ex, to be honest. If I had any idea who might have her, I would tell you." She's being honest. Susan Cartwright genuinely appears to want to help.

A pair of women walk past and take a seat opposite their table. Both of them stare hard at Megan before looking away. It's just a matter of time before they start gossiping.

Kathy rejoins them. "Is there anything you need to know about me or my husband, Susan?"

Megan listens as Susan asks Kathy similar questions about visitors to the house, but she zones out as she thinks about her mom dying without them having one last conversation. Who can she go to when all this is over and she can no longer stay at Kathy and Mitch's place? She's lost her job, so she won't be able to afford her apartment. It's unlikely Mitch will still help her out financially, not that she ever felt comfortable with that arrangement.

She always intended to take Charlie to meet her mom one day, and to apologize to her for everything she put her through as a teenager. She closes her eyes as she realizes that's never going to happen now.

FORTY-ONE

Chase races through red lights in order to get to the crime scene as fast as possible. He wants to beat any reporters so he can see for himself what's been found, and then notify Megan and Mitch before it's all over the news.

When he reaches the brewery, he skids to a halt, parking haphazardly near a rusting train carriage. He's quickly out of breath as he rushes from his car to the yellow crime-scene tape just beyond the rail tracks. The mid-morning sun is unforgiving as it beats down and reflects off of all the metal around. There's so much trash illegally dumped here that the air is filled with flies and putrid rotting smells. This brewery went bust years ago and has been a magnet for addicts and the homeless ever since.

He passes three dead rats before he sees the uniformed officers who are swarming the site, looking for evidence. He spots Detective Brown and Chief Wilkins standing together. Brown looks dejected.

"Hey," says Chase, slowing down. "Is it Charlie?"

Brown shrugs. "No way of telling in the body's current state. Let me show you so you can see for yourself."

Chase takes a deep breath, knowing the air here will be better than the air around the body. Chief Wilkins stays behind as he follows Brown to a metal shipping container near the brick building. "She's in there?"

"Afraid so. Follow me."

Inside, it's dark and it takes more than a few seconds for Chase's eyes to adjust from the bright sunlight outside. A God-awful smell quickly hits the back of his throat. The heat makes it worse. He pulls out a face mask and covers his mouth and nose with it. It doesn't really work against the smell; it's more of a psychological barrier.

Brown leads him to a dark corner of the near-empty container and points to a shape on the floor. "The medical examiner's on her way."

Chase switches his flashlight on. A small, headless female body has been dumped on the floor. The skin has a green tint to it and the corpse is bloated. He closes his eyes and says a silent prayer for her. He may be a lapsed Catholic, but he still finds comfort in having someone to pray to. Opening his eyes, he looks again. This body hasn't been here long. His limited experience of cadavers suggests it is relatively fresh. He shakes his head in disgust before leaning in to study the neck in order to figure out what might have been used to sever the head. The cut is messy, the skin shriveled, suggesting a handsaw.

"Hard to tell how long she's been here," says Brown.

Chase stands up. He thinks of Megan. How will she take the news? Without a head, they'll have to wait days for DNA to confirm the identity. It would be better not to tell her until they know whether or not it's Charlie, but that's not how this job works. The families always want to know any update, no matter what. It's only fair to tell her, but it won't feel good. She'll be a wreck. He thinks of Mitch and hopes the guy steps up for her. They might not be a couple, but they're Charlie's parents.

Chief Wilkins walks in. "The owner of the property is on his way. He doesn't have a record. I think we all know it's likely the body was dumped here by someone else. He's going to open the buildings for us so we can search for the rest of her."

"We need cadaver dogs asap," says Chase. "I'd prefer to find the head before I contact Megan Carter. If we can at least identify the child first, I'll know whether it's worth upsetting her with this."

The chief nods. "Good call. I'll notify the team and keep any reporters away. Let's hope we find something as fast as possible, because it won't take long for this to become the talk of the town."

Chase crosses his arms and sighs as the chief leaves the container.

"We've got one sick asshole on our hands," says Brown, removing his jacket.

He's right. These things don't happen in Maple Falls. Sure, there's crime here, same as the rest of America, but this? This is something Chase would expect in a big city, where no one knows each other and sadistic killers get away with living in plain sight because no one thinks to call the cops on the weirdo down the street. People like that would stand out in this town. "This might be the worst crime scene I've ever attended," he says. "There may be no blood and only one victim, but a *child?*" He shakes his head. "Who would do this to a little girl?"

They both stare hard at the naked corpse. Where are her clothes? He thinks of the photograph they shared with the media; the one where Charlie was grinning from ear to ear on the white pony at her cousins' birthday party. How can this little body in front of him be all that remains of her? Even if this is another child, it's just as horrific—and it could be that the same person took Charlie. "We've got to find the perp, Brown. Whatever it takes, we've got to find him."

Brown nods beside him. "I have a feeling this will be the one."

Chase turns to him. "The one?"

"The one that stays with us for the rest of our lives."

His mouth goes dry. He suspects Brown could be right.

FORTY-TWO

On the way home from the coffee shop, Kathy can tell Megan is upset. She's quiet and reserved. Worried about her, Kathy tries to make conversation as she drives. "I think Susan could be just what we need: fresh eyes to look at the case, a woman's perspective."

Megan nods.

"Did she ask you anything that Chase hasn't?"

Megan sighs. "She asked about my parents."

A red traffic light gives Kathy the chance to look at her, and she spots the tears running down Megan's face. She reaches for her hand. "What's wrong?"

"She found out my mom died last year. I had no idea." Megan starts sobbing.

A horn behind her makes Kathy jump. The lights have turned green. "I'm so sorry." She swallows hard and thinks of her own mom. Although she and Connie have a strained relationship, the stroke back in February scared her. She can't imagine her parents not being at the end of the phone. It must be harder for Megan, knowing how things ended between them.

She pulls up in front of the house and notices that the

number of reporters and news vans outside has halved again. Megan gets out first and they both rush to the front door to avoid being questioned.

Once inside, Mitch greets them. It's not even lunchtime yet, but he's holding an almost empty whiskey glass and taking a drag on a cigarette. He notices Megan's tear-stained face and his eyes widen with alarm. "Is there news?"

She shakes her head.

"Let me know if you need anything," says Kathy. Megan heads upstairs, so Kathy leads Mitch into the backyard. They take a seat at the glass table, which is thankfully in the shade. "She's just found out her mom died last year and no one told her."

He leans back in his seat and closes his eyes. "Terrible timing."

"How did it go with Fay?" she asks.

He finishes his drink. "Well, it turns out she already knew everything."

"What do you mean, she already knew? How?"

He takes a deep breath. "When Charlie arrived here after Christmas, Fay was confused. She said she couldn't understand where this little girl came from and why we didn't tell her in advance that we were adopting someone. Then she heard us arguing. A lot."

Kathy's heart sinks. No one deliberately argues in front of their child, and she thought she'd done a good job of keeping her voice down those first few weeks. Any arguments they had were taken outside or conducted in the privacy of their bedroom. But they obviously didn't do a good enough job of keeping quiet. Emotions were heightened, to say the least. "So she overheard that you'd slept with Megan?"

"She heard enough to put two and two together." He rubs his face with both hands. "She suspected all this time and never came to me to talk about it."

That could explain why Fay's never been a fan of Megan. She must blame her for tempting her father away from them.

"It's actually a testament to her character that she didn't take it out on Charlie," he says. "That she helped her settle in and feel part of the family."

Pride fills Kathy's chest. Fay's a good girl. She does everything they ask of her and more. Which is why the anxiety she experiences is so hard to watch. She should be proud of herself. "This must be why she's been so anxious these last few months."

Mitch looks at her. "Jesus, Kathy. You're blaming me for that? I already feel bad enough."

She's not in the mood to spare his feelings. It's difficult not to make the correlation and she finds herself resenting him for Fay's reaction. "What else did she say?"

"She lashed out at me. Told me I was a horrible person for cheating on you. She said she was hoping none of it was true. Having me confirm it really upset her. I don't think she'll ever look at me in the same way again." He lowers his eyes. "When she calmed down, she asked if we were getting divorced."

Kathy shifts in her seat. So here they are. The elephant in the room. "What did you tell her?"

He looks away and stays silent for the longest minute of her life. "I said it's inevitable after everything I've put you through."

Tears pool in her eyes. She nods, accepting that he's right. They can't stay together now. She doesn't feel the same about him. It hurts to finally acknowledge it. The upheaval they're about to go through will be painful for all of them. She covers her eyes with her palms and cries.

Mitch gets up and hugs her to him. "I'm sorry. I wish none of this had happened."

She feels his tears drop onto her hands and stands to hug him back. There's no way of saving their marriage but they can at least end it amicably.

When they step apart, she wipes her eyes. "Is she upstairs? I should go see her."

"No, she wanted to see Christine. I dropped her there about forty minutes ago. I'll collect her soon."

Kathy's relieved that Fay took it upon herself to request a therapy session. Maybe now that Mitch has come clean, Christine can help her explore her feelings for her father. With everything out in the open—to Fay, the media and the police—they might all be more comfortable around each other and can focus on getting through the family break-up and Charlie's disappearance.

She cringes. "If Fay's been telling Christine everything, what must she think of our family?"

Mitch smiles, embarrassed. "Probably that we'd all benefit from seeing a shrink."

Kathy groans. That's not something she would ever agree to again. "I guess one bonus of us splitting is that we never have to go to couples therapy again."

He laughs this time. "You're good at looking for positives, I'll give you that." He checks his watch. "I should probably fetch Fay."

"No, you get some work done. I'll get her."

"You're sure? I have some showings I need to reschedule."

"Go for it. I'll take her to lunch. It'll give Megan some time to herself in the house if we both go out. I'm sure she'd like some privacy right now."

He nods. "It feels like life is slowly returning to normal. Not the same kind of normal, but we're leaving the house more, not staring at our phones constantly for the police to call. I don't want it to seem to anyone that I'm not thinking about Charlie every second of the day, because I am. She's here now, like a ghost in the corner of the room. I feel like she follows me wherever I go." His voice catches at the end.

"That's how I feel too. Like her shadow is waiting for us to find her, to put it back with her physical body."

"Is it her ghost?" Mitch wipes his eyes with the back of his hand. "Is she dead, Kathy?"

The pain in his eyes is obvious. She hugs him again. "Until she's found, she's alive and well. Just don't give up on her."

He pulls away and takes a deep breath. With a weak smile, he goes inside to get his car keys. Kathy follows him and picks up her purse. She scrawls a note on the refrigerator pad for Megan.

You have the house to yourself for a couple of hours. Call me if you need anything at all, or if you hear from Chase.

FORTY-THREE

Progress Notes—Confidential

Client's description of the issues they are experiencing
Client was tearful and despondent on arrival. During the session she opened up and was able to talk herself down from her state of unrest. Recent revelations meant she had come to the conclusion that she can only depend on herself and not on her parents anymore, as they are capable of letting her down. This gave her some confidence in moving forward.

She appeared stoic by halfway through, with a perspective shift in the form of a new determination to get on with things regardless of how hurt she feels. This could be a defense mechanism in order to accept the latest drama unfolding in her life, in which case her anxiety is only temporarily abated.

She showed a much-increased level of trust in me and was the most open and honest she's been. However, she didn't want to discuss her disordered eating, preferring to believe her issues would go away on their own. As she appears to be a healthy weight, I didn't press on this.

Therapist's observations

Client is possibly creating a false sense of reality to help her cope with her most recent disappointment. Either that or for attention-seeking purposes. This could be normal teenage behavior.

Goals/objectives of client

For the first time the client refused to come up with any goals, feeling they are empty gestures.

Assessment of progress

Progress only in the sense that she has found a new coping mechanism—pretending everything is fine if she only relies on herself. On a personal note, I worry that she is turning to an alternate reality, so I will focus on this at our next session. It suggests she may become dishonest as a method of coping with rejection.

Any safety concerns

None.

Next appointment

Within a week.

FORTY-FOUR

After lunch at Fay's favorite diner downtown, Kathy drives them to Scott's house. They've all been invited over to see the boys. Mitch is taking Megan with him to get her out of the house, and Kathy just has to pray that Scott is polite to her this time. And although there's tension between herself and Cindy, she knows they all need to put their personal feelings aside and focus on what's important.

The atmosphere in the car is a little strained. Fay doesn't want to talk about the conversation with her dad or her therapy session, so Kathy stays quiet, not wanting to upset her.

"How long is Megan staying with us?" asks Fay as they pull away from the lights.

"I don't know the answer to that yet. She's getting stronger, but she has no one else to stay with."

"Will she go and live with Dad when he moves out?" Fay doesn't look up, which means she cares about the answer.

Kathy reaches for her hand, keeping her eyes mostly on the road. "They're not a couple, Fay. It was a one-off. They've both assured me of that and I believe them. You need to go a little easier on Megan. She's going through the worst thing imaginable right now."

"So are we, though." Fay pulls her hand away. "I liked having Charlie around, but once she's found, she'll go live with Megan. It'll just be me and you at home."

The thought of a near-empty house makes Kathy sad too. "Charlie's your half-sister and you'll be able to see her whenever you want." It feels wrong planning for something they have no control over, but she knows that if they don't have hope, it will be impossible to get through this.

Pulling into Scott's driveway, Fay is out of the car before her. The heat is oppressive and surely has to break sometime soon. Time slows down as Kathy follows Fay to Scott and Cindy's front door. Last time she was here was the day of the birthday party. She remembers Charlie running ahead of her. The last words Kathy said to her were "Be careful and stay away from the pool!" When she returned later that day, everything had changed.

Trying not to think about it, she tries the door. It's locked. That's unusual. When they're expecting company, they usually unlock it. Fay takes the lead and heads around the side of the house.

There's no sign of Mitch and Megan in the backyard, but Cindy's bringing out drinks and snacks and Scott is back at his favorite place, the grill. "Hey, kiddo!" he says to Fay. He gives her a hug. "The boys want to show you their diving skills. I should warn you they create quite a splash, so stand back."

Fay laughs. The twins spot her and both start talking to her at the same time. Austin eventually grabs her hand and leads her over to the pool. Thomas stays behind and looks at Kathy. "Is Charlie back yet?" he asks.

Kathy's surprised by the question. She kneels down to be level with him. "Not yet."

"We made her a card." Thomas wipes water from his face; it's dripping from his hair. "We wanted to say sorry for making fun of her."

Kathy swallows hard. She's glad Megan's not here yet. "That's very thoughtful, Thomas. Keep it in a safe place until she comes back, okay?"

He nods and then runs away, dive-bombing into the pool and covering Fay with water. After the initial shock, Fay laughs it off.

Cindy steps forward nervously. "I just want to say I'm sorry for telling a reporter you didn't go to the women's refuge Saturday afternoon. It was mean and I don't even know why I did it." She appears earnest. "Scott made me realize I was being a bitch."

Kathy smiles. "I'm sorry for throwing lasagna at you."

Cindy bursts out laughing. "You owe me an oven dish. And it wasn't cheap!"

Mitch appears behind them, closely followed by Megan. She's changed out of her sweatpants for the first time in a while and is wearing a denim skirt and a T-shirt. Her bruising is still evident, and Kathy wonders why she isn't wearing the scarf she gave her. Perhaps because of the heat.

"Hey." Mitch leans in for a kiss. It's automatic, and Kathy kisses him back. They both realize too late that they probably shouldn't be kissing each other now they've decided to split. The lines are blurred right now.

"Megan!" shouts Austin from the pool. "What happened?"

Kathy winces as she realizes the boys will be fixated on her bruises.

"I fought a dragon," says Megan, deadpan. "And if you think *I* look bad, you should see *him*." She winks, making the boys laugh. They go back to their pool games.

"Okay, take a seat, everyone," says Scott. "I have chicken

wings, ribs, beef patties, hot dogs. They'll be ready soon. Cindy, fix everyone a drink, would you?"

Cindy gets busy fetching more drinks and ice from the house. Kathy thinks about volunteering to help, but she's enjoying watching the boys and Fay play together. Megan leans back in her chair with her face to the sun. Kathy wonders if she's thinking about the party and where Charlie could've been snatched from. It's got to be in the back of all their minds.

As Cindy passes Kathy a huge glass of white wine that could last her all afternoon, a male voice behind them says, "Sorry to interrupt, guys."

Kathy turns. Her stomach flips with dread as she sees Chase. He's not smiling. Megan turns in her seat and her mouth opens.

"I tried knocking at the front." He walks toward them. He's alone. "I wouldn't have interrupted if it wasn't important."

Kathy, Mitch and Megan all stand.

"The cop's back!" says Austin behind them.

"He hasn't brought the dogs." Thomas sounds disappointed.

Chase looks at Megan and Mitch. "Can I have a word?"

"Go on inside," says Scott with a serious look on his face. "We'll keep the kids out here."

Kathy's hands start shaking as Mitch silently walks toward the house. Megan seems rooted to her spot. When she turns to look at her, the fear in her eyes makes Kathy go over and take her hand. Megan grips onto her tightly.

"Come on," says Kathy. "We're all here for you." She feels like her legs will give way, they're shaking so much.

Chase follows them inside. The house is cool, but Kathy feels sweaty with dread.

Chase takes a deep breath and looks primarily at Megan. "I'm sorry. This isn't the news I was hoping to deliver, but—"

"No!" says Megan. "No, please don't. Don't say it!" She covers her ears.

Kathy is helpless against her own tears. The look on Chase's face is awful.

Mitch puts an arm around Megan's shoulders.

With regret emanating from every pore, Chase says, "I can't confirm whether it's Charlie at this stage—there's still a chance it's not—but we found a child's body this morning, over at the old brewery."

"Jesus," says Mitch. He squeezes Megan tighter. She turns and hugs him, sobbing loudly. Kathy puts her hand on Mitch's back.

Quietly Chase adds, "I really wish I didn't have to tell you this, but the reason we can't be sure whether it's Charlie or not is because... her head was removed."

Kathy gasps. Megan lets go of Mitch, who says, "What?" He's clearly confused. "What are you saying?"

"The head is missing."

Megan silently sinks to the floor. Kathy crouches next to her, but she has no comforting words.

"I've got all my officers searching the area in the hope we can identify her as soon as possible. The medical examiner believes the body belongs to a female under eight, but that's all we know at this stage. I'm sorry." He takes a deep breath. "Something to keep in mind is that we're also still looking for Olivia Jenkins, so there's a possibility this could be her instead."

Mitch walks to the couch and sits down, speechless.

"Although we don't know whether it's Charlie or not, I had to tell you about it before you see it on the news. I was hoping to find something to confirm one way or the other before doing so, but news vans have already arrived at the scene. It's just a matter of time before speculation starts."

Megan's silent, as if in a daze. It worries Kathy.

"When will we know?" whispers Mitch.

"When we find clothes or... something else. But in the meantime, I'd like to take a DNA sample from both you and

Megan so the medical examiner can compare it with the child's."

Megan looks at Kathy, her eyes wide and wet as she whispers, "I can't believe this is happening."

Kathy strokes her hair away from her tear-stained face. "I know, honey. I know."

FORTY-FIVE

Waiting for the body to be identified is a whole new level of unbearable. Megan wanted to come home, to try to absorb the news privately, and they're all in a state of suspended animation while they wait for the phone to ring. Kathy considers fixing herself a drink to take the edge off her nerves. After all, Mitch is in the backyard sipping vodka and staring into space. But she should stay clear-headed in case she needs to drive anywhere. The thought of eating crosses her mind, but she doesn't feel hungry. She has a horrible feeling her old issues are rearing their head because of the strain she's under. She needs to try to eat more, if only to set a good example to her daughter.

Fay has gone to Jenna's house. She was devastated when Kathy told her the news. She let Scott comfort her while Cindy took the twins to their room so they couldn't overhear the gruesome details. Kathy considered keeping it from her, but she knew she'd find out online. Every sordid detail is already making headlines on the local and national news. Websites and social media are full of speculation. Short of locking Fay in her bedroom and taking away all internet and TV access, there's no way of protecting her. So when she asked to be with her friend, Kathy agreed. What else could she do?

She goes into Charlie's room to check on Megan for the third time. She's lying on the small bed. She keeps slipping into a fitful sleep and waking with a start. Kathy feels helpless, unable to help her or Mitch, because what do you say to someone who's waiting to find out whether a dead body is the remains of their five-year-old daughter?

"I want my mom," says Megan. She sits up on the bed and leans against the headboard. "Isn't that stupid? I'm twenty-seven years old and all I want is my mom."

"I don't think we ever stop needing our moms."

"Even when they're as irritating as yours?" She attempts a laugh.

Kathy smiles sadly. "My mom can certainly be... annoying, but she means well. I truly believe that."

Megan lowers her eyes. "Imagine if all the pain of pregnancy and childbirth and the years of worry that followed was for nothing. Imagine going through all that and having nothing to show for it in the end."

Kathy swallows hard. "Tell me about the day you gave birth to her. Did it go smoothly?"

"Are you kidding?" Megan wipes her eyes. "It hurt like a bitch! She took twenty-one hours to make an appearance and I barely had enough energy to hold her after. I just wanted to sleep."

Kathy smiles. "Don't worry, labor gets quicker with each child. Fay came out just an hour after I arrived at the hospital. She surprised everyone."

Megan frowns and is about to say something when her cell phone rings. She freezes, not daring to pick it up. "I don't know that number." When they immediately call again, she answers. "Hello?"

Kathy can hear the caller's voice.

"Megan, hi, Susan Cartwright. I've just had a call from Olivia's mother with news of the discovery. How are you holding up?"

She sniffs back her emotions. "As you'd expect, I guess."

"You're not alone, are you?"

"No. Kathy's with me. I think if I'd been alone through this, I would be high on coke right now."

Susan doesn't seem taken aback by the comment. "That's never the answer, Megan. Although I can see why you would be tempted." She pauses. "Listen, I wouldn't normally bother you at a time like this, but I've got some information that I'm not sure you're aware of."

Kathy and Megan share a look.

"You might want to hear it in private."

"What do you mean?" asks Megan.

Kathy stands up. She doesn't want to eavesdrop. With what she hopes is a reassuring smile, she silently leaves the room, closing the door behind her. She can't help wondering what Susan's discovered.

A loud knock at the front door sends her downstairs. Mitch has left the TV on low. He must be hoping to see any breaking news as soon as there's a development in the case.

She peeks out of the glass panel next to the door to check who's standing there. She doesn't want to speak to the reporters. They're all back outside since the news broke about the devastating find at the brewery.

Christine Stiles peers back at her and offers an apologetic smile.

Kathy opens the door and ushers her in.

"Mrs. Hamilton!" someone shouts from the street, a male reporter. "How is your husband feeling about the news of the dead body?"

Kathy winces. Does he have to be so crude? So uncaring? Before she closes the door, she spots one of her neighbors talking to a female reporter. Alarm runs through her. What on earth could she be telling her? She closes the door on them.

"I'm so sorry to stop by without calling first," says Christine. "I just wanted to check on Fay. I thought she might want to see me."

Kathy leads her to the kitchen and gestures to a stool at the breakfast bar. "I'm having a chamomile tea, would you like one?"

"If you're sure it's no trouble." Christine takes a seat.

"I appreciate you looking out for Fay. She's actually gone to her friend's house. The two of them are thick as thieves, and I think it's good for her to get some time away from us."

Christine nods and accepts the cup Kathy hands over. "She's going through a lot right now, so if she finds being with her friend helpful, it's the right thing to do."

Kathy leans against the counter, cup in one hand. "I won't lie, it feels a little strange to think you know every single thing about our family, yet I know nothing about you."

Christine blushes. "I doubt I know everything, Kathy. But I do think it's better that everything Fay suspected is now out in the open. For a teenager, there's nothing worse than the thought that they're being lied to by their parents. She was pretty devastated about her dad's affair, but I think she's strong enough to get through it." She sips her drink. "But I understand how it must feel to have me know private information about your family. You needn't worry, though; I take confidentiality extremely seriously. I would never speak to the press, for instance."

Kathy scoffs. "I don't think confidentiality applies to my family now everything is splashed across the news. But I appreciate the sentiment."

Mitch walks in, and after a quick look over his shoulder at the TV, he registers their guest. He appears surprised to see her.

"Hey, Christine." He puts his empty glass in the dishwasher. "Did you manage to find a house in the end?"

Kathy listens with interest. As far as she knew, Mitch has never met Christine before. He's dropped Fay outside the clinic a few times, but it's Kathy who organized the therapy and met with Christine to make sure she was right for their daughter. She feels a stab of jealousy go through her, which is ridiculous considering they're in the midst of splitting. But part of her is wondering if he didn't tell her they'd met because he has something to hide.

"Not yet, we're still looking," says Christine. "Sorry it didn't work out with the Wicker Lane property."

He waves a dismissive hand. "Think nothing of it. When you know, you know, right? You'll walk into a house one day and both of you will instantly fall in love with it. Don't settle for anything less."

Kathy's in awe at how he manages to slip into work mode so effortlessly after the news he's had, but she suspects he's a little drunk. She wonders why he never told her he'd shown Christine a house. It seems like the kind of thing he'd mention, considering he's shown lots of their acquaintances houses over the years and always told her if it was someone she'd know.

Christine smiles at him before saying, "I should go. I just wanted to check on Fay, but since she's with her friend, I'll catch up with her another time." At the door, she turns. "I'll be praying it's not Charlie they found today."

"Thank you." Mitch shows her out.

When she's gone, Kathy says, "I didn't know you two had met."

He raises his eyebrows. "Really? It was Christine and her partner I was showing the house to on Saturday night. I didn't know who she was until she introduced herself. I recognized her name."

Kathy watches him as he opens the fridge door. Is he being

too casual? She looks away. Paranoia is setting in again. She walks to the living room and watches the news. A whole team of officers is keeping people away from the dilapidated brewery. There are crime experts—behaviorists and ex-detectives—discussing what kind of person could decapitate a child.

Bile rises to her throat, but she finds herself listening with morbid fascination as they argue over whether it could be the regular clichéd loner with no friends who still lives in his mom's basement. They decide that, because of the way Charlie was snatched in the presence of so many people, it suggests he or she was confident of getting away with it. According to them, loners suffer with self-esteem issues and they mostly stalk their prey at night, with fewer people around. The person who grabbed Charlie was more likely a psychopath; someone living in plain sight. Someone with a partner and maybe even children. Someone who no one would think capable of such a heinous act because they've managed to manipulate everyone around them into believing they are what they portray. They finish by confirming it's highly likely to have been a man, not a woman, who did this.

Kathy glances at Mitch. He has his back to her. He's not capable of doing something like that. Is he?

FORTY-SIX

Chase goes home to shower, change and grab something to eat. He needs a short break from the crime scene because he knows he'll be working well into the night. Besides, the heat is wearing him down. Despite the clouds that are slowly appearing for the first time in days, the temperature remains unusually high, and the foul smell in the shipping container—the whole damn area —is sticking to him like sweat.

As he parks in front of his house, he notices Shannon's car is missing. It's early evening. Maybe she's gone grocery shopping.

Inside, his house is empty. There's a note on the refrigerator.

Patrick is with Luke. I've left my key on the counter. Keep an eye on my boy for me.

Chase sighs, worried that he's forced Shannon into making a decision she wasn't comfortable with, but also relieved that Patrick is with his dad at last. And who knows? Maybe she'll get her shit together and find someone or something that makes her happy. He'll check in on Patrick tomorrow. Not now. He's got too much to do.

He showers quickly and the cool water brings down his core temperature, making him not want to get out. After dressing, he heads to the kitchen. The house feels eerily quiet as he throws together ham, cheese and some wilting lettuce leaves. It's a little too quiet. Maybe he liked having house guests. Or maybe he should get a cat. A cat would be someone to talk to in the evenings. He laughs at the thought. "How about you get yourself a damn woman instead?" he says aloud.

Settling down to eat in front of the TV, he switches it on and sees the crime scene he just left. It looks busy, but the cameras don't pick up anything they shouldn't see. The body has been taken away already. He spots Brown walking away from the shipping container. It looks like he's making a call.

Chase's cell phone lights up and he has a split second to appreciate the weirdness of watching the caller. "Brown?" He puts his half-empty plate on the couch.

"Hey. I've just had a call from Kenny, the contractor who confirmed Mitch's alibi was a lie."

Chase frowns. "What did he want?"

On the TV, Brown turns away from the camera so Chase can't see his face anymore. "He says the reward money has prompted one of his team to come forward about something he found at Mitch and Scott's renovation property over in Glenwood."

Chase grips his phone harder. "What did he find?"

Brown pauses. "A little girl's cowboy hat."

Chase jumps out of his seat, his adrenaline kicking in. "You're kidding? Where was it found?"

"In a kitchen unit, on Sunday morning. He didn't come forward before now because he gave it to his daughter. Apparently he had no idea it was relevant."

Chase runs a hand through his hair, frustrated. "That was

two days ago! It'll be contaminated with his family's DNA by now."

"I know, right? Kenny told him to bring it to the station, but it doesn't look like he has yet. I'll pay the guy a visit and get him to hand it over. But I'll tell you now, Cooper: if this leads to us finding Charlie and this guy expects the reward money, I'll happily tell him myself where he can find it."

Chase smiles faintly. "I didn't know contractors worked Sundays."

"These guys do." Brown sighs. "Are you coming back here, or do you want to go check out Mitch Hamilton's fixer-upper? The contractors have downed tools for the day."

Chase takes a deep breath and thinks of Megan Carter. She needs to know whether the body they found is Charlie. The medical examiner suspects the girl has been dead slightly longer than Charlie's been missing, which should be good news, but that means that if the body is Olivia Jenkins, she was kept alive for the whole eight months after her abduction and only killed recently. What must she have gone through in that time? "Fetch the cowboy hat and get it tested for DNA asap. I'll go to Mitch's renovation project and see if I can find a reason to request a search warrant."

"What if Mitch is keeping her there, alive?" asks Brown.

He's assuming it's Mitch, but Chase thinks it could be anyone who knows about the place: Scott, Cindy, a party guest, or whoever was dressed as a clown at the party. No one's admitted to that, so he's asked forensics to cross-reference all the prints they took from Scott's house with the list of guests. If he can find prints for someone who wasn't a guest—the person dressed as the second clown—he might have a lead. Assuming that person has a criminal record. It's a long shot, but one worth taking. "It's unlikely," he replies. "He knows we know about the place, and the contractors would've seen or heard her."

"I don't know, Cooper. We've all seen those sex dungeons in

the news over the years. Some perps' wives don't even know they have one in their own basement until a kid escapes."

He's right. Chase needs to see the house for himself. "I'll head there now. Keep me updated."

FORTY-SEVEN

Megan's reeling from what Susan Cartwright has discovered, and she doesn't know what to do with the information. She's asked the reporter to triple-check her facts and get back to her. Meanwhile, she needs time to consider the news before she tells anyone. She's still trying to process the thought that her beautiful daughter might be dead. A numbness has settled over her in preparation for hearing the worst. Chase hasn't confirmed it yet, but she's barely holding onto her final thread of hope.

Kathy has brought her to the hospital for her scheduled follow-up consultation. Dr. Anders wants to check her injuries to make sure everything's healing as it should. Megan tried to get out of it, because after losing her job, there's no way she can afford the original bill, never mind aftercare, but Kathy's offered to pay. She insisted. Maybe she just wanted to get away from the house, and Megan wouldn't blame her. It's become a prison for all of them.

They're alone in a small consultation room. Dr. Anders has been delayed with an emergency. The nurse let them wait in here instead of in the waiting area so the other patients don't stare at Megan. The sympathetic look in the woman's eyes made her feel like everyone has given up hope of Charlie being found alive.

"How are you feeling?" asks Kathy.

She hesitates to find the right word. "Empty is the only way I can describe it."

Kathy nods like she completely understands.

A baby is crying loudly outside, and Megan wonders why no one is comforting it.

"I hate hospitals," says Kathy. "They give me anxiety."

"Why's that?"

Clutching her purse on her lap, she takes a deep breath. "I've just never had a positive experience, that's all."

"Really? But Fay was born in one. That must've been a happy day for you: the birth of your first child."

She glances at Megan. She appears nervous. "Although that was a quick birth, it was still traumatic for me." She lowers her eyes. "It brought back some upsetting memories."

Megan senses she's on the verge of disclosing something. She looks as if she's carrying a heavy burden. "I'm sorry to hear that." She considers changing the subject, but she needs to hear her say it. "Fay wasn't your first child, was she?"

Kathy doesn't look at her.

Gently Megan says, "In Charlie's bedroom earlier, you said labor tends to be quicker with subsequent children, and how Fay arrived quickly."

"I..." Kathy looks unsure of herself.

"I won't repeat anything you tell me, Kathy. You've been so good to me that I'd like to return the favor and be here for you. You don't need to feel ashamed of anything. Unlike everyone else in your life, I don't expect you to be perfect."

A tear runs down Kathy's face. Looking as if the words are too big to come out of her mouth, she struggles as she says, "It was so long ago. I rarely let myself think about her."

Megan feels tears build behind her eyes. She leans forward and touches Kathy's knee. "Tell me about her."

It takes a long time for Kathy to push past the wall of silence that's kept her from talking about her first daughter for so long. The words come fast and stilted. "I was too young. Only seventeen. It was my first time with anyone and I was unlucky enough to be caught out. I should've known better. I shouldn't have trusted the person. Mitch doesn't know."

Megan thinks of Chase Cooper. He must be the father. That must be why they split. Does he know? She doubts it. He seems like the kind of guy who would step up to the plate and take responsibility. Maybe Kathy didn't let him. Or maybe... "Let me guess, your mom made you give her up?"

Kathy nods as she wipes tears away with a tissue. "She couldn't bear the thought of me raising an illegitimate child." She scoffs. "I mean, imagine what people would say! What her church friends would think of her daughter having sex outside of marriage!" She shakes her head.

"So you had no say in the matter?"

"No. It was made clear there would be consequences if I didn't give her up. Keeping her wasn't an option, and neither was an abortion, not that I know whether I would have chosen that route if I'd had the chance. It's difficult to say all these years on. It took me months to build up the courage to tell my mom I was pregnant, and up until that day I enjoyed having a baby grow inside me. I didn't get any morning sickness, and I felt less alone. I'd sing to her. But once I started to show, I had to tell Mom. She broke it to my dad for me." She starts sobbing, and Megan is surprised by how raw her emotion is after all these years. "My dad was so disappointed he barely spoke to me until after I'd given birth. And then it was as if the baby didn't exist and none of it had ever happened. Everything went back to normal for my parents."

Megan passes Kathy more tissues. "But not for you."

She shakes her head. "The labor was traumatic because by then I knew I wanted to keep her but I also knew they'd never let me."

Megan can't imagine what she went through. "Did you get to name her at least?"

"Not officially. The family who adopted her chose their own name, but I was never told what that was. I knew that if she was a girl, I'd name her Hope. I thought Hope Hamilton sounded lovely."

It does. "What did she look like?"

Kathy smiles through her tears. "She was beautiful. Six pounds eight ounces, no hair at all, these big brown eyes... I was allowed just ten minutes with her before I had to give her up to the case worker. There was a couple waiting in the next room to take her home. I never got to meet them, to suggest the name I'd thought of."

Megan can't stop her own tears as she thinks about the couple who were waiting next door. About the life they were about to embark on together with this baby girl. "That must've been torture." It seems so barbaric to think someone can insist on taking your child away from you.

"The weeks and months afterwards were even worse," says Kathy, the words flooding out of her. "I couldn't get over the feeling of loneliness. Emptiness, I suppose, like you said. When you grow a baby inside you and you don't get to keep her, you're always looking for her. I'd wander from room to room. Did I put her here? Or here? It must sound stupid to you, because I was aware she didn't live with me, of course. But my arms ached some days, for someone to hold. Someone to feed. My breasts leaked for her." She looks down. "And having Fay later didn't help me forget. It just reminded me of the milestones I'd missed: her first step, her first word, taking her to her first day of school."

Megan can tell she's distraught. She struggles to find any comforting words that aren't meaningless, which makes her realize that's how people must feel around *her* while Charlie's missing.

A knock at the door makes them both jump. It opens without waiting for an answer. "Sorry to keep you waiting," says Dr. Anders. He notices they're both upset and stops in his tracks. "Would you like me to come back in a few minutes?"

Kathy shakes her head and stands up.

"No, it's fine," says Megan sadly, knowing it's anything but fine.

FORTY-EIGHT

WINTER 1994

Kathy's scared. The pain shooting through her body is excruciating. She had no idea giving birth would be this painful and undignified.

"I think one more push might just do it," says the doctor.

The nurses in the room keep throwing her sideways glances, determined to make her feel more ashamed than she already does. They've been judging her since the moment she arrived at the hospital. She's under no illusion that it's not just for getting pregnant so young, but also for giving her baby away. She feels like screaming at them, to tell them it's not her choice and it's none of their business, but she doesn't have the energy.

With one final push that feels as if it's splitting her entire body wide open, a hot searing pain is followed by the strangulated cries of a baby. *Her* baby.

The social worker steps forward from the corner of the room. "They'll clean her up and then you can have some time with her," she tells Kathy.

"It's a girl?" She was advised not to ask the gender at her last ultrasound. The social worker thought she'd get too attached. But that was naïve, because there was no way she wouldn't get attached to her baby. They were physically attached for nine months.

"I'll get your mom."

Before the woman can leave, Kathy grabs her arm. "No! Please don't get her. I don't want her in here until it's time."

The social worker appears uneasy with the request, but manages to find one ounce of decency—the first she's shown throughout the entire pregnancy—to allow her that.

The least judgmental nurse in the room hands over a swaddled baby to Kathy, and as she takes her in her arms, she's in awe of how natural it feels to hold her. The weight of her is reassuring, like she's a solid, healthy little girl. She looks down at her daughter and is at first alarmed by how reddish purple her skin is all over. She's completely bald too, which she didn't expect. She slips a finger into the baby's grip, and Hope Hamilton locks on tight. Then, slowly and cautiously, she opens her eyes and looks up at Kathy.

"Hello, Hope. I'm your mommy."

The social worker steps back and clears her throat, and Kathy knows what she's thinking. She warned Kathy not to name the baby. She said it would make it harder to let go emotionally, as if anything could make it easier.

Hope makes a light attempt at a cry while Kathy stares, in awe at what she's created. At the other end of the bed, the doctor is talking about placentas and stitches, and Kathy feels more contractions, but she doesn't want to give up Hope. Until she arrived here earlier today, she didn't even know what a placenta was. Upon arrival, the doctor explained what to expect during labor, and Kathy wanted to leave. She started hyperventilating and almost passed out. She still can't believe no one tells you about the mechanics of labor in school.

One of the nurses leaves the room, and shortly afterwards Kathy hears a cheer from next door, followed by clapping and laughing. The couple who will be adopting Hope are ecstatic.

She swallows back tears. She doesn't want to cry in front of the social worker. "Did they have to be in the next room?" she asks. "It doesn't feel very nice for me."

The social worker steps forward again. "I think it's time to hand her over now, Kathy. The longer you hold her, the harder it will be to give her up."

Kathy tenses, which makes her stomach hurt. "Not yet, please!"

"You're about to deliver the placenta," says the doctor with a sympathetic expression on his face. "You can't hold the baby through that."

"And she needs feeding," says a nurse.

Kathy cries harder. She knows it's no good. They'll take her baby no matter what she says. She kisses Hope all over her face and tastes her own tears. "Please don't forget me," she says. "I'll never forget you." As the social worker reaches in, Kathy whispers into her daughter's ear, "Come find me when you're older. I'll be waiting for you." She knows the baby can't understand her, but Hope has to know that she was wanted, that she was loved by her biological mother. And that she'll be loved forever, even if from a cruelly enforced distance.

The social worker gently takes her, leaving Kathy empty-handed. She slouches back against the pillows, all energy drained from her. It's only now that she becomes aware of the pain from all the pushing. A hot flush runs through her body and she's stinging down below.

As her daughter is carried out of the room, Kathy's mother enters. She walks to the side of the bed and squeezes Kathy's hand. "Well done, darling. I'm proud of you. Try not to worry about the baby, she'll be well cared for. The couple who are adopting her have gone through all kinds of checks to make sure they'll love her and give her anything she could ever need."

Kathy turns away. Surely all Hope needs is her real mother?

She feels another squeeze of the hand. "You can start afresh now, darling," her mom says breezily. "We can all move forward as if none of this ever happened. You can go to college and come back to church. You can stop being fussy with your food." A strained laugh. "You may not think it now, but you'll thank me when you're old enough to understand how keeping a baby at your age would have ruined your career prospects, never mind your opportunity to find a decent husband."

Kathy makes everyone in the room jump out of their skins by screaming at the top of her lungs. She vaguely hears the doctor telling her to push, and wishes it were another baby she was pushing out. One that she gets to keep.

FORTY-NINE

The sun is hidden behind large gray clouds that have gathered overhead as Chase arrives at Mitch and Scott's renovation property. He gets out of the car and rolls up his shirtsleeves, feeling a splatter of light raindrops on his forearms. He checks his windshield to be sure. It's definitely starting to rain. But the humidity is still stifling. He thinks of his mother, something he tends not to do often, considering she didn't play much of a role in his life. But if she were here, she would say they need a storm to clear the air, and she'd be right. A good thunderstorm and a heavy downpour is desperately needed to bring the heatwave to a dramatic end.

He hears rumbling in the distance. He looks up and smiles.

Stepping forward, he assesses the property. It's nice. Not Lexington Lane nice, but it's a good size and the front lawn is full of mature trees. There are no cars on the drive and all the windows are closed. He walks up the path and peers in at the window. He can see the clouds above reflected in the brand-new glass. Apart from the construction tools and offcuts of wood stacked up inside, the house appears to be empty.

He arranged to pick up a spare key from Kenny on his way

over here, swearing the guy to secrecy. Now he slips it into the lock and opens the door. Stepping inside, he closes it behind him and listens to the silence. Eventually he shouts, "This is Maple Falls PD. If there's anyone here, make yourself known!"

He cocks his head to listen hard, desperately wanting to hear a little girl's voice call out. But there's nothing. He steps into the room on his left: nothing. Cautiously he walks around the downstairs. It's messy with tools and dust blankets everywhere, and a small cement mixer in the hallway. In the kitchen, all the brand-new units are empty. It was a strange place for Charlie's cowboy hat to be found. Not exactly discreet.

Upstairs, half the floors are missing. There are floorboards leaning against walls, waiting to be fixed into place. The rain is pelting down now, hitting the windows hard. He walks to the master bedroom window and looks out at the quiet street beyond. Most of it is obscured by trees. The day suddenly feels like night as the clouds blacken. He sees a flash of lightning and waits for the subsequent thunder. It roars angrily above the house. The fast-moving storm makes him think about the browning lawn in his own backyard. He hopes the rain lasts long enough to help it spring back to life and cool down the air.

The last place he checks is the basement, Detective Brown's words about sex dungeons playing out in his head. With no windows, the basement is in darkness. He flips a light switch, but the power isn't connected yet. Instinct makes him shoot Brown a quick message to let him know he's at the house. Then he turns on his phone's flashlight. He should've brought one from the car.

Walking slowly, he shines the light across the floor and up the walls. The room is mostly empty. A few pots of unopened paint sit in one corner. He goes over to them and leans in, tipping one of them back slightly to see the color. Brilliant white. That should lighten the room well. His flashlight draws his attention to something under the can. Just a tiny bit of lint, he thinks. He blows at it, but it doesn't move. Kneeling down, he shifts the can of paint and tries to pick up whatever's there, but it's stuck.

He realizes that this corner of the floor has been repaired recently. The concrete here looks newer—a noticeably different color than the rest, and uneven in places. His arms break out in goosebumps as he moves his phone closer. It isn't lint he can see; it's a tiny piece of material, submerged in the concrete. And it's red.

"Shit."

Charlie was wearing a red dress at the birthday party.

He tries tugging on the material again, but it won't give. Dread fills his stomach as he tries not to jump to conclusions. He leans back slowly, painfully aware that he could be kneeling on Charlie Hamilton's grave.

FIFTY

The sudden storm catches everyone unawares, making the journey home from the hospital slow as people drive more carefully than normal, tires sloshing through the rainwater. The car's wiper blades work hard to keep the windshield clear. The thunder is directly overhead, and Kathy listens to it with a knot in her stomach. She's worried she's told Megan too much and that she might tell Mitch, or use the information against her somehow. Her mom always says she's too trusting.

Although it was difficult because of the ferocity of her pent-up emotions, it felt wonderful to talk about Hope. It brought the baby back to life. Kathy's discovered over the years that when you don't talk about a child who was taken away from you, it's like they never existed.

But now she needs to focus on Charlie and Fay. Maybe once all this is over and Mitch has moved out, she can look into what happened to her daughter. It won't be the first time. She's had several unsuccessful attempts to trace Hope over the years, but her mom told her it was a closed adoption, and therefore no information was shared about what happened once the baby was placed with her new family.

"Are you going to be okay?" asks Megan.

Kathy glances at her and smiles. "I think so. I've lasted this long after all."

As she turns onto their street, Megan gasps and sits up straight. "Oh God, you know what this means, don't you?"

There's a squad car with flashing lights parked diagonally across the driveway. Chase's Honda is in front of it.

"She might be home," says Kathy, offering the last scrap of hope possible in this awful situation.

"No," says Megan quietly. "They've confirmed the identity of the body they found."

Kathy is surprised by the acceptance in her voice. It suggests she's used to getting bad news. Megan is out of the car as soon as it stops, instantly soaked. Thankfully the reporters have been moved away from the house, but it doesn't stop them yelling their questions.

Kathy finds herself utterly drained of emotion and glued to her seat, gripping the steering wheel. She keeps the engine running with the wiper blades swiping the rain back and forth. She doesn't want to go inside. She wants to delay the bad news. And she wants to give Mitch and Megan some privacy as they find out whether the body is Charlie. This is about *their* loss. This is about the daughter they created, no matter how unintentionally. They both love Charlie dearly, that much is clear.

Time stands still as she waits in the car, paralyzed by grief. Eventually there's movement at the front door. A uniformed officer appears, followed by Mitch. He's in handcuffs.

"What?" she whispers, confused. Dread runs through her.

Chase is behind them, holding Megan back. She's trying to attack Mitch. Kathy's heart sinks. Was it really him? Has she been living with a child killer all this time?

Megan struggles free and picks up the heavy ceramic plant pot next to the front door. She throws it at Mitch's Lexus, shattering the windshield. Kathy gasps. A female officer appears from inside the house, pulling Megan away, out of sight of the cameras that are snapping away like crazy, capturing every sordid detail.

Chase looks over at Kathy, but she focuses on Mitch. The officer clutching him by the arm leads him to the cruiser, opens the door and pushes his head down so he can climb in. He slams the door shut behind her husband. Her soon to be *ex*-husband. The father of one of her daughters.

Her car door opens and she feels the rain hitting her thigh. Chase helps her out and leads her into the house, where Fay is crying in the armchair. Megan is sobbing on the living room floor. She looks as if she didn't quite make it to the couch. Kathy feels numb.

"I've arrested both Mitch and Scott on suspicion of abducting Charlie," says Chase. "I have reason to believe Charlie's body is buried in the basement of the house in Glenwood that they were renovating."

Kathy looks into his earnest eyes. "I don't know what to say."

"You don't have to say anything, unless you know anything that will help me in this investigation. If you've been covering up for Mitch—"

"What?" she snaps. "How can you even suggest that?"

He looks away. The expression on his face reflects his unhappiness at being in this position.

Going to Megan, she picks her up off the floor and sits beside her on the couch, holding her tight. She doesn't attempt any cheap platitudes. She just hugs her. Eventually she holds her arm out for Fay, who comes to her other side and leans in to be comforted. Fay's lost her half-sister, and now she'll lose her father to the prison system.

"I'll interview them right away," says Chase. "I have a team of experts at the house in order to confirm our suspicions as fast as possible." He takes a step toward them. "I'm sorry, Megan. I wish I..." He doesn't seem to know how to finish the thought. To Kathy, he says, "Are you able to stay with her?"

She nods. "I'll take care of her."

Megan doesn't look up. Fay reaches past Kathy and takes Megan's hand. Kathy kisses them both on their wet cheeks, clutching them as tight as she can.

Chase hesitates by the door before eventually leaving and closing it behind him.

"It may not feel like it now," says Kathy, looking at them each in turn, "but we're all strong enough to get through this."

She silently prays that she's right.

FIFTY-ONE

The house is still as the clock above the fireplace softly chimes midnight. It was a wedding anniversary gift from Kathy's parents, but one that neither she nor Mitch liked. It was more her mother's taste than either of theirs, but rather than tell her that, it seemed easier to stare at it for years.

Kathy sits in darkness with just the glow of the muted TV illuminating part of the room. Fay and Megan are asleep upstairs. She offered them both some of the sleeping pills she was prescribed earlier this year, when she was struggling to sleep due to news of Mitch's affair. She doubts Christine would approve, but Fay needed some reprieve from her emotions. Megan refused to take any, not wanting to jeopardize her sobriety, but Kathy saw how hard she stared at Mitch's whiskey bottles. Once Megan was upstairs, Kathy poured the liquor down the sink, wishing she'd done it before the girl moved in.

Her phone lights up with a new message.

We're here.

She waits for the front door to open. Her parents have a

spare key. She sees their shadows silently enter the house. They're being quiet because she asked them not to wake the girls. Her mom approaches her first and embraces her. "You'll be glad to know the storm has finally passed."

Kathy wonders whether she's talking about the weather.

Her dad places a comforting hand on her shoulder. "I'll make a pot of coffee." He shuffles off to the kitchen, suddenly appearing old to her.

Her mother sits next to her and winces as she bends her knees.

"Are you okay, Mom?"

"I'm just old and creaky. My bones don't like damp weather. It'll happen to you one day." She takes Kathy's hands. "I'm sorry. If I'd ever thought Mitch Bowers was capable of this, I would never have let you marry him."

Kathy rolls her eyes. "I was an adult when I married him; you wouldn't have been able to stop me." She softens. "It's no one's fault but his."

"Well, either way he's proved himself to be a murdering asshole."

Kathy chews her bottom lip. "I just can't see it. I can't see Mitch hurting Charlie in any way. He's such a good dad."

"Then maybe it was his brother. Your father never liked Scott. He thought he had shifty eyes. He thought it was strange the pair of them invested in a house together when it's clear they can't stand each other."

Kathy looks at her. "No. It must've been one of the construction workers, surely? Mitch told Chase they were the ones who poured the concrete."

Her mom considers it. "But how would one of the workers have lured Charlie away from the party? Do you think she would've just left with a complete stranger?"

Kathy lowers her eyes. Charlie was aware of stranger danger from lessons at school, and Megan would've told her more than once. "Maybe if they were dressed as a clown. They could have pretended to be Mitch in order to get her to go with them."

"I think we need to wait and see what the evidence tells us," says her dad. He brings over three coffees and switches on a side lamp. The orange glow gently lights the room. "Mitch is a part of the family, no matter what we think of him as a person. There's still a chance this wasn't him or Scott."

Kathy is surprised by her dad's attitude and grateful for some hope. "You really think so?"

"Sure. Let's wait until we've got all the facts. Because if it were you sitting in jail right now, I wouldn't automatically assume you were guilty. And I'd hope you'd do the same for me."

Her mom scoffs. "Come on, Jack. He's already proven himself an adulterer. That shows he has no moral compass. And he hates going to church. We know now that's because he has a guilty conscience."

Kathy's dad rolls his eyes. "Are you really saying that a guy who cheats on his wife is automatically capable of murder?"

The look of scorn her mom shoots him makes Kathy realize that her father had an affair at some point during their marriage, maybe more than one over the years. She wishes she could have more sympathy for her mother, but the way Connie rubbed it in when Kathy initially told her about Mitch's affair means there's no compassion in her.

According to Kathy's therapist, it was her parents' arguments when she was growing up that triggered her issues with food. They sent her to counseling to get better, but what they really should've done was act like civilized human beings around her. To shield her from their marriage problems. To split when her father strayed.

A terrible thought hits her. Maybe if she'd chosen to divorce Mitch after learning of his affair, instead of pretending nothing was wrong and keeping his secret, she could have somehow lessened Fay's anxiety and stopped her from needing a therapist. It dawns on her then that her own marriage has mirrored her parents', and that the effects on her as a teenager are mirrored in the effects on Fay.

She wipes her eyes, feeling as if she's finally seeing things clearly. She has to do better. She has to break the cycle.

Her mom and dad revert to their usual roles by changing the subject and making polite conversation, but Kathy tunes them out as she watches her cell phone, willing it to light up with the news that all this has been a terrible mistake. That Charlie's been found alive after wandering off into the woods by herself and getting lost.

But the dread in her chest tells her that's not going to happen.

FIFTY-TWO

The storm is a distant memory as Kathy arrives at the police station just after eight the next morning. The rising sun and cheery birdsong give the illusion that everything is fine. That Charlie is still alive and Mitch isn't a murderer. She finds herself wondering how the earth can still turn when there are such terrible things happening.

Chase told her that Mitch wants to see her, which she already knew due to the missed calls and answerphone messages from him overnight. She didn't answer because she needed time to think. She worries that being here now is the wrong thing to do.

"Kathy, hey." Chase approaches her. "How's Megan this morning? I was hoping she'd come with you so I can update her. She's not answering her phone."

"She's barely coping. She wasn't up when I left the house, so I thought it best to let her sleep in. Fay wanted to come with me, but I don't want her to see her dad in here. My parents are with her."

He nods. "I've got a room for us so we can talk in private."

She follows him past the front desk and along a corridor to

the back office, where the phones are ringing loudly. Several officers glance at her as they pass, and she sees sympathy in their eyes.

"Here we are." Chase motions to a seat and closes the door behind them. He sits opposite her.

"How are Mitch and Scott?" she asks. "I've spoken to Cindy this morning and she's angry. She's talking about hiring a lawyer to sue you and the department."

He shrugs like it's something he hears a lot. "It's a natural reaction, I guess. They're doing fine. They managed some sleep, but they've both lawyered up. Last night's questioning didn't yield any new information. I'm hoping they'll be more talkative this morning. They're both insisting they had no involvement in Charlie's disappearance."

"Do you believe them?" As soon as she asks, she wishes she hadn't. She's not prepared for what he might say.

"It doesn't matter what I believe. It's all about where the evidence points. We've still not identified the body found at the brewery, but as well as that..." he pauses, and his expression changes to one of sadness, "one of the contractors working at the house found a little girl's cowboy hat in the kitchen."

She closes her eyes and sees Charlie on the pony, cowboy hat balanced on top of her blonde pigtails. It feels like things are speeding up now, hurtling toward the inevitable.

"We've brought all the contractors who ever worked on that house in for questioning. Maybe they know something, or maybe it was one of them. Either way, I feel like we're getting closer to finding the truth."

She's nervous about asking the next question, but she has to know. "What about the basement? Do you know whether there's a body down there yet?"

He reaches for her hand. Gently he says, "Our forensics team are still there. But they brought in a ground-penetrating radar overnight, and it's indicated that something is buried in the newly poured concrete."

She wipes her wet eyes. There are now two bodies. It feels painfully inevitable that one of them will be Charlie. Images of what must have been her final moments flash through her mind. She can't stop them. Bile stings her throat and she worries she might vomit.

"I'll let you know as soon as I hear anything. There's still a chance it could just be clothing down there; it's difficult to tell with the radar." He pauses before removing his hand. "I wanted to show this to Megan last night, but everything happened so fast and she was pretty distraught. I didn't think it was the right time." He pulls out a small plastic bag from his case file. "This is a sample of the red material found poking out from the floor at the house. Let me know if you recognize it."

Instinct makes her turn away. "No. I don't want to."

He moves close to her. She can feel his body heat. "I'm sorry. I can't ask Megan because she's not here, and besides, she didn't see Charlie that day, so she might not recognize the dress she was wearing."

"She will recognize it," says Kathy, still turned away. "She bought it for her."

"Kathy, look at me. Please."

She slowly meets his gaze.

"Do you want Megan to have to identify it? Is she even up to it?"

She swallows, knowing he's right. It could be the final straw that sends Megan on a downward spiral back to addiction.

As he slides the bag in front of her, she can't contain a shocked sob. It's a tiny fragment of Charlie's dress. She recognizes the zebra head that should be a whole body. She pushes away from the table and goes to the corner of the room, burying her face in her hands.

Chase follows and hugs her to him. "I'm so sorry, Kathy. I wish I didn't have to do that."

She cries for what feels like forever, leaning into him as she doesn't trust her legs with the weight of the shocking truth. He doesn't rush her, and he's not embarrassed when another detective knocks on the door and slides something onto the table.

When he's gone, Chase pulls back. "I'm working on the assumption that Mitch and Scott were both involved."

She takes a seat, trying to calm her breathing.

"I think Scott could easily have dipped out of the party under the pretense of going to use the bathroom. While there, he could have changed into the clown costume, walked through the yard, playing the role for other kids, and then coaxed Charlie into the woods while she was waiting in line for another pony ride. Mitch could've been waiting there, unseen by any party guests. He could've taken Charlie off him, allowing Scott to ditch the clown costume and re-enter the yard."

"But that would mean Mitch was the one who killed her." When Chase doesn't reply, she shakes her head. She thought she wanted answers, but that hypothesis is devastating if true. "I can't believe he would do that."

Chase turns to the piece of paper left by the other detective and reads it. He takes a deep breath. "It will be of no comfort to you now, but this is confirmation that the body in the shipping container isn't Charlie."

If Charlie's dress hadn't subsequently been found somewhere else, that would've been good news. Instead, Kathy feels numb. "Is it Olivia Jenkins?"

He looks away and his face confirms it, even though he can't. He'll have to go see Olivia's mother shortly. She doesn't know how he does this job. *Why* he does it. She's grateful he does, though, because she can't imagine going through all this with a stranger.

A thought occurs to her. "Maybe whoever took Charlie was

the same person who took Olivia?" The thought gives her some hope. "There could be a serial killer out there, someone no one's considered for Charlie's disappearance! He needs finding so these accusations against my husband and brother-in-law can stop."

Chase gives her a look of pity now. He knows she's clutching at straws. "Kathy, that serial killer could be your husband."

Her mouth falls open. After a few seconds she says, "I need to see him."

Kathy's hands are sweating as she hears footsteps approaching the small room. The door opens and Mitch follows Chase in. He looks tired, and his clothes are badly creased.

Chase doesn't uncuff him. "You can have up to fifteen minutes." He looks at Kathy. "I'll be right outside. Shout if you need me." He doesn't close the door fully.

Mitch leans in for a hug, but Kathy turns away. Disappointed, he sits opposite her. "You think I'm guilty, don't you?"

"Actually, no, I don't. But none of it makes sense, so what do I know? Chase said you haven't been charged yet."

He scoffs. "*Yet*. They can do what they want, they'll find nothing tying me to Charlie's abduction. I'm not even convinced they'll find her in that basement. If they do, it has to be one of the construction guys who did it."

She's relieved at his confidence. Surely it points to his innocence? "Chase said the team left the premises at four o'clock on the afternoon Charlie went missing, and that they hadn't yet poured the concrete."

"Right, according to them. But who's to say one of them didn't go back after the others left and dumped Charlie's body there? Everything they needed was already on site. I was at the counseling session with you from four thirty until we got home at six, remember? So when would I have had the opportunity to do it?"

"After showing the house on Wicker Lane to Christine that evening."

"No, Kathy!" He grabs her hands, the cuffs straining. "I promise you I came straight home afterwards."

She studies his face. He looks tormented. If he's innocent, he's grieving for his daughter while fighting for his freedom. "Could it have been Scott? Are you covering for him?"

He pulls back and looks up at the ceiling in frustration. "Goddammit, I'm not covering for anyone and I don't know anything. I'm as confused as you are." His eyes fill with tears as he stares at her. "Please don't let Fay think I'm a murderer. Don't let her read the articles online or give her any reason to doubt me. I mean, just think what this will be doing to her."

She doesn't know whether he's using Fay to win her over, but her gut tells her he didn't take Charlie. And she doesn't believe Scott's capable of it either. He was perfectly relaxed with her at the birthday party; he even tried to get her to stay longer. He wouldn't have done that if he was planning Charlie's abduction.

"If it wasn't either of you, then who was it?" she asks.

He shakes his head. "I don't know. But if you don't help me find out, I'm afraid I'll go to prison for this. I'm afraid they'll give me life without parole." He rests his forehead on the table as he tries to hold back his fear.

Kathy goes to his side and rubs his back. "I'll do what I can." She lowers her voice. "But if I find out it *was* you, you'll *never* see me or Fay again."

FIFTY-THREE

Megan groans. Her whole body is aching. She's slowly sobering up and it's not a good feeling. Too many emotions are trying to overwhelm her, the same as in the early hours before she snuck out of the house. Her buzz has almost definitely evaporated, and was it even worth it? Yes. For a few hours of peace, it was. But as the cops chaperone her to Kathy's front door, embarrassment eats away at her.

Before they can knock, a car pulls into the driveway behind them. Megan turns to see Kathy's confused face.

"What's going on?" She slams her door shut and joins them.

The female officer speaks before Megan can. "We found her outside the liquor store downtown. She was drinking bourbon behind a dumpster. The manager complained."

Kathy's face softens. "Oh Megan. What have you done? All that hard work for nothing."

"I'm sorry," Megan mutters, her eyes on the ground. "I just needed something to take away the pain."

"I thought you were asleep when I left?" Kathy opens the door with her key.

Megan doesn't reply as she follows her inside.

"I'll keep an eye on her," says Kathy to the officers. "Thanks for bringing her home."

The male officer hands Megan a leaflet. It's a list of local AA meetings. Megan's been to a couple before, but they weren't for her. "There's no judgment there," he says. "They've all been through similar stuff and come out the other side."

"Really?" she snaps. "They've all lost children too?"

He doesn't care for her sarcasm. "Everyone has problems, Ms. Carter. It's how you choose to deal with them that matters. I'm sorry about your daughter, really I am. But she wouldn't want her mom getting wasted behind a dumpster and being brought home in a patrol car for the whole world to see."

Megan looks away. She's angry and ashamed. When the officers have left, she goes to the living room and finds Connie in there.

"Hello," says Connie. "I'd imagine you'd like some coffee?"

Megan hesitates. She's pleasantly surprised when Fay comes over with a glass of water and hands it to her. "Thanks." She drinks it down in one go, hoping it'll get rid of the sickly-sweet taste in her mouth.

"Where's Dad?" asks Kathy.

"He went to play golf," says Connie. "You know what he's like, he gets bored easily."

"They had another fight," says Fay.

Connie smiles, but you wouldn't know it from her eyes. "Don't be silly, Fay. We only had a small disagreement." With some trouble, she stands up. "I'd better be off. I hope you feel better soon, Megan. In future, I'd recommend clear spirits. They don't cause such a nasty hangover."

Kathy gasps. "Mom! She shouldn't be drinking anything."

Megan sits down. "It's fine. Your mother hates me, Kathy. I'm not stupid. I bet she wishes Mitch had never met me."

"I think the whole family wishes that, dear," says Connie.

"Mom, you need to leave. I can't believe how rude you're being!"

Connie snorts. "That's not rude. Telling her what a terrible mother she is would be rude, but have I ever done that? No. I've kept my opinions to myself. And I've been proven right."

Megan shakes her head. She's used to assholes like Connie Hamilton, so she refuses to let it bother her. "Just because you have money doesn't make you better than me. You didn't even work for it; it's family money you inherited. You haven't done a day's work in your entire life."

Connie looks like she's about to answer, but Kathy leads her to the front door before she can, forcing her to walk quicker than she looks comfortable with. It must have been terrible for Kathy growing up with that woman as her mother. Never being able to please her no matter how much she does what she's told. Megan rubs her face. She's in desperate need of a shower. The only good thing about last night was that she didn't score any drugs. She was tempted, but for some reason she stopped at liquor. Maybe it was the thought of letting Kathy down.

After walking Connie out to her car, Kathy joins Megan on the couch. Fay sits opposite them. "I'm so sorry, Megan. I don't share any of her opinions about you, you know that, right?"

Megan waves a dismissive hand, but she's unable to reply. She couldn't be feeling any lower than she does right now.

"I've been to see Chase," says Kathy, changing the subject. "I saw Mitch briefly too."

"Is Dad okay?" asks Fay.

"Yes. He's adamant he had nothing to do with any of this. He doesn't think Uncle Scott did either. And I believe him."

Relief swamps Fay's face. "I believe him too."

Megan knows they want him to be innocent, but she's less sure.

"While I was there Chase received confirmation that the child in the shipping container isn't Charlie."

Megan looks up at her. "It's Olivia Jenkins, isn't it?" Her poor mother. What that little girl must have gone through doesn't bear thinking about.

"He wouldn't confirm it, but I think so. He also said they don't know yet whether Charlie is... at the house. He said he'll let me know as soon as he finds out one way or another."

Megan wipes away a tear. She wants to remain hopeful, but it's too hard.

"What about the red material they found there?" asks Fay. "Did he describe it?"

Kathy glances at Megan in a way that suggest she's keeping something from her, probably to spare her feelings. "I don't know, he didn't mention that," she says.

Megan takes a deep breath. It's time she faced her other problem head-on. "There's something I need to tell you, Kathy, but I think it's best done in private." They both look at Fay, and Megan says, "It's not about your dad or Charlie. It's something about me that I need to share with your mom."

To her credit, Fay doesn't appear upset at being dismissed. A sign of being brought up well. "I'll be in my room."

"Thanks, and sorry for all this," Megan says. "I appreciate you being nice to me and all, even after what me and your dad did."

Fay offers a nervous smile before leaving them alone. Kathy moves closer. "What is it?"

Megan feels her hands shaking. "Susan Cartwright told me something and I wasn't sure whether to believe her, so I asked her to go away and triple-check it." She runs a hand through her tangled hair. "Last night she emailed me proof. So now I know it's true. But you won't like it."

Kathy takes her hands. "It's okay, Megan. Whatever it is. You don't have to get yourself worked up over it."

Megan's breathing has become short and shallow and her heart's beating out of her chest. She's nervous to see how Kathy will react. "But that's just it. You might not think it's okay when you hear it. Because it's about you too. And I wasn't going to tell you, because it's screwed up, and you'll probably be so disappointed that you'll make me leave, and I... I don't know if I could bear it." She's talking too fast.

Kathy's frowning. She pulls her hands away as if she's expecting bad news. "I'm confused. Just tell me what she discovered."

Megan feels like she's going to vomit, but she's come this far and she has to finish it now. No matter what the consequences. "Okay. So I'm pretty sure I never mentioned this, because we've never really been that close except for the last few days, where I've felt we're starting to get to know each other, you know?"

Kathy nods.

"So, you already know that Susan told me my mom died last year. That's why she didn't get in touch even after my attack being all over the news."

"Right," says Kathy.

"But Jeanette wasn't my real mom." She pauses, and finally makes eye contact with Kathy. "I was adopted as a baby."

Kathy looks surprised. "Oh."

"I never knew my real parents, so I only ever mention Jeanette when anyone asks about my family."

"Did you ever learn their names, at least?"

Megan doesn't think Kathy has cottoned on yet. "No. It would seem they didn't want me to know who they were."

Kathy nods with sympathy in her eyes. "The adoption process can be cruel."

Megan swallows. "Jeanette told me they didn't want a relationship with me. That messed me up as a teenager, because I was at that age where I wanted to find out who I really was. Now, I'm no shrink, but I'm pretty sure it was that rejection that sent me on a downward spiral. It's why I started drinking. Then I started smoking weed and trying pills..."

"I'm sorry to hear that." Kathy's starting to look nervous.

"When we met with Susan at the coffee shop, she asked about my biological family while you were in the restroom. And, well, she's managed to find out who one of my parents is." Megan takes a deep breath. "She couldn't find my father; he's not listed on the birth certificate and there's no record of him ever being mentioned as part of the adoption process."

Kathy sits back. She looks like she's going to be sick. The color has vanished from her face.

Megan reaches out and takes her hands. "Susan told me the name of my birth mother." Tears are streaming down her face now. "I'm so sorry."

"What are you saying?" whispers Kathy. She shudders as if she's cold.

"My real name's not Megan Carter." Megan wipes her eyes. "Thanks to you, I know now that it's Hope Hamilton."

FIFTY-FOUR

Kathy's heart is pounding against her chest. She does the math based on Megan's age. It fits.

"I'm so sorry to be a massive disappointment after everything you went through back then," says Megan.

Kathy feels dizzy. Her face is soaked with tears. Can it be true? That all these years, her daughter has been living so close, in the next town over? She struggles to breathe.

Megan pulls her phone out with trembling hands and shows her a child services document Susan sent her that lists Megan's date of birth, the hospital where she was born, her weight and her mother's name. *Kathy Hamilton*. It also gives the names of the couple who took her home from the hospital. Bob and Jeanette Carter.

"They're my adoptive parents," says Megan with fear in her eyes. "They split when I was still young, and Jeanette raised me alone until she asked me to move out."

Kathy studies Megan's face. Her brown eyes. Her dyed black hair that shows lighter roots emerging. "My mom always told me black hair coloring ages a woman, so I wasn't allowed to try it," she says.

Megan pulls up a photograph on her phone. It's a copy of a print of her as a toddler. She has long auburn hair and a smile that reminds Kathy of both Fay and Charlie.

Kathy takes Megan's face in her hands. She struggles to speak. "You're Hope? You're my daughter?" She feels like her heart might burst.

Megan breaks down completely then, unable to speak through her tears. Kathy pulls her into an embrace, hugging her tight. "But Megan, it's a miracle. I thought I'd never find you."

Eventually Megan pulls away. "You looked for me?"

"Of course I did! But no one would tell me anything. I bought you a birthday card every single year and wrote all my hopes and dreams for you inside in case I could give them to you one day. They're in a box in the attic."

Megan's face is filled with relief. Kathy grabs some tissues from the coffee table, and they're both eager to talk as they wipe away their tears.

"You're not disappointed in how I turned out?"

Kathy takes her hands. "You turned out perfectly."

A cloud crosses Megan's face. "But this means Mitch is technically my stepfather."

Kathy hasn't realized the implications. She worries for a second. "Not really. He didn't raise you. He was a stranger to you. But he's going to feel even more guilty for the affair when he finds out." She remembers Mitch telling her he was initially attracted to Megan because she reminded him of her. Could he have subconsciously noticed a resemblance?

Megan nods before smiling sadly. "And Charlie's your granddaughter."

Kathy gasps as the full consequences hit her. Her heart flutters. "That's right. I'm a grandmother!" She chokes back a sob. "My God. I couldn't have asked for a more wonderful granddaughter. I fell in love with her the day I met her."

"You don't have to say that."

"But I mean it! She's so funny and vibrant and kind. Even Fay fell for her immediately." She stops for a second. "You're Fay's half-sister."

Megan smiles. "I always wanted a brother or sister. But she might not be as happy when she finds out."

Kathy's stomach lurches with dread. She'll have to explain to Fay and Mitch about being a teenage mother and giving away her baby. How will that impact Fay? She thinks of Christine. Maybe Kathy could arrange to tell Fay in a session, with Christine there to help her deal with the news. "Fay is Charlie's aunt, as well as her half-sister."

Megan looks surprised. "I hadn't even thought of that." After a few minutes' silence, she suddenly grins through her tears. "Can I be the one to tell your mom that she's my grandmother?"

Kathy surprises herself by laughing. "Oh my God, she'll go nuts. Can you even imagine the look on her face!"

"She's not going to be happy, that's for sure." Megan turns serious. "Do you think she might try to keep us apart? I mean, she was the one who made you give me up, right?"

Kathy feels sick at the thought of having this conversation with her mother. Connie will hate it if news gets out about Kathy having an illegitimate daughter, never mind the fact that it's Megan. She tries to offer a reassuring smile. "She's more compassionate than you think. I'm hopeful she'll surprise us and be glad to see you back with the family."

Megan doesn't look convinced. "I'll have to take your word for it, but I can't see it myself." She cocks her head as more implications hit her. "I guess this means that Chase Cooper is my biological dad?"

Kathy's smile fades. She leans back and takes a deep breath. "No. He's not your father. Believe me, I wish he was."

"He's not? Then who is?"

She looks away. "I've never spoken about that to anyone." Her elation at discovering her long-lost daughter drains away as she realizes she'll have to discuss the person who got her pregnant.

FIFTY-FIVE

SPRING 1994

The counseling room is bright but small. A window looks out over the street below, and the shelves are full of books. A picture of a summer meadow almost fills the wall opposite the couch, presumably placed there so unhappy clients can try to forget their problems.

Kathy slumps onto the couch and sighs. She's cried almost non-stop since her mom found her waiting for Chase at the hotel two nights ago. It's left her feeling drained. Losing him as a boyfriend is devastating, but now she's focusing on the other girlfriends he's said to have, and she's angry. She wants to hurt him back, but she doesn't know how.

"How are you today?" asks her therapist. He's only twenty-eight, and Kathy's one of his first clients since qualifying.

"Fine."

He smiles knowingly. "Now, Kathy, I can tell that's not true. Your face is all blotchy and you look exhausted. Has something happened at home? Are your parents fighting again?"

She rolls her eyes. "They're always fighting, and lying to me, but I don't care what they do. This has nothing to do with them."

He leans in and touches her knee. "Come on. Tell me what's wrong. You can trust me, remember?"

A thrill goes through her at his touch. He's flirted with her before in their sessions, and at first she thought she was imagining it—surely it's against his oath or whatever they agree to? But now she wonders if she was right. With just an eleven-year age gap, they hit it off straight away. They have stuff in common. He knows the music she listens to and what TV shows she watches. Plus, he's attractive, with his geeky glasses and quick smile.

It's nice not having an older therapist for once, one who doesn't remember what it's like to be a teenager. She's had her share of them over the years and never felt a connection. She also didn't trust that they wouldn't tell her mom everything she disclosed. But her current therapist has promised he would never do that. He's like a secret-keeper for her. She can say whatever she feels and he doesn't seem to be shocked. "I broke up with my boyfriend. I found out he's been cheating on me." She manages to say it without crying.

He leans back in his seat. "I'm sorry to hear that. Do your parents know?"

Embarrassment causes her to blush when she thinks about her mom finding her at the hotel. She nods. "They didn't know I even had a boyfriend until my mom listened in to our phone conversations from the extension in the bedroom."

"And how are you coping? Have you eaten much since then?"

"I've actually been overeating." She grimaces. "It's disgusting how much food I can put away."

"Are you purging afterwards?"

"No. I'm too scared I'll choke. I hate being sick."

"That's not the only reason you shouldn't do it, Kathy." He sighs. "I warned you having a boyfriend would end in tears, didn't I?"

She doesn't reply.

He moves his chair closer; their knees are touching. "Is there anything I can do to make you feel better? Because you know I don't like to see you sad."

A small shiver travels through her. Is he interested in her? Surely not. "You're my therapist. Shouldn't you be giving me coping mechanisms or something?"

He laughs. "My dad always says the best way to cope with a break-up is to move on with someone else as fast as possible. Although I won't tell you the phrase he actually uses."

"Well, I've got to tell you there aren't that many boys lining up to take his place. I mean, look at me."

"I *am* looking at you. I see an intelligent, beautiful young girl on the cusp of adulthood who can be whoever she wants to be if only she'd cut herself some slack."

Kathy looks away. His stare is intense. She feels like they're doing something wrong. She considers what he said. Is that really how he sees her? Not the beautiful part—she knows that's not true. She's too thin, all the boys make fun of her red hair, and her skin is so pale it burns quickly in the sun. Besides, if she was beautiful, Chase wouldn't be cheating on her, would he? Tears rush to her eyes. She feels stupid for assuming he wouldn't do that to her.

Handing her a tissue, her therapist says, "Don't cry over a teenage boy. First loves never last. At least you got yours over with early on in your life. This can teach you valuable lessons for the future."

He seems dismissive, and she wonders what she's done wrong. He moves away slightly. Has she ruined this too?

"I think it's best you see a different therapist from now on," he says, picking up her file.

"What?" Alarmed, she leans forward. "No, I like seeing you. I can be myself here."

He's silent for at least a minute, and she thinks he's going to end the session early and tell her to leave. Instead, he smiles. "But if you remain my client, you can't meet Bailey, my new dog."

She's confused. "What do you mean?"

"I rescued him from the animal shelter, and he's got a lot of energy, so he needs regular walks in the woods. I was hoping you'd join us, but if I'm your therapist, I'm not allowed to spend time with you outside of our sessions."

She looks away, suddenly shy. He may only be eleven years older than her, but he's been through college, he's had older girl-friends. He's more experienced than her. Besides, she doesn't want to cheat on Chase, as crazy as the thought sounds to her. She isn't looking for another relationship. That's not why she's here.

On the other hand, when she thinks of Chase with his girl-friends, she feels angry again. She thinks about how dating an older guy would piss him off. It would show him she can do better than him. Her mother might even approve of this rela-tionship, what with him being a doctor and all.

She looks back at him and smiles nervously. "I'd love to join you."

"Great," he says. "But not a word to anyone. People might think it inappropriate until you turn eighteen and some time has passed since you were my client. My reputation is on the line here, Kathy."

Chewing her bottom lip, she nods.

"I already know you can keep a secret," he says, "because you hid your ex-boyfriend from your parents for so long. But it's a little more serious that you keep our date secret. You understand?"

"Sure."

"Good." He stands up. "You know what? I don't even think you need therapy anymore. I think you're a perfectly well-rounded young woman who's capable of making your own decisions. That's what I'll tell your mother. There's no need for you to see anyone else. Okay?"

She nods. "Okay." She's relieved he has so much confidence in her, because she'd love to stop therapy for good.

He writes something down before slipping her the piece of paper. "Here's where we should meet, at seven tonight. You know it?"

She smiles. The woods aren't that far from her house. "Sure."

He leans in to kiss her, taking her by surprise. He doesn't kiss like Chase. There's nothing soft and tender about it. It's hungry, almost. Forceful. It scares her. He pulls away and smiles. "You'd best get home. I need to write up our final session notes."

As she walks out the door, she feels confused by the whole encounter. She hesitates in the waiting room, wondering if she should say something to someone. The receptionist smiles at her. "Your mom's waiting outside."

Kathy's heart hardens immediately. Can't her mom leave her alone for one hour? She didn't ask for a ride home. It's her mother's way of controlling her, making sure she doesn't see Chase. The sight of her mom smiling behind the windshield as Kathy walks out of the building strengthens her resolve. She's going to meet with Dr. Harris tonight. She's going to do whatever she wants from now on.

FIFTY-SIX

Progress Notes—Confidential

Client's description of the issues they are experiencing
Client stated she had split with her boyfriend. She's been keeping him a secret from her parents, and when asked previously about whether she felt comfortable lying to them, she said she had to because they were so controlling. Client was clearly distraught over the split and said she had been coping by overeating. No purging, though. She was unable to offer much introspection today and unwilling to see things from her parents' perspective.

Therapist's observations
Overeating, secrecy, deviousness. When she doesn't want to be guided by me on certain topics, she switches off and focuses on me instead, which leads me to believe she isn't benefiting from our sessions. As touched on in the notes from my previous session with her, I still worry that she is capable of making things up, possibly for attention, because she's not getting the attention she craves from her parents. Her atten-

tion turned toward me early on in the session, to the point where I now feel uncomfortable assisting her alone. I feel she may be harboring inappropriate feelings for me. As a result, I feel I'm not best placed to help her going forward. She should seek a different therapist if she decides to continue with sessions.

I've informed the client this is my last session with her and she agreed that would be best and that she doesn't feel therapy is necessary any longer. I did advise she should see someone else in case her food issues get worse, but she seemed reluctant. I advised her to discuss the matter carefully with her parents.

Goals/objectives of client
    N/A

Assessment of progress
    See above.

Any safety concerns
    None.

Next appointment
    N/A

FIFTY-SEVEN

Chase is in the basement of the house in Glenwood. The excavation work has begun. He has a guy carefully drilling around the object in the concrete, and the dust is getting stuck in his throat and drying out his eyes. There are a lot of people down here watching and waiting. The mood is somber and no one wants to say anything.

"Did I miss anything?" whispers Detective Brown, out of breath. He's only just arrived.

"No. Do we have results on the cowboy hat yet?"

"Not yet. I'll let you know as soon as they come in."

Chase nods. He leaves the basement and walks through the kitchen and out to the backyard, craving some clean air. He looks at his phone. It's been quiet for the last hour, which is unusual. It's probably because most of his team are here.

Mitch Hamilton and his brother are still denying everything, and Chase is worried their lawyers will get them released before he can confirm whether it's Charlie down there. Even then, he needs physical evidence of their involvement—something other than the fact that they own this place and that Mitch's alibi for Saturday hasn't yet been corroborated. If his theory is correct and Scott handed Charlie over to Mitch in the woods behind the house, it's Mitch who killed her. He'd be facing life without parole.

Chase has a team of officers scouring the property inside and out. The contractors have all sworn blind they found nothing else at the house other than the cowboy hat. And all of them have alibis for Saturday afternoon and evening. Shaking his head in frustration, he wishes his job was more like the cop shows on TV, where clues are found every twenty minutes until the final discovery of the body. He pulls his tie loose and rolls up his sleeves, trying to cool down, but the midday sun is strong.

"Cooper!"

He turns around to face the house. Brown is there. "You better come take a look."

He doesn't have the luxury of taking a minute to brace himself for whatever they've discovered. He runs into the house and follows Brown down the stairs, back into the airless basement. Everyone except the forensics team is turned away from the corner where the red material was found.

A smell reaches him, and although it's not as bad as the one inside the shipping container, it's undeniably the smell of putrid gases from a decaying body. He covers his mouth with his arm. His feet feel like lead as he steps toward the chunk of concrete they've excavated. The forensics techs get off their knees and move out of his way.

His heart skips a beat and he blinks hard, trying to get Megan and Kathy out of his head. They can't see her like this. They'll never get over it. They'll never forget it. He knows he won't.

He kneels down and spots the yellow shorts sticking out of the slab of concrete where her hips would be. "Jesus."

The rest of her is still entombed. The medical examiner, with the help of the forensics team, will need to recover the body carefully, officially confirm the identity and find a cause of death. He stands up and walks away, everyone moving aside for him. He hears Detective Brown follow him up the stairs and out of the house.

Brown pulls out a cigarette and lights it with shaky hands.

Chase looks up at the sky. "His own daughter."

"Sick bastard," says Brown between hard drags on the cigarette. "But we need evidence."

Chase looks at him. "We'll get it. I intend to nail the son of a bitch for this."

Brown exhales smoke. "If we do this right, he'll never get out of prison."

Chase can feel the pressure weighing him down, but his need for justice fuels his determination. "That's the goal."

FIFTY-EIGHT

Fay takes the news that Megan is her half-sister surprisingly
well. It makes Kathy wary. "Are you sure you're okay? You don't
want to talk it through with Christine?"

They've come to sit in the backyard for a change of scenery,
sick of waiting for news in the house and not wanting to brave
the reporters outside. Megan and Fay are sipping Diet Cokes.
Kathy has sparkling water. Their cell phones are lined up on
the table in front of them so they don't miss anything.

"I'm fine," says Fay. "It's pretty cool to have an older sister,
and at least I already know you. Maybe you could come to
school with me one day and silence a couple of bitches. 'Cause
you're pretty badass with those tattoos and all."

"Fay, don't swear!" says Kathy.

Megan smiles broadly, giving her gaunt pale skin a hint of
color. "Consider it done."

"Cool. Does it mean you're going to move in with us when
Dad moves out?"

Megan glances at Kathy, embarrassed. "I don't..."

Kathy realizes that Megan still doesn't know whether she's
wanted here, even though she's her daughter. "I think that's a

great idea," she says. "We have plenty of room and you're welcome to stay as long as you want." Her heart couldn't be more torn right now. She has her two beautiful daughters in front of her, but the empty fourth chair at the table speaks volumes. They're missing Charlie. If she could just come home to them, Kathy's family would be complete for the first time ever.

"So who's your real dad?" asks Fay with a frown.

Trust a teenager to get right to the heart of the matter. Kathy realizes it's time to give up her last secret. It's something she never expected to have to talk about. "This is strictly between us, okay?"

They nod.

"When I was younger, my parents made me see therapists. They were worried about me because I wasn't eating enough and I kept burning myself out by studying hard, trying to stay a straight-A student to make them happy."

A fleeting look of recognition and understanding passes across Fay's face, making Kathy take her hands. "I'm sorry. I've done the same to you. I didn't want you to see anyone, but Mitch insisted; he thought therapy would help you. I was hesitant, to say the least, but when you started losing weight, I had to try something. You don't have to go back if you don't want to."

"That's okay," says Fay. "I like Christine. We just chat; it's not like I'm crying the whole time or anything."

Kathy's relieved about that. "The last therapist I saw was newly qualified. He was only twenty-eight, if I remember right. Anyway, to cut a long story short, we ended up having a stupid one-night stand." She looks away. "It was my first time with anyone, and I regretted it immediately."

Megan clutches the arms of her chair and leans forward, aghast. "Are you serious?"

Kathy's a little taken aback by her reaction. "I was seventeen, it was legal."

"Legal maybe, but totally and utterly immoral of him to take advantage of you! He was your therapist and eleven years your senior!"

Her reaction brings back the shame and doubt Kathy felt back then. "I agreed, though."

"Okay, so tell me this. Did it feel right at the time?"

Kathy is keenly aware of Fay's stare. "We'd agreed to stop therapy that same day so that it wasn't unethical. He asked me on a date." She doesn't want to think about the so-called date. She notices her hands are shaking. This is a subject she never dwells on.

"You're avoiding the question, Mom," says Fay. "What happened?"

Kathy sips her water. "He invited me to walk his dog with him in the woods."

"Oh my God." Megan clutches her head in her hands like she's dreading what's coming.

"Look, we fooled around a little and it led to sex. I'm not proud of it for a variety of reasons, but I'd had such a bad time with my parents, and I'd broken up with Chase two days before. I was an emotional wreck."

Megan puts a gentle hand on her shoulder. "Stop trying to justify what he did. He took advantage of you. He was your *therapist*, Kathy. Your goddam therapist! He knew you were in a vulnerable position and he abused his power." She shakes her head. "Let me guess, that was the last you ever saw of him. There was no follow-up date, am I right?"

Kathy bites her lip. She's right back to feeling like the naïve schoolgirl she was. "He said he didn't think we should see each other again. He thought I couldn't be trusted to keep it a secret." The shame was unbearable. She blamed herself and knew no one would feel sorry for her because she'd willingly gone with him. She didn't expect to have sex with him, not on their first date and not out in the woods. She was going by her experience with Chase, who never pressured her into anything she wasn't ready for.

Fay gets out of her seat and hugs her from behind. "I'm sorry you experienced that, Mom."

Kathy's surprised by her own tears. "How can it still affect me all these years later?" She attempts to laugh. "I mean, it was just sex, right?"

"Rape more like," says Megan. It's obvious she's angry on Kathy's behalf. "Does the slimeball still live around here?"

Kathy doesn't want to give up his identity, because she's still fearful he could claim she was lying about the whole thing. Nothing good can come of naming him. "No, I don't think so."

"I can't believe my biological father is a goddam rapist," spits Megan.

"Please don't say that," says Kathy. "He didn't rape me. Yes, with hindsight he could be accused of abusing his position, but we were both young and the sex was consensual."

"Well let me ask you this," says Megan. "Imagine Fay's just turned seventeen. Would you consider it consensual if she was seeing a male therapist and he talked her into a one-night stand?"

Kathy gasps at the thought. "Of course I wouldn't! But that's different. Fay's my daughter, and times have changed..."

Megan and Fay share a look. Fay returns to her seat as she says, "But Mom, that doesn't make any sense. If it would be wrong for it to happen to me, it was wrong for it to happen to you."

Kathy sips her water again. They're confusing her. "It's a gray area. I didn't feel like I was raped." But there's no getting away from the fact that it didn't feel right either. It was a horrible, awkward experience. "Please don't mention this to anyone. My mother would go mad if she found out it was one of my therapists who got me pregnant. She'd probably sue him, and it would cause all kinds of problems for his career, especially as he's just made tenure at the university." She cringes when she realizes she's slipped up.

Frowning, Fay says, "Tenure? Wait, he's a *professor* now?"

Kathy gets up. "I don't want to talk about this."

"Why?" Megan asks Fay. "Do you know him?"

Fay's eyes are wide. "Christine's partner just made tenure at the University of Vermont. She was celebrating Sunday night."

Kathy stops dead in her tracks. "What's her partner's name?"

"Evan something. I forget his last name."

She leans forward with dizziness as goosebumps cover her arms. "That's him," she whispers. "Evan Harris, Dr. Harris to me back then. I had no idea he was your therapist's partner. He's so much older than her. My God, I would never have let you see her. I would've insisted on someone else." Chills run through her body.

"But why?" asks Megan. "What am I missing?"

Instead of answering her, Kathy looks at Fay. "How much did you tell Christine about our family once Charlie moved in with us?"

Fay looks scared. "Everything. I mean, isn't that the whole point of therapy? I told her I thought Dad had cheated on you with Megan and that Charlie was their child. Then I confirmed it after he came clean to me."

"She might've told Evan," says Kathy. "He might have taken Charlie."

"Why would he, though?" asks Megan.

Kathy tries to think. "I don't know. Could he have somehow realized that you were his daughter and Charlie his granddaughter? Maybe he wanted rid of you both for that reason, so no one would find out what he'd done to me."

"But *you* didn't even know that until today," says Megan. "So how could he?"

Kathy nods, trying to piece everything together. "You're right. If I didn't know your true identity, there's no way he would've. I never saw him again after that night, and once I knew I was pregnant, I became reclusive, so he would never have seen me with a bump." Relief washes over her. She was jumping to absurd conclusions again.

"Did I do something wrong?" asks Fay with tears in her eyes.

Kathy goes to her. "No, honey. I'm sorry. I was just shocked at the connection between Christine and Dr. Harris, that's all. I had no idea they were together. It's just a little too close for comfort. I wish I'd checked her out better before agreeing you could see her, but I didn't know she was dating him. I mean, he must be at least fifteen, sixteen years older than her!"

Megan leans back in her chair, looking exhausted. "This town is so messed up."

Stroking Fay's hair, Kathy nods. "You can say that again."

A loud knock at the door makes them go still. None of them move.

"It might be Dad," says Fay. "He could've been released."

Kathy doubts it. He'd have his keys. It's more likely Chase with the results of the excavation. She remains frozen to the spot.

FIFTY-NINE

It takes three knocks before someone opens the door. It's Megan. The fresh breakouts on her cheeks and her bloodshot eyes tell Chase everything he needs to know about how she's coping. When she sees him standing there, she recoils. Chase tries not to give anything away until he's out of reach of the cameras.

Megan steps aside and he walks in without saying a word. Kathy has her arm around Fay. They're standing in the kitchen.

"There's no way of breaking this to you gently." He looks at them all before focusing on Megan. "I'm so sorry, Megan, but we've found your daughter's body. Her identity has been confirmed by DNA. She was encased in concrete in the basement of Mitch and Scott's empty house."

Kathy and Fay quickly embrace her.

"I have so many questions," says Megan before her face inevitably crumples. "But I can't right now." She covers her face with her hands before breaking down.

Allowing them some privacy, he walks into the living room and sits on the couch. He rests his head in his hands as he struggles to remain composed while listening to Megan's gut-

wrenching sobs. He feels for them all so damn much. Olivia
Jenkins' mother broke down when he told her the body in the
shipping container was her daughter. After absorbing the news,
she went to the kitchen for a knife and started slashing her
wrists. Detective Brown caught her before she seriously hurt
herself. He's with her at the hospital now until she can be seen
by someone.

It's been one of the worst days in Chase's whole career. He
rubs his face. What he'd give for a drink right now. A drink and
a new job, something where he doesn't have to deliver death
notifications to distraught parents.

Eventually Kathy joins him on the couch as Megan heads
upstairs. "She doesn't want to know the details yet. She needs
some time. Fay's going to stay with her."

He nods. "Of course. Are you going to be okay?"

She lowers her eyes. "I have no idea. Part of me knew it was
inevitable the minute I saw Charlie's dress at the station." He
rubs her back and she leans into his shoulder. "Was it Mitch?"
she whispers.

"So far we haven't found anything linking him or Scott to
the site. She was probably killed elsewhere, so I'll be pulling all
the surveillance footage I can find—from the whole town if I
have to. Someone would've caught the killer driving to the
house. Maybe even entering it. I won't give up until I know who
did this."

Kathy pulls away. "Thanks, Chase. I'm so glad you're
looking out for us. I can't imagine taking this news from anyone
else."

He studies her face. He wishes he could do something to
help. He wishes their lives had been different.

She looks him in the eye. "There's something you should
know about Megan and Charlie."

His hands tense. He isn't sure what she's about to say.

"Come with me." She leads him outside and they stand in

the shade of a huge maple tree. Out here in the bright sunshine, with the buzz of a lawnmower in the distance, you'd be forgiven for thinking that everything was fine, and that little girls didn't get murdered.

Kathy faces him. She looks exhausted. "You wanted to know why I cut you off after that night you stood me up all those years ago, right?"

He leans against the tree trunk. "I didn't stand you up, Kathy. I was pulled over by the cops for something I didn't do." He pauses. "Your mother organized it."

She frowns. "How do you know?"

"When I first joined the department, one of the old-timers told me Connie had had a word in Chief Ingham's ear. Remember him? He was close with your mom before he retired and moved to Florida."

She nods.

"He arranged for me to be pulled over that night as a favor. She must've found out somehow that I was on my way to you."

Kathy looks away. "I discovered she was listening in on our phone conversations from the extension. She must've heard us discussing the arrangements."

He scoffs, "Why doesn't that surprise me? I wasn't lying. The car I was driving was my boss's. He'd loaned it to me. The cop who arrested me knew that, but he was told to pull me over anyway, to give your mom time to collect you. He told me to stay away from the Hamiltons unless I wanted to get arrested again. The son of a bitch even slapped me around a little in case the message wasn't clear enough."

A look of realization crosses her face. "That's why you turned up at school a week later with fading bruises."

He runs a hand through his hair. "Right. And I didn't have any other girlfriends, Kathy, that was bullshit. You were enough for me." She's always been enough for him, but he doesn't say that. "We don't have to discuss this now. Today's not about me."

"But I want to." She says it so tenderly that he's drawn in.

"Okay then, if we're being honest. The truth is, I've never stopped wondering why you never spoke to me again after that night."

She takes a deep breath. "Because two days later, I lost my virginity to someone I shouldn't have."

Two days? Was that how long it took her to get over him? Even after all these years, it hurts to know that. He tries hard not to react.

"Every single time you came to the house, causing a scene with your attempts at being Romeo, I listened and I wanted to let you in," she says. "I wanted to run away with you."

"So why didn't you? I wouldn't have held that against you." He's not lying. He could've moved past it.

She smiles sadly. "Because I got pregnant."

Chase blinks. His mouth opens but he doesn't know what to say.

"I was growing bigger over those months you were pursuing answers. If I'd spoken to you, you would've seen. You wouldn't have wanted me anyway, so there was no point talking to you. I felt like I'd betrayed you. I went through a deep depression that whole year. Especially after my parents made me give up my baby girl for adoption."

"They *what?*" He shakes his head, angry on her behalf. Her parents are assholes.

"The baby's father never knew I got pregnant, but he wouldn't have wanted anything to do with us even if he had. I never saw him again after we'd had sex that one time. He made false promises about wanting a relationship, promises I would see right through now, but back then... Well, I fell for it."

He pulls her to him and they hug while he considers what she's telling him. What she went through. How could her parents have made her do that?

"I'm so sorry, Chase."

He pulls back, then takes her face in his hands and tenderly kisses her forehead. "I would have raised the baby with you. We could've been a family. We could've moved far away from your asshole parents and brought her up together."

Kathy's crying now. "Don't do that! Don't tell me what could've been. I can't bear it! That's all I ever wanted."

He wipes her tears away. "I'm sorry you had to give her up. I can't even imagine what that did to you."

She steps back. "That's not where the story ends." She hesitates as if she can't believe what she's about to say. "My daughter found her way back to me." She swallows. "I just found out that Megan is the baby I had to give up."

Chase frowns. But Megan slept with Kathy's husband, who technically is her stepfather. Still, it wouldn't be the first time he's heard of that happening, as well as a hell of a lot worse.

Then he considers something else. What if Megan is just some random woman playing on Kathy's emotions and lying about being her daughter? Kathy wouldn't be able to tell she was being duped, not while all this has been going on with Charlie. She's vulnerable right now. "How do you know?" he asks. "Do you have evidence?"

She smiles. "I knew you'd ask that. Yes. You don't have to worry: I've seen the proof. Susan Cartwright found out for us."

He knows Susan. She's a skilled reporter and a pain in the ass most of the time. She usually gets information quicker than anyone in his department can, and he has no idea how. If she has proof that Megan is Kathy's daughter, that means it's legit. His face softens as he realizes the implications. "Charlie was your granddaughter?"

Tears stream down her face as she nods. "I know. Isn't that wonderful? Isn't it great that I got to meet her? To spend time with her before..." She can't finish the sentence.

All Chase can do is hug her again. He thinks about all the wasted years he and Kathy spent apart because of Connie stopping them from being together. He meant what he said: he would've raised Kathy's baby as his own. He would've loved to have had a family. But he has to accept the fact that it wasn't meant to be. Something's bothering him, though. "Who was the guy you slept with?"

She pulls away and wipes her eyes with a used tissue. "You don't know him."

He wonders if it was someone they went to school with. "You said it was someone you shouldn't have. What did you mean by that?"

Shame clouds her face. "It's taken me so long to talk about all this. And I'd bet if Charlie hadn't been taken I would never have opened up to anyone. I would never have got to know Megan properly. We would never have had Susan Cartwright looking into our backgrounds and realizing our connection. You wouldn't be in my life again." She smiles. "Charlie did all this. Charlie has brought us all back together."

She's right, but she clearly doesn't want to tell him who she slept with. It makes Chase want to know even more. Was it even consensual?

"It was her therapist," says Megan.

They both turn their heads and see Megan and Fay behind them. He wonders how long they've been there.

He looks back at Kathy. "Your therapist?" Alarm bells start ringing. "What the fuck, Kathy?" He's assuming the worst: that she was groomed by an older guy. A guy who was hired to help her.

"And Dad showed him the house on Wicker Lane the night Charlie vanished," says Fay.

Kathy gasps. "Girls, why are you saying this?"

Chase steps forward. "Professor Harris? That's who you slept with? He was your therapist back then?"

Kathy looks nervous. "Yes, but he wasn't much older than

me and I agreed to it. Chase, please don't make a big deal out of this. He could lose his job."

Megan says, "Me and Fay have been talking about it, and we think it's a pretty big coincidence that my biological dad viewed one of Mitch's listings on the night Charlie vanished. I mean, Charlie is this guy's granddaughter! Add to that the fact that he lives with Fay's therapist and could've got inside information about what was going on here, and it looks pretty damning to me."

"Who's your therapist?" Chase asks Fay.

"Christine Stiles."

His mind is in overdrive. "I need to find Harris."

"No, Chase, please. He couldn't have known I got pregnant back then, so there's no way he would know who Megan and Charlie were before I found out. Besides, even if he did know, why would he kill his own granddaughter?"

"Don't forget someone tried to kill me too," says Megan.

A potential motive springs to Chase's mind. "Because Megan and Charlie were proof that he groomed you for sex. They share his DNA. If you'd ever told anyone about what he did, my department would've done a DNA test and found he was Megan's father."

"No one's listening to me," says Kathy, frustrated. "It was consensual! And I wasn't underage!"

Chase steps forward and takes her hands in his. "Kathy, he was your therapist. No professional who wasn't a creep would sleep with their client, and that's before we even consider your age at the time. It may not be illegal, but it was immoral, which suggests he could have done it before and he could have done it since."

"What? To other young girls?" She swallows. She obviously hasn't considered that.

"Girls *and* boys," he says. "These men don't discriminate. He could have a history of abusing kids. Maybe other clients have come forward over the years. I don't know. He can't have any convictions or he wouldn't be in his job, but I need to get to the station, check if he has a record of allegations against him. And then I'm going to pay him a visit."

"Don't let him know about Megan," begs Kathy. "If he finds out she's his, he might want to be in her life. I don't think I could bear that."

"Honestly, Kathy? My gut's telling me he already knows."

She looks pained, and he wonders how much more she can take in a week that's already changed her life forever.

"Stay here, all of you, and don't speak to anyone. Not the press, not Susan, not anyone. You understand?"

They all nod, but Kathy says, "Can I tell my parents? I need to break it to them about Charlie before they hear it on the news. And obviously I need to tell them who Megan is."

"Sure. But no one else. If Evan Harris is our guy, I get one shot to do this without anyone tipping him off."

Megan grabs his arm; her eyes are pleading. "If it's him, don't let him get away. I don't care that he's my real dad. Lock him up. For Charlie."

He realizes how much they're all relying on him, and the pressure weighs him down. He can't screw this up. "I'll call when I have news."

He rushes out of the house.

SIXTY

After checking Evan Harris's criminal record at the station, Chase speeds to the university campus. He's relieved to have a different suspect for Charlie's murder. He'd prefer it wasn't Mitch or Scott who killed her, for their family's sake. The background check revealed that Harris has one allegation of sexual assault against him, back in 1997, when he would've been thirty-one years old and just four years into his role as a psychotherapist. He was working at a different clinic to the one Kathy saw him at, and Chase wonders if he regularly switched employers to avoid co-workers figuring out what he was up to. It's a common tactic amongst sexual predators, along with moving house regularly too, in an attempt to leave their old victims behind before they find the courage to speak out.

Whoever wrote the case file for the allegation wasn't diligent, as it was short and detailed only the basics, including the victim's name and age—a fifteen-year-old boy. The charges were soon dropped when the boy retracted his allegations. Perhaps Evan intimidated him, or offered him money for his silence. Or perhaps the poor kid wasn't up to reliving the ordeal in court. Chase wouldn't blame him. He's seen first-hand how brutal it is for victims of sexual assault to testify about their experiences, no matter how old they are when they manage to find the strength to come forward.

His mind is buzzing as he enters the campus grounds. Is he being too hard on the professor? Is he jumping to conclusions because he's desperate to tell Megan he has Charlie's killer? One dropped allegation doesn't prove the guy's a criminal. It could've been a messed-up kid who was lashing out at his therapist, making false accusations.

He shakes his head. No, he's never let that be his first assumption about anyone who makes a serious allegation like sexual assault. And dropping charges isn't necessarily a sign the crime never happened. It's sometimes indicative that the judicial system needs to work harder for the victims. To advocate for them and support them in the process of securing a conviction. In his experience, the system is already skewed in the perp's favor.

He slows at the campus security gate and flashes his badge. He considers telling the guard to stop Professor Harris from exiting the grounds, but he'd be overstepping the mark. Right now, there's no evidence to confirm he's their guy; just a hunch. So instead, he drives on and finds a parking spot. The minute he's parked, he rushes into the building, climbs two flights of stairs and walks along the corridor to the assistant's office. Inside, he notices that the door that leads to Evan's office is closed.

"Hi, can I help you?" A young woman dressed in jeans and a baggy shirt is boxing up some heavy-duty books on the floor.

"Hi, I don't think you were here last time I visited. I'm Detective Chase Cooper." He flashes his badge. "Is Professor Harris available?"

She stops what she's doing and frowns. "No, I'm sorry, he left about twenty minutes ago. Is everything okay?"

Shit. "Do you know where he's headed?"

"No, he was in a rush and he didn't say. He has a conference in Boston tomorrow, so you won't be able to see him until next week."

Chase thinks about going after him, but he has no cause to arrest him yet. He looks around the small room. "How come you're boxing all this up? Moving offices?"

She laughs. "No, we're having the offices decorated over the summer. It's been years since they were last touched. It's my job to declutter."

He nods. As she's being helpful, he decides to risk asking her a few probing questions. "What's Professor Harris like to work with?"

She laughs. "Why do people always ask me that?"

"What do you mean?"

"Oh," she waves a dismissive hand, "it's just that he has a bit of a reputation, so the other staff are always asking what he's really like and whether the rumors are true."

Chase tenses. "The rumors about his wandering hands?" It's a guess, but her reaction will be telling.

"You've heard them too, I see." She turns serious. "I've got to say, he's been nothing but nice to me."

Feeling like he's onto something, he says, "You wouldn't happen to have found a clown mask or costume in here while you were cleaning out, would you?"

Her face lights up. "How did you know that?"

He takes a step forward as a surge of adrenaline rushes through him. "Just a hunch. I hear the guy likes to dress up at kids' parties."

She scrunches her eyebrows together. "Really? I can't see him doing that. I didn't even know he had any kids in his family."

He runs a hand over his jaw and resists crossing his fingers as he asks, "You didn't throw it out, did you?"

"No, I only found it this morning. It was stuffed under the

armchair in his office." She stands up. "Give me a second. I can't remember which box I put it in."

Chase's hands sweat while he waits. He tries really hard not to rush her as she wades through box after box.

"Oh, here it is." She pulls it out and smiles. "It's a little creepy."

All he can think about is the DNA he can pull from it. And how her DNA is going to be on it now. He doesn't have any latex gloves on him, so he grabs a pen and uses it to take the mask off her. "I need to take this."

She laughs, confused. "Are you afraid of clowns or something?" As soon as she says it, a realization comes over her. "Oh my God, you're treating it as evidence." Her hands go to her mouth. "What did he do?"

Chase needs to get out of here, but he doesn't want her tipping Evan off about what he's taking with him. "Nothing to be alarmed about, it's purely precautionary. I need you to keep this to yourself."

Someone at the door interrupts them—a smartly dressed older woman of about sixty. "Are you here about Jacqueline Weston's murder?" she asks.

Where does he know that name from? He suddenly remembers: the first time he visited the professor at work, Evan Harris mentioned a student who had gone missing last year and was later found dead in her home state. He remembers her name from the news surrounding the case.

"I don't know what you're investigating him for," says the woman, "but you need to look into Jacqueline's murder. Her boyfriend was convicted for it, but some of us believe it wasn't him who killed her. You see, she was sleeping with Evan before she went missing, but the local police wouldn't even consider him as a person of interest."

Chase walks over to her, careful not to drop the mask that's hanging off his pen. "Thanks for making me aware. I can tell you I will one hundred percent be looking into that. Do you know where the professor might have taken off to?"

"I was in his office with him when he took a call," she says. "His face went white and he said he had to leave. He was gone within two minutes of answering the phone."

Someone's tipped him off. But that would have to be Kathy, Megan or Fay. They're the only ones who know. Unless... Fay might have wanted to talk to her therapist after Chase left them. She could've called her and told her everything, giving Christine the chance to tip Evan off. Dammit. "I need to know what car he drives."

"I just renewed his insurance," says the younger woman. She pulls out the paperwork from the top drawer of her desk and hands it over. It lists the make and license plate of Evan's car.

"Thanks. You've both been really helpful. You can guarantee we'll be speaking again in the near future, but in the meantime, keep this between us if you don't want to ruin our chances of getting a conviction at trial."

The younger woman gasps, but the older one looks satisfied, like she's been waiting a long time for this day.

Chase runs down the staircases out into the parking lot, holding the mask out in front of him. He opens his trunk, pulls out an evidence bag and carefully shoves the mask in. It needs to go to forensics asap, but he needs to track Evan down faster.

Pulling out his cell phone, he calls dispatch, who answer in two seconds. He gives them his name and barely takes a breath before explaining, "I need all units in the vicinity of the University of Vermont and surrounding areas to locate a black Cadillac CT5 with the following license plate." He reads it off the insurance paperwork. "The owner is an Evan Harris and he's wanted in connection with the murder of five-year-old Charlotte Hamilton. I believe he's absconded and may be heading for an airport."

"Understood, Detective. Notifying all units now."

"I don't know if he's armed."

"Copy that."

Chase ends the call and tears open the car door. He slips in and starts the engine, determined to find the son of a bitch before he can get away with murder.

SIXTY-ONE

It's only mid afternoon, but Kathy sips from a small glass of white wine, alone in the kitchen. The girls were asked to stay upstairs while she told her parents everything: about Charlie's body being found, about who it was who got Kathy pregnant as a teenager, and about the identity of the baby she gave up for adoption. She didn't relish telling her mom that Megan—the woman Connie Hamilton has looked down on ever since she came into their lives—is her long-lost daughter. As expected, it didn't go well, and Kathy's a mess. Her hands are trembling, her eyes feel like sandpaper from all the crying and her nerves are shot.

After finishing off the glass of wine, she picks up a tray of coffees and walks through the living room and out to the yard. Her dad is pacing at the end of the lawn, trying to get his head around the fact that it was the therapist they paid to help their teenage daughter who got her pregnant. Until today, he was always convinced it was Chase. He says he feels responsible for exposing her to someone who took advantage of her, and nothing she says helps him feel otherwise.

"Here you go." Kathy places a mug in front of her mom,

who puts her cell phone face down on the glass table. Sitting next to her, Kathy says, "You've been very quiet. What do you think about all this?"

Her mom looks out over the lawn, occasionally following her husband with her eyes. "I think if you'd controlled your sexual desires as a youngster, none of this mess would've happened."

Kathy leans in. "Mom! I was *seventeen*."

Connie turns to her with a cold stare. "We all make choices in life, Kathy. And you chose to let that man touch you. Age isn't an excuse. You went against everything I'd ever taught you was right. All those years of attending church and you still sinned at the first opportunity."

Kathy's shocked. She doesn't want to hear this from her own mother. "It wasn't the first opportunity. I was with Chase for months and we never slept together. I wanted to, but you ruined that for me."

"You let me down," her mom continues. "I had such high hopes for you. But because of your poor decision to let your therapist violate you, you felt so worthless that you married Mitch Bowers of all people. You could've done better. You chose not to."

That angers Kathy. "Maybe if I hadn't grown up in such a screwed-up household, I wouldn't have needed a therapist in the first place. Did you ever consider that?"

Her mom doesn't acknowledge her. "I knew that baby would destroy our family eventually."

"No, Mom. *You* destroyed our family when you made me give her up. When you took away my choice, it affected not just my life but Megan's too. Don't you even realize that if you'd let me be with Chase that night at the hotel, none of this would have happened? I wouldn't have slept with Dr. Harris at all." With bitterness in her tone, she asks, "Tell me something, if the baby had been a boy, would I have been allowed to keep it?"

A derisive snort. "Well of course, dear. I could have raised him as my own. He could've carried on the Hamilton name."

Kathy's mouth falls open. "I can't believe how callous you are. You're all about protecting the Hamilton name, but it doesn't stand for anything good anymore! You've destroyed that with your controlling, manipulative behavior."

A flicker of emotion crosses her mom's face. "I did what I had to in order to protect the family. That means you. You're my family. Fay is my family. We can't have trash like Megan Carter and her child coming in and claiming what isn't theirs! My grandfather didn't work all day every day building the railroad so that some drug addict could drink and smoke it all away in a heartbeat!"

Kathy's confused. What is her mom saying? "You can't blame Megan and Charlie for our family's problems. We were messed up *way* before they came along."

"I disagree. I was perfectly happy before you told me your stupid husband had slept with his own stepdaughter and got her pregnant, of all things. I could just imagine what Reverend Stanley would say. And our family friends... they'd have a field day. They'd look down their noses at me, reveling in the fact that *their* families were better than mine. Just the thought of it was enough to give me a stroke."

Kathy swallows. She must be misunderstanding. "We didn't know Megan was related to us when I told you about Mitch's affair in February. I've literally only just found out myself."

Her mom finally looks at her. There's a dangerous smile on her lips. "You might have only just found out, dear. But I've known the entire time."

Kathy leans back in her seat, incredulous. "That's not possible." A knot of dread weighs on her chest. Because the implications don't bear thinking about.

SIXTY-TWO

Kathy watches her mom pull a cigarette from her purse and light it. She's never smoked in front of her before.

"I knew who got you pregnant the minute you told me about your positive test," Connie says. "I mean, it wasn't hard to figure out. You refused to ever see a therapist again, and he recommended you didn't need one, completely out of the blue. I made sure he didn't find out you were pregnant, of course. I didn't want him talking you into keeping it, although I suspect someone as unscrupulous as to impregnate their young client would prefer a termination, which I don't believe in, of course."

Kathy doesn't want to hear this.

"I watched him advance in his career over the years, and when I saw that he was being offered tenure by the university, it stuck in my throat." Connie sucks on the cigarette and inhales deeply. "I also knew the names of the couple who adopted your baby. You see, they wanted it to be an open adoption from the very beginning, where you could stay in touch by sharing letters and photographs, perhaps even the occasional visit."

Kathy gasps. "But you said they didn't! You said it was closed!" She's devastated at discovering that she could have watched Megan grow up. She could have been a part of her daughter's life. "You lied to me!"

"Well of course I lied." Her mom stops to sip her coffee, as if they're having a mundane conversation about the weather. "You needed closure in order to move on from it. And people would've found out. I thought a complete break was the right thing for everyone. The mother—Jeanette, I think her name was —was persistent over the years, sending photographs of the girl growing up."

Kathy can't believe what she's hearing. Her mom had photographs of Megan as a child and she never shared them. "Do you still have them?" she whispers as tears stream down her face.

"No. I burned them."

Kathy closes her eyes against her rage. She could slap her mother right now.

"Your father didn't know any of this, of course; he was too busy sleeping with other women to care about what you and I were going through." Connie takes another drag on her cigarette. "So when *your* husband slept with Megan Carter, of all people, and then invited their love child to come live with you!" She shakes her head in disgust. "Well, I had to take matters into my own hands. I had to stop you finding out who she and the child really were."

Kathy slowly looks at her. "What are you saying?"

Her dad approaches them. "Kathy? Is everything okay, honey?" He puts his hand on Kathy's back, but she shakes it off, too angry to even look at him.

She jumps out of her seat and looms over her mother. "Tell me, Mom! Tell me what you did!"

"What are you talking about, Connie?" asks Kathy's father. "You're upsetting her with this rubbish."

"It's not rubbish, Jack. I heard that the university had offered Evan Harris tenure before it was confirmed in the newspaper, and I realized he had a lot to lose if word ever got out about how he liked to prey on vulnerable young girls."

Kathy's heart beats hard against her chest. She wants her mother to stop saying these things.

"You see, Kathy, I knew from a friend of a friend that you weren't the only client he's coerced over the years, so you needn't feel stupid about that. Unless you felt special, in which case..."

"You knew he was the one who got our daughter pregnant and you never told me?" says Kathy's dad, his fists balled in anger. "I would've had the son of a bitch arrested!"

Her mom waves a dismissive hand. "It wasn't illegal. You would've hit him and got yourself arrested. I couldn't risk it getting out to anyone. It was like something from a soap opera. People would've gossiped about Kathy for years. And what would they have thought of me, letting it happen?"

Kathy's dad glances at her with a look of disbelief on his face.

It dawns on Kathy then. "You met with him, didn't you?" she whispers. "You met with Evan Harris."

After another puff on her cigarette, Connie says, "Yes. I arranged to meet him under the pretense of donating to the psychology department at the university. He knew who I was, of course, but so many years had passed since your therapy that he didn't bring it up, and he didn't know that I'd guessed what had happened between you two." She gives Kathy a cursory glance. "He genuinely thought I was there to blow smoke up his ass and hand over a big fat check. I insisted on meeting him at his home, so no one would see us together, but his partner surprised us. She came home for something."

Christine saw them together. "What did you tell him?" Kathy asks. She has to hear it for herself.

"When his partner left us alone, I told him everything: about your baby and who she had grown up to be. About how she was now slowly inserting herself into your life through Charlie—his granddaughter."

Kathy experiences a heavy sinking feeling as she listens to her mother's admissions.

"I made it clear that if you ever found out who Megan was and revealed to her that he was her father, he could be exposed. I got the impression he's a man with a lot to hide. That he's enjoyed abusing his power over the years. So I pointed out that Megan and the child were proof of what he'd done to you. After all, they shared his DNA, they were walking evidence."

"Stop calling her 'the child'!" screams Kathy. "Her name was *Charlie*! She was your great-granddaughter!"

Her mom looks taken aback. "Don't scream, Kathy. It's unbecoming. It makes you look hysterical."

Kathy slaps her hard across the face.

"Kathy!" Her dad grabs her arm and then realizes he's on her side. He tries to comfort her by rubbing her back.

Her mom is shaken by the slap. The mean-spirited smile playing at her lips is gone. "I warned you you'd turn feral hanging around that woman."

Her dad pulls Kathy away from her mother before saying, "Connie, we're leaving."

"No, Jack. It's time this all came out. Then Kathy can decide where her loyalties lie. Whether she wants to remain a Hamilton or not. Because I'm not having that drug addict in my family."

"For God's sake, woman!" shouts Jack. "There's nothing special about being a Hamilton! Not anymore."

Kathy glances at her father. He's had enough. This is the final straw for him, and Kathy sees he's been controlled by her mother over the years too. Suddenly she doesn't blame him for cheating. Instead, she hopes he found other avenues of happiness over his lifetime with Connie. She turns back to her mother. "You put the idea in Evan's head to kill Charlie and Megan? To hide the trail?"

Connie looks her in the eye. "I merely advised that he should eliminate the problem, darling. I didn't say *how*."

Kathy takes a step back as she realizes how badly her mother has betrayed her. It's like a punch to the gut. Connie ruined her relationship with Chase and took away her daughter unnecessarily. Then she told the man who'd got her pregnant that he needed to eliminate Charlie and Megan. Which means the only reason she offered a reward for information was because she knew it would probably never be claimed. Kathy is too overwhelmed to even begin to know how to process that level of treachery. "You told him to frame Mitch, didn't you? Not only would you get Megan and Charlie out of our lives, you'd get Mitch imprisoned at the same time. You'd let him serve a life sentence for crimes he didn't commit."

Her mom doesn't reply at first. Eventually she says, "I never spoke to Evan again. I made it clear that I'd deny the conversation ever happened."

Kathy has heard enough. She can't stay another second anywhere near her mother. "Dad? Would you watch the girls for me?"

His eyes show concern. "That depends. Where are you going?"

She swallows hard before answering. "There's someone I need to see."

SIXTY-THREE

Kathy grips the steering wheel hard in an attempt to stop the trembling in her hands. She drives fast, but when she can no longer contain her disgust, she pulls over by the side of the road, opens the driver's door and vomits. A pedestrian is passing, but he doesn't offer her any assistance. He just shakes his head, probably assuming she's drunk.

She waits until everything's out before she leans back against the headrest and wipes her mouth with a tissue. With her mother's words circling her head, she needs answers. And Christine Stiles might be best placed to answer them. Pulling out her cell phone, she tries calling the clinic to see if Christine's at work, but the receptionist informs her she's gone home early. She doesn't disclose the reason, but Kathy thinks she can guess. When the receptionist asks if she wants to book an appointment for another day, Kathy ends the call with a brief "No thanks."

Maybe Christine's planning her getaway with Evan right now. Maybe Kathy's too late and they've already fled the state, if not the country. Feeling utterly defeated, she considers returning home and telling Megan and Fay how badly their grandmother has let them down. But just thinking of the girls makes her angry. They'll want answers, and she's determined to get them.

Pulling away from the sidewalk, she races to Christine's house, intending to go straight to Evan's next if she's not there. The newspaper named the street he lives on when they announced his tenure, and Kathy thinks it would be easy to find out which house is his. She could knock on a few doors if she has to. But she's in luck. Her stomach flutters when she sees Christine's car parked outside the house. She considers calling Chase to let him know what her mother has admitted to, but Evan's car isn't here so she's not in any immediate danger, and she wants this chance to talk to Christine herself first. The woman might open up to her if she tries a gentle approach. There might be more to the story than Connie let on.

She gets out of her car and approaches Christine's front door. It opens almost immediately. Christine doesn't ask why she's there; she simply turns and walks back inside the house. Kathy follows her, closing the door behind her, but not before taking a cautious look around in case Evan is there after all. He isn't.

In the living room, Christine sits on the couch, looking disheveled. She has a tissue in her hand and some papers in front of her. Kathy takes a tentative step inside the room. "Did you help him?" she asks in a shaky voice. "Did you help him kill Charlie?"

Christine looks up at her. Her eye makeup has been wiped away with tears, and as a result, she appears younger. "How can you even think that?" She looks lost, and that's when Kathy notices a near-empty bottle of white wine on the coffee table.

"What am I supposed to think? You're Fay's therapist! And you're dating that creep."

Christine snorts derisively and takes a long gulp of her wine before saying, "Dating? You have no idea."

There's obviously more to the story. Kathy senses that

Christine is a victim in all this too. She takes a step forward and crouches down in front of her. "Tell me. Tell me what's going on. My mother paid him a visit, didn't she?"

A sharp glance. "How do you know that?"

"She told me she gave him the idea to kill Megan and Charlie. To cover up the fact that he abused his authority."

Christine blinks. She looks surprised. "He took advantage of Megan?"

Kathy breaks eye contact and slowly shakes her head. "No, not Megan. Me." She leans back. "He was my therapist when I was seventeen. We had sex, and Megan was the result of our one-night stand. He's Megan's father, and Charlie's grandfather."

Christine's mouth opens now. "I only recently found out he was your therapist back then, but I had no idea who Megan and Charlie really were. It all makes sense now." She rifles through the papers in front of her and pulls out a batch. "I accessed his safe when I started suspecting he might be involved in Charlie's disappearance. These are his progress reports on you." She holds them out.

Kathy doesn't want to take them. She doesn't want to read what he wrote about her all those years ago.

"At least read the last one."

Taking it slowly, she skims the page. Certain phrases jump out at her.

I still worry that she is capable of making things up.

Her attention turned toward me... I now feel uncomfortable assisting her alone.

I feel she may be harboring inappropriate feelings for me.

Kathy can't believe the way he's misrepresented her. "This wasn't how it happened. I wasn't a liar. He wasn't uncomfortable around me."

Christine scoffs. "Oh, I believe you. Unfortunately, I've been there."

Kathy looks her in the eye, and suddenly it dawns on her. The age gap. "You were his client too."

Christine nods. "I was just thirteen when I was assigned to him. He was twenty-nine." Her eyes fill with tears. "I was fourteen the first time he raped me."

Kathy closes her eyes. "Oh my God."

"All these years later, and he's never let me go," she continues. "He has this psychological hold over me, more so when I was younger. I've been trying hard to break it, because the more I talk to victims in my line of work, the more I realize I'm giving them the kind of advice I should be taking myself." She wipes away tears. "I don't know how he does it. But I was so young and impressionable back then. And he's helped me over the years, as a kind of twisted reward for keeping quiet about what he's done to me. He paid toward my qualification. He helped me get my job." She shakes her head. "The deeper into our perverse arrangement I got, the less I could exist independently."

Kathy reaches out and takes her hand. "He groomed you, Christine, from a young age. It's not your fault." She can tell Christine believes it is, though. That's how some abusers get away with their crimes. They make their victims feel implicated. They prey on their feelings of shame and guilt. "Your relationship with him was never really consensual."

"I wouldn't call it a relationship. I'm just someone he doesn't know what to do with anymore. As long as I toe the line, everything's fine. The minute I stop..." Christine hesitates. "I fear I'll end up like Charlie."

Kathy's heart goes out to her. Leaning in to hug her, she says into her ear, "It's not your fault. You, me and Charlie are all victims of that man. And now I need to make sure he doesn't get the opportunity to hurt anyone else." She stands up. "It won't be long before he learns that Charlie's body has been found, if he doesn't know already. Do you have any idea where he would go to hide from the police?"

Christine looks up at her through wet eyelashes. "He'll want to destroy any evidence that could put him away." She swallows. "He'll either come here to kill me, or he'll..."

Kathy leans in. "Or he'll what?"

Christine won't finish her thought. Frustrated, Kathy says, "Please, you have to tell me so I can tell Detective Cooper."

Tears are running down Christine's face again. "Or he'll finish what he started with Megan."

Kathy takes a step back and swallows. Megan and Fay are at home *together*. They're both in danger. Not wanting to believe it, she says, "He wouldn't dare. My parents are with the girls."

"If your mom has already betrayed you, she could tip him off about Charlie's body being discovered, and Megan's current location."

Her stomach flips as if she wants to vomit again. Connie had been messaging on her phone before Kathy confronted her. She's at home with Fay and Megan now. She could let Evan into the house. Spinning around, Kathy races for the front door, shouting, "Get somewhere safe! I need to go and protect the girls."

She's out of the house and into her car so fast she doesn't have time to dwell on the fact that she might already be too late.

SIXTY-FOUR

Chase is racing to Evan Harris's house. It's safe to assume he'd need to collect some clothes, his passport and any valuables before he flees, and his head start wasn't long enough to get to an airport already. When Chase's cell phone rings, he slows down a little, but not much. Using speakerphone he barks, "This is Cooper."

"Chase? It's Kathy. It was Evan! Evan Harris killed Charlie!" She's out of breath and clearly in a panic.

"I know. How did you find out?"

"Christine Stiles. She's another of his victims. I'll explain later. She thinks he'll try to destroy any evidence that could put him away." She's not stopping for breath and he hears a loud car horn through the phone.

"You're not driving, are you? Pull over, Kathy. You could have an accident."

"I can't!" she shouts. "Chase, you don't understand. I think he's on his way to my house. He wants to kill Megan!"

His mouth goes dry as he swings the car into a high-speed U-turn in the middle of the intersection. "I'm on my way. Is anyone with her?"

"Fay and my parents. I've tried calling both the girls, but they're not picking up. I'll try my dad next, but Chase, my mom..."

"What is it?" he asks, trying to keep his eyes on the road.

"My mom might let Evan in. She hates Megan. It was her idea for him to kill Megan and Charlie. She knows Megan was the baby I gave up for adoption. She's always known."

Chase's mouth drops open and for once he's speechless.

"Are you there?" she asks down the line.

He shakes his head, trying to focus. "Yeah. I'll get officers to your house right away, and I'm about a ten-minute drive away. If you get there before me, do *not* go inside, Kathy. You understand?"

There's a pause. "Just get there as fast as you can, Chase. I can't lose my daughters as well as Charlie." She ends the call.

"Shit." He has a feeling she's not going to wait for him, which means she could get herself killed.

He calls dispatch and updates them on the suspect's location and the fact that he could be armed. If Harris is going to Kathy's house, he'll want to be in and out quick, leaving no trace behind. Which means he might take out everyone present to avoid witnesses.

Stepping on the gas, Chase races through downtown. He hears sirens in the distance and that gives him some comfort, but his hands are sweating and he can't stop thinking about losing Kathy for a second time. That can't happen.

When he finally makes it to her street, he notices almost all the reporters have gone. That'll work in Harris's favor. Kathy's driveway is empty, and he allows himself to relax just a little. He beat her here.

Then his blood runs cold as he spots a black Cadillac CT5 parked at the end of the street, at least eight houses down. "No." He jumps out of his car, leaving the door open behind him, and runs to Kathy's front door, which is closed. Pulling his weapon, he listens in. He can't hear any raised voices inside. He tries the door, but it's locked, so he has no way in without announcing himself. Seconds later, Kathy's car swings into the driveway, closely followed by a patrol car, its lights and siren blazing. Harris will know they're here now.

Kathy looks exhausted and terrified as she approaches him. "That car down the street isn't normally there," she whispers.

He nods. "Give me your key."

As she fishes it out of her pocket, he tells the two patrol officers who get out of the cruiser to go around the rear of the house. Kathy hands her keys over and shows the officers how to open the lock to the side gate.

"Stay back," says Chase. "I mean it, Kathy. You're no good to me or the girls in there."

She studies his face before nodding.

When he's sure she appreciates what he's saying, he gently slides her key into the lock and opens the front door. It's eerily silent inside. With four people supposedly in there, and possibly Harris, there should be some noise. It suggests he could be too late.

He steps inside and closes the door behind him, making sure to lock it.

Edging forward along the hallway, he clears the kitchen first. There's a broken glass on the porcelain-tiled floor. It looks like it contained orange juice. He's getting a bad feeling about this.

He walks into the living room, gun out ahead of him, but there's no one here either. He stops to listen. The whole house is silent.

When something crosses his peripheral vision, he turns to look out the sliding doors that lead to the backyard. That's when he hears voices approaching.

"He definitely went that way." It's Kathy's dad.

Chase is overwhelmed with relief when he sees Jack

approaching the deck with both Megan and Fay. He steps outside. Connie Hamilton is sitting at the table puffing on a cigarette.

"You missed him," says Jack. "The son of a bitch just took off over next door's fence."

"Is everyone okay?" asks Chase. They don't appear to be hurt, though Megan looks shaken.

"I guess that was my dad," she says.

Chase watches the officers dart off in the direction of the neighbor's house, one of them calling for backup. He needs to go with them, but before he can leave, Kathy appears from the side gate. She runs up to Megan and Fay and hugs them tight. "Oh, thank God!" she sobs. "I thought he'd hurt you."

Jack puts a hand on her back. "He was scared off by the sirens. Stupid asshole didn't even make it into the house."

Chase smiles faintly. Until he notices that Connie is showing no emotion at all. He remembers what Kathy told him: that she was involved in Charlie's murder and the attempted murder of Megan. He walks up to where she's sitting.

She gives him a silent cold stare while finishing her cigarette.

"Kathy tells me this is all your fault," he says. "That you wanted Megan and Charlie dead. Which means I have to take you in for questioning."

Kathy's dad turns away with his hands to his head. "My God, what is happening?"

Connie slowly pushes her seat back and struggles to stand. "It would have to be you, wouldn't it, Chase Cooper?" She practically spits his name. "I suppose you're going to take this opportunity to handcuff me in order to embarrass me in front of the news crews?"

Chase steps forward. "No, Mrs. Hamilton. Not everyone plays dirty."

Megan looks shocked. "*You* were behind all this? I can't

believe it. What did Charlie and I ever do to you? She was a beautiful, innocent little girl who would've brought so much joy into your life if you'd let her. Instead, you're the same bitter old woman you've always been." She's sobbing now. "You're a killer!"

Connie is unmoved by her words, but she can't look at her.

Chase nods at Jack, then at Kathy, who has tears streaming down her face, before leading Connie into the house and out through the front door, where another patrol car is waiting. To the female officer he says, "Take her in."

As the officer leads Connie to the back seat, a dark figure darts out between the two houses opposite. He's heading for the neighbor's backyard. Pulling his weapon, Chase runs after him. When he sees an older woman peer out of the living room window, he mouths, "Stay inside." Alarmed, she nods and takes a step back.

He picks up speed as he runs past the side of the house. When he gets to the backyard, he looks around but can't see anyone. He doesn't know which direction to head in until Evan Harris steps out from behind a huge maple tree and makes a run for it. He tries to scale the fence at the bottom of the yard.

"Stop! Police!"

Evan doesn't listen, and Chase sprints to the end of the yard, reaching him just in time to pull him back down to the ground. Evan goes down hard on his back and kicks out at Chase, knocking the gun from his hand.

Chase drops on top of him and tries to turn him over so he can pull his arms behind his back, but Evan is strong and he's resisting. "Get off me!"

Chase is about to lose his grip as Evan heaves with his full force in a bid to get up. Suddenly a gunshot rings out close by, scaring birds out of the trees above them and making Chase wince. He instinctively braces for impact, but he hasn't been hit.

Evan goes limp underneath him and Chase assumes the worst: that one of the officers shot him without a warning. But when he cranes his neck, he sees Kathy standing behind him. She's pointing his gun up to the sky and her face is deathly pale. Chase uses the distraction to pull Evan's hands behind his back and pins them down with the weight of his body. He doesn't have any cuffs on him, but he knows the nearby officers will follow the sound of the gunshot and be here in seconds.

Kathy walks slowly forward to look down at Evan, but she doesn't drop the gun. "I should kill you for what you did to Charlie. For what you've done to my whole family." Her voice falters and tears run down her cheeks. "But then I'd be no better than you."

Evan turns his head away, giving in to Chase's grip. He remains still, face-down on the ground, and he doesn't say a word.

"Put the gun down, ma'am!" shouts an officer behind them. Chase is relieved to see three of them approaching. One is pointing his weapon at Kathy.

"It's okay, she's not going to fire it!" he shouts. He gets off Evan as one of the officers cuffs him and hauls him up. Going to Kathy, he takes the gun from her and pulls her to him, stroking her hair. "We've got him, Kathy. We've got him."

But his work isn't over yet. Catching a suspect is the easy part. Proving they're a killer is something altogether more difficult.

SIXTY-FIVE

Chase enters Maple Falls PD with the weight of the world on his shoulders. He has one chance to prove that Evan Harris killed Charlie Hamilton. It's not that he doubts his own ability, but this case is personal for him, which means he needs to keep emotion out of it.

As he makes his way to the briefing room, it's clear everyone at the station has been waiting for him to arrive. Eyes follow him as he passes desks. No one knows the full story of what just went down; they only know that Chase requested backup at Kathy Hamilton's house. Once inside the briefing room, he nods at Detective Brown and asks for various arrest and search warrants to be requested. It's then that Chief Wilkins walks in.

"I hear you've been busy," says Wilkins. "I want a full update, but before that, you should know we've cut Scott Bowers and Mitch Hamilton loose. Couldn't keep them any longer without charging them, and the DA's office won't allow any charges without firm evidence they were involved."

Chase nods.

"Mitch's cell phone records are in," says Brown. "They show he sent Kathy a text message just after one o'clock on

Saturday afternoon to remind her about their couples therapy. The cell provider confirmed it was sent from the overlook hiking trail."

So Mitch *was* there on Saturday. "How did he take the news about Charlie's body being positively ID'd?"

"Honestly?" says Brown, exhaling. "He was devastated. I thought the guy was going to punch me at first, but then he collapsed into his chair and sobbed. His brother's taking him to his house for a few days to give Kathy and Megan some space. Mitch spoke to his daughter on the phone before he left the station. She wanted to see him, so she's meeting him at Scott's place. I've told the brothers to stay in town until they're no longer persons of interest."

Chase nods again. "It's looking like they weren't involved." He updates Brown and the chief on everything that's happened this afternoon. They don't register much shock—they've been in law enforcement too long to be shocked—but they do shake their heads in unison at the realization that Evan Harris wanted his daughter and granddaughter dead to save his own skin.

Chief Wilkins claps Chase on the back. "Good work, Cooper. Now finish this."

Chase glances at Brown, who raises his eyebrows and smiles. "You heard the guy. Finish it."

Chase walks toward the interview room, aware that all eyes are still on him. When a child is killed, the whole department feels it keenly. It happened on their watch. They failed to protect someone. In reality, they can't be in all places at all times, and they all know that deep down, but the way they're portrayed in the media during a case like this—especially when there's no evidence to follow and suspects have to be let go—can be harsh. So he's praying he finally has the right person in custody.

In the room next door to where Evan Harris is waiting, Chase looks at the monitor on the desk. There's a camera fixed on the guy. He's sitting with his legs apart and his arms resting on his knees. His head hangs low, as if he's overwhelmed.

Chase has interviewed three killers in his time as a detective, as well as eleven rapists and sixteen sex offenders. Those are just the ones who were eventually convicted by a jury. There were others who got released without charge, but that doesn't mean they were innocent. What he's learnt from them is that everyone reacts differently to being caught. You have those who plead their innocence all day long even after they're convicted—hell, even when they're at the end of their life in the prison infirmary after serving decades inside. Even when all the evidence proves they were guilty, they still can't admit it.

Then there are others who, the minute he sits opposite them in the interview room, want to spill their guts, admit everything and just get it over with. It's almost a relief to them. They plead guilty in court and minimize the victims' pain by not forcing them to go through the often humiliating and degrading experience of reliving their nightmare in front of a room full of strangers. But that's not why they plead guilty. Most of them want a reduced sentence. Most of them accept a deal. Deals often lead to perpetrators giving up much-needed answers about what they did and where the bodies are buried.

As he stares at Evan Harris, he thinks about how this guy coerced Kathy into sex at seventeen. There's no changing the fact that he's capable of manipulating young people. He's the father of Kathy's child, and he was Charlie's grandfather. Did he know that? It all depends on how much Connie Hamilton was involved.

"I'll be in here if you need me," says Brown, slipping on headphones.

Chase stands outside the door of the interview room. He takes a deep breath, then opens it fast and loud. Evan jumps. He sits up straight and watches as Chase takes a seat across from him and lays out the case file on the table. "Recovered from your sprint?"

The guy's clearly unamused. He gives a blank stare.

"Okay," says Chase, "I'm going to get straight to it. You've been apprehended for the abduction and murder of Charlotte Hamilton on June twelfth of this year. I also believe you attempted to murder Megan Carter by strangulation on the same day."

Evan leans back. "I'm waiting for my attorney to arrive before we discuss this."

Chase resists the urge to roll his eyes. Waiting for his lawyer is smart—it's what he would do if he ever found himself arrested —but it's frustrating. "Interesting. I don't hear a denial from you. That gives me hope that you're going to be honest with me and save Charlie's family more suffering."

Evan's gaze is steely. "I didn't kill anyone and I'm waiting for my attorney. Is that clear enough for you?"

"No? So what were you doing at Kathy Hamilton's house uninvited? And why'd you run away when the cops showed up?"

Silence.

"Fine." Chase collects the case file and abruptly stands up. "You can wait in a holding cell."

"A holding cell?" Evan asks. "Why can't I wait here?"

Chase laughs. "Because it's not a hotel, it's a police station. I need this room to interview your co-workers from over the years. Starting with the clinic where you were Kathy Hamilton's therapist, all the way through to the board who offered you tenure."

Evan suddenly looks less sure of himself, but only for a second. "You can't do that. You need evidence first."

Chase shakes his head. "You don't watch many crime shows, do you? The whole point of questioning people is to *gain* evidence. Kathy's already told me what you did to her when she was just seventeen, so I'm thinking I'll start with Matthew Stuart, the fifteen-year-old client who accused you of sexual assault in 1997." He pauses for effect, but the professor doesn't flinch at the name. "So you need to get out of this room and wait downstairs in the cells with all the other criminals. Don't worry, there's only eleven other guys down there at this moment in time. I'm sure they'll all agree to look away while you take a crap in public." He shouldn't have added that last bit. It was unnecessary. But it felt good.

Evan tries for a disarming smile and holds his hands up. "I'll answer your questions now, Detective. We can get this misunderstanding straightened out in no time. There's no need to go bringing in my patients and clients from over the years. That wouldn't be fair on them." He shifts in his seat. "Most of them are suffering with serious mental illnesses, so I don't want to put them through the ordeal of coming to a police station when they don't have to."

"Wow," says Chase. "You're such a nice guy, putting their needs first and all." He hopes the sarcasm in his voice is evident. He throws the file back on the table and sits down again. "I need you to confirm for the camera that you understand you have the right to remain silent and to wait for your lawyer to be present. And that I'm not forcing you to speak now and I've given you the opportunity to wait for your lawyer."

Evan takes a deep breath as he considers it. "I understand and agree."

Relief washes over Chase. He has a chance to extract the truth before a lawyer advises Evan to zip it. "Let me tell you where I'm at. Charlie Hamilton was just shy of her sixth birthday when she went missing on Saturday afternoon. Based on my investigation, I believe she was abducted by a male assailant and that he murdered her probably within hours of taking her." He meets Evan's gaze. "Give me your perspective as a person with a far deeper understanding of human psychology than me: what kind of person do you think could do something like that?"

"You want me to psychoanalyze your killer?" Evan laughs. "It's impossible without studying the man—his childhood, his parents and siblings, his motivations."

Chase nods thoughtfully. "Okay, but help me understand the kind of guy I should be looking for. Just give me a generalized outline of the kinds of issues that make a human being want to kill someone."

Evan shifts in his seat. "That would depend on whether it's someone who kills as a one-off, such as a husband or wife who kills their spouse out of jealousy or hatred, or someone who kills repeatedly. Serial killers only represent about one to two percent of all homicides out there, even though the media would have us believe it's a lot more. If the person who took this girl—"

"Charlie," Chase interrupts. "Her name was Charlie." He knows he needs to let this guy talk himself into revealing some detail that places him in the timeline of Charlie's death, but it's hard to hear him refer to her as "this girl" when he thinks of her family.

"If he was a serial killer," continues Evan, unmoved, "his motivations are known only to him until he's caught. *If* he's caught. And even then, he might not disclose them to the likes of you."

"So *when* he's caught—because it's just a matter of time— what kind of punishment does he deserve for killing a little girl who loved animals and who wrote stories to tell her friends and family? A little girl who is sorely missed by her mom, as well as her dad, her grandmother and her half-sister. What sentence would you pass on him so he didn't do this again?"

His face blank, Evan says, "That's for a judge and jury to decide."

"You don't think someone that deranged should be locked

up for life so he doesn't do it to another child? Because—and tell me if I'm wrong here, because you're the expert—I think he probably *will* strike again. I think the guy can't help himself. I think he's probably a psychopath or a sociopath." He frowns. "I can never remember the difference between those two. Care to enlighten me?"

Evan crosses his arms. "I'm not here to teach you Psychology 101, Detective. Stop wasting my precious time and get to the point."

"Fine." Chase sits straight and raises his voice. "Talk me through your whereabouts for the whole of Saturday, June twelfth. I want every single second accounted for."

SIXTY-SIX

Evan doesn't miss a beat. "I was in my office at the university all day. I'm currently researching my next academic text, which has a tight deadline, so I don't have much time for a social life. I'm always at work these days."

He must be banking on his staff covering for him. His look is smug and his body language is confident. He's not shying away from meeting Chase's gaze. But his profession is probably helping him mask any telltale signs of guilt, because he'll know what Chase is looking for. He wouldn't be surprised if the guy could pass a polygraph.

"Can anyone corroborate that? And before you speak, you should know I met a few of your co-workers earlier, and I've got to say, I don't think they like you much."

Evan's smile falters. He's wondering who has said what about him. "I was there alone all day. With it being a June weekend, the campus was quiet. That evening I met up with my partner, Christine, and we toured a house. But you already know that, because you questioned me about it."

"I do," says Chase. "But you lied about one detail."

"No."

"Yes, actually. You said you saw Mitch Hamilton drive away in the direction of Glenwood after your showing."

"That's because I did."

"No, you didn't. He told me he didn't head to Glenwood, and I've been able to verify that." Chase spoke to the cashier in the liquor store, and although the trash can outside the store had since been emptied, the security footage corroborated Mitch's claim about dropping in to buy whiskey before he headed home.

Evan looks away for the first time, trying to be dismissive. "I must've been mistaken."

"More like you tried to pin this on him. I'll admit, he makes a good suspect. I even brought him in twice."

Evan shakes his head. "Look, just tell me why you've arrested me, Detective. What evidence you think you have against me. Because I don't have time to sit here playing your games. I'm a busy man."

His attitude astounds Chase. He's ready to hit him with some truths. "You're here because we've found Charlie's body."

Evan licks his lips. His eyes are back on Chase, but he gives nothing away.

"We excavated her remains from the freshly laid concrete in the basement of a residential property in Glenwood owned by Mitch Hamilton and his brother."

Silence. Until: "So why aren't they sitting here right now, instead of me?"

Unbelievable. He hasn't shown any sympathy for Charlie. Even if he didn't kill her, he should be horrified by that information.

Chase leaves the room to go next door. He grabs Charlie's cowboy hat, which is in a fresh evidence bag after being processed for DNA. He returns to the interview room and places it on the table in front of Evan, where it looks small and childish. "I'm guessing you left this where it would easily be found by a construction worker. You were counting on them going to the police, where the finger of suspicion would instantly fall on Mitch, or maybe his brother."

Evan tries to look bored by the accusation.

"But you didn't bank on one of the contractors taking this home for his daughter. We only found out about it recently."

"I don't know what you're talking about."

Chase ignores him. "I'm guessing you found out about the renovation property during your first tour of the house on Wicker Lane. I'm sure Mitch would've run through his entire portfolio with you while he had your attention. You went to scope out the Glenwood property and saw the hole in the basement waiting to be filled. You thought you could hide Charlie's body there and pin it on Mitch. And if not him, then hell, a construction worker could take the blame. Anyone as long as it wasn't you. Am I right?"

Evan remains silent, but Chase thinks he sees fear in his eyes.

"Then you arranged a second tour of the Wicker Lane property for the evening of Charlie's disappearance. Why was that?"

Silence.

"So you had an alibi? Or so you could later tell me that Mitch was acting strange and send me off on a wild goose chase? Presumably you'd already buried Charlie by that point."

Evan crosses his legs at the knee and with feigned patience says, "Don't you think the construction team would have noticed if someone else had filled a hole in the floor?"

Chase mimics his body language. "Oh, they noticed, Professor, but the foreman didn't want to tell Mitch about it, because whoever had done it had made such a crappy job of it he thought Mitch would fire the whole team." Kenny told Detective Brown that they were planning on fixing it before Mitch noticed.

Chase leans in. "I believe you abducted Charlie from the

birthday party, and then later that day you went to the fixer-upper and laid her lifeless body in the basement—at least I hope to God she was already dead—then mixed up the concrete that was already on site and poured it over her. Over your own granddaughter."

Evan scoffs. "What are you talking about? I don't have any children, and I've never seen the girl before in my life. I only know who she is now because of the news."

Chase feels like he's getting nowhere. This guy is going to be one of those who cries innocence for the rest of his life. He clearly values his reputation over anything else and he believes he's untouchable. Chase stands. "I'll be right back."

He heads next door, where Brown is reading a piece of paper. With a satisfied look on his face, the detective says, "Forensics found Charlie's DNA on the mask."

"No way?" Chase steps forward.

"Her skin cells are all over it. She must've tried hard to push him away."

Relief swamps his body and his mind goes into overdrive. "We need a sample of Harris's DNA to see if he ever wore the mask. Finding it in his office isn't strong enough evidence on its own. His lawyer would claim it was planted."

"Agreed."

Chase goes back into the interview room with a spring in his step.

"I'd like to leave now," says Evan. He's standing.

"Sit down. I'm not done."

Evan remains on his feet.

"You remember those co-workers I mentioned? Well, they were pretty helpful earlier. One of them found a clown mask in your office."

The color drains from the guy's face, and it's a couple of seconds before he visibly pulls himself together. "I don't know what you're talking about. I don't own a clown mask. It must be my assistant's." His voice isn't as confident now.

"Huh. Funny that. Because she told me she found it stuffed under a chair in your office, like someone was trying to hide it. I guess you forgot to destroy it when you fled this afternoon. After you were tipped off."

Evan sits down and Chase can tell his knees are barely holding out. He has him right where he wants him, so he continues. "The one person I haven't been able to locate from the birthday party is the second clown." He pauses for effect, and Evan lowers his eyes. "He wasn't hired by the family and he didn't ask for payment before he disappeared. So I'm guessing he's the person who coaxed Charlie away from the party."

Silence.

"I've just been told that Charlie's DNA is all over the mask I took from your office. You want to tell me how it got there?"

Evan visibly slumps.

"Tell me something. Did you rape her before you killed her?"

He looks up with contempt in his eyes. "How dare you? I didn't touch her that way. She was my *granddaughter*." As soon as he says it, his entire face flushes red.

Chase leans back, finally relaxing. He's got him. And Evan knows it. He lowers his eyes again, and beads of sweat pop out all over his forehead.

Three whole minutes go by with neither of them saying anything. Chase daren't move. He's at the most delicate part of the interview. Eventually he says, "Listen, the more you tell me now, the better things will be for you. So tell me, how did you convince her to go with you?"

Evan swallows so hard it sounds like a gulp. He rubs his hands together as if he's cold, even though it's sweltering in here. Finally he mumbles, "Unicorns."

Chase leans in. "What's that?"

Evan doesn't look up as he speaks. "She didn't want to see another pony because she'd already got one in front of her. But when I mentioned there was a unicorn in the woods, she ran straight toward me and took my hand. She was so trusting." He sneers. "It's like her mother never taught her anything about strangers."

Chase closes his eyes. It's bad enough the guy killed her, but to blame Megan for how trusting Charlie was? She was at a family birthday party. She thought she was safe. The man is a scumbag. "Once you got her into the woods, how did you kill her?"

"The same way I thought I'd killed her mother."

"You strangled her."

Evan doesn't react.

Chase knows he's on borrowed time, so he has to ask the pertinent questions before the guy's lawyer turns up and makes him retract everything. "How did you even know Megan and Charlie were related to you when Kathy never told you she was pregnant? I mean, even she didn't know Megan was her daughter."

Evan looks up at last. He meets Chase's gaze. "Connie Hamilton."

And there it is. The damning link. Could it also have been Connie, rather than Christine, who tipped him off that Chase was on to him? He thinks so. He wishes he was more surprised, but in his heart he knows what that woman is capable of. "She knew and she told you. And I'll bet your first thought wasn't how happy and grateful you were that you had a daughter and a granddaughter you never knew about. You were terrified that if Kathy ever told anyone that you'd taken advantage of her— which she might do now that Megan was back in her life and would inevitably ask who her biological father was—you'd lose your job, your wealth and possibly your freedom."

Evan doesn't deny it, so Chase continues with his theory.

"Especially if it was in the news for other victims to see what you'd done to her. They might have come forward and alerted authorities about how you'd taken advantage of them too. Which means my department might find there was a pattern of offending." He exhales. "I'm guessing your victims were all teenagers, or perhaps even younger. To discredit their potential allegations, you had to remove all evidence of what you'd done to Kathy. And the only evidence was damning DNA in the form of Megan and Charlie."

Evan stands and walks to the wall. He wipes the sweat from his brow and appears to be panicking. Before he can ask for his lawyer again, Chase says, "What about Jacqueline Weston, the college student who was murdered? And Olivia Jenkins? Were they your work too?"

Evan spins around. "I'm not a *serial killer*," he spits, as if killing a single child is better than killing a whole bunch of people. "I had nothing to do with either of them. I have no idea what happened to the Jenkins girl."

Unless he can find a link between Evan and Olivia Jenkins, Chase can't arrest him for that. The state of Olivia's body suggests she was killed by someone else, especially as she was kept alive somewhere for eight months. She doesn't fit Harris's MO. Olivia's killer must've been spooked by all the law enforcement agencies out looking for Charlie, and dumped her before he originally planned to. If Charlie hadn't gone missing, Olivia might have endured even longer with her abductor. It doesn't bear thinking about. But Chase will *have* to think about it, because once he puts away Charlie's killer, he'll be looking for Olivia's.

"As for Jacqueline," Evan continues, "her boyfriend found out she was sleeping with me. Turns out he was the jealous type. That's on him." With a new look of determination on his face, he paces the small room. "You put words into my mouth. You can't prove any of it, and I don't care that you're filming this. Any jury would see you coerced me into saying it. That I was under duress. It wouldn't be the first time police have extracted false confessions. I have an excellent attorney, and if I'm charged, I'll plead not guilty."

Chase stares at him with contempt. "I had Scott Bowers' property dusted for prints the night Charlie went missing. If you were there that day, I'll soon know about it. So your confession will just add to the evidence I'm already accumulating."

Evan looks away, a shadow of doubt on his face. He's trying to recall if he touched anything while he was there.

"You might not remember this," says Chase, "but when you were Kathy Hamilton's therapist, she was seeing a boy her own age."

"So what?" Evan stops pacing.

"That boy was me."

The professor opens his mouth in shock. "*You're* the poor kid who had her in a spin? The one she tried to hide from her parents because she knew they'd be disgusted with her for wasting her time with a no-hoper?"

Rage runs through Chase's veins. "That's me. We broke up because of her mother. Kathy went to see you because she was so cut up over it and didn't know how to cope. She went to you for help. Instead, you groomed her. You took advantage of her in every way a therapist shouldn't. In every way a human being shouldn't."

Evan looks away. "She never said no. It wasn't illegal."

Chase's grip on the table tightens. He has to fight the urge to go over there and shove the guy's face through the wall.

The door behind him opens and Detective Brown walks in. "He's not worth it," he whispers into Chase's ear. Followed by "Search warrants have been authorized."

"I'm glad you told me that," says Evan, turning to Chase with a wolf's smile on his face. "Now my lawyer can convince a jury that this is personal for you. That the uneducated boy from a loveless family is upset that his rich girlfriend didn't give it up for him the way she did for me. I mean, it's obvious to me now that you've set me up out of some deep-seated revenge for taking your girlfriend's virginity all those years ago."

Chase stands. With trembling hands that barely contain his anger, he pulls his case file together. "You're the biggest piece of shit I've ever met. Not only did you try to kill your own daughter, and actually murder your granddaughter, you also took advantage of vulnerable people in your care and you don't even have the balls to own any of it." He shakes his head. "I may not be as educated as you, and I obviously don't know as much as you do about how the mind works, but I do know you're one of the most depraved assholes I've ever arrested. You know why?" He doesn't pause for a response. "Because you still think you're better than me. Even after everything you've done."

He walks right up to Evan's face and hears Brown step forward behind him, ready to pull him away if necessary. "I have officers on their way to search your office and home right now. I intend to read through every single case note for every patient and client you ever saw as a therapist. I'll find evidence of your grooming."

"You can't do that." There's panic in Evan's eyes.

"The judge who just signed my search warrants would disagree." Chase finds satisfaction in knowing he's rattled the guy. "I'll find every patient you ever abused, and together with Kathy's testimony of how you groomed her like a common pedophile, and all the evidence I'll unearth to prove you killed Charlie and strangled Megan, we'll make sure you get put away for life."

He turns around and follows Brown out of the interview room, slamming the door shut behind him.

EPILOGUE

Three weeks later, the heatwave has abated but it's still a glorious day. The sky is cloudless and there's a gentle breeze making the long grass sway. The cemetery is quiet except for the chirping of birds and crickets, along with the hushed voices of the congregation walking away from the grave.

The graveside is surrounded by flowers and stuffed animals, mainly horses. One red balloon filled with glitter is floating above, slowly ascending away from them. Kathy squeezes Megan's hand. "Are you okay?"

Megan nods. "That wasn't what I expected. It was... comforting. Is that the right word?"

"Yes. The minister's words were perfect." Kathy feels a stab of guilt for ever thinking Reverend Stanley could've harmed Charlie. She believes him now that he didn't gift Charlie those toys she brought home. Charlie must've taken them from the church. She had plenty of her own since she moved in with them, but sometimes children can't avoid temptation. She turns to Mitch. "You described Charlie and the light she brought into our lives perfectly."

Megan nods. "I wish I could've spoken, but I couldn't get my shit together. I didn't want to cause a scene."

Mitch puts a hand on her shoulder. "We all know how much you loved her. She was lucky to have you as her mom. You made the difficult decision to let her live with us when you couldn't look after her yourself. A lot of parents wouldn't do that."

Megan wipes her eyes. "I'm so glad I have somewhere to come and talk to her."

Kathy nods. It's a lovely spot in the cemetery. She hesitates, before saying, "How would you feel about me changing my last name so that I'm Kathy Carter?"

Megan's mouth falls open. "You'd do that?"

"I want to." Kathy turns to her father. "Is that okay with you, Dad?"

Jack smiles, but it doesn't mask the pain in his eyes. He's struggled over the last few weeks, and feels terrible about what his wife did right under his nose. "I think that's a great idea."

Kathy looks at her younger daughter. "Fay Carter has a nice ring to it, don't you think?" Fay's still coming to terms with the level of betrayal Connie has shown them, but she's already said she doesn't want to be a Hamilton anymore. The name has lost its former prestige now.

Kathy talked to Mitch about it yesterday, and he's keen to ditch the Hamilton name and go back to Bowers. He's ready for a fresh start too. It's clear he's felt even more ashamed about the affair with Megan since he found out she was Kathy's daughter. He's also found it hard to accept that Kathy didn't feel she could confide in him about what happened to her as a teenager. She's tried to reassure him that she wasn't ready to talk about it and it doesn't mean she never loved him, but he's got a lot to work through.

He's moved out of the family home, but instead of staying with Scott, he's got his own place. It has a spare room for Fay to sleep over whenever she wants, which is a lot at the moment. She's giving Kathy and Megan time to get to know each other properly, but she also wants to be with Mitch while he's grieving, so that he isn't alone.

Fay smiles. "Sounds good to me."

Megan hugs Kathy and Fay before taking a step back to address all of them. "I'm so glad you all got to know Charlie."

Mitch nods. "She was one of a kind." It's clear he wants to say more, but he's too overwhelmed with grief.

Scott slowly approaches. "Are you all ready to come back to the house?"

"Sure," says Mitch. He leads Fay, Megan and Jack toward the waiting cars.

Scott and Cindy have kindly offered to host a reception. Not at their house on Lexington Lane—that's already up for sale because of what happened there—but at their new rental. They only moved in yesterday, but Cindy's worked her magic by getting staff in to prepare food and serve drinks. Jack has offered to help out too. He's a single man now and has already started divorce proceedings. Connie will never be allowed to see any of them again. She hasn't been charged with anything yet, but it's probably just a matter of time. Kathy doesn't know, because she doesn't ask.

Standing alone at the grave, she watches her family walk away together. She imagines Charlie following them in her cowboy hat and boots, and not for the first time today, tears spring to her eyes.

She thinks of Christine Stiles. Christine insisted during questioning that she didn't know anything about Evan's involvement in Charlie's murder, but she confirmed she'd walked in on Kathy's mom and Evan together at home one day. Evan asked her to leave them alone while they talked, and then later used the excuse her mom had given: that she was there to make a donation to the university. Christine is an important witness for the prosecution, not just for placing those two together, but also for confirming that she disclosed to Evan some of what Fay had told her about what she was going through at home. It was unprofessional, but Evan clearly had a hold over her and took an interest when he found out she was counseling Fay. She's already agreed to testify at his murder trial, and hopefully that will go some way to setting herself free of his influence.

As Kathy wipes her eyes with her last dry tissue, Chase approaches. Until now, he's kept a respectable distance. She smiles at him.

"You okay?" he asks.

She takes his hand. It feels perfectly natural. "I will be."

"Want a ride to the house, or are you going with the kids?"

She smiles at that. Megan's twenty-seven and Fay is almost seventeen, but they *are* her kids. They always were and they always will be. "I'll go with you if you'll have me?"

His face lights up and she sees the teenage boy who kissed her by the creek all those years ago. "You know I'd never turn you down," he says.

She can tell he wants to kiss her but is holding back, thinking it wouldn't be appropriate here. She briefly wonders what people would think, but realizes she doesn't care. Charlie wouldn't mind, so why should they? Without checking who's watching, she leans in and kisses his soft lips. Just once. It's enough for now. She feels butterflies in her stomach.

They slowly walk hand in hand toward his old Honda. She turns to him and smiles. "I'm guessing that thing doesn't have A/C?"

He rolls his eyes with a smile on his face. "You're still high maintenance, I see."

Kathy laughs, and for the first time in her life, she feels free to be herself.

A LETTER FROM WENDY

I'd like to thank my loyal readers first of all. Some of you have been with me since the very beginning, with my Dean Matheson series (oh, I still miss Dean and Rocky even all these years later...), and some of you are newer and have recently discovered my Detective Madison Harper series. Some of you will be *brand* new, and *The Birthday Party* will be the first book of mine that you've tried. Either way, thank you all for coming on this journey with me.

If you'd like to, you can keep in touch with me and get updates about my future releases by signing up to my newsletter here, and by following me on social media.

www.bookouture.com/wendy-dranfield

The Birthday Party touches on the sensitive topics of grooming and sexual and emotional abuse. I understand the sensitivity involved when using any kind of abuse in my storylines, especially sexual abuse of children. It's something I experienced throughout the whole of my childhood, so I try to portray it as honestly as I can. All abuse survivors handle their experiences differently, but hopefully this book portrays the message that it's *never* the victim's fault; it's always *one hundred percent* the abuser's.

Aside from the difficult topics, I hope you enjoyed spending time in Maple Falls, and learning about Kathy's life. I don't know about you, but I'm glad she and Chase finally reunited after all those years apart. Writers often become attached to certain characters, and I have to tell you that I have a soft spot for Chase Cooper!

If you enjoyed this book, please do leave a rating or review (no matter how brief) as this helps it to stand out amongst the thousands of books that are published each day, thereby allowing it to reach more readers.

Thanks again, and hopefully see you next time!

Wendy x

www.wendydranfield.co.uk

facebook.com/WendyDranfield1
twitter.com/WendyDranfield

ACKNOWLEDGMENTS

Thank you to everyone at Bookouture who worked on this book: my editor, the copy editor, proofreader, cover designer, social media team and everyone involved behind the scenes. A book is made better with an experienced team behind it.

A special mention to the advanced readers, book bloggers and everyone who interacts with me on social media. I love reading your enthusiastic reviews and comments, so don't ever feel you're not appreciated. I can be going through massive self-doubt with my plot one day, but when I get tagged by one of you on social media with a review or a lovely comment about one of my books, it reminds me that there are readers out there enjoying them.

Finally, thanks to my husband, who researches for me and reads the first drafts of all my books. During the COVID pandemic he's been working from home alongside me, and the normally lonely task of writing has been made so much better by having him here. Because there's only so much conversation you can have with a cat. Even when you have three of them!

Printed in Great Britain
by Amazon

78010440R00215